Walkin’ Man

BOOKS

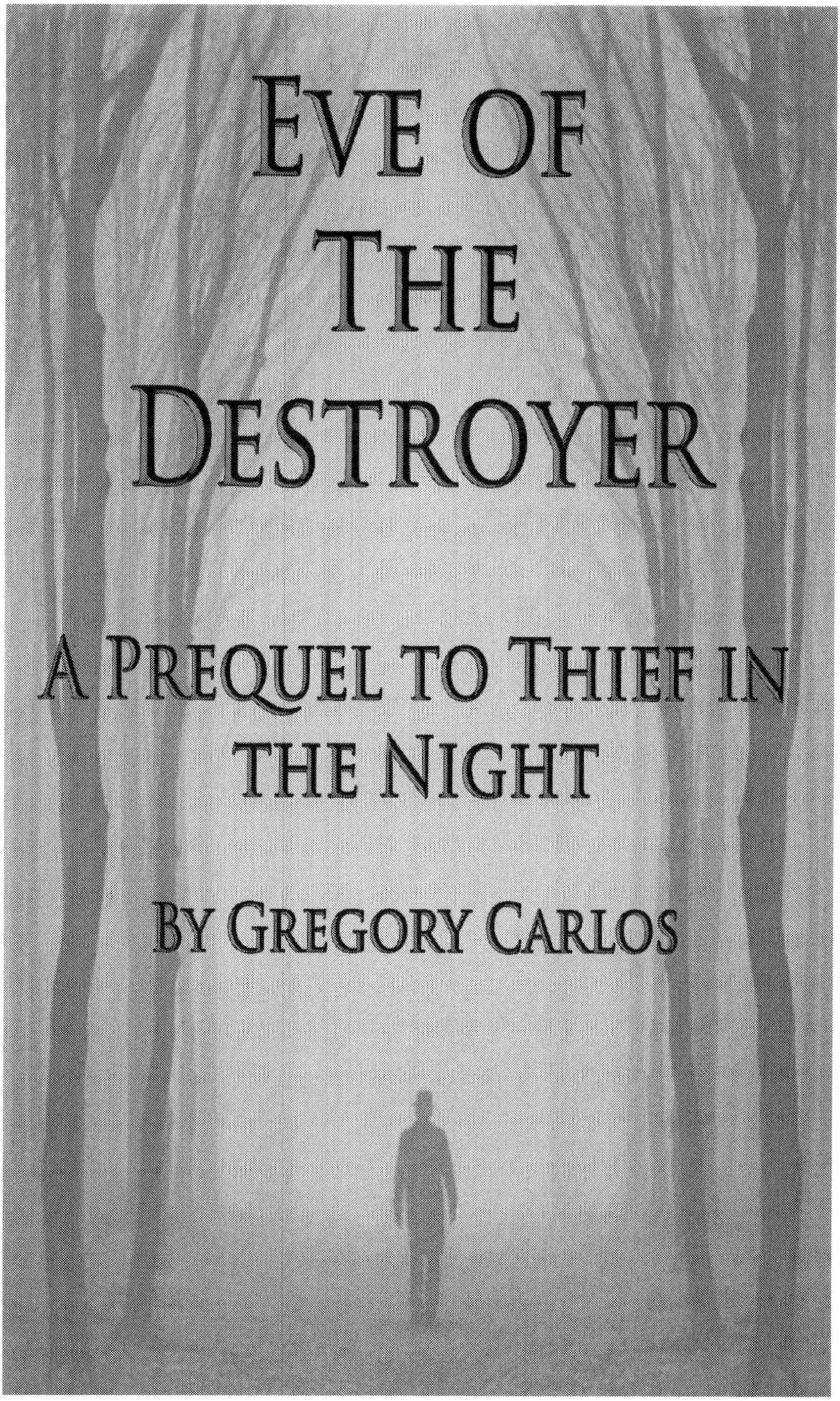
Eve of The Destroyer
A Prequel to Thief in the Night
By Gregory Carlos

Cover by: thebookcoverdesigner.com/designers/betibup33 & S. Caparella (i)

"Eschatology 101" excerpts used with permission from Chuck Missler & Koinonia Institue.

"Unconditional," Song by S. Caparella & Phace

"En-Dor" Poem by Rudyard Kipling, 1916

Written 2012-2015

First edition 2023

Dedication:

For Gregory Carlos Norris, the original Walkin' Man.

You opened my eyes to foreign film, fine scotch, and a chessboard.

'Perfect Day.'

RIP

Eve of The Destroyer

Ad Finem

Sirens howled as police cars rolled up to a high-rise in Upper Manhattan. As an officer got out of his cruiser, his radio squawked. "Suspect is a white male in his 30s, with brown hair, blue jeans, and brown jacket. He was last seen entering the building with the child in his arms. Officers are in pursuit." The radio crackled, "we have the suspect ahead of us. He just entered stairwell B."

A man burst through a door into the hall of a Madison Ave high-rise, out of breath. A child was crying in his arms. He turned and ran for an open elevator. Before entering, he hit the down arrow on the opposite elevator and then hurried into the open one as both elevators shut. He was still breathing heavily as he looked at the child, "This is what's best for you, Son."

Officers hit the hall and radioed in, "Suspect may be in elevator two going down. We're on our way to check the roof."

The radio squawked, "Ten-four, officers are stationed at all exits on the first floor."

The elevator door opened on the top floor. He hit the 3rd-floor button to send the elevator back down as he exited.

The man spotted a sign that read 'Rooftop Access' and charged in that direction with the child floundering in his arms. He stumbled and almost fell as he ran out onto the roof.

The man looked back and heard the sounds of police coming up the stairwell. Grabbing for a better hold on the crying child, he ran to the corner edge of the rooftop and sat on the short wall.

The man looked back at the open door and swung one leg over the edge straddling the short wall with the child in his arms. The sounds of agitated police were now coming from the door. He imagined angry army ants erupting in defense a colony.

The man looked at the child. "I love you, Bub." He held him tight against his chest, tears welling. "I would never want anything bad to happen to you. Please forgive me."

Five police officers emptied onto the roof, guns drawn. "Step away from the edge and put the child down."

They slowly made an arch around him with guns trained. The man stiffened, ready to plummet over the edge, and spoke in a choked voice, "Please, stop where you are. I'm trying to save my son."

The lead officer put a hand up, begging him—wait. "Sir, can you explain to me how this is saving your son?"

More police cars pulled up down below. The man looked over the edge to see a crowd forming.

More ants.

His gaze darted around before landing back on the lead officer. The lead signaled the other officers to holster their guns and holstered his own.

"Stanley, to me," he said.

Stanley, a red-headed man in his mid-twenties, came over to him, and they spoke. Officer Stanley withdrew into the building.

The radio buzzed, "This is Thompson; what's your status, Norton?"

The lead officer toggled his shoulder mic, "We're on the roof. The suspect has the child in his arms and is sitting on the ledge. I'm trying to speak to him now."

The voice returned, "Keep us informed. Richardson is assuming command."

The officers seemed restless, waiting for something to happen.

Another officer moved up to speak with Norton, startling the man on the ledge. He postured closer to the edge in response. Everyone tensed, one officer placing his hand on his gun again.

Norton put a hand out towards the other officers—*stay cool.*

Officer Stanley returned, came back up to Officer Norton, and said something the man on the ledge couldn't hear. Norton nodded toward a hard-looking Hispanic officer and said, "Take Rodriguez."

Officer Stanley walked over and spoke to Rodriguez for a moment then both officers retreated into the building. Officer Norton looked at the man on the ledge,

"My name is Tim, I don't want to cause you more stress than you're already feeling, but can we get you to sit on this side of the wall and talk?"

The man shook his head. "I feel more comfortable right here, just let me speak to my son for a moment, and then I'll consider your request."

Officer Norton was a tall, muscular man with a sharp military cut and a perfectly fit uniform. His gaze was steady, and his stance prepared. Yet, at the same time, there was compassion in his face. Officer Norton backed off with a nod and started talking to other officers. The man sat on the ledge and calmed the child, who was now more curious than afraid.

"It's okay, Sam, everything will be okay."

He stroked the back of the child's head and looked him in the eyes. The toddler smiled at him, "Da." Though 47 stories above the hard ground, Sam was at home in the man's arms.

The radio came to life again, "This is Richardson. Talk to me, Norton."

"This is Norton, are you informed of the situation?"

"Yes, Thomson has brought me up to speed. Our negotiator is on the way. Is there anything you need?"

Officer Norton looked at the man. The man shook his head.

Norton toggled his mic, "Not at the moment, Sir. Rodriguez and Stanley are on alpha two. They can update you further on our status."

"Got it, Norton, on two."

"This is Stanley, Rodriguez and I are in position."

"Good, stand by for Richardson," Norton answered.

"Ten-four."

Norton walked back over to the man and wiped the sweat off his brow. “It’s going to be a hot one today.”

The man on the ledge started to speak, “I am—”

The radio interrupted him.

“Someone here claims to know the suspect,” Richardson said over the radio. Officer Norton backed up, hitting his shoulder mic without taking his eyes off the man. “What’s the plan, Sir?”

He turned to the man on the ledge. “I believe there’s someone you know here. Would you talk to them?”

The radio squawked before the man could answer, “He is a friend of the suspect. He says he wants to speak to him. Tell—What? His name is Stephen? Tell the man his friend, Peter, is coming up.”

“Did you hear that?” Norton asked.

The man on the ledge nodded.

Norton took another step. “Will you wait for your friend?”

The man nodded again, “As long as you back up the three steps you just crept and stay there.”

Norton backed up with a smile. “Okay, so Peter claims your name is Stephen, this true?”

The man on the ledge nodded again and then looked at all the police below. “I’m a good father.”

“I’m not judging you. I only want you and your child to come out of this safely. Do you believe that?”

Stephen nodded.

“Good, just relax until your friend gets here.” Norton clicked his mic, “are you sending him up now?”

Thompson replied this time, “Hey, Norton, yeah, I’m escorting him up myself. We will be there momentarily.”

Stephen and the officers waited.

Angelos Aiónios

We should probably start at the beginning. However, as the highest historian in earth's history, I can attest to the fact that time is not linear, and more often than not, the stories I've documented end closer to where they began.

Consider the Bible; it is told from the past and with a historical memory of your future. In this same way Stephen Meyers' precarious moment on this roof is a central moment that drew powers of light and darkness into battle. None the less, let me bring you back to *A* beginning.

Stephen Meyers' adoptive mother named him after a martyr in the Bible. He grew up believing that—although a sweet loving woman— she was wrong with all the talk about a creator. Understand, I have been watching him all of his life. I am no guardian, in fact, my power is limited in how I may interact with humanity, and for most of history only the purest of hearts have heard my stories.

My master leaves no room for error when empowering His servants. I'm a scholar, a storyteller. I have total access to every moment in humanity's existence and travel back and forth as I please. Only my Master and I have this ability and because I have such power, my ability to physically intervene has been taken from me. I cannot walk among you, like so many of my kind do. Mine is to document the story of earth, and the powers that surround all from beginning to end.

Stephen's story is just one part in the whole, just as your story too, becomes part of it as well. Yes, I know you. From your first tear, to what you will smell drawing in your last breath, and you also, have an effect on this story. You are a part of it. This story was written for you, about you, and I knew you would be right where you are now, when you began to read it. I know what you will think of it now and how it will impact you in a year when… well, I'll leave that for later.

I am the keeper of time, of your story, as well. I cannot write my true name in your language, but I have been called Olam by the Hebrews and later Aiónios, by the Greeks. Either is acceptable to me, if a name is what you require to hear the story I have delivered to you.

Stephen was a writer, living in San Diego, when I took notice of his story's significance on the future. The exact moment I looked in on him he was toying with that great mystery—where do we come from?

He believed there was probably a higher power, but that was where he left it: out-of-sight, out-of-mind. He was doing research on demons and the occult because there had been a rash of violent murders linked to the occult all across the West Coast. He had written a piece that got great reviews, and was asked to follow it up with a book. He traveled to New York to get access to a larger library, and was in New York's largest when everything in his life changed.

New York

(1991)

And it shall come to pass afterward, that
I will pour out my spirit upon all flesh;
and your sons and your daughters shall prophesy,
your old men shall dream dreams,
your young men shall see visions:
—Joel 2:28

Stephen sat in The New York Public Library, in the city's Theater District, with a table full of Babylonian, Hebrew, and Greek texts opened before him. He noticed a story told in several ancient histories about a demon-possessed man who overpowered and assaulted several priests in an ancient city called Ephesus.

He had his nose buried in a Greek manuscript when a man cleared his throat, startling him. He looked up to see a well-dressed man, in his mid-fifties, sitting across from him. The man chuckled at something he was reading, and Stephen smiled as the man looked over. He was elegant looking with chiseled features exuding his time on planet. The man smiled back, then returned to his reading. Stephen tried doing the same. The man looked like he came from money. Most definitely well-educated. Stephen was distracted by him.

In truth, Stephen was bored with the manuscript he was reading. It spoke of a man named Paul, a teacher or healer of some kind. His stomach was grumbling, and his eyes were beginning to feel the strain from all the texts. The man laughed again, drawing everyone's attention. He gave a humbled nod to the other library patrons, then turned to Stephen and spoke in a low voice, "I forgot where I was for a moment, my apologies."

Stephen nodded and then continued his search. The library was now quiet again, and every turn of the old pages echoed.

Where is it?

The man spoke again. "I think what you are looking for is in the book of Acts in the New Testament."

Stephen looked up at him, confused. He had books opened up to pictures of demons and hell. There was also a stack of books on exorcisms, the occult, and ghosts sitting next to him.

Stephen smiled, "I'm looking for a story about a demon-possessed man who attacked and injured several Rabbi in ancient Rome." Stephen raised an eyebrow in anticipation of the man's response.

The stranger smiled and nodded at the large Bible to Stephen's right, "Yes, Acts is the place to look. Chapter 19, I believe."

Stephen nodded but did not turn to the place the man recommended. Instead, he decided to take a break from his research and start a conversation with the man to be polite. He interlaced his hands in front of him, looking at the man's book. "Satan and Demonism, I've read that."

The man folded the cover towards him and looked at it. He nodded, "Oh, yes, of course, I find it entertaining. So many try to speculate on the subject, yet few can agree. My favorite saying about our ominous friend is 'The best trick the devil ever pulled off was convincing the world he did not exist.'" The man smiled with extremely white teeth. Stephen could smell the cigar smoke on him.

He must work hard at keeping that smile so bright.

Stephen re-arranged some of the books in front of him and asked, "Do you believe the devil exists?"

The man set the book on his lap. "Oh yes, I believe he exists; however, the little red fellow with the horns and the pitchfork, I rather doubt, is his accurate description. Nor do I agree with many of the ideas and folklore surrounding him."

Stephen nodded in acknowledgment. "I'm doing a study on demonism and the occult. The devil seems to go hand in hand in everything I read on the subjects."

The man slapped his book on his knee. “My point exactly, ‘the devil made me do it.’ I really doubt all that is true.”

He turned to face Stephen, laying the book on the table in front of him. “My research has focused less on folk-lore and old wives’ tales and more on real documentation such as Archeological data and documents like that book on ancient Babylonian artifacts next to you.”

Stephen’s eyes grew wide. “Really, so you research this subject as well?”

The man leaned closer, noticing a librarian’s unfriendly stare, and whispered, “I did, but now I’m mostly retired. I own an antique shop uptown from here, ‘Things Of Old,’ perhaps you’ve heard of it?”

“No, I’m not too familiar with New York. I’m just here doing some research and then returning to San Diego. I will try and make that one of my stops on my way out of town, though.”

The stranger smiled with a nod and then looked at Stephen’s pile of papers. “The story you are looking for is an interesting one. I have found several accounts of it from different civilizations. The real story is rather exciting and a little frightful.”

“Really?” I would love to hear it.” Stephen replied.

“Stop by my shop sometime,” The man said, “Maybe we can chat in a more comfortable environment.”

Stephen leaned back in his chair. “That sounds like a plan.”

The man reached into his sport coat, removing a gold business card holder. He opened it, pulled out a card, and handed it across to Stephen.

“Things Of Old,” Stephen read aloud. It looked like real gold leaf lettering. The card was beautiful, probably the most exquisite card Stephen had ever seen. “Who does your business cards?” he asked, “They’re amazing.”

The man looked pleased. “I have them made by a man in Italy. He is one of my clients and insisted I give him a chance to make them for me.”

Stephen carefully placed the card in his wallet and began to organize his workspace. “I will make sure to see your shop before I leave. My Name is Stephen, Stephen Meyers, by the way.” He held out his hand.

The man extended his own hand and gave Stephen's a solid squeeze.

"Charles Rutherford," he said, "Glad to meet you, Stephen."

For a moment, as they shook hands, Charles appeared older, more like a man in his seventies than fifties. He had a depth of wisdom in his eyes, like he knew far more than anyone Stephen had met.

"Are you the Meyers that wrote, "Dangerous Superstitions?" he asked.

Stephen's eyes were wide, "I am. You read that?"

"I did and enjoyed it. I read seven papers keeping up on things here in the states and a few publications overseas. I would love to talk more on the subject; however, I must be going. I have a client stopping by this afternoon. It was a pleasure meeting you, Stephen."

Stephen nodded, "You too, Charles; it was my pleasure."

Charles turned as he walked away, "Don't forget to feed the body as well as the mind, my friend," smiling with a final wave as he left the library.

Not today, Stephen thought. *He has a client coming.*

His research was finished for the day. He was too excited about seeing Charles' shop and learning more. Stephen decided to head back to The Paramount Hotel before going to dinner.

A Troubled Soul

(1991)

Monstrous screams fade.

A howling in the sky above dissipated with cold burning in his skin as Mitchel Falcone awoke. He shielded his face from shards of jade glass falling out of nowhere, covering him and a woman in the bed. He sat up, looking around the room as everything settled. The woman jumped out of bed and backed into the corner, holding a sheet against her.

"Get out," he said as he swung his feet out of bed and reached for a smoke.

"What are y—"

"GET OUT!" He barked again, lighting a cigarette. His back was to her as she slid across the wall stepping carefully around broken glass. She managed her underwear, grabbing the rest of her clothes as she backed out the door.

Hours blurred by in this moment with only the movement of shadows across walls and cigarette butts multiplying in an ashtray, the man unmoving. The day passed like a blur, time in fast forward.

Horns blared as pedestrians shuffled along San Diego's Lamplight District, breaking the silence in the room. The sun was now setting, and the sky flaunted its last colors of the day as people got ready for Saturday evening on 5th Avenue. Lights blinked to life all over the city. Restaurants were seating their first dinner guests, and nightclubs that made up much of this part of Fifth were coming to life all around this brick building; within, a tiny motel sat atop a dress boutique and coffee shop.

His motel room was no bigger than a child's bedroom, but this was all he needed. The rooms were meant for short-term guests, and short-term had come and gone for Mitch. Inside room {19} sat the man in his thirties. He ran his fingers through his short dark hair as he blew out a large puff of smoke. Mitch brushed ash off the knee of his dark slacks and adjusted the collar of his starched white shirt, looking in the reflection of the now-darkening window. Only the orange glow of his cigarette illuminated the room like a dying heart beating its last.

Another night at the Onyx.

Mitch looked over and swiped the clusters of green glass off the nightstand, picking a more significant piece up to take a closer look.

I've been here too long..... how long had he made this place his world? *Two years in this coffin.* Had it been that long?

Now his mind battled with memories of fire and a dead wife and child. The intent was to be here long enough to drink himself to death or waste away until he had the guts to pull the trigger. His money, too, was giving way, He kept only enough cash to keep him fed, bed, and buzzed until the end, *but here I am still…alive.*

He looked around the room. There was no intention of leaving it, spending the first year without his girls, right here, drinking his sorrows away. Something kept him from finishing the game and ending his miserable life. He had looked down the barrel of his gun on many a drunken night, seeing the shimmer of the copper-clad bullet staring back at him. Taunting him. Daring him to pull the trigger and say goodbye to the pain and misery of this loss, to the guilt that crushed his soul.

Why can't I do it? Something deep within him always stopped him.

What if you could see them again? It would say.

Is there an afterlife?

These questions always stayed his hand from letting go. Now this lingering like a ghost had forced him to find a remedial job at the club down the street, and though he remained closed off, the other fractured people he encountered there fed his continuance if only out of curiosity and the desire for answers.

Darkness surrounded the man, hate enveloped him, and his heart was cold and unfeeling. It was the only way he knew how to exist now—not feeling but moving, eating when the body demanded, drinking always, screwing when the opportunity presented—but never caring.

No, never care again.

Drunken one-night stands were the easiest. The women at the clubs seemed to fill that need, and it was rare that another word was even necessary in the morning.

Demons lived here with him, in this room. They were drawn to his misery and guilt, feeding on it somehow. The blame he wore for the house that cooked his family. His self-loathing was a delicacy these dark weeds thrived upon. Mitch was still too hard-willed to allow them to possess him, or maybe the small fire of love for his wife and nine-year-old daughter remaining within prevented them access. They tried, though.

Oh, do they try.

He felt like whatever was keeping them out was breaking down, weakening. That deeply buried love was like acid to them. Still, unable to have him, they could afflict him; torment him with the manipulated ghosts of his family. The demons followed him everywhere he went, attached now to his dying heart.

He was still, sitting silent on his bed, when his mind returned to the present. He listened to the noises coming from his open window now. He looked down into his lap, and there in his hand was his revolver.

When did I pull this out?

Behind him stood a dark being made of shadows. Its form appeared, legs and arms, like a human, but no color, only blackness. Wisps of darkness rose from it like smoke as it grew closer to Mitch. Some tendrils of shadowy smoke crawled like a wicked ivy along the floors and up the walls to the ceiling. All this darkness, now filling the room, sprouted from the dark being and seemed to grow into the walls and furniture like black veins pulsing with deadly blood. Mitch was oblivious to the demon standing behind him. His focus was on the gun now. He tumbled it from side to side, admiring its cold beauty—a changer of lives, a destroyer of joy—its cargo, the teeth of death.

The shadow put a ghostly hand on Mitch's shoulder. Its fingers had tentacles of black smoke rolling from them that slithered all over Mitch like tiny snakes. The demon leaned down and spoke near the man's ear. Mitch barely reacted. The demon began to take form and solidify. Its shape grew slender. Hair formed, long and dark. Its skin had color now. It was a woman, and she was naked, standing behind him. Her body was beautiful, her hands delicate and soft. Her eyes were a glowing hazel, and her features flawless. Her lips grew full of color, and her face softened—a silk negligée forming over her naked body. Mitch lifted the revolver to his temple and closed his eyes. The beautiful woman touched the gun delicately as if to see if it was real. Wisps of darkness from her fingertips crawled all over it, exploring its inner workings, and then withdrew.

Mitch pulled the trigger.

The cold sound of metal-on-metal, from the hammer's fruitless drop, echoed in the room. The dark woman came around him, gently pulling the gun down. Mitch opened his eyes to see his dead wife standing before him.

"You're not real," he stammered.

She only smiled lovingly at him and put her other hand on his face.

"Not yet, Dear," she spoke in a soft voice. "We'll be together soon enough, but first, you have things to do."

Mitch looked down at the gun resting in his lap and closed his eyes.

"Leave me alone," he said in a cold voice.

His eyes were now tightly closed, fighting feelings.

Why, God, why did you let this happen? What did I do wrong? The darkness vanished all at once. Mitch opened his eyes to find the woman gone. He looked around the room; it was empty.

Alone.

The shadows slowly returned, growing up around him. The room became a dark crypt again, slithering darkness crawling up all the walls once more. Voices came from all around him as he stared out the window.

Why should anyone feel love?

The world is full of phonies, the voices whispered.

Mitch opened the cylinder of the gun, revealing rounds in each slot. The gun was loaded, and there was a dimple in one cartridge where the pin had struck.

Why didn't you fire? He thought as he pulled the fired cartridge out of its slot. He closed the revolver's cylinder with a snap of his wrist and set the gun down. Mitch lay down, rolling the bullet casing between his fingers, examining it.

"A dud."

The voices seemed to quiet with Mitch's disregard. Maybe he was learning to tune them out as time went on. Their tormenting words did not seem to pierce him tonight. Tonight, he felt stronger somehow. Maybe it was because He called out to God, if only to complain.

Maybe...

He and God were not on good terms. They never really were. Mitch never believed in God to begin with, so why would He want to help him now?

Mitch was soon walking down Fifth Avenue towards his work. He stopped, picked up a pack of cigarettes, and stood on the street corner packing them.

"Daddy! Daddy!" called a familiar voice from beside him. He turned and saw his little girl, as beautiful as he remembered her. She had her locks tied in pigtails and wore a beautiful dress with ruffles on the bottom. She was smiling, holding her hands up for him to lift her into his arms. Mitch looked away, peeled the cellophane from his pack of Camels, and pulled a smoke from the pack.

"You're not real," he said as he laid a smoke on his lip and lit it.

The ghosts of his wife and daughter had besieged him longer than he could remember. "You're something else," he finished as he puffed on the smoke.

"Daddy!" the little voice returned, a little disheartened. "Please, daddy, don't you love me anymore?" She was now crying.

The light changed, and Mitch stepped off the curb to cross.

"DADDY!" She screamed with a little girl's temper. "Daddy, why did you let me die?" she cried, her voice distorting into something bigger, darker.

Mitch turned, startled by the change. She was standing on the curb's edge, charred like a burnt roast, smoke rising off her. Her dress was mostly gone, some of it still melted into the girl. The skin on the right side of her neck and face was gone, revealing only remnants of charred flesh and bone. Her eyes were dark, shriveled balls, moving sightlessly in their sockets.

"You piece of shit!" It yelled at him in a mangled version of the girl's voice. "This is your fault."

A horn blared at Mitch, dislodging his gaze from his dead daughter. The light had changed, and he was in the middle of the intersection. He crossed the street and then looked back at the place where his daughter was standing, but she was gone. He was worn out and tired of these insane moments, where sometimes hours were stolen from him by the ghosts of his dead family.

déjà vu,

French: "Already seen."
1. An impression of having seen or experienced something before.
2. A recollection of a fragment from one's past, or alternate time path.
3. A merging of frequencies from an alternate universe, time, or layer of reality.

Stephen awoke early the following day from a bad dream. All he could remember by the time he made it to the bathroom was screaming. He looked in the mirror and saw dark circles accenting his eyes. He ran his fingers through his wavy brown hair, scratching the scruff on his jaw. He tried on a smile but was not impressed with it.

"A hot shower will fix this," he said to the man in the mirror and undressed. He tried to remember the dream but could not. He showered, shaved, and put on slacks and a dress shirt, slipping on a pair of square-tipped Madden's before heading to the door. Stephen stopped and smiled at himself in the vanity mirror on the way out.

He had breakfast at Chelsea's Diner, in the Garment District nearby, and then took a cab up to Central Park to kill some time before heading to Charles' shop.

Stephen noticed a few people stretching. Two women in their twenties were eyeing him as they jogged by. After a walk around the park, he headed back to the main street to catch a cab. He stopped when he noticed a man looking intently at him. The man was dressed in what looked like a robe.

"That can't be good."

He decided to walk a little farther before turning toward Central Park South. He wanted to avoid the crazies, if possible, on this trip. Stephen hailed a cab and then asked the cab driver to stop at the nearest souvenir shop along their route so he could pick up a gift. He bought a New York snow globe for his girlfriend,

Heather, and was back in a cab again headed to the Upper Westside when his phone rang.

It was her. Heather was a beautiful 26-year-old Architect with a magnetic personality. She had long raven hair and gorgeous green eyes, which made his heart race every time he looked into them. She was an optimistic person to be around, yet, commanded respect with her professionalism and intelligence. She was not only what he desired but what he needed in a mate.

Stephen answered, "Hey Babe, are your feelers twitching?"

"No, why, should they be?"

"Well, I just finished buying you a gift when you called me."

She laughed, "That's women's intuition, my Dear; we always know when our men have their wallets out."

They both laughed.

"Hey baby, I just wanted to say I miss you and can't wait to see you tomorrow."

Stephen's face brightened, "I miss you too, Honey. I'm on my way to meet a fascinating man who may have a lot of information about the story I'm writing. I met him yesterday at the library."

Heather was interrupted by someone in the background, then responded, "Oh Babe, that's great, I... I have to go, work calls. I just wanted to hear your voice and wish you a good day. Be safe and call me tonight, okay?"

"I will, Honey. You have a good day too. I love you."

"You too, Lover." It sounded like she was walking into a busy meeting as she hung up.

A moment later, his phone rang again. When he answered, it was quiet for a moment. As he was about to repeat a hello, she spoke in a low but possessive voice, "Stephen…"

"Yes, Love?"

"Stephen….I love you darling, and…" her voice grew even lower. "I miss waking up next to you."

"And I you, Love."

"I gotta go, Babe, their looking for me," she whispered before hanging up.

Stephen sighed. The driver, an Irishman in his late fifties with scruff for a beard, gave him an enquiring look in the mirror and then pulled over. "Do you mind walking a bit? There's an accident ahead, so I may be stuck if we go any further."

Stephen handed him some cash. "Not at all, thanks for the lift," and stepped out onto Columbus Avenue. As he walked, he noticed some very nice shops, thinking they were all out of his price range. *Charlie must have some nice wares to afford the rent.*

About a block from Charles's shop, he noticed a lunatic shouting at the crowd of pedestrians across the street. He could not hear what the stranger was saying, but the man was getting the same nervous look from all who hurried by him. This person was also wearing some kind of robe or *Is it a tunic?*

As he grew closer, the man looked more and more like the stranger in the park.

"There's no way," he whispered.

At that moment, the lunatic stopped speaking to the people around him and just looked across the street at Stephen. The man smiled and waved as if they were friends. It gave Stephen a chill, so he faced forward, ignoring the strange man's gaze. The stranger continued speaking, now clearly preaching.

"The end is near; turn to Christ before it's too late."

Stephen chuckled. "Okay, now the robe makes sense."

He was eased by this notion and slowed his pace. The lunatic seemed to get louder.

"Narrow is the path to your salvation. Turn away from your wicked ways."

"The path I'm on leads to an antique store, you nut," Stephen muttered.

The lunatic continued preaching as the distance between them grew. "The path you're on leads to death, Steve."

Startled at the sound of his name, Stephen turned and looked back. The robed man was not facing him anymore, but a crowd of people who had stopped to listen. Stephen could not make out what the man was saying anymore.

He didn't just say my name...I need sleep. Stephen let the thought go and continued walking down the street.

"What a kook."

He arrived at the front door of Charles's shop. The door had large gold lettering: 'Things Of Old' and below those letters, 'By appointment only.' He pushed the intercom button and waited for a reply. Stephen looked in the window and saw furniture and other antiques packed in tightly. Though they seemed like lovely pieces, he could not imagine them affording Charles such a nice address.

"One man's treasure," he said to himself.

"Hello," crackled a voice over the intercom. "May I help you?"

Stephen leaned toward the box. "Yes, it's Stephen Meyers; we met at the Library?"

There was silence, then a crackle of the box again. "Oh yes, Stephen, glad you could stop by. I will buzz you in. Make your way straight back to my office if you would."

There was a loud buzzing sound as the electric lock disengaged. He grabbed the handle looking back once more to see his crazy monk friend quietly staring at him. He entered the shop. "Weirdo."

As he walked toward the back, he looked around. There were some exquisite pieces of furniture: old roll-top desks, plush chairs, and an old miner's cart. Everything had been restored to pristine condition.

Stephen soon found his way to a set of double doors, where Charles held one open with a smile.

"Good to see you. Did you have trouble finding us?"

"Not at all. I actually walked that last couple blocks because of an accident, and it gave me a chance to look at all the shops you have around here."

Charles's smile grew, "Yes, I chose a good spot, I do believe. Well, come on back. I was finishing a cup of tea. Have you eaten?"

Stephen nodded, "Yes, thank you."

They walked back into a sitting room filled with more antiques and a small desk with a computer off to one side. Behind the desk was another set of double doors.

"So, this is your shop, it... it's nice."

Charles smiled at him. "You're being polite, and thank you, but no, the front of the shop is there for the average joe who gets it into their head that an old piece will make them seem more refined. The real treasures are beyond those doors." Charles pointed behind him at the double doors. "I have a few designers who like to peruse the front end for their clients, but for my better clientele, I find pieces that match who they are and join them with their new owners."

"Oh, so the good stuff's behind door number two," Stephen said with a smirk.

Charles gave a patient look, "Yes, so to speak, we'll head through that way to my study, where it's a little more comfortable."

Charles made a note at the desk before walking to the doors. He led Stephen back farther into the back of his store.

"This is what pays the bills," Charles said.

Stephen's jaw dropped as he entered a small museum-like warehouse of ancient artifacts and antiques.

"Talk about things of old," he said.

Charles looked pleased as he led on. The pieces were all very old or the best knock-offs Stephen had ever laid his eyes on. From his perspective, it looked like pieces of ancient Egypt, Greece, Israel, as well China. All of humanity's history seemed to be represented in this gallery. All the pieces were set together from their region of the world and era.

"So you choose the pieces?" Stephen asked.

"Well, my clients are welcome to come choose a piece, and some do; most just tell me the part of the world or time they would be interested in and leave it to me. I always see where the piece will be displayed ahead of time. Some clients give me artistic license to choose a piece that would complement who they are. My best clients trust me emphatically with the choice."

Stephen pointed at what appeared to be a Babylonian stone with cuneiform carvings all over it. "Is this stuff legal?" His eyes exploring Charles for the truth.

"Of course," Charles replied, "All the most important pieces are brokered to museums around the world, but many are allotted for private ownership. Museums even sell some of their lesser valued pieces they choose not to display to private collectors. I work closely with all the museums as well consult from time to time."

Stephen looked all around in amazement. "I had no idea I would be walking into a room like this."

"Few do."

Charles continued leading them back. "I would love to show you more when we have time, but I believe you were interested in what I know about that story, am I correct?"

Stephen nodded, still looking around at all the relics. He followed Charles into yet another room filled with beautiful pieces of furniture: chairs, love seats, tables, and art on all the walls. The room was arranged into a pleasant-looking study. A fire was burning in the fireplace; the lighting was dimmed to a comfortable level.

I could easily take a nap in here....

A large desk was set off to the left, appearing to be from the 1700s. It was made of beautifully carved wood, with an exquisite chair sitting behind it. In front of the fireplace were four high-backed leather chairs with glimmering silver stands between each pair. Charles gestured to one just to the left of the fireplace, and Stephen sat. He watched as his host went over to a roll-top desk and opened it up, revealing a small bar.

Pulling out a pair of rock glasses, he asked, "Would you like to join me for a drink?"

Stephen nodded, "That would be nice, Charles."

Charles picked up a beautiful crystal decanter, "Scotch, okay?"

Stephen nodded. Charles poured, then picked up a box of cigars and opened it for Stephen, "Cigar?"

Stephen took the drink and then a cigar from the box, giving his host a grateful nod as he did. Charles walked over to the chair opposite him and sat. He pointed to a cigar cutter and lighter sitting on the silver ashtray next to Stephen as he lit his own cigar; everything was beautiful. The v-cutter was of the finest quality, as well, as the lighter, which carried the weight and glimmer of white gold, and the *S.T. DuPont Paris* logo confirming. The standing silver ashtrays were polished without blemish.

Stephen lit his cigar and then tasted his drink. The scotch had a smooth, smoky flavor, and the cigar was the finest he had ever smoked. His host sat back just out of the firelight, his face in shadow, puffing large clouds of smoke. The two sat silent for a few moments enjoying their drinks and cigars.

Charles leaned forward, revealing his bright, blue eyes.

"How's the scotch, my friend?"

"It's wonderful, thank you," Stephen answered.

Weren't his eyes brown?

Charles held up his glass in salute, "I know you have many questions and little time, so I thought it best we sit here and chat. You depart for San Francisco tomorrow, yes?"

Stephen's expression grew perplexed, "Umm, yeah, I fly out at 11 tomorrow, but it's San Diego, not San Francisco; I don't recall telling you my departure date?"

Charles leaned back into shadow, "Oh, my mistake; you mentioned being here for three days from the West Coast when we met."

"I did? I don't remember telling you that, but yes, I'm afraid that's all the time I could afford to be away."

Charles puffed on his cigar, "Whatever the case may be, let us make the best of your time, shall we?"

Stephen nodded. "I was intrigued by what you said about the story."

Charles took a sip of his scotch, a long puff on his cigar, and then began.

"I'm going to tell you the story as I know it and believe it to have happened."

Stephen smiled, "Okay, sounds good, Charles. I'm your captive audience."

Charles chuckled, "Are you familiar with the Mediterranean Coast?"

Stephen nodded.

"Good," Charles said, "This story begins in an ancient city in the Roman Empire on the coast of the Aegean Sea."

Charles set his glass down, pulled a beautiful gold coin out of his breast pocket, and started rolling it back and forth across the top of his right hand. It sparkled brightly as it rolled in the reflection of the firelight.

"Money, my friend, is the motivation of most everything in this world and has been since people have been telling stories. In this story, many were trying to capitalize on the new religion sweeping the land. This fellow, Jesus, had caused such a stir that many turned to this new belief in droves.

Because of this, others who made their living as fortune-tellers, mystics, and diviners were losing income and had to change their racket. Only with this new religion, there were no relics to sell or carved images to peddle. Many became exorcists and prophets of god, instead. Some of these were actual Jews who were attempting to keep a hold of their power over the people.

The men in this story were self-proclaimed apostles, declaring they had the authority of God and the new church behind them, but in truth, they were the equivalent of traveling medicine men."

Stephen could not take his eyes off the dazzling coin as Charles continued.

"It was a warm spring day, and there was a mild breeze blowing in the city of Ephesus."

Ephesus A.D. 55

Ephesus was one of the larger cities in the Roman Empire. It was located on the western coast of what is now Turkey, with a population of over 250,000. Ephesus was beautifully built with the style and grace of any modern Roman city. The city had stunning views of the Mediterranean and Aegean Seas and an excellent climate.

The bustling metropolis was known for its great luxury, as well debauchery. Ephesus was full of major monuments and great amphitheaters and one of the seven wonders of the ancient world: The Temple Artemis, dedicated to the goddess Diana. It was a city of great trade and wealth in the area and was an international tourist destination so profitable its leaders opened the first World Bank here.

In one of Ephesus' market districts, there was a group of men walking through the streets having a discussion. It was a warm spring day, with a cool breeze scented with a mix of the sea and the wonderful foods sold in the market. The men were making plans for a feast with the local church. These men all looked like prominent Hebrew scholars and rabbis ranging from early thirties to late sixties, with their fine cloaks and head coverings. It was obvious the elder three were the leaders of the group, surrounded by their apprentices.

One of the elders at the front of the group turned to the other, "Zadok, I heard this, Paul, from Tarsus, and his companions are headed this way. The rumor from Antioch and Iconium is that these men can heal all kinds of disease. Some say this Paul can send his personal handkerchief blessed to heal the one that is sick upon its touch."

All the other men started to grumble at this and speak their opinions on the subject amongst themselves.

Zadok Laughed, "That is preposterous, Simeon. Still, we could use this. We will have Cohen have several handkerchiefs made up for us to bless, as well."

Cohen, a thin young man with curly dark hair, was the son of Zadok. He was a very hard worker and zealous in his position. Zadok and Simeon were brothers, both in their sixties, with dark curly hair that was greying. Both men had long greying beards; however, Zadok was a thin man with the look of many years of stress on his face, and Simeon, the plumper of the two, had a more youthful, happy look to him.

Simeon nodded, "yes, I was also of the mind that we should offer to bless their homes as well. Of course, this will take much prayer and fasting on our part to accomplish such a feat, and we will need compensation for our pains.

Zadok smiled, "Simeon, you speak true. Are we to eat with this new church today?

Simeon looked back to the crowd of men walking with them. "Nabal, are all the arrangements made for the meal?"

Nabal was a strong, good-looking man with wavy black hair. He was known for acting hastily at times but very eager to learn. He caught up to his two Rabbis'.

"Yes, teacher, we are to meet with the church body for prayer and be the guests of honor at the feast afterward.

Zadok smiled, "Good, good, this will be a wonderful evening, my friends."

The men continued on to the market. Two of the younger men walking in the group were talking. One, a darker-skinned man of Egyptian descent named Abimelech, and the other, the son of Simeon, a hulking man with dark wavy hair named Uzzi.

Abimelech turned to his friend, "I thought they stoned this Paul to death?"

Uzzi said, "Yes, and the next day he was seen alive and well in that very city."

They all continued walking as they talked about the rumors. Zechariah, another of the elders, was walking at the group's rear, speaking to his son Jeriah. Zechariah was a wise-looking man in his sixties with brown hair and a prestigious beard. His son, Jeriah, was his spitting image, only younger at thirty-one years old.

Zechariah looked at his son, "Jeriah, I want you to listen to my words. I have spent most of my life studying the Torah and practicing the laws of God, and I am disturbed and concerned by what I am hearing. I believe there is much merit to the claims that our Messiah has come, yet I still advise we step carefully as there are so many false teachers about. It is better we are slow to speak our opinions and quick to listen for right now."

"If the claims of this Paul and other brothers are true, a great tragedy has happened. I will go further and say that our Jewish brothers in Jerusalem have committed a travesty against God if Iesus was truly our Christ."

Jeriah, Spoke in a low voice, "I feel the others have made their choice and are embracing this Iesus and his disciples, as long as they follow our laws. Are you saying not to be a part of this?"

"No, my son," Zechariah said, looking intently at him. "I only say, look and listen and be careful not to follow a crowd into a hunter's pit. The miracles are clearly Yahweh's work, yet so much is still unknown. I am saying, embrace these new brothers but with care not to offend Yahweh in the choices you make. Do you remember what I taught you about the wisest man in an assembly?"

Jeriah, Smiled. "Of course, father, the wisest man in an assembly is often the one sitting quietly, listening to everything everyone else is revealing. Not only their opinions and knowledge but their hidden motivations."

"Yes! son, this is true, and what else do you remember about a wise man?"

Jeriah thought for a moment, slowing his pace, then looked up with a bright look. "The foolish tell you all they know, and the wise tell you only what they need to satisfy."

Zechariah smiled. "Yes, this is counsel you should think on as all this unfolds. In addition, I advise you not partake in any of this venturing out to do miracles in the name of anyone other than Yahweh. Speaking with authority about something we know little about is foolish."

Jeriah's brow creased. "So you do not support the authority of Paul or Iesus?"

Zechariah put one hand on Jeriah's shoulder, the other out in a gesture to pick up their pace. “Speaking with authority on any subject, when you know little about it, is dangerous. I would like to speak with the church leader, Aquila, who is a friend to this Paul, about all of this before trying to accomplish anything of our own power. Do you understand my caveat, son?”

Jeriah picked up his pace, noticing the others slowing and looking back at them, “Yes, father, I understand, but if Yahweh is with us and Iesus is of Yahweh, then we are all of one mind and should not fear.”

“We are to fear our Father, and in this reverence, walk carefully. Only this will He smile upon.”

“I will heed your counsel, father; you have always been wise in what you teach. I only hope we will soon have a full understanding of these things and can be a part of the great miracles that are being accomplished.”

The group called back to them to hurry, waving them up.

Zadok called, “Zechariah, brother, come speak with us. We want your opinion on what we have planned.”

Zechariah looked at Jeriah once more. “Just remember my words, my son.”

He patted his son on the shoulder and joined the other elders up front. Zechariah and his son were from Ephesus and welcomed these men when they arrived, but Zechariah was reserving his final judgment of them after more time had passed. The younger men started speaking with Jeriah as he met back up with the group, and they continued making plans as they walked.

***

A blood-curdling scream resounding for several blocks echoed from a distant part of the city. It came from a small house at the end of a dark backstreet. The meager dwelling rested in a corner of the city near a broken wall, revealing a cliff and ocean beyond.

The door to the house crashed open, and a half-naked woman rushed out, screaming and gasping for breath. She stumbled and looked back in terror as if being pursued, though no one was following her. The woman clambered back to her feet, running in a staggered run. She made no attempt to cover herself with what was left of her clothing. It hung off her tattered as she ran yelling, "Demon, my God, my God, help me, demon!"

The woman was covered in blood, running down the right side of her face. She made it to a group of people in the center of that district and collapsed. Several women came to her aid, covering her and getting her out of the middle of the alley.

As they comforted her, one called out, "Call for the magistrate; call Aquila as well!"

Two bystanders ran off in different directions. One was a young boy around the age of thirteen. He ran non-stop for the church until he collided with the group of rabbis walking together.

"Rabbi, Rabbi," the boy choked, entirely out of breath and falling before their feet. "Please come, a woman has been attacked, and they are calling for Aquila and the Magistrate."

Zadok picked the exhausted child up by the shoulders. "Boy, calm down and explain to me what has transpired?"

The boy, still heaving deeply, explained what he saw and how people called for him to go for help. All the men started to talk amongst themselves.

Zechariah stepped forward. "Nabal, go to the church and bring Aquila or whatever church leader you find, and make sure they have told the local Magistrate."

Simeon said, "Wait! Nabal, before disturbing the church, we will go see what this is about. They are in preparations for tonight's festivities."

Zechariah nodded in concession but was clearly dissatisfied. Zadok put his hands up to quiet everyone, "Quiet, quiet! All of you, listen, we shall go look in on this woman as we are here to serve the people and then decide what is best. Alexander, will you meet with Hymenaeus to ensure everything for tonight is in order?"

Alexander nodded and continued on in the direction they had been walking. The entire group gathered around the boy.

Simeon leaned down to the boy's level. "Lead us, child."

The group headed back the way the boy had come. Zechariah looked at Jeriah with a concerned look on his face as they followed. A few minutes later, the men arrived at the scene where a small crowd was forming. The young men in the group immediately started disbursing them. "Everyone, move along to where you are needed; we will take care of this," said Jeriah.

Cohen and Marcus walked into the crowd speaking to the people, "Please move on so the woman can be helped."

Marcus was a Greek man in his late twenties-with green eyes, dawning short brown hair-who always had a smile on his face. He had joined up with the group the day they arrived in Ephesus, wanting to learn as much as possible under Zadok's tutelage. He was very good at dealing with people and was liked by most, and they listened to him and backed away from the scene.

A voice from the crowd said, "Who are you? I know Zechariah and his son Jeriah, but we don't know the rest of you."

Zechariah said, "My friends, these are great men of God who have come here to minister to our city and check on the church. We are all here to help resolve this issue."

Another voice in the crowd yelled, "You will need God himself with you to resolve this, I fear."

Simeon stood facing the crowd and said, "My friends and neighbors, we are the sons of Sceva, come all the way from the church in Jerusalem to serve Ephesus. Truly I say to you, if we are here, God is here with you as well."

Some people drifted off but then reformed a crowd farther away. This allowed room for the group of rabbis to reach the woman. She was surrounded by her nursing neighbors, who protected and consoled her. Zadok leaned down, looked at her bloody face, cringed, and then looked up at his companions. The woman was missing her right eye, which looked as if it had been gouged out. There was dried blood all over her face from the wound. One woman, named Zara, was wiping blood away with a wet cloth. There was a profuse smell of blood and sweat, mingled with urine coming from the victim.

Simeon said, "Woman, can you speak?"

There was no reply; she only shook and trembled in shock as the aids wrapped her up in a cloak someone had donated. One of the women looked over at Zechariah and said, "She only repeats the word demon and then calls out to God."

Zadok stood up and spoke with a loud voice, "Who can show me the place this horror has transpired?"

Many of the crowd simply pointed down the alley. Another woman lending aid to the victim spoke. "The end of the block, near the broken wall," and pointed down the alley. "No one will go near it. The man has been crazed for weeks and attacks any who come near the house."

Another old woman in the crowd spoke up. "He has a spirit, and it has taken all the goodness from him."

An older man raised his hand and said, "I'll show you where it is. I know the man, or I knew him. His name is Meraioth, and the injured girl is his daughter, Tamar. He was a good man once; who he is now, I know not."

The hunched-over man was in his seventies and balding. His head was burnt from the sun; he had a weathered face from years of hard labor, and he used a cane to walk as he stepped out in front of the crowd.

At that moment, the injured Tamar started to scream again and struggled free of the aids around her. She backed herself up against the wall and seemed to be looking at something or someone who was not there.

"Please, please, no more, I... I will not disobey again," nodding her head back and forth as she tried to back away from the unseen terror down the alley.

Simeon said, "Woman, we will not harm you. You are safe now."

Tamar looked in his direction for a moment and then back at whatever unseen thing stole her peace. The other women rejoined her to help. Zechariah turned to his left and looked in the direction she was staring. He could see the long walk down an alley, but no one was there.

The sun was beginning its departure for the day, and the horizon reddened.

Zechariah looked at Zadok and Simeon, "If we are going to deal with this man, I think it best we go while we still have light of day."

The assembly of men began walking down the alley. At that moment, the two Magistrates arrived and called the crowd's attention. Zechariah put his hand up and looked back to halt his group.

"Where is this victim we've been called here for?" said the taller of the two soldiers. He was a man in his thirties, wearing the armor and gear of a well-paid Roman soldier. He was muscular with short brown hair. The other, in his twenties, was a little thinner, with short curly hair. The smaller soldier looked at Tamar and seemed nervous and unsure of himself. He also wore armor, though of a lesser quality than his superior officer.

The crowd pointed to Tamar lying on the ground. The Magistrate walked over to her with his first officer following behind.

"Can she speak?" He questioned one of the women.

Zara, who was still attending to Tamar's wounds, shook her head. She looked at Zechariah and then back at the soldier. "These men were on their way to see the one responsible for this when you arrived." She continued to wash the blood off Tamar's injured face.

Zechariah moved to the front of his group. "We've been told that the father of the victim did this. Will you see that justice is served?"

The soldier nodded, looked at his subordinate, and said, "Make sure this woman is taken someplace indoors and cared for properly, and then follow after me."

He then knelt near the woman and looked at her. "What are we expected to find down this alley?" He looked up at Zechariah.

Zadok stepped forward, "The crowd says a demon-possessed man, I expect nothing more than a drunken fool who has lost his way." Zadok stood there with his hands folded on his chest in the hems of his fine cloak and then pointed to the old man. "This man here has offered to lead us to the house."

The soldier looked past Zadok and then to Zechariah. "Zechariah, you are admired among the people. Do you agree with what this man has said? Is this simply a drunken fool abusing his daughter?"

Zadok began to respond, but Zechariah put a hand on his arm and stopped him. "I know all that you know, Calimus, nothing more. I suggest you and your officer both come, and armed."

Zadok's face tightened, "We can handle this, Zechariah; why bother Rome over every disturbance we have? We are not children who still need to suckle from our mother's teat."

The crowd of men behind Zadok chuckled.

"We will go deal with this unruly man and be done with it." Zadok said in a loud voice, "Remember, we have a feast to join very soon." Zadok put his hands on the shoulders of two of the young men in their group as he turned and headed down the alley. The group of men turned with him and started walking. Jeriah was the only one who remained. He looked at Zechariah and Calimus. Calimus turned to his first officer, "Trophimus, leave the woman to us. Go bring me four armed men and two sets of shackles."

Trophimus stood and was off without another word. Jeriah postured in a desire to follow Zadok and the others, and Zechariah nodded.

"I only want to see what transpires. I will not get involved," Jeriah said.

Zechariah gave in with a look of frustrated consent. Jeriah smiled at his father as he ran after the men. Zechariah crossed his arms and looked at Calimus.

"I can call them back if you think it best." Calimus put a palm out toward the men in question.

"No, I am not an expert in any of the matters before us. My opinion is simply one opinion. Zadok comes highly endorsed from Jerusalem and seems to be comfortable dealing with situations like this. Still, I'm glad you will bring men, to be sure."

Calimus put a hand on Zechariah's shoulder. "Come, my friend, let us help these women get this poor blind wretch someplace safe, and then we will dispel all your concerns and be sitting with a warm meal in both our bellies."

Calimus handed Zechariah his cloak and picked Tamar up in his arms. "Lead me someplace safe to lay her." He said, looking at all the women who were helping her. They looked at each other bewildered.

"LEAD! NOW!" Calimus said.

The women scurried together down the alley to the main street, looking back nervously and talking amongst themselves.

Zara looked back and said, "We will go to my home. Will you explain to my husband that you have demanded a place for this woman?"

Calimus nodded impatiently, "Yes, now lead!" He looked at Zechariah as they followed the women along. Zechariah looked at the woman and then at Calimus. "Her name is Zara, and her husband is a brut, himself. You may need to take the time to make it clear to him that she is under orders from Rome. Will you do her this kindness?"

Calimus nodded, "I will," as he carried the injured woman.

Just before they turned onto the main road, Zechariah looked back once more. Jeriah had just caught up with the group near the end of the alley.

✦ The House ✦

Shadows were growing long in the alley where the group of men stopped. The sky was developing a deeper red as the sun began to set. The ocean breeze had become a blustery wind, which threatened to become more. Something nasty seemed headed their way.

Simeon was the first to speak. "Bring the lanterns up front."

Two younger men, Marcus and Uzzi, came forward holding lamps. Marcus handed one to Simeon and lit it, then lit his own. Marcus turned to Uzzi and lit the two he was holding. Zadok took one out of Uzzi's hand and nodded intolerantly for him to move to the door. "Let us be done with this. We have plans this eve.

Simeon walked up to the door with Uzzi and Marcus and pushed it open. They covered their faces with their cloaks, offended by the profuse smell of decay and human waste. The house was dark and seemed empty as the nine men crowded the doorway. Jeriah was at the back with Nabal and lit his own lamp.

"Can you see anything?" said Nabal.

Simeon was the first to enter, followed by his son Uzzi and Marcus. As the light of their lanterns illuminated the front part of the home, they could distinguish evidence of a violent altercation. The rest of the men filed in.

Zadok and Abimelech went to the left, followed by the old man who led them there. Simeon and Marcus had moved to the right, as they entered. Uzzi was in the center, with Jeriah and Nabal bringing up the rear. Stools were toppled, and broken pottery lay strewn all over the place. They were in a rectangular room, with another adjoining room, a kitchen, in the back left corner. A fireplace was to the right, now behind them. There were no windows in the front part of the house. The entire group of men was now facing the kitchen.

"Bring your light over here to the table," Zadok ordered.

Marcus came closer, followed by Simeon, bringing the group into a semi-circle. Revealed by the light of their lamps was a naked man slumped on a stool.

His knees were wide, exposing his distended belly and genitals. His right arm rested over a large jar, his left rested on a table. Jeriah came up behind them and peered over the shoulders of Nabal and Uzzi to get a better look.

BOOM!

The front door slammed shut so hard it rattled everything. The wind had picked up to a gale and started to howl outside. Jeriah immediately felt a chill come over him as all the warmth left the room. There was a deep darkness here.

"Let us go, Nabal said. "This weather is going to be bad soon. The man is asleep. We need not disturb him until he sobers up. Deal with him then."

"Quiet boy!" Zadok said, looking back at the grotesque man who started to laugh in a low guttural way. The Laugh came from deep within him, yet Jeriah could feel it echo in his skull. The group backed up as the man lifted his head and smiled in such a way it made their hair stand up. The skin on his face was sunken, and his eyes seemed to bulge from their sockets. They were icy azure eyes, so unnatural they could not be mistaken for human.

Marcus backed into Uzzi, stepping on his foot, and Uzzi groaned, dropping his lamp. The group of men jostled to recover themselves and the lamp. The frightful-looking man fell into shadow for a moment, revealing a flicker of yellow luminescence from his eyes. Jeriah's gaze was locked with his. *You are no man, are you?*

The man seemed to grow and stretch along the wall from the shadows he was casting. He stared at Jeriah and, for a moment, looked puzzled. His gaze soon returned to the men in front.

"Why leave…you just got here?" The man said.

He let out a growling moan as if an animal was stretching after a long nap, then gave them an in-humanly wide smile. It reached from one ear to the other and looked as if the ends of his lips were torn to accomplish this. Meraioth had what looked like dried blood all over him. From his mouth to his groin was a wide flow of blood and saliva. Meraioth stared at Zadok to his right and then looked up at the ceiling, resting his head on the wall behind him.

"No, you'll stay."

He started to relieve himself right where he sat. A healthy flow of urine arced out between his open legs; it became a puddle on the ground between his feet. The men cringed. Marcus tried backing up again, but they were too crowded to accommodate this move. Simeon moved to the right, and Cohen followed him, creating more space around the demon-possessed man. Jeriah was now able to come closer.

He came up beside Marcus putting a hand on his shoulder. Marcus started. "We should leave."

"QUIET! Everyone," Zadok scolded and looked intently at the mess of a man before him. Jeriah's added light illuminated the man with more detail. He had crusted dirt and blood all over him, and it looked as if there were feces on the floor next to his feet. Jeriah felt a deep sense of fear come over him. He could see his father's eyes and wished he had heeded his warning to stay behind.

Zadok started to speak. "We are the sons of Scev—"

"SHUT YOUR JAW FOOL!" shouted Meraioth, in a voice that seemed more animal than man. The house shook as if from a mild earthquake, though Jeriah doubted anyone outside this house felt a thing. Marcus and Nabal retreated to the door, clearly shaken by what they were witnessing. Both men fought unsuccessfully to open it.

"It is locked. Somehow this monster has locked us in here!" Nabal bellowed, rattling the door to get it open.

Jeriah slowly backed up towards the right side of the room behind everyone and blew out his lamp.

"Hah hah hah hah hah," The thing chuckled. It was no longer a man.

Jeriah could feel the buzz of energy flying about the room, causing the hair on his head to stand up.

"Let me try," squealed Marcus, pushing in next to Nabal. He tried to get the door open. Thunk, clunk, thunk, clunk, the door rattled with no success.

Zadok spoke again. "We are the sons of Sceva, and you—"

"I SAID SHUT YOUR JAW, WORM!" It roared.

The Wall behind the Meraioth cracked, and the ground trembled.

In an instant, Meraioth was up and in front of Zadok carried by an unseen force. Zadok flew across the room and hit the ceiling and part of the wall before landing lifeless in the corner near the door.

Their guide screamed as he turned to run away from the creature but was not fast enough. It grabbed the old man and twisted his head all the way around to face him. The room resounded with the twisting crack of the old man's spine as his neck broke. Meraioth looked into the eyes of the old man as his body hung below, twitching in its final death throws.

"I told you to go away, old man. Now, look what your disobedience has earned you."

Meraioth threw the dead man into the corner next to him. Then he turned to Abimelech, who screamed and turned to run as well. It jumped on his back, taking him to the ground. All the men were in shock by everything they just saw. Uzzi grabbed the creature's left forearm to keep it from attacking his friend. It bit deeply into Abimelech's back and shoulder, drawing a flow of blood and screams from the helpless man. The creature ripped at his cloak, shredding it with what now appeared to be claws protruding from his once-human hand.

Uzzi yelled, "Help me!"

Jeriah was the first to react. He ran to the creature's right side and grabbed its other arm. Both men pulled with all their strength in an attempt to keep the thing off Abimelech. Simeon and Cohen remained still, paralyzed where they stood. Marcus and Nabal doubled their efforts to get the door open to no avail.

Clunk, clunk, clunk, clunk, the door sounded as they rattled it back and forth as one. The creature started to shake and vibrate in their hands, but they did not let go. Cohen ran to their aid. There was a horrible sound of cracking bones as the monster twisted its head all the way around. It now faced the men holding it from the back. It snapped at both men with its sharp teeth. Jeriah let go in horror at seeing this.

He backed away, his face turning pallid, as Cohen took his place, holding onto the creature's right forearm. The demon grimaced as more cracking and dislocations occurred within its now grotesque body. Its arms twisted to face backward. It grabbed hold of both Uzzi and Cohen's collars. Abimelech struggled to crawl from under the thing as it slammed Uzzi and Cohen into each other like a child clanking toy blocks. A sick joy on its face.

"GREERRROOOLLL!" It roared and then threw both men in opposite directions. Cohen hit the wall and landed dazed on top of the old man's corpse. Uzzi flew across the room, slamming into the western wall. The hulk of a man cracked the wall with his impact, allowing wind from outside to howl into the house near Zadok's body. The demon contorted its arms and head back into position as Abimelech scurried out from under it. He crawled towards the door to his friends who were working to get it open.

"It will not budge," yelled Marcus.

He began beating on the door and slamming into it. BOOM! BOOM! BOOM! The door remained solid.

Simeon called out to them, "Nabal, Marcus, to me, we must be united!"

Marcus gave up on the door and went to Simeon, followed by Nabal. Jeriah ran around to Abimelech and helped him to the door.

The demon rolled over onto its back and started to cackle loudly. The sound felt like it came from a deep cavern. Jeriah tried the door once, then went over to check on Zadok.

"We are the sons of Sceva," Simeon shouted again. "We come with the authority of the Lord God of Abraham."

The thing rolled onto its side in the center of the room and looked at Simeon narrowly. Its eyes reflected a yellow glimmer of light.

Simeon continued. "We adjure you in the name of God and command you to leave this man you have infested, unclean spirit!"

The creature seemed assaulted by the words and writhed in pain on the floor. It pulled itself into the fetal position and covered its face with its long clawed hands. The house began to shake again, and a swirl of wind circled about, picking up dust and debris. Simeon smiled at his students, who seemed encouraged by this. All three stepped closer to the thing.

At the same moment, Cohen came out of his daze and sat up.

"In the name of Paul's Iesus!" Simeon continued, echoed by the others. "And our God, we adjure you. We banish you from this place."

Cohen cringed as he realized he was sitting on a dead man, got up, and stood on the opposite side of the demon with his hands up.

All four men repeated, "In the name of Paul and Iesus, be gone!"

The thing squirmed on the ground in pain, its face still covered by hideous hands.

It spoke in a little girl's voice, "Please, no, I do not want to go."

Cohen's eyes were wide when he looked at Simeon and the others and edged towards the door. Abimelech was on the ground near the threshold holding his right arm, his shoulder bleeding profusely.

The creature stopped squirming and just lay there for several moments. Everyone grew silent, wondering if it was over.

The little girl's voice spoke again. "Please don't make me go; I'll be good."

"BE GONE, DEMON!" Simeon shouted.

The thing uncovered its face, now contorted and elongated with a horrible grin. It revealed rows of sharp teeth. Its jaw was agape so wide it could fit a man's head in its bite. It no longer resembled a human; its face long, eyes spread apart larger than normal, with dead-pale-eyes.

Its neck was almost a foot long and hands longer than a man's forearm, ending with talons. The monstrosity's chest cracked as it distended and rose in the shape of a bird's. Its legs contorted and crackled as they stretched in length before the men's eyes.

The demon started to laugh, first guttural, then becoming louder. The voice was like a man and beast in one. Simeon looked at the others, fear and confusion washing over his face. He started to edge around the creature, towards Jeriah and the door. The others followed him, keeping their eyes on this new thing on the ground before them.

The demon was up instantly, its head hanging down like a bull ready to charge. It eyed Simeon and rotated in place as the men circled it.

"Paul, I know… Iesus……I know… but you .... Who are you? All I see are fools." The creature said. "You know not of what you speak."

Cohen fought the door with all his might, but it would not open. The creature leaped without taking its eyes off Simeon, smashed Cohen's head into the door, cracking it down to the bottom, and then smashed his head into the doorjamb with a horrible sound. Cohen's hands splayed out, and his body stiffened before dropping to the ground.

Before anyone could react, the demon stomped on Abimelech's good arm crushing the bone with a crunch. Abimelech screamed in agony, rolling onto his back and pushing himself away from the creature with his feet.

Jeriah moved to Uzzi and checked his condition. The others froze where they stood, not knowing where to run. Jeriah was terrified, looking all around for another way to escape. Then he looked back at the hideous thing as Abimelech screamed for help. The demon had picked him up by his hair and was holding him dangling off the ground in front of it. The creature stood nearly seven feet tall now; it examined Abimelech for a moment before tossing him into the door, where he lay crumpled next to the body of Cohen.

The creature turned towards Simeon and the others. They split, running in different directions like deer spotting a predator. It shot its left hand out, smashing nothing but air, but Nabal flew across the room, slamming into the back wall, landing on the table.

A split second later, it leaped forward, grabbed Simeon by the chin and the back of the head, and pulled Simeon's face to within an inch of its own.

"You should have stayed and polished the silver like your father wanted, Worm."

Simeon squirmed and attempted a stifled response. Jeriah could see the fear in his eyes and felt rage well up inside of him.

Simeon managed a muted, "please, let me go; I did not know who you were."

It laughed. "So you know who I am now, do you?"

Simeon looked past his captor, his eyes pierced Jeriah's, then moved to Uzzi. Jeriah knew what he was thinking, "Get my son out of here." Simeon felt the hold on his jaw slacken and yelled in the thing's face, spittle flying.

"Yes, you are the Destroy—"

Blood splashed on the wall behind the creature as Simeon's twitching body staggered and dropped to the ground.

Marcus fell to the ground next to Jeriah, who stuttered to stand back up. The thing turned towards them. It smiled, face covered in bright red blood save for its eyes and jagged teeth.

Jeriah backed against the wall as he saw Simeon. Marcus crawled for the door once more, looking back at the nightmare. Jeriah touched Uzzi to see if he was alive, and the large man looked at him, confused but okay. Uzzi sat up, saw his father, and fell back again in shock.

Jeriah closed his eyes and prayed while he waited for the blow that would take his life. When it did not come, he opened his eyes and saw It moving towards the table where Nabal lay dazed. It picked Nabal up by his cloak. Nabal's feet dangled off the floor. He reared away in revulsion as the thing brought his face close.

"No, you will not do either," it said and then shook him back and forth, slamming him into the walls. Nabal only gained freedom as his clothing ripped. He dropped to the ground half-naked and bound for the door.

Marcus was now beating and kicking at the widening crack in it. Jeriah ran to help the two get the door open and turned back, only to see the creature was gone. Jeriah scanned the room as the others beat at the door, then screamed, "Hurry, it's on the ceiling!"

They all looked up to see the thing, now resembling a spider, crawl toward them. The creature dropped from the ceiling right behind them, grabbed Marcus by his cloak, and swung him back and forth. Marcus yelped as he was repeatedly slammed into the wall. The other two men dropped to their knees to dodge being hit by the flying-man-projectile, then backed away from the door. It kicked at the two, crawling away, sending them sprawling to the ground. Marcus used the brief reprieve of being shaken to drop out of his cloak and escape.

Still on the threshold, Abimelech tried to crawl through a new hole at the bottom of the door. The creature grabbed one of his legs and he screamed,

"Noooo!"

Uzzi charged at it with a large piece of firewood held over head. "DIE!"

He hit the demon upside the head with all his strength. There was a crack as its head folded sideways from the blow. The creature dropped where it stood. Uzzi swung repeatedly, crushing bones with each blow.

Jeriah grabbed him. "It's dead; help us here."

Jeriah, Nabal, and Marcus worked frantically to break the door down. Uzzi dropped the wood in his hand and went to work on the door. He pulled at a piece of wood that finally gave, causing the door to cave in the middle. At the same moment, the room filled with the sound of bones cracking and popping. Uzzi looked back to see the thing standing again; the hideous smile full of jagged teeth had returned to its face.

Before anyone could react, Uzzi turned, fists above his head, and ran at the thing screaming, "Die demon!"

Jeriah watched as Uzzi pummeled it. Marcus tried to grab him and pull him to the door, but he would not leave. Marcus gave up trying to get Jeriah to come, grabbed Abimelech, and started to pull him out the door. Jeriah's gaze was locked hopelessly on the battle as the creature grabbed both Uzzi's arms and spread them out. With its greater strength and reach, the creature stretched the man's arms to the point of dislocation. Uzzi's face contorted as he groaned in agony. He tried to kick the demon, but his efforts were futile. He stared at it with a look of defeat, and then the demon head-butted him repeatedly.

It threw the man at the doorway, knocking Marcus and Abimelech outside and sprawling to the ground.

The house began to shake again, and the wind howled like a tormented soul. The thing picked Nabal up and threw him out the door. Nabal flew across the alley and hit a wall, crashing to the ground. Marcus was dragging Abimelech down the alley to safety but stopped when he saw Nabal hit the wall.

He set Abimelech up against a wall. "You are safe, I must go help the others." Abimelech, barely conscious, nodded and was out again.

Marcus ran to where Nabal had landed and started dragging him down the alley. The creature grabbed Uzzi, who swung and missed. It smiled at him. "You I like, I could use ten thousand more just like you when war begins."

It threw Uzzi against the back wall, and he landed atop his dead father. It looked at Jeriah, who was crawling around him towards the door, and said, "Stay!"

At that instant, the door reconstructed itself from its broken halves. The creature jumped on Uzzi and beat him repeatedly. Uzzi screamed in agony until growing silent.

Jeriah knelt again in fear and pleaded with God to spare his life or to make his death quick. It stood, back to Jeriah, looking down on the beaten giant of a man. "This man was worthy... Of all of you, he was the only one."

Jeriah's eyes were now full of tears. "God help me."

It spoke in a more human voice without turning back to Jeriah. "You will die an old man if only for the plans for your offspring."

The creature turned to face Jeriah, now shrinking in size a little. Its face no longer elongated, its eyes no longer bulging. It lifted one hand and watched it shrink back to a man's. Its stature changed as well. The thing's face was still covered in blood, but the eyes were becoming Meraioth's again.

Meraioth walked over to Jeriah, shaking, but instead of grabbing him, passed him and picked up the body of Zadok. Meraioth returned to the table on the other side of the room. He laid Zadok down on the table and grabbed the dead man's head in his hands. There was a popping sound as he twisted the man's neck back into place.

Meraioth looked back at Jeriah once more, then back to Zadok's body.

"Yes, you will have much offspring, and one day one of your descendants will play an important role in this war. For a future some foolishly believe is already set."

Jeriah was stricken dumb, not knowing what to say or do. He just sat there watching this creature as he moved the body around and looked into its dead eyes.

Meraioth turned around and began to shake. His knees knocked and gave out, and he fell to the floor, hands out like a dog, shaking. A cloud of black dust started coming from his mouth and nose. The man seemed to be coughing and choking it up. It was darkness in its purest form, becoming a cloud in front of the shaking man.

The cloud began to take shape before him. It first took on the form of a bird, then a serpent, and finally began to solidify into what looked like a giant gargoyle. Its wings stretched out to touch both walls, its head looked like some kind of hideous lion or panther with long sharp fangs. The creature looked like it was made of charcoal and ashes. Only the eyes had color, an icy, blue.

It moved and breathed like a living creature but also looked like stone. Its arms ended with deadly hands. Its wings were enormous, filling the entire room. This brought Jeriah back to his knees. The beast's wings folded behind its back as it stepped toward the terrified man. Jeriah got up and sidestepped to the door, only taking his eyes off the beast for a moment to avoid stumbling. Before Jeriah could make it there, the beast started to fill with light from within. The light seemed to pierce through cracks in its skin, which spread like fracturing faults in the earth's crust. The beast was slowly exploding into a white ball of fire—a supernova.

Jeriah fell to the ground and covered his face as the light became blinding. His arms felt like they were on fire from the heat but cooled as the blinding light subsided. He uncovered his eyes to see a being clothed in brilliant white, whiter than any garment Jeriah could have ever imagined. Straight platinum hair framed a flawlessly beautiful face. Its skin was smooth and perfect, almost translucent. It had beautiful eyes that looked like Sapphires, their aqua-blue radiance reflecting light like precious stones.

The entire room was alight, yet Jeriah could not tell from where this light source came. The being was the most beautiful Jeriah had ever looked upon. It captivated him, imprisoned him in its gaze. Its clothing seemed to be made of millions of tiny platinum fibers, with Diamonds lining every hem. It smiled at Jeriah as it came closer.

"The terror has left your face, I see."

Jeriah was speechless and just stared. This could only be God himself come to rescue him, or an angel of God at the very least.

"There was a demon here before, but now it is gone." Jeriah stuttered, "Are you, God?"

The being laughed. Its voice was like the sound of the most beautiful music Jeriah had ever heard. "Some would say that I am God. That depends on what side you are on."

As the being came closer to Jeriah, he could see tiny pulses of energy moving beneath the skin. The beings' eyes were so brilliant. The pupils were not round but shaped like stars ✦ encircled by Irises of Sapphire.

"You, Worm, are stuck in the middle of a family feud."

It turned away from him, looking about the room, and continued, "Like a pet torn between two masters calling it to their sides."

Jeriah sat up on his knees, "I do not understand," still gazing at the being of light.

"You are incapable of understanding; it is beyond that feeble mind to grasp your gods. Go! Before I have a change of heart and end you now."

Meraioth, now a small shell of what he was, lay whimpering on the ground. The being went to him and touched his head, and he quieted. Jeriah got up and backed to the wall, making his way to the door with the beings back turned to him. The door fell into pieces before him, and he edged outside, still within view of the being. Jeriah now thought it was an angel, though not one who stood by God in this war of which it spoke.

Could this angel be the demon I saw, or did the demon leave when the angel appeared?

Jeriah saw a crowd far-off, which was headed his way with torches. He saw Marcus about ten meters down the alley pulling Nabal back to safety. Marcus stopped and waved for him to come. "Hurry, Jeriah, run!"

Jeriah put a hand up, looked back into the doorway, and spoke to the angel within. "You are the being that was in Meraioth, are you not?"

The man-of-light ignored him, its focus on Zadok.

"I think I do understand some of this, though much is still beyond my grasp," Jeriah said.. "What confuses me is how a being of such beauty and radiance can be capable of such cruelty and darkness?"

"Go!" shouted the being in a louder, more monstrous voice. Its body shimmered with dark flashes of that profound darkness as if its rage snuffed out the light within it.

Jeriah turned and left, not running but a tired walk. He could see his father and soldiers, now twenty meters away, approaching quickly. A crowd of people, all carrying torches, followed them. Jeriah looked back after about fifteen paces and saw the light in the room vanish as if a light were blown out. He reached Marcus and helped him move Nabal next to Abimelech. His father and the soldiers were almost there now. He put his hand on Abimelech's chest. "You are safe now, my friend, rest."

Jeriah stood and looked at Marcus, who looked at him with disbelief.

"What have we witnessed tonight, Jeriah?"

"A lesson in humility, my friend," Jeriah replied.

Marcus looked down the alley and shivered as the sound of the crowd grabbed their attention. They were now only steps away when Jeriah walked to them.

Zechariah came first; with open arms, he grabbed his son. "You are well my son. Thank God you are well. I hope these men are the worst of it."

Jeriah looked at him gravely. "This is the least, father."

Zechariah checked him for injuries and held him in his arms for a moment. Calimus and his soldiers came around them. The crowd was getting louder. Calimus put a hand on Jeriah's shoulder and asked, "The others?"

Jeriah shook his head and looked over at Marcus and the two injured men. "We are all that is left. The rest are dead."

A few men and women from the crowd went to aid Abimelech and Nabal. Marcus walked up to Calimus and Jeriah.

"It ripped us to pieces, and we could do nothing to harm it."

Calimus looked down the alley, "Is it still inside?"

Marcus nodded, looking at Jeriah for confirmation.

Jeriah put a hand up in warning. "You don't have enough men."

Others began to crowd in, becoming a mob.

Jeriah looked at Calimus, "With respect, Magistrate, and for your safety, I suggest you wait for church leaders. They know how to combat such things as this, or I hope they do." Jeriah looked at his father and sighed, "Your advice of early today could not ring truer, father. Of wisdom and the understanding of things we do not know." Looking back down the alley he continued, "Aquila and this Paul who is coming know things we would be wise to learn."

CRASH!

A clay jar exploded against the wall of the alley. Another flew out of the house into the alley and shattered.

Meraioth ran out of the house screaming, "Aaaaarrrh GAAAH!"

His hands flailed about over his head. He stopped and looked at the crowd in surprise, then turned screaming again and ran towards the end of the alley where the wall was broken.

Four soldiers immediately ran after him, drawing their swords as they ran. Meraioth did not stop at the broken wall; he continued screaming until his figure just dropped off the edge. "Arrrraaaa youuuuu baaaaaaaaaaaaaa…"

Calimus and others in the crowd followed the four soldiers. They had made it to the edge and were looking down, shaking their heads. One looked back with a perplexed look on his face.

Zechariah touched Jeriah's arm and said, "It is over, son. We will move on from this."

"I will never move on from this father, nor do I want to. I believe it best I never forget what I witnessed tonight. I know now, without doubt, that we are surrounded by beings beyond our understanding."

Zechariah looked up at the sky, now dark and full of stars. "Yahweh rules over all of them, son, do not forget this."

Jeriah looked back at his father. "Does He father? Does he rule, or is this all a struggle for who will rule?"

Zechariah took his son by the shoulders. "Never doubt that Yahweh rules over all, son. Do not allow the deceiver to trick you with his deceptions."

"He is a destroyer father, one that is very powerful. I pray God is that much more powerful, or we are doomed."

Calimus and one of his soldiers entered the house with torches, followed by a couple of neighbors carrying out the bodies.

Calimus shouted, "One is alive!" Another soldier entered, and the crowd came around the entrance, trying to get a look.

Jeriah looked at his father perplexed, "Who? They are all dead, I am sure."

"Did you check them all?" Zechariah replied.

"I did, father, well, I... Uzzi and Cohen were obviously dead, father; just look at them. As well, Simeon lost his head."

"MAKE ROOM!" shouted a soldier. "MAKE ROOM, PEOPLE!"

Calimus exited the house, followed by two soldiers carrying Zadok on a blanket. He was moaning and had a hand on his face as they came out. Jeriah pushed through the crowd to get a closer look, followed by his father.

Calimus shouted to his men, "Secure this area now! Trophimus, you are in charge here."

One soldier handed his side off to Marcus who now carried Zadok along with the help of the other soldier.

As Zadok passed by Jeriah, he turned his head and opened his eyes. For the briefest of moments, they were a pale azure. Jeriah stumbled back and looked at his father.

"Did you see that?"

"See what, son?"

"His eyes!" Jeriah answered.

They both looked back at Zadok as he was carried off.

Jeriah ran up to him, "Wait!"

Marcus and the Soldier stopped.

He touched Zadok and said, "Rabbi?"

Zadok's eyes were now brown, and Jeriah looked at him with confusion. Reality was a shattered mess around him, and he was unsure of anything at the moment.

Zadok spoke in a raspy voice, but Jeriah could not make out what he said.

"There will be time for talk later," said the soldier. "We need to get these injured men to a physician."

Jeriah turned and went to the edge of the cliff. He could not see to the bottom clear enough to see the body, but he knew there was no way anyone could have survived that fall. He stared out at the ocean and could hear the crashing of waves on the shore below. The wind was beginning to calm some but was still boisterous.

Zechariah called to him. "Jeriah, come back here."

No answer came; he only stared out to sea. "Jeriah, do you hear me?" his father called again, "Jeriah … Jeri—"

Charles voice echoed … waking him.

Begin Again

A woman's scream startled Stephen as he awoke. He sat up and looked around his hotel room. The dream was cloudy, but lingering. He got up and looked out his hotel room window. There was a crowd forming around a body in the street, and police sirens were calling out from nearby.

"What a dream."

Stephen got up and found himself in front of the mirror again. This time déjà vu hit as his memory of the dream co-mingled with the events of the morning. Everything was the same until he reached for a shirt. He remembered a blue silk dress shirt in the dream and had his hand on it for a moment, then moved past it and put on a white one.

Did I change my mind in the dream? He was not sure now. The dream was pale in his mind, and he could not remember what shirt he actually put on anymore as if reliving it combined the two worlds, convoluting them.

He ate breakfast and went to the park without any more confusion, though he had a strong feeling all of this was the same as well. As he walked through the park, he heard the footfalls of two runners coming up behind him, and without looking he spoke.

"Morning, ladies."

The words fell from his lips at the exact moment the two girls past him by, both smiling in the same way. The rest of his walk in the park was identical to his dream, right up until he made the turn to grab a taxi.

"And cue the Mr. Crazy." Stephen turned and stopped in surprise when the man in the robe was not there. This was the first detail of the day that did not match his dream. He decided to continue along his original path anyway in order to follow the path he had taken in the dream. The taxi driver was the same and Stephen found himself back on track, buying the same snow globe, and getting back in the taxi to go to Things of Old. Everything was the same. He pulled out his phone and looked at it.

"Cue, phone call."

It rang.

The rest of his journey to the shop was exactly the same, save for a bewildered look from the taxi driver when Stephen finished his sentence handing him the money with a smile.

However, again, no street preacher. The same people were on the street walking to various destinations, but those Stephen remembered having to carefully navigate around the man simply walked through the space he had occupied. Stephen put it out of his mind and made it to the shop pushing the buzzer as he came to the door with a familiarity he did not have the first time.

Was there a first time?

Charles buzzed him in, and soon they were in their chairs, cigars in hand. Charles started to tell the story of Ephesus, as he did before, only this time Stephen was less focused on it and more on the man. Charles was mysterious. Sometimes he revealed a severity of age, and at other moments, youthfulness. The man was invigorating, and Stephen enjoyed being in his presence even though a repeat was playing out.

It was when Charles got to the house in the story that things deviated from the path in his memory. Charles' version was different, in many ways, mostly in that the creature Jeriah discovers was more benevolent. This new version was less violent and did not end with a possessed Zadok. What surprised Stephen the most though, was that he again fell asleep.

When Stephen opened his eyes Charles was leaning over him with his hand on his shoulder.

Charles smiled, "There you are. I guess I'm not the storyteller I use to be if I put my listeners to sleep."

Stephen still half in and half out of the dream tried to catch up. "Um…no, I was listening, I just dosed at the end there, I guess. It's so comfortable in here. I didn't get enough sleep last night. Forgive me, Charles."

Charles smiled and sat back in his chair. Not to worry, I've taken many a nap in this room myself."

Stephen stretched and was coming out of the darkness of sleep. He looked around the room. "So, the last thing I remember was the demon-possessed man running off a cliff. Did I miss anything important after that?"

Charles looked at him intently for a moment, then smiled, "No that was basically where I left off."

Charles held up the gold coin and waited for Stephen to acknowledge.

Stephen sat up and gave a nod, and Charles flicked the coin across the room to him. He caught it and felt its weight. It was cold, and heavy in his hand. It felt real, tangible, reminding him that he was now in reality, not another dream. Stephen opened his hand and looked at the coin. It had a Roman profile on one side. There were Greek characters around both edges. The coin looked old yet was in amazingly good condition for its apparent age. His first thought was that it must be a replica minting of an ancient Roman currency.

"That coin is said to be the one used to pay the man who executed Paul of Tarsus. Those were called—"

"Staters," Stephen finished for him, a little surprised he knew this.

How do I know this?

Charles' eyes widened for a moment, then he smiled, examining his guest, "Yes that is correct, very good. That is Nero's profile on the front. There are several relics like that one, which are not made known or available to the public. I have not been able to prove whether it is truly the coin it is claimed, but I have authenticated it as true currency of that time. That one was a gift from a friend. It is now my gift to you, Stephen."

Stephen shook his head, "Oh Charles, I couldn't accept this. We've only just met, and this must be worth—"

"Nonsense," interrupted Charles. "I am well-off. I give gifts as it pleases me.

To refuse, would only be an insult to a bright new friendship."

Stephen looked at the coin again and cringed at its value, then held it up to Charles and said, "I am very grateful for the gift, Charles. I could never afford a gift that matched your generosity."

Charles nodded, satisfied, then got up and stoked the fire before walking over to the bar. He lifted his glass in question, and Stephen shook his head. Charles poured himself another.

"I have many questions Charles and I have no idea where to begin. What happened to Zadok, And what about the young man and his father, for starters?"

"I could go on for hours talking about people from the past, but I don't think that's the question you wanted to ask."

Stephen got up, placed the coin in his pocket, and walked around the room looking at the art. "Was it a demon, or an angel?"

"Both," said Charles, "Or, all of the above, I'd rather say."

"I don't follow you."

"Well, you asked if it was a demon or an angel, but that was not all that Jeriah believed the being might be, was it?"

Charles walked over to his desk and opened a drawer; he was looking for something. Stephen came back near the fireplace and stood next to the mantel.

"He also thought it was God for a moment."

Charles pulled out a little leatherbound journal. He walked back to his chair and sat. "There are many in my field, or at my point in their research, that believe that it was also a god or God-himself."

Stephen gave him a doubting look as he sat.

"Now hear me out, I am not saying Yahweh, or Jehovah as many call him was there possessing the man but that Lucifer himself was. What I am saying, is that many believe Lucifer is either, another son of the Father-God or his brother."

"Where would you get an idea like that? I mean every piece of literature I've ever read contradicts this."

Charles opened the book and read to himself for a moment then spoke. "Well, some believe in a theory that puts Lucifer and Yahweh at the center of a great explosion, like the big bang. They believe the two were formed from this big bang or were transported to our universe in an explosion. This disoriented and dazed both of them.

Yahweh recovered first, and attacked Lucifer, subduing him, before he could fully rouse. With both their memories shattered from whatever brought them here, Yahweh claimed to be Lucifer's creat—"

"Wait a minute, hold up there," Stephen interrupted, "Let me get this straight. The big bang is now a reality again? Don't get me wrong Charles, but you're losing me here completely. I don't want to get into a debate over science but the best of them, I'm talking atheists like Francis Crick, the father of micro-biology agre—"

"Yes," Charles cut in, "Frances Crick, and what was his partner's name? Watson, I believe, James Watson, yes that's it. They discovered the double helix DNA strand. Crick went from believing evolution infallible to denouncing it and claiming Aliens planted us here like seeds, right? This left yet another question unanswered, 'who created the aliens?" Charles gave him a hard smile.

Stephen ignored him and continued. "Yes, well, anyway, the probability that we evolved would be likened to a tornado moving through a junkyard and reassembling a fully functional 747 aircraft by chance."

Charles chuckled, expecting the reaction. "We have a preacher in the room, ladies and gentlemen."

Stephen shook his head. "I disagree with religion. I believe it's something man made up to make a buck and to make weeping widows feel better at their husband's graves. However, my ancestors were not monkeys. That theory is the most ridiculous thing I have ever heard…."

"It is the mark of an educated mind to be able to entertain a thought without accepting it." Charles challenged.

"Aristotle…" Stephen returned.

Charles smiled with a nod.

Stephen put his hands out, indicating his surroundings. "I don't see any being wonderful enough to be able to put all of this together, beginning by chance, for one."

"Well, I don't think it *is* by chance, Charles insisted. "I said, many theories point in that direction. What *I* believe, is no one, knows what happened before that moment, no one on earth, anyway. I believe the two were locked in battle in another universe or dimension, and through both their power's being exerted at the same time, they created a powerful force like never before. Both were violently transported into our universe, or maybe it created this universe. All I know is they are both here and seem to be at war. Now you must admit, if God was the all-powerful creator of Lucifer, why wouldn't he just point and poof, bad guy gone?"

Stephen nodded, "I'm listening."

"That does not mean we all came from that explosion. Charles asserted. "I still believe we were created, but I believe we were created as a challenge between the two in an attempt to settle an otherwise eternal battle between them. Even many modern day Christians believe we were created by God to prove that His justice was righteous. In addition, through humanity having free will and choosing to be good rather than evil, Yahweh's is proven right. On the other hand, when humanity chooses to be evil or to do what pleases, they are proving Lucifer's point. That Yahweh was unfair in condemning Lucifer for wanting his freedom to live the way he pleased, instead of as a servant."

Charles put his elbows on his knees, leaned forward, and continued. "My theory is very much the same, with the exception of the roles of the two watching this play out. I believe two brothers, or gods, are wagered. They both are supposed to allow us free will to prove their side, yet they both tamper and coerce humanity for their own cause."

Stephen stood again and walked around the room, thinking about this. Some of it made sense, and some seemed to be reaching, yet much of what he already knew was also making leaps. There was some logic to what Charles said, but Stephen still had difficulty swallowing powerful beings floating around trying to sway humanity.

"Well, Charles, you have not failed to deliver on what I hoped to be an interesting morning…"he paused then added, "a person's mind stretched to a new idea never goes back to its original dimensions."

"That quote would have to be from Oliver Wendell Holmes," Charles answered.

Stephen smiled. "I will ponder these thoughts. I promise you that. What's more, I am indebted to you for sharing the story. Of course, I still have questions about the sources; if you would be willing to share that information with me."

Charles nodded.

Stephen leaned on the back of his chair. "So, two equally powerful beings engaged in battle started all this. Then created us to finish this war because they were incapable of killing each other or something?"

"Something like that," Charles answered.

Stephen came around and sat. "Well, it's fascinating, I'll give you that. At the very least, it could make for a good book."

Charles eyes lit briefly and he looked intently at Stephen. "This is my journey, the real story, not man's rendition. Would you be interested in helping me write such a book? I think with your writing ability and my research, we could be a marvelous team."

Stephen was caught off guard. He had no inkling that Charles was even considering a book when he made the comment.

"Um .... Ah ... well ... Really?

"Yes, why not? I have been struggling with how to put together all the research I have, and for the life of me could not figure out how to start.

"Well, okay, I guess… I'm in," Stephen said. "I will still need to be on the west coast much of the time, though. Will that be a problem?"

"Not at all; in fact, I am in the market for a place out west as we speak."

"Really?"

"Yes, I have my daughter Lucy heading up the search. She has been working with different real estate groups trying to find the perfect place. I simply detest realtors. To be honest, realtors and politicians. These are my least favorite people on earth." Charles smirked.

He really is a pleasant fellow…

"Well, let me know if I can be of any help, Charles. I know the best parts of town south of LA if you're not sure about a neighborhood."

Charles stood and looked at his watch. "Listen; let us conclude for the day if that is okay with you. Go enjoy the city for the remainder of your stay and call me next week. We can iron out all the details then."

"Sure, that sounds fine; I'll do that. So, the number on your card is the best way to reach you?"

"Yes, that is forwarded when I am away. Do you have a card for me, Stephen?"

"Yes," Stephen pulled out his wallet and handed Charles his business card.

"Simple and to the point, I like that," Charles said. He put the card in his pocket.

"I planned on making up something flashier but just never got around to it." Stephen apologized. "It seemed to be sufficient for dealing with the newspapers and magazines I've been writing for."

"Let us get our venture started, and I'll introduce you to Lorenzo, my friend who makes my cards. He can make you something a little flashier if you like."

Stephen shook his head, already feeling out of balance in this relationship. "That's okay, Charles; I can get something made up. I don't want to trouble you."

"Nonsense," Charles said, "If we are to be partners, we should reflect the image we want our audience to see. It is no trouble; a simple phone call with your information, and we will have them free of charge."

"Free of charge?" Stephen questioned.

"Yes, free of charge. You forget, I deal in wares that fetch hundreds of thousands of dollars. A few cards are nothing more than asking for a beer while at a friend's home."

Stephen laughed. "Okay, maybe I should lighten up. Just don't forget to call on me if you need any help regarding home shopping. I do have a few friends of my own in California."

Charles looked at him with a question, then waved it off.

"No, what? Stephen prodded. "We're partners now, right? Just ask, and I'll do my best to help, if I can."

"Well, Charles said, "I will be in need of someone to assist my daughter with things as she tries to set up the house there. She will be the primary resident when I am not there. We plan to make a separate level or wing for myself; the rest will be hers. Oh, and she said she wanted to get the name of a good designer too."

Stephen's smile grew. "Well, my friend, for once today, I can now help you. I just so happen to know one of the best on the west coast, and that's not just my opinion. Her name is Heather Swan, and she is my girlfriend."

Charles's face warmed. "How great. I always like to do business by word of mouth; it turns out better that way. Keep it in the family, I always say."

"I agree," Stephen said, "Heather will be happy to help out, and she is one of the best."

Charles started to walk them out to the front of the store. "Please tell Heather I say hello, and that my daughter and I look forward to meeting her. I will have Lucy call you to set up a lunch to get acquainted, if that is acceptable?"

"Of Course," Stephen said, "That would be great. I'll invite Heather as well. I know just the place."

"Good, then it is settled. Let us get together next weekend. Hopefully you will have been able to meet Lucy by then." Charles walked Stephen out.

"That will be fine. I'll leave the weekend open. I'm glad I ran into you. I feel we are about to embark on a great adventure." Stephen said.

Charles opened the door. "I do too, my friend, I do too. Watch out for the crazy down the street. I think he dropped one too many tabs of the LSD. He seems to have decided my street is his new playground this month."

"Crazy?" Stephen looked, and there he was, *right where I left you...*

He slid his hand into his pocket, feeling the cold of the coin and confirmation this was real.

"Oh, yes, I noticed him coming up. I'll stay on my side of the street, believe me. There was another one in Central Park this morning too."

"Big cities Stephen, you've got to love them," Charles said. "Be safe, my friend. You have a cab right there if you need." Charles waved at the cab driver behind Stephen, who pulled over.

"Okay, Charles, thanks again for a wonderful morning and for the Stater. I look forward to seeing you out west next weekend."

Stephen gave one more wave to Charles as he got in the cab. Charles waved back, then looked at the robed man down the street, a scowl forming. Stephen looked over his shoulder in the back seat and saw the man just staring at him.

He felt deja vu flush over him, a ripple, breaking the peace of a pond.

"Where to, Buddy," Said the cab driver.

"Actually, anywhere near the Empire State Building will do."

The cabbie nodded and pulled out, blasting the horn as another cab almost side-swiped them.

"Watch it!" He shouted, flipping the other driver, the bird, out the window. "Man, they will give a license to just about any fool nowadays."

Stephen grabbed the front seat as the driver pulled out into traffic.

***

Mitch walked down 5th avenue to his job, drawing his cigarette down to the filter and snubbing it out as he entered the bar. The place was empty, save for one bartender named Brad. He always passed work off onto Mitch, and Mitch was cool with this because it would leave him alone in the bar. Brad was an arrogant kid, who thought he had life by the jewels, but in truth, had no clue. Mitch sometimes pictured the guy in his 50s, balding, still hanging around bars trying to pick up uninterested women with tired one-liners, until one day realizing he was a waste of DNA and blowing his brains out. This thought always made Mitch smile.

Brad ran off with the usual excuses that he had to run a bar errand, and Mitch went to the back to grab the liquor for the bar. He sat on a case of vodka and lit another smoke. The place was dark and quiet. It smelled of sticky spills and wild nights. He pulled out a bottle of J&B from a stash he had and took two long swigs.

He sat there puffing on his smoke, waiting for the calming effect of alcohol to flow through his veins. It took a couple more pulls off the scotch and another smoke before the world was once again flat. Most nights enough liquor, and the touch of a stranger, pushed off the molesting assault of his misery. Although it was taking more and more booze and greater adventures with women to sate his, need to forget.

"Hello," a woman's voice called out from the front.

It was Brandy, the owner's girlfriend. She worked as one of the VIP girls and assistant manager of the nightclub.

"I'm back here," Mitch answered.

He got up, walked into the employee bathroom, and splashed water on his face. When he stood up, she was smiling at him in the mirror.

"Hey there, Sexy. How's my favorite bouncer?"

Mitch smiled. "Another day in paradise, sweet cheeks."

Brandy was a gorgeous redhead in her twenties who was allowing her college aspirations to fall by the wayside for the bar industry. She was smart, and Mitch liked her because she had substance. He often told her she needed to blow this life and go get a real one. She would always smile and say, 'what would you do without me?' Mitch cared, but then again, he didn't, so it never went past the occasional rebuke.

She sauntered up next to him, pulled out her compact, and worked a line of cocaine out of a vial.

"You want a bump, Sweetie?"

"Na, I'm already wound up enough."

She rolled up a twenty and smiled at him. She was wearing skintight short-shorts that revealed every curve and shape beneath, and Mitch took note as she bent over and crammed the crud up her nose. She stood, checked her nose for signs of trouble, and then gave him another look.

Solitaire

Stephen entered his room, now beginning to darken. He placed his shoulder bag on the chair nearest the bed and set a finely folded shopping bag with a gold emblem on the table. He went to the window and drew the shades open to let in the last of the day's sunlight. Stephen opened the bag, pulled out a blue felt-covered jewelry box, and sat on the hotel bed. He was in deep thought for a moment with the box out in front of him.

When to ask Heather.

This had been long overdue. He hoped this new deal was only the beginning of success for them. As he opened the jewelry box, Stephen began to imagine how he might ask her. The ring was gorgeous, sparkling in the setting sunlight. The stone was a princess-cut diamond. The dealer had explained all the details, which Stephen barely understood as he listened. He was too distracted by the rings calling to him. Stephen did not care; when he walked up, he knew immediately that it was Heather's ring.

After looking in two other stores with no luck, he had given up the search. He only entered the third after failing to catch a cab and found her ring seconds after entering the store. In the end, Stephen put almost eight grand on credit. He had assured himself that he could sell his motorcycle to cover the ring cost if the book deal did not pan out.

As Stephen stared at the ring's radiance and allowed the financial commitment and future with Heather to sink in, he felt at peace about the decision.

His eyes began to feel heavy; he had not slept well the night before. With any luck, a short nap would recharge his batteries before dinner. He set the ring, still in the open box, on the nightstand facing him and laid down looking at it. As he faded out, he thought he heard his phone ring but ignored it.

A dream had taken hold of him and dragged him away to a distant place or time...

***

The club was soon pumping, and the bar was packed with thirsty fools needing Mitch's services. He did his job quickly, and soon the two bartenders had things well in hand. Mitch went to the back and lit a smoke as Porcia and Brandy came in giggling.

"Those guys are such fools, but I love them because they always tip me on top of the gratuity in the bill."

Brandy smiled at Mitch as they passed him on the way to the employee's bathroom. Porcia was a beautiful strawberry blonde, in her twenties, with all the right curves and the attitude that came with them.

"You best be careful; they may look at that receipt sober and come back here hot." He warned.

"That's their problem. I didn't tell them to overpay me."

The two girls did a couple of lines and fixed themselves up in the mirror. Porcia looked at Mitch in the mirror and then smiled as she turned around. She leaned up against the sink and started caressing Brandy's rear.

"You like that, Mitch?" She gave him a wicked smile. "What's your deal, Man? Why are you such a mystery?"

Mitch finished his smoke and looked at Brandy as she touched up her makeup. She gave him a wink. Porcia continued caressing Brandy's rear and staring him down.

"Leave him alone, Porcia. He's just picky, that's all, huh, Mitch?"

Mitch smiled at her in the mirror, then looked at Porcia.

"What do you want to know?"

"I know what you want; it's in your eyes, Mr. mystery man," she bit.

"Sweet-tits, you couldn't handle a grown-up; best stick to the boys you been playing with."

Mitch lit another smoke and sat down. Porcia gave him a scowl and was about to say something when Brandy grabbed her by the chin and kissed her briefly on the lips. "Come on, Babes, we got enough men to tangle with out there, and they're all dying to hand over their wallets."

Porcia gave Mitch a sneer as the two walked out. Brandy smiled at him as they passed.

"Besides, Mitch is right; he'd rock your socks and have you spinning, Darling."

She shot Mitch a wink from the door before disappearing with her friend. Mitch rested his head against the wall of the empty room. A moment later, he felt someone looking at him. He turned his head to see Porcia leaning against the doorway. She just looked at him with a serious look for a moment before turning to walk away.

"Prove it." She said from the hall as she went out front.

I might just do that.

New York Dreams

It was dark, and there was screaming echoing all around. Stephen's eyes seemed to open on a scene of chaos and destruction. He was standing in the middle of a residential street on the crest of a steep hill. Ahead, in the distance, was what Stephen thought might be the Interstate 5 freeway.

I'm back in San Diego.

There were explosions occurring all around him like a horrific symphony. He could see the landing lights to San Diego International Airport past the freeway.

There was another scream, a second, followed by a third, all from different directions. Several cars were losing control on the freeway below. Both the North and South bound lanes were becoming a horrid pile-up, with cars flipping end over end. A truck slammed into a Greyhound bus, pushing them both over the edge down into the streets below.

There were static explosions all over the sky like balls of lightning popping. No bolts reached the ground but instead traveled across the sky before vanishing.

A jetliner's engines screamed as it dropped into a steep dive above high-rises to the south. Stephen looked in that direction. He could see part of downtown from where he was standing. The airliner pitched a hard left and straight down, heading for the NBC building. There was another boom with screeching tires and crushing metal behind him. It sounded like it was only a block away. He cringed but kept his eyes focused on downtown. The airliner crashed nose-first into the top of the NBC building. A massive plume of fire exploded through the building and out the top ten floors.

He thought of the crooked attorney who had burnt him a couple of years back. "There goes one dirtbag." He said, then felt guilty for the words.

Before Stephen could give it another thought, there were two more large explosions. One erupted from the Southbound lane, then a second from the Northbound, a little further north. The screams came from men, women, and children. There were sounds of great pain and anguish all around him. Stephen felt sick, and confusion overtook him. All of this was unfolding in a matter of moments, and he felt his blood pulled from his face. He had no time to react or feel anything.

A louder scream came from behind. Maybe this was some kind of terrorist attack. *That doesn't explain the cars losing control all over the place.*

At that moment, another airliner dropped from the sky. Its engines screamed from the excess force of the dive. It pitched sideways and was almost upside down when it crashed into San Diego's flight-control tower. A huge fireball erupted from the building with a shockwave that Stephen felt on his face. He stepped back in horror at what he was seeing.

"Heather!" he shouted, "Where is Heather?"

He looked in the direction of their loft but could not see that part of the city. Screams were sounding all along the freeway. Lights flickered, then went out downtown, followed by all the lights where Stephen was standing.

The airport lights flickered off, and then the runway lights came back on.

Another loud explosion behind him caught his attention, and he turned to see a woman staggering around the corner. She was sobbing, tears running down her face, making dark tracks down her cheeks. Both arms were out at her side as if for balance. There was another loud explosion from behind the building where the woman appeared. Stephen cringed and almost fell over. The woman was now only a few feet away when he called out to her.

"Are you okay?"

Sirens were blaring everywhere now. "What's going on?" Stephen asked her.

Her sobbing words barely made sense, but he still understood. "They're gone; they're all gone."

"Who Are—"

Boom! Another explosion let loose from a building, shattering the windows on his side filling the building with fire. He stumbled backward but kept his footing. The blast knocked the woman off the curb as if hit upside the head by the concussion. She stumbled sideways like a drunk. She kept walking down the hill, but now there was a shard of glass lodged in the side of her head. She ignored it, obviously in shock. Stephen reached out to help her, grabbing for her hand, but the moment he touched her, she pulled away in shock, as if seeing him for the first time.

Her arms were badly cut from the inside of her elbow to her wrists, like red ribbons of blood. She ran down the hill screaming. "No, Please, No…"

Stephen felt pain in his left forearm and looked down to see a small piece of glass embedded in it. He pulled the glass out and inspected himself to ensure there were no other injuries. He watched the woman run out of sight, then turned and saw a creature ten yards away, looking at him. It was the black monster he had envisioned while listening to Charles' story. Stephen's heart was pounding in his chest. The two stared at each other for a moment, and then the dark-winged horror sprung at him. Its arms outstretched, ready to rip him limb from limb as it charged. Stephen stood, frozen with fear. *If this is a dream, it had better be at its end.*

Time seemed to slow as the creature lunged for his throat, and Stephen fell backward. The creature's open mouth full of sharp teeth followed, snapping after him as he fell. It froze for a second in surprise, eyes wide, before flying backward. Stephen watched as the creature crashed into the windshield of a truck 50 feet away. The monster's departure revealed another being, but this one was made of the whitest light and had a form more like a giant man.

Fire engulfed the building next to him as the other explosions continued throughout the city. Stephen looked in amazement at both creatures as they looked first at him, then each other. The being that had just saved him was stunning, white like a star. It was the angel, both of them were here now. He tried to calm himself by rationalizing, *It's just a dream.*

These were the creatures from the story; this made sense. However, he was still terrified. Stephen's Protector was brightly clothed in radiance, as before, only this time it seemed brighter than before. Its hair was platinum with shimmers of the purest gold within. This was not the same being-of-light but another of its kind.

The dark beast roared so loud that Stephen felt the ground rattle as it readied to charge his guardian. It was so beautiful and powerful that Stephen was awestruck. The angel grew in size, and great fiery-white wings unfolded from behind it. Its bright clothing solidified into armor of gold and platinum. A great breastplate lined with diamonds formed to protect its chest, and a huge double-edged sword materialized in the angel's hand. The blade shimmered like a mirror and looked deadly.

The angel looked at Stephen and pointed down the hill. This, Stephen was sure, was an order for him to flee, but he remained frozen, sitting on the ground in the middle of the street. His guardian's free hand was engulfed in a silvery mist that formed into a beautiful shield of platinum and gold. It shimmered like a liquid yet held its shape as the angel swung it over its head. This move was just in time to deflect a massive blow from the dark creature's sword.

Clang!

There was an explosion of lightning, like fire, from the clash of sword and shield. Bolts of lightning shot out in two directions, taking out a power transformer and igniting a car in flames.

The dark gargoyle was now assuming a humanoid form similar to the angel. It too was brightly clothed. Yet next to his protector, it looked dim. Stephen could not put a finger on it.

Is it light or color I am seeing?

Their swords and shields clashed with great speed and power. Each collision emitted great sparks of fiery lightning, which jumped to cars and houses, engulfing them in flames. Their movements were fast and dexterous, almost like a ballet. Only this was a ballet of light, a dance of death, in which both were very proficient. The darker angel's armor was similar to his protectors, only it had less gold and what looked like black onyx and other dark gemstones throughout. This angel also wore greaves and leggings that looked like onyx.

The ground shook as if hit by a giant meteor, as the dark angel slammed Stephen's guardian to the ground producing a crater in the road. The guardian recovered quickly and backhanded the dark angel in the face with its shield. The dark angel flew backward again, only this time not landing in a windshield. Its great wings brought it to flight, and It flew up and then straight back down to its enemy with fiery rage in its eyes. The impact sent both angels into the side of a building reducing the doorway and wall to rubble as they fought.

At that moment, a hand grabbed Stephen's shoulder. "Stephen," the voice behind him spoke. He looked up and saw the crazy monk from the streets of New York. He was not wearing a robe anymore. He was wearing faded blue jeans and a light-grey tee shirt.

"You must go," the man repeated.

Stephen was so confused by all of this. *What was all of this about? Mom would understand all of this.* He was sure it was the same man, but he looked normal now.

"Go, Stephen, this is not your time."

Another loud boom shook him. The two angels were now on the other side of the street in a new pile of rubble, which resembled a burning apartment building. There were flames all around them as they fought, licking at them like cheering fans.

Explosions still rocked the night from all directions. San Diego was now a blaze. Bright orange glows lit Downtown, as well, several places north.

A howl came from behind. Stephen turned, and the dark angel lunged toward him. Its hands outstretched to grab his throat. It came within millimeters of its goal before being hit by what looked like a freight train of light. Stephen felt the sting of a cut across his neck as it happened. The two angels were across the street once more. The building engulfed them as it collapsed.

Stephen awoke, grasping for his throat and covered in sweat. He looked over at the nightstand. The clock read 3:30 A.M. *There's no way. I just went to sleep.* He had been out nine hours. He looked for the ring. Its case was now closed, but it was where he had left it.

He got up and went to the window. Looking down onto 46th street, he saw the man dressed in a robe walking east. He had curly brown hair and a short beard, just like in the dream. The man stopped and looked right up at his window. Stephen darted back, startled, then thought better.

This guy has some explaining to do.

He decided to go down there to confront the man, but when he looked back out the window, the man was gone. Stephen felt like he was losing his mind. He went to his bag, pulled out his notebook, and sat on the edge of the bed, writing everything he could remember from the dream.

After finishing his writing, he flipped on the television and walked into the bathroom. The news was on, and a reporter was talking about guerilla warfare happening in Rwanda. Stephen started the shower and got in. He recognized the street from the dream. He thought about the woman, also.

Who were all gone?

Stephen let hot water rain down on him, calming him. "The Rapture!" Stephen said aloud. *I dreamt of the rapture. But what about the angels?* He could not remember a thing about angels fighting during the rapture. He thought about Sunday school and his time in private school. There were many lessons on the end of days, yet nothing about angels fighting in the street. He remembered hearing about great battles after that but not when the rapture came.

You really should have paid better attention, son. His mother's voice returned.

He did remember that subject being more exciting than all the other stuff, and there was no mention of angels fighting in the streets, this much he was sure of. *Dreams don't have rules.*

He looked down to see a little red in the water by his feet. Stephen was startled and looked all over for an injury and found one. A tiny little cut on his neck. "There's no way!" But there it was, right where that thing had reached for his throat.

I must have done that in my sleep.

What about the time? That dream didn't last nine hours.

He put it out of his mind, rationalizing other answers for injury to his neck. He finished his shower and then put on a bathrobe as he walked over to the mini-bar. He pulled out all several mini-bottles of whiskey and a can of Ginger Ale. He chugged two bottles, chased by some Ginger Ale, and then topped the can off with whiskey after each drink. He turned off the television and sat in the dark.

"It was so real," he whispered to the dark room as he poured the last bottle of whiskey into the Ginger Ale. He felt calmer, a little buzzed. He thought about calling Heather, but it was far too late. He lay back down and was soon asleep.

San Diego

Heather Swan

She sat removed in a crowded conference room, nodding every few moments in agreement as her department head spoke. In reality, her mind was somewhere else, along with her heart. Heather knew her man's flight would be touching down within minutes, and she wanted to be there and touch him the moment he opened the door. She had work to complete, though. She always prided herself on being reliable.

She glanced at the clock again.

Heather had loved Stephen ever since she was a teen. She recalled the moment she knew this. She and her missionary parents went to China when she was twelve, but after one year there, she was so miserable that they allowed her to return to the states and board with Stephen's family, who were the church leaders overseeing their mission trips.

The two got along well as children, but the actual romance was not born until high school. This was a time in Heather's life when she needed love more than ever. It was in her first year of high school that her parents both died in a small plane crash. Heather was devastated. She stopped eating and became very ill, causing everyone concern. The Meyers did everything they could to comfort her, but it was Stephen who broke through her misery. His mother sent him into her room one day to try to get her to eat, and the seed of their love grew from there. These quiet moments shared between them anchored her. Soon she came through it and was able to move on. His understanding helped her through the roughest time in her life.

She spun her watch around on her wrist, checking its version of time with the clock on the wall. A man was droning on about the budget now.

She did not sleep well when Stephen traveled, and she'd gotten very little the last few days. The two of them shared everything and felt a close bond both being orphans. The Meyers were a great family, but there was only so much they could offer. Heather and Stephen filled the void left with each other's love.

Two clients were eyeing her across the room. She had already put one of the men in his place at a soft opening last year. The other elbowed the first and whispered something. Heather was used to this kind of behavior from many of the clients that her company worked with. She was an attractive woman but refused to use her looks.

The client leaned over to his friend. "So what's the deal with the brunette?"

"Off limits, Man, don't even try. She's all business."

"Too bad, she's a looker." He smiled at her, but she didn't notice. She was in the past. Heather designed nightclubs and restaurants, some of the nicest places on the West Coast. Her focus was usually solid, and she gave one hundred percent while at work, but today, she was ovulating.

"So what's the deal, Man? She the boss's girl?" the first man asked.

"Boss's, girl?" the other man snickered. "She owns the design firm downstairs and is the senior executive at this office."

She nibbled on her lip, wondering if it was too soon to bring up kids again. She wanted a family badly but always acted casual about the subject when it came up. That would not do anymore. Her clock was spinning, and thirty was just four years away.

I want a child by then. Now that she was making good money, and Stephen's writing was beginning to payout.

A family should logically follow.

Heather looked at the clock again. Five past ten.

Damn, only five minutes have passed? Time was creeping along at an unbearable rate for her.

She noticed the lustful client across the table and shook her head.

Nope.

He read her loud and clear, a little squashed. His friend smiled.

She drifted off again, imagining her future.

"So if we can get the zoning changed, this will allow the project to move forward as we originally envisioned. Miss Swan, can bring us up to speed on the mezzanine level and floating stage. Miss Swan…Miss Swan?"

Heather startled. Everyone was looking at her.

"Yes, I'm sorry. I was recalling the load calculations for the stage."

Lie.

"I am very excited about how things are progressing," *another lie.*

"Our German friends at Disco-Designs have finished the mock-up for the dance floor and hydraulics for the stage, And it looks like what was only a dream a year ago will soon be a reality."

The room erupted in applause. Heather ignored them and continued. "We were concerned that we would lose the ability for a pressure-sensitive dance floor, but with the new, lighter- technology offered through Matrix Systems, we can achieve our goal without exceeding our weight limits."

Heather walked around to the end of the long conference table. She was wearing a sleek cream-colored skirt-suit that clung in flattering remark to her figure yet was still professional. Her long hair was rolled in a braided bun in the back. She pointed to an easel, where she had a drawing of a stage that appeared to be floating on a small pond inside a glass-walled building.

"As you can see in this drawing, the stage is out over the water. All hydraulic systems are worked from behind, so they cannot be seen from any seating areas or dance floor."

Heather flipped a page on the easel.

"This is the stage back in position to be used as an extended dining area or VIP space. The dance floor can be set in several different programs. Examples include: single color, slow glow, changing with the beat of the music, and now, with the interaction of the dancer's footsteps."

This was followed by more applause from the executives around the table.

A Gift

Porcia slowly opened her eyes, and the midday light instantly caused her to close them again. Her head was throbbing, and so was her Vagina.

Other than the hangover and sexual soreness, she felt really good, though. Having him inside her felt, so right. It was the right moment for her. She wished it had been more romantic and less drunken, but she had wanted Mitch so badly when it happened that it was bliss, and that would be the memory she clung to when she recalled it.

Did I really say I loved him?

She knew she couldn't love a guy she barely knew and felt stupid for the words that spilled out of her mouth while she climaxed in his tiny bed. She looked over at Mitch, sound asleep next to her, and wished this could be more. She wanted to call her mom and talk about it.

The Loft

Stephens's flight was in a holding pattern, circling downtown San Diego. He looked out his window and tried to find the loft as the plane banked left. He looked forward to being home and getting some rest. Their loft was in the Southeast part of the city, with views of the bay and high-rises. It was located on the top floor of a four-story building, which Heather's company had renovated. The intent, when designing it, was to create a comfortable living space for the artistic mind, with ample parking and storage on the first floor—two things in short supply downtown.

Two artists bought the third-floor units and set up home studios. A novelist bought one of the second-floor units after a heated battle over the top floor with Heather and Stephen. Heather would not cave when pressured, and she and Stephen took both top-floor units. They converted both units into one large loft with offices on the other side for Heather's design company. The front of the design loft was divided into two adjoining offices for Stephen and Heather. A guest room and bath joined the offices and their home loft. The third and fourth floors were faced with eight-foot windows revealing San Diego to its residents. Heather's architectural company used the other unit on the second floor for their San Diego office, and the headquarters moved to Newport that same year. This was a great blessing for Heather because her office was now only an elevator ride away instead of a rush hour commute.

Stephen thought about all the love he and Heather put into setting up their Lair, as they liked to call it. Heather was the designer, but she was adamant about their home being a living extension of them both, so the two spent eight months in the design and decor of their home. It was spacious and modern, though much of the furniture had ended up coming from Ikea because they were up to their necks in debt in getting the place and investing in her design business. It took all of Heather's inheritance and much of their combined savings to accomplish, but the investment was beginning to pay off.

As he entered, Stephen dropped his bags just inside the door, walked over to the entertainment system, and turned it on. Smooth Jazz came to life, filling the air with a relaxing serenade of sax and piano as he proceeded to the bedroom. Entering the loft, one would find an open kitchen to the right with a large island cooktop and bar, surrounded by seats. Beyond the kitchen, to the right, was a pantry and wine closet. Separating the kitchen from the open lounge area was a dining table. To the left, Felix's cat castle sat along the wall separating the two lofts, followed by the double doors leading into the guest area and offices.

In the main lounge area was an entertainment system, pool table, and lots of seating, which made for great house parties. Heather often held parties there for her company. Beyond the kitchen and lounge area lay the double doors to the master bedroom room. It was spacious with its own view of the city. There was a large bed, with a small loveseat and chair facing the window. As one entered the room, to the right was a glass-walled bathroom with separate shower and Jacuzzi tub. The only solid wall in the bathroom was for the toilet, hidden off in the corner and out of site. Beyond the bathroom was a walk-in closet with a long seat in the middle. That was all Heather's design. Stephen just asked for a spot towards the front so he would not get lost.

He kicked off his shoes and fell backward onto the bed, exhausted.

No dreams, just sleep, please.

He was unsure how long he had been lying there when she came, but it felt like only moments. He heard the click of their bedroom door being carefully closed but did not open his eyes. He could smell her. His lover was in the room. He could tell she was now standing near the bed to his left, and he imagined the smile on her face. Stephen was so relaxed that he just lay there, focusing on the stillness in the room and her presence. He could hear her undress, and this excited him. The sound of jewelry being placed on her vanity came next, then the gentle movement of the bed as she climbed up beside him. He opened his eyes to see her lay down in the crook of his outstretched arm.

"I didn't mean to wake you, Hun. I just wanted to snuggle."

Stephen closed his eyes and took a deep breath as he pulled her close to him. "You didn't Love. I was just resting."

She put her hand on his chest and one of her legs crossed over his waist as she cuddled up to him. "I missed you, Stephen."

He squeezed her tight, "And I you, Love."

They lay there quiet for a while, her smell engulfing him. It was like the smell of spring flowers, like being in a field of them on a perfect day. It was not her perfume, he could tell the difference, and she never wore it to work. She said it wasn't professional, that she wanted respect from her co-workers, not proposals. Stephen was sure she still got both everywhere she went. This smell was hers, and it was wonderful, filling him with peace. It was the smell she gave off when they would work out or play together, the smell that filled the room when they made love—it was her. He opened his eyes and looked at her. Heather's silky dark hair was pulled back into a ponytail now, and her fair skin flushed in her cheeks. Her eyes were closed. He listened to her breathe, loving her.

She was wearing nothing but a pink tank top and a pair of white panties. Stephen admired her long slender legs and kissed her forehead, "I love you," he whispered.

"Forever?" she responded.

He smiled. "Yes, Baby, forever." They were soon both asleep.

A few hours later, Stephen woke to Heather playing with his hair. She loved to twirl his locks in her fingers, a habit she picked up back in high school, while morning her parents' deaths. Stephen would sit on the floor by her bed and tell her stories while she played with his hair on the nights she could not sleep. This comforted her, and Stephen loved being this security for her. Felix, Heather's amazing cat, knocked over something in the kitchen. By the sound, it was most likely her purse. She barked at Felix in her sleepy voice, never opening her eyes.

"Felix, leave my keys alone!"

Felix, was Heather's baby. He was black with a brushstroke of white on his belly. Felix was the smartest cat Stephen had ever known; not that Stephen had known many cats, but this cat was intelligent and had personality. However, Felix had a problem; his problem was that he was a kleptomaniac. He would steal things that were shiny or valuable, like keys and jewelry. Felix had a carpeted castle in the other room where he would stash his booty, and over the last year, Stephen managed to train him, or as Heather put it, bribe him into returning the last item stolen. Stephen would open a special jar of treats, hold one out, and then say the magic words. "Return the booty." The odd thing was, if there was something odder than a thieving cat, that this only worked for the last item stolen. No matter what Stephen tried, he could never get the cat to return anything else. It was as if, in Felix's mind, the other items were now his after so long in his castle.

"So, how was the interview with the man you went to see," Heather asked.

"It was good, very good. In fact, it was great." Stephen answered.

"You had me a little worried when we spoke on the phone last night. You sounded odd."

"So we did talk last night?" Stephen asked. "I wasn't sure; I was so out of it. I didn't sleep very well. I kept having bad dreams. I even fell asleep in Charles' study while he was talking."

"Oh, Honey," she kissed his cheek. "Did you miss your mamma?"

Stephen rolled toward her, their noses almost touching. He looked into her eyes; they glistened as her shy smile grew.

"I did miss my mamma," He gave her a wolfish grin and then a gentle squeeze to her rear.

She kissed his nose and forehead, "I don't sleep well when you're away, either." She said, kissing him more slowly. He gently bit her lower lip. She gave him an eager smile and then hugged him. "So you were sleeping when I called? That was early."

"Yeah, I got back to the hotel and laid down, planning on a short power nap, but I didn't wake until almost four in the morning. I vaguely remember my phone ringing, but that's it."

"You sounded tired. I didn't want to bother you."

"You never bother me."

"So it went great, huh, the meeting? Did you get all the info you hoped for?"

"Oh yeah, and more; in fact, I've got another book deal developing out of it and some business for you."

"Really? Wow! Sounds like a productive trip. I want to hear everything, Baby, but after I take a shower. Would you like to join me? You can wash my back."

Her smile faded into a wanton look. He pulled her against him, and she straddled him in response. They kissed passionately for a moment, and then she sat up on top of him and started unbuttoning his shirt.

"This new deal will change everything for us, Heather."

She looked at him briefly, then back at her task, pulling his shirt open.

"Oh…how?"

"Well, for one, I will be making the kind of money I hoped to be making so we could get married."

She froze, then flopped onto her back next to him, looking at the ceiling.

"Did I say something wrong?" Stephen asked. He cuddled up to her pulling her close again. She turned toward him, tears building in her eyes. She put one leg over his and stared at him. The emotion in her eyes was vast.

"What's wrong, Babe?"

She hugged him, her cheek against his. "Nothing's wrong, Stephen; I have everything I could ever ask for. I love you so much." Her lips tickled his ear as she spoke. Stephen relaxed, realizing he was miss-reading the tears, then hugged her again, putting one hand under her tank top and rubbing her lower back gently. "I love you too.

"So, when?"

"So when what?" he replied.

"When do you want to get married?"

Stephen smiled and let out a short laugh, "Well, whenever you want. I mean, I planned to take you someplace and ask you first and figured we would set aside money while we plan the wedding, don't you think?"

"Why wait?

"I don't kn-"

"I have enough money for the dress, and we can afford the rings. We can afford a simple wedding; why wait?"

Her response caught Stephen off guard. Heather was a very secure and independent woman. He knew she was more than ready to take the next step in their relationship, what with the hidden bridal magazines behind the laundry supplies and the baby magazines behind her shoe rack. He had no doubt it was time, but he always thought she would want a big wedding.

"Don't you want something formal?"

"No, I don't want all that. I want you, with our loved ones, somewhere beautiful. I want a beautiful dress and a handsome groom, and that's it."

"Babe, whatever you want is what I want. I just want you to feel special."

She was still holding him tight, and he could not see her face. He felt her tears on his temple as she spoke. Stephen tried to pull back so he could look at her, but she clenched. Her heart was beating fast, and Stephen could feel it pounding against his chest. "Are you sure you're okay," he questioned.

"Yes, I'm okay," Her voice was trembling, more beautiful than ever to him.

"So, ask me."

"Right now, like this, you in your underwear?"

"Yes, right now. I can take the underwear off, if you like."

Stephen laughed, "That sounds promising, Hun, but I wanted my proposal to be special for you."

"You're special to me. You make my life special. That's all I need. What would be more special than this?"

"Can we at least go out to dinner someplace nice, make an evening of it? I don't even have the ring on me."

"No, there's no—"

She stopped mid-sentence and drew back with shock in her eyes; she was gorgeous. Stephens's heart was pounding now.

"You bought a ring?" Her cheeks were flushed entirely."WHERE?"

Heather jumped up in a poised position beside Stephen. She was on her hands and knees like a puppy, ready to pounce. "Where is it, Stephen," she demanded. A serious look overtook her expression, which caused him to bust out in laughter. He loved this; it was already worth the eight grand he spent on the ring. She was like a little girl. He decided to mess with her a little. “Well…. I’m not sure. I think I left it lying arou-”

“STOP IT, Stephen, don’t play with me.” She was now standing on the bed, looking down on him like a mother scolding her child. Her beauty mesmerized him.

She has no idea how beautiful she looks right now.

She stood there with her hands on her hips. Stephen admired her body while she stood there, glowing like... *an angel.*

She pounced. Time was up, she landed on top of him again, knocking the wind out of him. Her face was now inches away from his own. “Where, Stephen?” she said, rolling his collar in her fist.

Stephen knew she meant business; still, he could not help but laugh even harder. Her serious look turned to a reluctant smile.

“STEPHEN!” she shouted, closing her eyes in frustration.

“Okay, Babe, Okay, I’ll tell you, but it will cost you two things, wait, no, three.”

“What are they?” eyes bright again.

“First, I want a kiss; second, I need you to go get me something; and third, well…we’ll talk about that later.

“I’m sure you were going get the third anyway, but what do you want me to get?”

He smiled, “If you get my bag, then I’ll tell you where—”

She was off the bed, then darted back and kissed him before rushing out the door. Stephen sighed, finishing his sentence.

“—it Is. . .”

He could hear her riffling through his bag out by the front door. “Hey, I said get my bag, not rip it to shreds.”

He lay there knowing it was no use; she was going to do it anyway.

“Move! Felix,” she barked at the cat, who was probably circling between her feet as she squatted on the floor, looking for her prize. Then there was silence.

Bingo. He grinned.

She took a deep breath and blew it out, “Stephen!” sounding winded.

“Yes, Dear?”

There was no reply.

“Stephen!” she said again, but sounding closer.

“Yes, Dear,” he repeated.

She entered the room with the open jewelry box in her palm; her eyes were wide. She pulled the ring out, letting the box drop to the floor, almost crowning poor Felix, who was following at her feet. The cat grabbed the box and scurried into the other room. Heather slowly approached the bed, putting the ring on. Its brilliant diamond shimmered in the light. Stephen could see its sparkle in his lover’s eyes; the two complimented each other. She sat staring at it, leaned over onto her side, and pulled her legs up onto the bed. Stephen put a hand on her stomach and pulled her against him. She looked at the ring on her hand as they lay there spooning. Stephen kissed her neck, then her shoulder. She was quiet.

“Do you like it?”

“Yes,” she whispered as if a secret.

Stephen watched as she moved her hand around, modeling the ring. He sat up on one elbow and looked at her. Her eyes were now closed. She held her ringed hand against her chest. Stephen tried to roll her on her back to look at her, but she became ridged, refusing the move.

“Ask me, Stephen, and tell me what you want... with me.”

Stephen laid back down and held her in his arms. “I want your love, I want your trust, and I want your companionship. I want your body—”

She giggled as he caressed her soft skin and kissed her neck up to the underside of her chin. She sighed, enjoying it.

“What else?” she asked.

“I want to give you my love, my life. I want to share it all with you, the good and the bad.”

She turned onto her back and looked into his eyes, still holding the hand the ring was on. They stared at each other for a few moments, and then she spoke. "What else do you want, Stephen Meyers?"

He kissed her. "I want to spend the rest of my life with you."

Tears filled her eyes again; a tear streamed down the side of her face and rested on the edge of her ear, glimmering in the sunlight from the window.

"Will you marry me, Heather Swan?"

She kissed him and put her arms around him, whispering in his ear, "Yes, Babe."

***

Felix was laying on the counter, looking out the window at all the city lights. The shower was running, and muffled giggles could be heard coming from under the closed door. Felix jumped down, sauntered over to the entertainment system, and lay on top of it, licking one of his paws. Jazz still poured out of the speakers. The phone rang, startling Felix. He looked in the direction of the answering machine as the outgoing message played, followed by a beep.

"Hello, Stephen, this is Lucy Rutherford. My father gave me this number regarding some help he said you were offering. I have found two houses I adore, but I would love to hear your opinion on the neighborhoods. Also, He told me you know a good interior designer. Call me when you get a chance. I'm sure you're still unwinding from your trip, so don't worry about getting right back to me." She finished by giving her contact information and schedule while in California.

Felix got up, startled by something, and scurried under the loveseat. He peered out toward the front door and hissed, then backed farther under the seat. A shadow fell near the bottom of the door, then disappeared without a sound from the hall. A few minutes later, Felix crept around the room into the kitchen and approached the door sniffing the ground. He jumped up onto the counter and resumed looking out at the downtown cityscape.

Bloodlines

Mitch stirred in his bed. It was late in the afternoon. He could smell Porcia in the room still. He had pretended to be asleep when she left hours ago to avoid an uncomfortable moment. He liked her smell, and this bothered him. *No attachments.*

Warmth stirred within him, too, and he felt anger for this. A demon was smiling at him from across the room. An empty beer bottle on his nightstand made it across and into a wall shattering. The room grew darker though the sun was blasting in the window.

"Now, Now, Dear," the demon spoke. "You are only human… or mostly human." It chuckled. Now becoming his dead wife again and touching his hair. He slapped the hand away, and it exploded into dark dust and reformed. "Darling, you can have all the fun you want with whores, but you are still mine." It said.

"Ours," another voice added. His dead daughter now standing next to the other demon. "they're all whores, Mitchel, all of them, and whores need to be punished, don't they?"

He got out of bed, waving them out of his way like smoke as he went to the fridge and grabbed a beer. He stepped on a piece of glass, drawing blood as he returned to the bed and sat facing the window. He pulled out the shard flicking it away and opened the new beer, guzzling it.

The little demon picked up the shard, intent on tasting the blood, but the moment it touched it to its mouth, it burned, and the thing screamed in agony and vanished into nothing, reappearing on the ceiling and touching its now wounded face. "What is he?" it asked the other demon.

"Nephilim," it answered. "Our instrument." It crawled up the wall and watched Mitch staring out the window. He ignored them.

New Friends

Heather came out of the bathroom with a towel wrapped around her and kissed Stephen as she passed. He admired her as she let the towel drop. She stood there for a moment, allowing him to before pulling on her robe and sitting down at her vanity. The two had spent the last few days alone at home, only leaving once to pick up takeout. Stephen pulled on a dress shirt and tucked it in. The doorbell rang, and he looked at Heather, "She's early."

Heather looked at her clock and then back to him, "Can you keep her company while I finish getting ready?"

"Sure," he answered as he finished buttoning up his shirt. He ran his fingers through his hair a couple of times and winked at her before leaving the room. Stephen went to the door and opened it. He was stunned at what he saw. Lucy was a gorgeous platinum blond with long legs and beautiful hazel eyes. She was wearing a light blue silk dress, which clung to her. It had thin straps and was cut low in the front, loosely covering her chest.

"Stephen?" she asked.

Um, yes, I'm sorry," Stephen finally spoke, "I...We didn't expect you until six."

"Oh, I'm sorry. I always try to get an early start when going to new places. It did not take as long as I had thought it would. I hope I have not come at an inopportune time."

"No, no, it's fine. Heather is in the room getting ready. Come in, please." He opened the door wider and put out a hand. Lucy entered, smiling at him as she passed close. She entered the loft, looked around, then turned and put out her hand to introduce herself. "Lucy Rutherford."

Stephen shook her hand. "Stephen Meyers, it's so good to meet you, Lucy. Heather will be out in just a moment."

"I Love your loft. It is gorgeous," Lucy said as she looked around.

From the bedroom came Heather's voice. Both Lucy and Stephen turned to see her peeking out. "Hi, Lucy; I'll be out shortly."

The two girls smiled at each other, then Heather looked at Stephen, "Babe, offer our guest a drink, would you?"

"Sure thing, Love. Lucy, would you like a glass of wine? We just opened a great cab."

"That sounds nice. Thank you," Lucy said.

Heather withdrew to finish getting ready, and Stephen went into the kitchen to pour Lucy a glass. "So, are you enjoying California?"

"Oh, yes, I love the weather, especially." Lucy walked around the room, taking in the view. Stephen soon joined her with two glasses of wine and handed her one. Holding his up, he offered a toasted "To new friends."

Lucy smiled, looking at him fixedly, "New friends."

The two touched glasses and stole looks at each other.

"It's wonderful, Stephen. Thank you."

"You're welcome; this is one of Heather's favorites. We found it wine-tasting near San Luis Obispo, and Heather bought two cases on the spot. We receive J.LOHR's wine every month."

"Well, Heather has great taste, which is all I need say." She smiled at Stephen again, then walked over to the window. The sun was setting, and the light shone through her dress, revealing the curves of her body. Stephen stared at the beautiful woman for a moment, then broke away and walked toward the bedroom. "I will be right back, Lucy; I must finish getting ready myself. Please make yourself at home. Play some music if you like."

Lucy gave a nod. He entered the room, and Heather looked at him with a stunned look. He raised his eyebrows in reply, then walked over to where she was sitting on her stool. He kissed her on the neck. "You look amazing, Honey."

Heather smiled at him as she put on her earrings. "So where are we going? You never told me."

"I made reservations at the Marine Room."

Her eyes lit up, "I love that place."

"I know." He took in her smell.

Heather looked towards the door and spoke in a lower voice, "So that's Charles' daughter? She's a hottie."

Stephen knelt behind her and put his free hand around her waist. He handed her the glass of wine with the other. "Yes, she is, my Dear."

"She could be a model," Heather added, looking at him in the mirror.

"She probably could be, Dear," Stephen replied.

Heather scrunched her nose and squinted at him. "Do you think she's hot?"

"Yeah, Lucy's smoke'n Babe," Stephen said in a serious voice. Lucy heard that coming from the cracked door and moved towards the stereo with a slight blush in her cheeks. Heather slapped Stephen's hand. "Stop it, Stephen."

"No, really, Babe, the three of us could get along well here You and Lucy could split the room with me. Lucy could sleep in here Mondays, Wednesdays, and Fridays, and you could sleep in here Tuesdays, Thursdays, and Saturdays. It would be fun." He tried to remain serious, looking at her in the mirror. Heather was annoyed with him but smiled, refusing him the victory

"No, I'm a Monday, Wednesday, Friday girl, and what about Sundays, Smartass?"

Stephen gave her a wolfish grin. "We could all share." His serious look gave way to a grin. Heather reached out to pinch his nose, catching the tip as he pulled away just in time.

"Don't even think about it. You know what I'm saying."

At that moment, the stereo came to life at a deafening level; it was Johnny Cash's Ring of Fire. The volume soon dropped to a bearable level.

"Sorry," Lucy called out from the other room.

Heather looked at Stephen, eyes wide. "She better not have heard your mockery, Buddy."

"Honey, this isn't like you to be so insecure."

"I'm not being insecure," Heather got up and walked over to the closet. She dropped her robe, and pulled her cocktail dress over her, then adjusted it in the mirror. She turned, looking enticing. "I was just surprised and also curious, how a girl so attractive is single, is all."

She sauntered past him to the bed with heels in her hand and sat to put them on. Stephen smiled and then shouted, "Hey, Lucy?"

"Yes?"

"Are you seeing anyone?"

Heather shot him 'The Look.' "Stephen!" she whispered sharply.

He gave her an innocent look.

"Not at the moment," came from near the door, and then Lucy knocked. She pushed it a little wider, "I hope I'm not intruding, why do you ask?"

Heather looked reproachfully at Stephen then, then smiled at Lucy. "No, you're not. Come in. We're decent, or at least I am. My fiancé is being rambunctious, but I'll dole out his punishment later."

Stephen walked over to Heather and kissed her shoulder. "No, I thought it would be fun to go sailing tomorrow afternoon. We are supposed to have some good wind, and our friend Peter will be going. I didn't want to make you uncomfortable by asking if you wanted to make it a double date."

Lucy smiled, "Well, what would be more uncomfortable than a blind date? Sounds like fun. I love to sail."

"It wouldn't have to be a date," Heather corrected. "Although Peter would probably be falling all over himself over you. Stephen and I were talking about how beautiful you are. Weren't we, Stephen?"

"Yep, we agreed on that, wondering how such a beautiful girl could be single."

Lucy's eyes pierced Stephen's for a moment, "I'm picky."

She looked at Heather and winked. "I love the loft, Heather. Is this your design?"

Heather got up, took her glass from Stephen's hand, and the two girls walked out of the bedroom together. "Well, Stephen and I worked on the interior design together. I wanted it to be both of ours. We both have put a lot of love into our home." She looked back and stuck her tongue out at Stephen.

"I love the open feel and how the kitchen is a part of the lounge area," Lucy said.

The two girls walked around talking about the layout of the loft. Stephen looked down at Felix. "It's all German to me, sport. So, what do you think of Lucy?" The cat just looked at him.

Cat's Eye

Felix woke from a nap hours later, stretched, and then jumped down from the stereo. He walked to the entryway, smelling along the bottom of the door, then ran and jumped up on top of his cat castle as the elevator ding came from the hall outside. Stephen and the girls entered the loft laughing as the phone rang. Heather and Lucy plowed forward to the lounge, and Stephen picked up the cordless.

"Hey, Pete, How they hanging, buddy?"

Felix climbed down and visited Heather, narrowly avoiding Lucy's attempted pat by arching his back and moving outside her reach. He meowed at Heather, who ignored him, then went over and marked Stephen's legs by rubbing against him, stopping to smell all the weird smells on his pant legs and shoes.

"The evening was wonderful, Man," Stephen said into the phone as he walked into the bedroom. "Honestly, I am kind of a third wheel at this point. The two are like besties already. Heather even invited her to the wedding."

Felix followed him, climbing up on the bed and used his leg for a backrest so he could groom his private parts.

"Babe, bring us some wine when you come back," Heather shouted from the other room. Felix looked up at Stephen, listening attentively on the phone, then resumed grooming.

"No, Lucy is just going to stay the night and go with us tomorrow…..Right now, I think they are talking about shopping for bathing suites together in the morning, so I'd say let's you and me meet down there and get the boat ready."

"Babe?" Heather said again.

"Yes, Honey, I'll be right out. Peter says hi." Stephen replied.

"Hi, Pete! Heather said.

"Yes, Hi, Peter," Lucy Added.

"Oh, you're going to dig her, Bro. Very hot and super smart. She's a sharp one." Stephen said.

Felix grew bored and gave Stephen's thigh a bite. Stephen responded with a brief stroke of his back but did not satisfy Felix's need for facial messaging, so he got up and decided to return to the girls for some loving.

Felix climbed up next to Heather, keeping the strange new human on the other side of his mom. Heather gave him some scratching around his face and a kiss, which made him recoil and need a good cleaning again. He retreated into his castle and started to lick his paw and clean off the smelly lipstick smell from his face.

"So I think your color schemes are exciting and brave," Heather said. "I can't wait to go over and see the place. We should make a day of it Monday. My schedule is light enough. I could push a meeting and take the entire day.

"Sounds great," Lucy said."

Stephen decided to call it a night, delivering two glasses of wine to Heather and Lucy. Both girls kissed him on the cheek, and Stephen grabbed Heather and picked her up in his arms, "Do you know how much I love you, drunkie?"

Heather giggled. "I love you too, Babe."

"We'll see you in the morning, Lucy. It was a pleasure to meet you. Please make yourself at home."

"I will, thank you," Lucy said.

"I'll be in soon, Honey, Heather said.

"Whenever you want love, have fun, girls."

Stephen was soon undressed and in bed, his breathing rhythmic, growing quieter. Felix followed him deeper and deeper into the grey dream world, curled up by his leg, listening to the girl's faint voices as sleep took hold of them both.

More Dreams

Stephen sat up in bed, startled awake. It was twilight, and Heather wasn't beside him. He looked towards the window and noticed the faint morning light coming through the closed blinds. It seemed to be fluctuating.

That can't be the sunrise.

There was a flash of brighter light from behind the blinds, followed by a loud boom. He jumped out of bed and went to the window.

"Heather?" he shouted.

He walked to the window and pulled open the blinds. He had to shield his eyes from the bright light.

"It's on fire," he whispered.

The entire city was in flames. Some buildings were crumbling heaps, and others raged like giant pillars of fire.

What is this?

"Heather!" He shouted again as he looked out at the city in devastation. He ran out of their bedroom into the lounge area.

Everything was changed.

The furniture was gone. Heather was nowhere to be seen; neither was Felix. This was his home, but it was different.

"Heather?"

Stephen walked up to the windows in the lounge and drew the blinds, revealing the same horrible cityscape in flames. The burning city looked like it was ground zero in every direction.

What is this? What is going on here?

"You are being shown a future, Stephen," a voice answered from behind him.

Stephen jumped and turned to see the man from New York leaning against the counter.

"It's you!" Stephen accused. "Where's my...where's Heather?...What happened to my home?"

The man put out a hand to calm him. Stephen lunged forward.

"Who are you?" He grabbed the man by his shirt and pushed him back.

Everything went dark.

There was no light. Stephen reached out, feeling nothing in front of him, realized his eyes were closed, and opened them. He was back in bed and staring at the ceiling above his bed.

A dream.

He turned towards Heather's side of the bed, feeling for her. She was not there. There was a loud explosion, and it shook the bed. The windows rattled, sounding like giant drums as they vibrated to the tune of their conductor. He could smell burning chemicals and plastics. Something toxic was in the air, and the room was becoming very hot. Stephen looked towards the window to see the same light glowing brightly from the gaps in the blinds. The irregular light cast strange shapes around the room, like sprites in a choreographed dance.

He got up and went to the window, feeling deja vu.

"Heather," he spoke aloud but with less conviction.

She did not answer.

"Where are you, Honey?" He whispered.

"The future," a voice said from behind him.

Stephen was startled, turning to see the man from New York standing in the doorway.

"I'm dreaming, aren't I?"

"In a way, yes, you are dreaming," the man answered. "That would be the easiest explanation without getting into quantum physics, and interdimensional boundaries. This dream, though, has a purpose, and I am your guide."

The man looked like he did in Stephen's dreams: the same wavy brown hair, short beard, blue jeans, and tee shirt.

"Why are you harassing me?"

The man smiled but said nothing.

Stephen stepped toward him. "Who are y-"

"You can call me Gabe," the man interrupted. "I am here to show you the truth."

"What truth?" Stephen snapped. "Why is my house changed? Where is my fiancé?"

"Stephen, sit down, we don't have much time, and there are some important rules you need to be aware of here, in this place."

Stephen did not move. He looked at Gabe with frustration on his face.

"This is no longer your home. As I said before, this is a future."

Stephen sat on the edge of his bed, bewildered. He put his head in his hands and let out a deep breath, then looked back up at Gabe.

"Where is Heather? How can this not be my home?"

"Stephen, I need you to listen to what I say carefully and trust that I am here to help you. This is *a* future, but not *your* future. That is all you need to know for now. This future is your son's. They will battle, and many will die. You are key to-"

"Who will battle?" Stephen interrupted.

"I know a lot of this may be hard to understand, much you will understand in time. Just know that God has chosen to reveal important truths to you, and you will pass some of them on to those he has chosen to stand."

"Wait a minute; I thought God chose His faithful servants to reveal things. Why would God choose me when I have not chosen Him?"

"God uses whom He pleases for His plans. The great Pharaoh of Egypt foretold the future of famine in the land through dreams given him by God and translated by Joseph. Also, the King of Babylon dreamed of his future and a future shortly to come that Daniel translated for him."

"I don't want any of this, and I don't believe in any of that stuff." Stephen rejoined, "Please leave me alone."

"Stephen, you are in danger, and I am here to help you. You need to listen-"

"What kind of Dang—"

Stephen froze. A deep chill washed over him. The temperature in the room dropped dramatically. Everything seemed to grow darker. Out the window, the flames still raged, but they changed color, now a negative hue. They were purple and dark. Only the smoke was bright. A putrid smell of decaying flesh and rotten eggs overwhelmed his senses. He looked at Gabe with alarm and saw a similar look on his mysterious guide's face. This made him panic even more. His heart was pounding in his chest, and he began to sweat, even though it was so cold he could see his breath.

"What's going on?" Stephen asked him.

"We must go. We are no longer alone," Gabe said, grabbing Stephen's arm.

He led Stephen to a door and stopped. "The next time you see me, you must focus on remaining calm and not allowing fear to take control. It is the key to your safety here."

Stephen opened his mouth to speak but was cut off.

"You have been chosen, and fighting it will only make things harder. Listen to my words, and note all you learn. When you see the door with light spilling from its edges, run for your life, and don't look back."

"What's going on, Gabe?" Stephen shouted.

"It's here, RUN!" Gabe screamed, pushing Stephen through a door.

He was now in a long hall full of doors. The door slammed behind him, and Stephen felt dizzying vertigo momentarily as the hall stretched out before him. He turned and tried to get back into the door Gabe had pushed him through, but it was solidly secured from the other side. There was a war cry from behind the door, followed by another animalistic roar.

Stephen turned and ran down the long hallway, looking from side to side at the doors as he passed by. None of them had light spilling from beneath. He began to run faster down the long hall. He could faintly see a door at the end with bright white light bursting from all around. There was a loud boom, followed by a crash from behind. Stephen ran faster, looking over his shoulder. What he saw caused him to stumble. He faltered, then regained his stride.

The thing behind him was darkness. Real darkness. It seemed to have many shapes, but they began to consolidate into one form with wings. Giant clawed hands emerged outstretched as it charged after him. It seemed to steal all light from the hall as it came, and its darkness preceded it, devouring the floor, walls, and ceiling. Stephen ran as fast as he could. He could feel the cold darkness passing him up along the walls and ceiling above. It was as if it was trying to beat him to the door of light. Its head, now solidified, like a dragon and wolf combined.

Stephen looked back once more to see the creature, a hideous thing nearly on top of him. Its eyes glowed like burning embers of a fire full of yellows and reds. There was no way he would make it before this thing caught him.

He screamed, grasping for the air as he ran. The thing howled a horrifying scream, and Stephen looked back once more. It was slowing down. Something was holding the thing back like a vicious dog at the end of its tether.

Stephen was almost to the door when it howled again, breaking free. It was now crawling on the ceiling and walls, circling as it came. Its face was turning a dark red. Horns were protruding from the sides of its head. Its mouth was wide and full of teeth. Smoke exploded from its nostrils in powered puffs.

Stephen stumbled again but recovered. He could see the door pulsating with light from behind now. A new terrified scream came from the monster, and Stephen slammed into the door and looked back.

The creature was battling with a being of pure light. The being of light took form as it struggled with the beast, which clawed and groped to get past. It was the same being from his dream. A beautiful bright warrior of light, clad in pearlescent armor. A white fire, like lightning, grew like tree foliage from his protector's back. It branched out into brilliant, white wings.

His guardian's wings engulfed itself, and the evil creature in a giant egg-like shell that filled the hallway. The darkness that had painted the hall floor to ceiling dissolved away, revealing white again. Stephen could not look away but knew he had to do what Gabe said, so he felt around the door keeping his eyes fixed on the battle. There was a blood-curdling scream from the dark creature within the angel's grasp. A sound first angry and then changing to agony as the creature was consumed in some kind of painful end. The light from within the guardian's wings radiated brighter and brighter—a supernova.

Stephen shielded his eyes as his hand touched a cold doorknob. At that moment, he was sucked through smallness into darkness. It was quiet, and he passed out.

Stephen opened his eyes and recognized the familiar ceiling above his bed. He turned to the window to see the faintest blue light coming from behind the blinds. He turned and saw Heather sleeping next to him. His heart calmed, and peace washed over him. He touched her and felt her warmth. He relaxed and pulled her into his arms, and closed his eyes.

Friendship

Stephen was up and showered long before anyone else in the loft. Sleep was something lacking the last few days, and he wanted answers. He made breakfast for himself and set aside some for the girls. He set out two large glasses of water, along with a bottle of vitamins and aspirin. The girls would probably need them to recover from the night before. He called Peter and then sat down and thumbed through his research. Lucy was the first to emerge from the guest area. She came out to the kitchen looking groggy, shielding her eyes from the sunlight that flooded the room.

She was in her underwear, wearing one of Stephen's tee shirts. He stole a brief look at her, then back to his work. She was a gorgeous woman, and he found it hard not to be drawn in. However, his heart was Heather's.

"Morning Princes, how you feeling?" he said as he turned a page

"Uugh, not like a princess, that's for sure."

She rubbed her eyes as Stephen pointed to the water without looking up.

"You two really tied one on last night, eh?"

She took a couple healthy gulps of water, then a deep breath. "Um ... Yeah, you could say that."

Stephen looked over at her. She was sitting half on a bar stool and tugged at the tee shirt, giving him a better glimpse of what was underneath. "I hope you don't mind," she said.

"Not at all."

"All I had with me was my dress. Heather gave me the shirt."

"That's fine. Heather wears some of my shirts more than I do."

Lucy went to a couch and sat cross-legged. She caught his eyes on her and gave him a receptive gaze. He turned back to his research. He thought of Heather, clearing his mind.

"Thank you, Stephen, for everything, really. The warm reception and wonderful dinner were very welcoming. I can see why my father likes you so much."

"It was nothing, Lucy; we enjoyed your company too."

Lucy leaned back, pulling her feet up and her knees close to her chest. "Heather .... She's great. I think we are going to be great friends." She looked at him, waiting for a response as he turned toward her again.

"She really likes you too, Lucy. I can tell." He smiled, "Just don't steal her from me."

She laughed and then put a hand to her aching head. "I doubt that would be possible, Stephen. That woman adores you." She got up and walked directly towards him, looking into his eyes as she approached. Lucy reached past him, too close for comfort, and set her glass on the counter. She was standing in his space, examining him.

This woman is not shy. Her stare was magnetic.

"You're both fortunate to have one another, Stephen." Her gaze remained locked on his for another moment, and then she touched his arm. She was reading him but finally broke away. She smiled, then turned and walked back to the double doors leading guest area.

"A shower will bring me back to life. You mind?" she stopped at the doors and looked back.

"Not at all; make yourself at home. Mi casa es su casa." He replied.

She disappeared into the hall.

A few moments later, she called out. "You have no towels in the bathroom, Stephen. Is there a linen closet or something?"

He got up and walked over to the laundry room. "I will put some in your room."

He soon heard the shower turn on. He grabbed two folded stacks on the shelf and went to the hallway. He stopped there and called out to her. "I'll set them on your bed, Okay?"

"Could you bring them to the bathroom Stephen?"

He went to the bathroom and turned to set them on the floor by the door. It was open, and Lucy stood there naked in the mirror's reflection.

She was putting her long blonde hair up, and for a moment, he stared, exploring her nakedness in the mirror. When he got to her eyes, she gave him an amorous smile.

"I'm so sorry I didn't think—"

"For what?"

"I didn't mean to walk in on you like this." He dropped the towels on the floor near the door and turned his back to the door.

"I didn't intend on walking in on you undressed. I'm sorry for the intrusion."

He turned and walked away. As he was turning the corner, she called to him.

"Stephen."

He turned and looked. She was standing outside the door with one of the towels held up, partially covering her.

"It's not a big deal, I'm very comfortable in my skin, and I'm used to being free to walk around like this. I'm sorry if I made you feel nervous."

"I'm not nervous, I just...well… I just didn't expect to see you like that when I went to the door." "You didn't? What? Think I would be undressing to get in a running shower?"

He was silent. *You are trouble.*

"Well, I'm sorry, Stephen. I'll be more careful. I'm just a very free spirit."

"You have no need to apologize; it's fine. Let's forget it even happened. Make yourself comfortable here. Everything's fine."

She giggled at his nervous response. "You're a cute one." She went back into the bathroom and closed the door. Stephen stood there stunned.

What the hell just happened?

He returned to the island and sat looking at Felix, now lying on his open book.

"That was awkward, buddy."

Heather's head was pounding when Stephen sat on the bed next to her. She opened her eyes and squinted, “Hi, baby,” she said in a groggy voice.

“How you feeling?”

“Like hell, Babe, I drank too much.” She rolled onto her back and rubbed her temples. Stephen set a glass of water and some pills on the nightstand.

“I’ll draw you a bath before I leave if you like.”

“Leave; where you going?”

“I’m going down to the marina and doing some work on the boat. Peter’s already on his way.”

“Oh, crap, Babe! Sailing. I’m sorry; I didn’t mean to get so drunk last night.” Heather sat up and grabbed the glass of water.

“It’s okay, Honey, really. I have some things I’ve been meaning to work on anyway, and Peter is easy to talk into the boatswain’s chair.” He smiled at Heather and kissed her on the forehead.

“Has Lucy shown signs of life?” Heather questioned as she plucked the pills off the nightstand.

“Oh, you could say that,” Stephen answered.

“What’s that mean?

“Nothing, she’s fine or at least getting there. She’s in the shower now. I think you both will need to take it easy this morning until you feel human again.”

“Oh Babe, I was really looking forward to sailing today. I think I can rough it.”

Heather finished her glass of water and pushed Stephen aside to get out of bed. She grabbed her head and rested her elbows on her knees.

“I’m sure you could, Dear, but that’s what it would be, is roughing it. Besides, what about Lucy? She’ll have her head hung over the side the entire time.”

She moaned, holding her head in her hands. “Yeah, you’re right.”

“Go have a fun day with her; maybe call the girls to come meet you. You can go by her place.”

“Oh Babe, I’ll miss you.” She gave him a melancholy look. Pushing her lower lip out.

“You’ll be fine. Pete and I will get some needed maintenance done on the boat, giving me a chance to talk to him about something."

"Are you sure, baby? I feel bad." She took his hand.

"I'm sure, Love. Enjoy a relaxing day, and if you're feeling better, later we can barbeque."

She smiled at him. "Okay, that sounds good. How about we make a plan for next Saturday, for sailing?"

He planted a kiss on her nose, walked to the bathroom, and gave her a look. She got up and grabbed her head again.

"Maybe a bath would be good."

He smiled and walked into the bathroom. "I'll draw you one, and then I'm out. There's food already made in the kitchen if you're hungry."

"Thank you, Honey." She grabbed him around the waist and hung onto him while he adjusted the water temperature.

On The Dock

Stephen walked down the dock, waving to his friend Peter as he walked up to his 30-foot sloop. The word Serenity was painted on the stern of the boat.

"Hey man, been here long?" Stephen asked.

"Got here around ten or so. It's so easy to lose track of time down here. I love being on the water, Man," Peter answered.

"True dat, true dat." Stephen returned. "You ready to try out the new spinnaker?"

Peter was already on-board getting things ready. Stephen threw his bag onboard as he climbed on.

"So, what's up, Man? You want to take her out on the bay or open ocean to try this?" Peter asked.

"Well, the open ocean would give us more room to move. I'm not too confident using a spinnaker yet. What do you think?"

"It's your call. I'm cool either way. So, the girls are hurtin'?"

"For certin'. They're crawling, though. You disappointed?"

"Na, not really. I'm going sailing, Man. They're the ones missing out. I am looking forward to meeting Lucy, though. Heather says she's hot."

"She did? When did you talk to her?"

Stephen pulled several rolls of line out of a seat locker and threw two at Peter before unrolling the rest. Peter caught them and sat unrolling line and draping it over a winch.

"They drunk-dialed me last night."

Stephen laughed. "Okay, that makes sense. They were having fun last night."

"Sounded like it when they called." Peter threw a jack-line over to Stephen, walked his end over to the bow, and attached it. Stephen rolled the last sheet around the starboard winch and tied his end of the jack-line off at the stern.

"So, is she?" Peter asked.

"Is she what?"

"A hottie, Man?

Stephen laughed, "Um, yeah, she's hot. A very forward too, Pete. I'd watch yourself with that one if I were you."

"What do you mean?" Peter walked back to the stern and waited for his answer. Stephen pulled up the main cabin's hatch cover and handed it to Peter. He smiled at him and then patted him on the shoulder as he went downstairs.

"Take it easy with her, Man; see how things go. From what I've seen so far, she seems like a heartbreaker."

Peter gave him a sly smile, "You know me, Man, I'm mister cool."

"Yeah, I do know you, and that's why I'm warning you. Just don't get blinded by the light."

Stephen flipped all the toggle switches that powered the systems on the boat. There was a beeping as the radios and chart plotters came to life, doing self-tests.

"Man, God's my guide, Steveo, you know that. That's why I'm such a joy to have around."

"This is true, Pete, you are always happy; that's another reason I thought it would be best just the two of us went out today."

"What, you need some pointers from your Bro?"

Peter flexed his biceps and then smiled.

"Um, no, Tough Guy. Well… kind of, but don't let it go to your head."

Peter's smile faded. "You and Heather are okay, right? You're not having wedding jitters, are you?"

"No way, Buddy; Heather is the surest thing in my life. No, I just have a few questions about God, or along those lines anyway."

Peter brightened. "Really? I was—"

"Don't get all excited. I just want to talk about some dreams I've been having and see what you think. Don't get your hopes up thinking I'm gonna join the choir."

Peter laughed, "Dude, you're funny. I wouldn't expect anything like that. First off, you can't sing to save your life."

Peter sat at the helm and started the motor. He looked up at Stephen as he climbed out of the cabin.

"So, we ready to go?

"Yeah, let's get underway. I'll cast off. You want to pull her out of the slip?"

Peter gave him a nod and readied himself at the helm. Stephen cast off all the lines and gave the boat a little push as he jumped aboard. The two were soon sailing out of San Diego Bay into the Pacific Ocean. They had been out for a couple of hours when Stephen felt ready to talk. He was at the helm, and Peter was trimming the sails. Good wind came out of the Northwest, and they were close-hauled, riding the rail.

"So, what do you think, Steveo, about there? Peter asked, looking up at the foresail.

"She looks happy to me. Maybe tighten the main a little, though."

Peter grabbed the main sheet and winched it in until the tail tales blew true, then he cleated off the line. The boat was moving fast, the ocean spray blasting over the bow as the waves hit. The sun was shining on the men's faces.

"This is living, Man," Stephen said.

"It is amazing; God is good," Peter answered. "Hey, I'm going down for my shades. You need anything?"

"Yeah, grab me a Ginger Ale while you're down there."

Stephen steered the boat off enough to right the boat on a calmer tack. As Peter descended into the cabin, Stephen steered the boat back into an aggressive angel and sent Peter flying onto his rear. He landed on the couch with his feet over his head and shot Stephen a nasty look. Stephen busted into laughter, and then Peter joined in. Peter regained his balance and stood feet wide, putting on his sunglasses. Before opening the refrigerator, he shot Stephen another look. Stephen saluted him with a smile. Peter grabbed a Ginger Ale and ascended the steps.

"Real funny, Man. Don't blame me if your Ginger Ale blows up in your face."

"Just keeping you on your toes, Dude." Stephen had a victorious smile on his face. He set the autopilot and let out the sails, putting them on a gentle course.

Peter came up and sat across from Stephen, handing him his drink as he sat. "So, are you ready for this wedding, captain?"

"Yes, more than ready; Heather is everything good in my life, Pete. I only wish Mom could be here to see us tie the knot."

"She will be, and I'm sure she is proud of you both."

The two men were silent for a few minutes, looking out across the ocean and San Diego's coastline.

Stephen looked at Peter. "Do you really believe that, Man? I mean, don't you ever doubt?"

Peter smiled, "Never. The world makes no sense without God. There would be no point in any of this without Him. Have you ever heard the term 'The devil is in the details?'"

Stephen nodded.

"Well, I believe it's the other way around. Every time you witness a stranger, do something nice for another. The things that warm your heart, like someone risking their life to save another. You know what I mean, right?"

Stephen nodded.

"The things that tug at people's hearts, love, and beauty, that's God. He is revealed through human compassion and kindness. He's revealed through the mercy of someone forgiving the murder of their child. I believe God is the essence of love, and love is the source of all goodness in the world."

Stephen looked at Peter intently for a moment. "I know there must be some higher power when I think about real love, art, and music, when I look at all the beauty around us, especially the beauty hidden in tragedy, like you said, Pete. All this demands it, but I don't get all the rest. Religion really rubs me the wrong way, man."

Rubbed Jesus the wrong way, too, Bro," Peter said.

"Hah…yeah. Never thought about it like that. He was quiet a moment. "No, really, the most selfish people I've ever met are Christians, though. They are the biggest asses too. No offense, not all of them."

Peter smiled, then sighed, "Yes, I know and agree with the statement, but that's exactly what the devil wants you to see. First, Bro, the biggest difference between believers and unbelievers is one simple thing: forgiveness. Believers are still sinners. We still have the desires of darkness to battle with, just like everyone else. The difference, though, is we are forgiven."

Stephen thought about what Peter was trying to point out. He looked at the water as Peter continued. "Christians still sin, but they repent and strive to stop, grow, and be better. Their sin stands out more because you expect better from them. More importantly, Satan tries harder to take them down because they threaten his plan. So he constantly attacks us and manipulates us in order to accomplish this. Bro, what I'm trying to say is, being a Christian does not make one perfect. We simply acknowledge the evil in our hearts and try to be more. We're all evil man; it's human nature; we're just forgiven."

"And I'm not?" Stephen frowned, then smirked.

"Have you ever asked God for forgiveness? That would be a requirement for anyone else to forgive. Why wouldn't God be entitled to the same penance any human would require to forgive?"

"Anyway, that's not what I want to talk about." Stephen returned.

"I'm all ears," Peter answered.

Stephen adjusted the autopilot and then looked at Peter. "I'm not sure where to begin."

"What's going on? Start there," Peter said.

"Dreams, Homie, dreams. Do you believe God speaks to people in dreams? I mean, like in the Bible?"

Peter was silent.

"I've been having strange dreams." Stephen finally finished.

Peter leaned forward, "Bro, the stories in the Bible are true. Do you realize that? The Bible is full of prophecies that have already been fulfilled, down to every detail. Down to the very day. The world is full of stories of other prophets like Nostradamus and movies, but the world refuses to acknowledge that the Bible's prophecies have been coming true left and right. The greatest of which is shortly to come."

"The rapture? Armageddon?" Stephen cut in.

"Yes, the end-of-days, Man. The greatest period of death and destruction this world has ever seen. I don't talk about it all the time because I don't want to force my beliefs on you. I believe the end is near, and anyone who really wants to know the truth need only study the scriptures to see this."

Stephen's eyes narrowed, but he chose silence because he was interested.

"I think most just don't want to face the truth. The Bible says that the evil one will blind many. The only way this blindness can be removed is for one to seek after God."

"So, what you're saying is Lucifer or the Devil is blinding me to the truth?"

"Tell me about the dreams. Let's start there."

"Well, simply put, I think I'm dreaming about the end of the world. This end of days the Bible refers to."

Stephen waited for Peter's reaction. Peter only nodded as if this was par for the course, so he continued. He told him about the crazy-looking man in New York and the dream in the hotel. He told him how this man, named Gabe, portrayed himself as some kind of a spirit guide. He described the creatures and what he thought was his guardian angel.

Peter sat patiently listening. He seemed to understand much more about what Stephen was saying. This set him at ease. After Stephen finished, they sailed quietly for a while, and the boat headed toward home.

When the marina was in sight, Stephen climbed up and started wrapping up the mainsail, putting its cover on. Peter dropped the throttle to a crawl and looked up at him.

"The dark creatures could be demons, but it also sounds like you are seeing fallen angels. You should talk to Leroy."

"Leroy? Why him? I haven't seen him since my mother's funeral."

"Dude, you are so in your own world. Leroy is still very close with your sisters and asks about you all the time. You're just never around."

"I know. I've just been so wrapped up in my career and helping Heather get her business going."

"Well, put it on your list, people miss you. Anyway, guilt trip aside, Leroy is teaching at the college, has been for a while. He's done extensive research on demons and angels; it's like his hobby."

"I thought he went to the Middle East on some dig or something?"

"Um, yeah, years ago, Dude." Peter snapped. "You should call him. It could also help you with the research you're doing for your book. I think he was a little disappointed you didn't interview him when you were doing that piece on the occult."

"I had no idea he had anything to add. I'll call him if only to say hi."

"That would be good, and I know he can enlighten you as to what these dreams may mean. Don't think you're going crazy, Man. I think God is trying to get through to you for something important."

"Really?"

"Really."

"Well, it does feel good to talk about it." Stephen's expression relaxed.

"You haven't told Heather?" Peter asked.

"No, I don't want to bother her about it. She is so happy with planning our wedding and everything. I don't want to rain on her parade."

"Okay, calling Leroy is a step in the right direction anyway. Take the helm; I don't like parking this thing."

Peter stood up, giving the helm to his friend. He went up to the bow with a line in hand, ready to jump off. Stephen cut the engine, turned the wheel, and Serenity glided into her slip. He jumped off and tied off the stern to the dock as Peter secured the bow. He was reaching for the spring lines when his phone rang. Stephen jumped on board and answered.

"Hello"

"Hey, Baby, how's the water?" Heather's voice carried from the phone.

"It's good, Love; we fixed the spreader light—"

"I fixed it; you hauled me up," Peter yelled from the bow.

"Yes, Peter changed the bulb out, and I did the hoisting. We had some nice wind, so we went out after. We just got back when you called."

"Awesome, Babe. Tell Pete I said Hi, and thanks for helping us out."

"Heather says hi, and thanks for being my be-atch," Stephen bellowed.

"I didn't call him that!" Heather said.

Peter gave Stephen a sharp look.

"Okay, she said thanks for being our hero and fixing the spreader-light."

Peter walked up to him and reached for the phone as Stephen dodged the move.

"So, how was your day, Honey?"

"It was good. Lucy and I finally got our butts moving and went to the house in Ocean Beach, then shopping for bikinis. You're going to love my new one; it's a little risqué but cute."

"I look forward to a private showing later, Sexy." Stephen turned his back to Peter.

Peter climbed onboard the boat.

"The house is gorgeous, Stephen. Some eccentric architect built it. It's amazing! She signed the deal today."

"That's great. I love O B. I think she'll be happy there."

"Hey Babe, I told Lucy she could stay in our guest room until escrow closes. That's okay with you, right?"

"Um ... well ... s—"

"He is happy to have you, Lucy. I told you there would be no problem." Heather spoke to Lucy in the background, and Stephen looked at Peter with a bewildered look.

"Um, yeah, that's fine; how long will that be, Love?" Stephen asked.

"We'll talk about all the details later. Baby, Lucy and I are setting up to barbecue. Hurry home, Hun. Bring Pete. Love you, Doll."

"Um ... Okay, sounds good. Love you too." Stephen placed the phone in his pocket and looked at Peter. "You up for barbecue? Lucy will be there."

Peter smiled, "Sure, sounds good to me. Let's button up the boat and fly.

***

It was dark when Stephen and Peter made it to the loft. Two neighbors were there when they came out onto the rooftop deck. They shared a drink and visited for a little while, then left. The roof had a small co-op deck with patio furniture and a barbecue, which all the unit owners chipped in to have built. The rooftop had a beautiful view of the city and bay.

Peter and Lucy sat talking mostly of San Diego, and Stephen was reclined on one of the patio seats with Heather resting against his chest. The two added the occasional comment to the other's conversation but, for the most part, were in their own world.

"You can see it from here if you look closely," Peter explained, getting up and taking Lucy's hand. He guided her to a small wall at the edge of the roof.

"Come on. I'll show you."

She looked at Stephen and then smiled at Heather as she allowed Peter to escort her. Peter stood behind her with a hand on the small of her back and pointed towards the marinas. Lucy looked back again, then to the various places Peter was pointing out. Occasionally she laughed at something Peter would say. Her laugh was contagious.

"Babe, we have a good life, don't we," Heather said in his ear.

Stephen thought that Heather's was the most contagious voice of all.

"Yes, we do, Love," He replied.

"I love you." Heather turned her head and looked up at him. She was so beautiful, her eyes shining in the moonlight. Her lips begged for his kiss, and more. Stephen set his drink down and pulled her tight against himself, looking into her eyes. "You are my life, Honey."

They kissed then continued to watch Peter and Lucy.

"They seem to be hitting it off, don't you think?" Heather asked him.

"Yeah, I guess, but I don't think anything will develop between them, though."

"Oh, why is that?"

"Well, they are very different. Peter is very conservative. Hell, he doesn't even drink. And Lucy, well ... She's ... a very free spirit."

"You act as if you've known her a long time," Heather questioned.

"No, I can just tell, Honey; plus, she said as much this morning."

"You're probably right, Babe. Peter has always been straight-laced. He's a good one, Stephen. I hope he finds a girl who will adore him as much as I do you."

"I do too, Love. He will, one of these days. He's young still."

Every few minutes Lucy would look back at Stephen and Heather as if not wanting to lose sight of them. Heather lifted her glass to her, and she smiled back.

"I know why you think she's a free spirit, and it's not just what she said… is it?"

Stephen was surprised by the question and took pause for a moment. "No, I guess it's not, but it's nothing big."

"It's okay, Stephen, she told me."

Stephen looked down at Heather's upturned face, "She did? What exactly did she tell you?"

"She told me you brought her towels, and she greeted you in the buff and that you were so cute and embarrassed."

"I wasn't embarrassed. I'm glad the two of you are enjoying this."

Heather put a hand up, pulling his head down and kissed him. "Oh, my baby is so cute. What a gentleman."

"I am not a gentleman. I walked in on her naked and tried to be respectful, that's it."

"You're so adorable, Stephen." She kissed him again, crawling onto his lap and straddling him.

"You're a gentleman…" He mumbled, not looking at her.

Heather burst out in laughter, and his frown finally broke, and he laughed too.

Lucy and Peter looked back briefly, confused, and then returned to their conversation.

"You're not bothered at all? He finally asked.

Heather smiled and ran her fingers through his hair. "She was honest with me about it. Why should I be? If anything, I feel better about her than I did before because she's an honest person who clearly doesn't play games. In the spirit of honesty, I love Kimberly to death, but two drinks and she cannot keep her hands off you. Lucy respects our relationship, and I like that about her."

"Wow, I didn't expect any of this. I'm glad you and Lucy are getting along, but I didn't expect you two to become best friends overnight."

"Besties Baby, Besties." Heather laughed and took a drink of her wine. A bout of laughter came from Lucy and Peter, catching their attention, and Heather laid her head on Stephen's shoulder, looking back at them. The two watched Lucy and Peter interact for a few moments.

"Stephen, I get the feeling she was raised coddled but also alienated from friends growing up. She talked about schooling and all the places she traveled to, and I don't see how a kid could develop any meaningful friendships that way."

"Wow, you two really talked. I can only imagine how much you must have shared with her."

"I shared too; that's the thing. I just felt so comfortable with her right away. She is special, Stephen, and I'm sure she will be a close friend for years to come."

"Well, I'm glad that you are happy. That is what matters to me."

"I *am* happy, Stephen, and you are the best part of it."

She sat back up, stared into his eyes for a long moment, and then laid back. He held her in his arms, caressing the nape of her neck as he watched Peter and Lucy talking. Lucy sat on the wall facing Stephen, with Peter's back to him. Lucy's eyes moved to Stephen often as she listened to Peter talk. Her looks were powerful. Stephen was unsure what it was about her, but somehow, she had a way of getting under his skin, and his fiancés. Those eyes and even the sound of her voice were captivating.

I hope you're not going to be trouble. He thought to himself.

Heather lifted her head and whispered in his ear. "I want you, Stephen. You know where to find me," She got up, grabbing her wine glass and lifted it to the others. "Make yourselves at home, you two. I'm going to retire."

Lucy and Peter waved from where they were. She gave Stephen an amorous look, begging he follow as she walked away. He got up and picked up their plates from the table.

"You two enjoy yourselves," he said.

Lucy looked at Peter, "You want to play a game of pool?"

"Yeah, sure, that sounds like fun,"

Lucy looked back at Stephen as he stacked plates and silverware. "Stephen, leave that; we'll get it. You have done enough."

He gave her a nod and waved to them as he went to the door. When Stephen entered the loft, music was pouring throughout the house, and He could hear the bath running. He entered the bedroom, closing the door behind him. The bed was pulled back, and candles were burning around the room. He turned to his right to see his fiancé. She placed a lit candle next to the tub and turned, looking at him.

So beautiful.

She had her hair pulled up and was wearing a silk robe. She pulled the robe back and let it drop to the floor, leaving her naked before him. He gazed at her, admiring her. She stood there letting him enjoy her. The more he stared, the more excited it made her. She smiled at him through the glass wall. He undressed where he stood, and her heart beat faster. His deep blue eyes conveying his love and desire pushed her to oblivion. Her body quivered with anticipation of his touch.

He opened the door, "Hi there."

She was trembling. "Hi," She whispered back.

She was tingling all over as he came closer. She admired his muscular body as he came. He touched her neck, and Heather felt she would lose it. She pulled him against her and kissed him.

"Make love to me." She begged.

They fell to the floor. This was the night everything changed.

***

Peter and Lucy brought down all the dishes and worked together, cleaning up, giggling, and playing as they worked. Occasionally, they would hear the passion from the bedroom and get quiet. Lucy finally went over, turned up the stereo, and smiled at Peter. "Say, Peter, do you mind if we take a rain-check on pool? I'm feeling a little tired myself."

"Not at all. I should probably be heading home soon anyway."

She got up and went over to the double doors leading into the guest quarters. She looked at Peter as if considering something, then opened the doors and walked in. "Peter, you can join me if you like."

He followed her voice down the hall to the guest room, where he stopped at the entrance.

"I enjoyed meeting you tonight, Lucy," he said.

"Me too, Peter. You seem like a really nice guy," she answered from behind the door of her walk-in closet. She stepped out, wearing nothing but lace panties and a bra, and sat on the edge of her bed. She looked up at him casually, removing a bracelet and putting it on the nightstand. Peter was rocked and turned away. Lucy giggled at him, making him turn back.

"I'm not going to bite Peter; this is all I have to sleep in. do I make you nervous?"

"Yes, very, Lucy, you're one of the most beautiful women I've ever met, and I'm taken back, to be blunt."

"You're cute Peter, like Stephen, seems like San Diego, is full of true gentleman."

"I wouldn't say that," he blurted out.

She giggled again. Her voice was so intoxicating.

"You can stay the night here if you like, Peter."

His heart was pounding, and a thousand things flew through his mind, including the idea of running. She just sat there, one leg crossed over the other, as if she were fully clothed and having a conversation at the office.

He looked at the bed and then back at Lucy, "I would love to stay the night, believe me, but I should go .... I... have work early tomorrow."

He fiddled with his hand behind his back.

Be cool.

"Peter, Dear, do you not find me attractive?" She gave him a pouting look, which just about melted him in place. She smiled at him.

"No ... I mean, yes, I find you attractive. I mean ... you're perfect, I just... Well, I'm not sure how to say it."

"You're a virgin." She finished for him. He turned bright red and looked like he was going to faint. Lucy got up and walked up to him, taking him by the hand. She led him to the bed and sat next to him. He looked at her.

Lucy smiled, "That's adorable, Peter. Let's just say that sex is not on the table, but I would love your company. Would you want to stay, then?"

Peter's shoulders lowered. "Well, yes, I guess."

"Good, I would like it if you stayed. We can talk until we fall asleep."

She pulled her legs up past him, tucked them under the covers, and slid over to the other side of the bed. "Come cuddle with me and tell me a story about how you met Stephen and Heather."

Peter pulled off his shoes and climbed into bed next to her, fully clothed. She pulled his arm around her, and he cuddled up behind her.

"Could you turn off the light next to you, Peter?"

He did, and they lay there quiet for a moment.

"What do you want to know?" He finally whispered.

"Just tell me a story about when you first met Stephen and Heather."

Peter shared with brief responses from Lucy. They lay quiet for a while. Peter was falling asleep when she spoke again.

"Peter, are you awake?"

"Yeah."

"Have you ever felt like your life was on a track you couldn't change?"

"I'm not sure what you mean," Peter responded.

"Well, my entire life has always been planned for me. I mean, daddy is sweet. He treats me well and always has, but I was always preparing for this great future with schooling and travel. I always felt like I was on an unstoppable train headed to a future I didn't agree to."

"Well, Lucy, your future is in front of you now, and you can do whatever you want. Are there dreams you have not gone after?"

"Yes, I guess, I never felt like I had time to think of any of my own, really, but I think if I were allowed to, I would have some of my own."

"I know people don't always like to hear it, but I get all my answers through prayer. God guides me when I am not sure what to do."

"You're a smart one, Peter. I can tell. You are so innocent in some ways, but something tells me that's a choice."

"Thank you, Lucy, that means a lot to me. You're right; it is a choice."

"We are very different, Peter, but right now, I wish that were not so."

"Well, I don't think we're all that different," Peter answered.

"That's because you don't know me."

He did not respond. She was right. They had only just met.

Lucy pulled his arm, bringing him closer to her. "Peter?"

"Yes, Lucy?"

"You want to know a secret about me?"

"Yeah."

"I am a virgin, also."

They were silent for several moments.

"Goodnight, Peter," She whispered.

"Goodnight, Lucy."

The two were soon asleep, and the house quiet.

Out in the main room, Felix sat peering under the front door. Shadows were fluttering back and forth, and the cat hissed and let out a small cry. He stayed there listening by the door for a moment, then a shadow fell outside with a stomp, and Felix hissed again and scurried away, looking back at the door from under the couch.

Boiling Blood

Stephen awoke in a strange place. He was in a city he did not recognize. It reminded him of Vancouver, Washington, with its quiet residential streets, only different somehow. He thought that it might be a city near the East Coast. There were vintage homes set high on their lots and trees all along the street on both sides, wreaking havoc on the sidewalks from beneath. There were Ash and Maple trees, and the neighborhood was quiet. Looking down the other end of the street, it opened up to a downtown cityscape. Stephen still could not tell where he was. The sun was high in the sky, and he felt very warm as he walked toward the city. After about thirty minutes, he noticed a few people walking along a cross street with bags in their arms. They gave him leery looks, then turned and vanished between houses. Stephen stopped at the next block and looked both ways. On his right, he saw two men in plain clothes walking towards him. They were still about two blocks away. They both carried assault rifles of some kind. As he crossed the street, he looked over at them. They were stopped one block away, rifles at their chests. The two men just stared at him but did not move.

They're guarding their homes.

Stephen continued towards the city. He was soon leaving the residential neighborhood and entering a more commercial part of town. He saw more people here and there, some looting a store and running with handfuls of food and others fighting with each other. Some of them seemed to notice him, but none seemed to care. Ahead, two men started brawling over a grocery cart half-full of food and other items. Two others came and joined in, beating one of them over the head with a pipe, then helping the first roll the cart away. Three more ran from an alley after the ones with the cart, and all six began to fight on the side of the road. Stephen stepped off the curb and walked down the center of the road to avoid them as he passed. A young man and a teenage girl grabbed the cart and ran, wheeling it away from the brawling group. They soon noticed, stopped fighting, and ran after them. One pulled out a gun and shot at the two, hitting the teenage girl in the leg. She fell, crying out in pain as the young man continued running with the cart. Stephen's gut clenched. He wanted to help the girl but was afraid to leave his tack. He was sure this was another dream and wanted to let it play out. The crowd caught up to the young man and started beating him. The man who shot at the girl used the gun to beat him in the head. The victors finally rolled the cart back to where the teenage girl was lying, leaving the young man dead on the ground. Two of the group grabbed the girl, who screamed and tied her hands. Another punched her in the face a couple of times until she was quiet, threw the girl over his shoulder, and started walking behind the others who were wheeling the cart away. Stephen decided, dream or no dream, he had to help and started after them.

"Hey, Sto—"

an SUV screeched to a stop, almost hitting him. There was a man and woman inside. The man had both hands on the wheel; one hand also held a gun. The woman looked distraught. She rolled the passenger's window halfway down, looking at the driver for confirmation. Stephen walked around to her side. The man lifted the gun in warning, and Stephen stopped.

"Have you seen a little blonde girl around here?" she asked, worry in her eyes.

Stephen shook his head, and her eyes grew even more devastated. He looked to where the man had kidnapped the teenager, and they were now gone, around a corner.

"My little girl is missing. Are you sure?"

The woman held up a picture of a girl.

"No, I'm sorry," Stephen answered, "But if I see her, I will be sure to get her to the authorities."

The woman looked horrified by what Stephen said. "You bastard!" she yelled at him.

Right then, there was a bright flash in the sky. All the blue vanished and became a blinding orange. Stephen and the couple cringed and covered their eyes.

There was a pop sound from the SUV, and it stalled. It was extremely hot, and Stephen heard screams from the surrounding area. He ran for the closest building, hearing explosions erupt all around him as he ran for cover. He looked back and saw the SUV starting to smoke and the couple clambering to get into the back seat. The sky was unbearably bright, and the temperature was hotter than Stephen had ever felt. Pops and booms sounded all around. The roof of the building made creaking and snapping sounds from over his head. The dashboard began to melt, smoke rose from all over the SUV, and the tires exploded, first one, then the other three in quick succession. Everything was igniting and exploding. The couple began screaming, and the entire SUV burst into flames. Stephen was in the shade of the building, looking out a roll-up door, but still, the heat started to cook his lungs, and he couldn't breathe. His eyes burned, and the sky turned a sunset red. The building he was in burst into flames, and he fell to the ground in agony. He felt his skin crack and char as he cooked and smelled his hair burning. He could feel the viscosity of his blood change as it began to boil in his body. Stephen cried out in pain, falling forward. Then everything grew quiet.

He was now lying face down in sand. It was no longer hot but cool. He lifted his head to see he was somewhere new. It was night, and the sky no longer burned but was full of the brightest stars. There were no buildings around, and he was in the middle of a desert. He scanned the sky, trying to get his bearings, and recognized Orion, except it was different now. The center star in the belt was a new nebula of bright colors as if Alnilam had exploded. He double-checked the sky, finding his way back to Orion's belt, and it was missing a star. He turned and looked up at the moon, which was growing brighter and brighter in its reflected light. The ground rumbled beneath his feet, and the moon's color changed to yellow and then orange in the sky. The moon continued to change to a deep red, then darkened. Several stars in the sky appeared to blink out of existence. One star in the northern sky seemed to grow brighter than all the rest as if it were growing or moving closer. Stephen stared at it, and it was getting brighter and bigger. It was pulsating, and he dropped to his knees in awe of what he was seeing.

It's not growing; it's coming closer!

There was a deep vibration all around. He could feel it resonate in his bones. The deepest bass sound was overtaking everything like distant thunder but louder and deeper. A loud Contrabass-Tuba was driving in his head. Sand in his lifted hand dance out of it. And his heart vibrated in his chest. The star grew so bright he had to shield his eyes. The thunderous horn that was sounding became deafening. He covered his head and laid his face in the sand. A feeling of peace and overwhelming joy washed over him, and then nothing.

Silence...

Stephen opened his eyes. At first, he could not make anything out because of the halos in his vision. He realized he was back in his room and felt for Heather. She was there, fast asleep. He still could not see enough to move, but he wasn't afraid this time. This peace had overtaken him like a drug. Soon the blue halos began to subside, and he could make out furniture and other things in the room. He looked over at the clock. It was 4:30 A.M. He got up, went to the kitchen, turned on the coffee pot, and sat down at the island. Stephen stared out the window until the smell of coffee started to fill the room.

God, if you're really out there, why can't you just say what you need to say?

He sat quiet for a moment as if expecting a response and then got up and poured himself a cup of coffee. He took a sip and walked over to the double doors leading to the guest quarters and offices. He walked into the hall entry and noticed Lucy's door was open. Lucy was fast asleep, and two glowing green orbs appeared next to her. Felix got up, stretched, jumped off the bed, and trotted over to his feet.

Stephen closed Lucy's door and returned to the kitchen. He pulled out a can of cat food.

"You hungry, Buddy?"

Felix gave him a meow, then a figure eight around his feet.

"You okay with all the changes around this place?" Stephen asked the cat.

Felix just stared up at him. He put Felix's food down by his cat castle and then knelt down to see what booty the cat had stolen over the past few days.

"Nothing?"

He looked at the cat, who sat beside him, ignoring his food. "You okay,

Felix?"

He stroked the cat's head and back. Felix closed his eyes and purred.

"Your two favorite pastimes, eating and thieving, and neither are of interest to you? You're going to worry your momma."

As if in understanding, the cat walked to his dish and started to eat a little bit of his food. Stephen got up and sat on a stool at the island, watching the cat eat. Felix stopped eating and looked at Stephen with a twist of his head. He trotted over to the double doors and meowed.

"You want back in with Aunt Lucy?"

Stephen got up, walked back into the hall, and was going to open Lucy's door when Felix turned left and ran down the hall towards the guest bath and office entrance. He removed his hand from Lucy's doorknob and took a step toward Felix. The cat looked down the next hall towards the offices and then darted in that direction.

"What is your deal, Buddy?"

He took another sip of his coffee, and Felix continued to meow, so Stephen followed him to the office entrance. The cat pawed at the door.

"Okay, buddy, I'll bite. Let's see where this leads."

Stephen opened the door, and Felix darted into the design area. He followed the cat first into reception, then into the meeting room, where he turned on a light. All seemed as it should. Felix darted on, and Stephen followed his guide first through the design areas and then through the work cubicles to his and Heather's offices. The cat was licking himself in front of Stephen's office door. Felix looked up at him, meowed, and pawed at the door. Stephen obliged the cat once more, opening the door. The cat disappeared into the office as soon as the door was cracked. As the lights flickered to life, Felix jumped up on Stephen's desk and sat on his address book. Stephen walked up to the desk and gave Felix a caress. The cat got up off his address book and sat beside it, cleaning himself.

"You want me to make a call, Bub?"

He set down his coffee and started thumbing through the address book. There were many names which he had not thought of in a while. Felix walked across the desk and knocked over a picture. Stephen picked up the picture and looked at it. He gave the cat an amazed look,

"You're freaking me out, Felix."

It was Stephen's favorite picture of his mother, Betty. The photograph was from one of her last birthdays. His sisters had gathered friends from over the years for the largest birthday she had ever had. She was sitting next to one of her closest friends, Leroy. Stephen sat looking at the picture for a while, missing his mother. Felix climbed into his lap and lay purring.

"I'll call him Buddy, I promise."

He was confused about everything that was going on: the dreams, what Peter had said, and the conversation with Charles about God. He didn't want to deal with any of this. His life was just where he wanted it to be, and he just wanted to be left in peace. The words 'you have been chosen' flashed through his mind.

Why does all this have to happen now when my life is perfect?

Stephen returned the picture to its place, picked up his coffee, and thumbed to Leroy's number. He pulled out a notepad, wrote down the needed information, and then wrote out all the details he could remember about his last dream. As he got up to leave, Felix gave another meow. He was now leaning against the adjoining door to Heather's office. Felix led Stephen over to a bookshelf, where he jumped up and sat on top of two books. Stephen picked up both books and sat down at Heather's desk. The first was a book he had not seen since his mother's funeral. It was her journal. She took up writing it over the last few years of her life. Stephen remembered her telling all her children it was full of things she wanted all of them to remember and some things they would one day need to hear. She left the journal to Heather with instructions for her to pass it on after she started her family. At first, this had caused some hurt feelings with her daughters, but when Heather offered to give it to them, they refused.

He thumbed through the book and stopped on a reference titled 'The Destroyer.' She talked about the end times, the antichrist, and signs of the end, some of which blew him away.

The world will begin to unfold. Crime will become rampant, and our nation's moral standard will become naught. Greed, corruption, and evil will become the driving force of our government. Sexual morality will fall, by the way, family values will disappear, and the sanctity of marriage will cease to exist. Crime and War will rule the news, and natural disasters will increase exponentially. The sea will take many lives, both in its depths and upon land. Disease and famine will become commonplace.

As America rejects God in our government, schools, and homes, His blessings and protection will be removed, and God will curse our land. The final blow will be when we no longer act as a true friend to Israel. The Bible quotes God's irrevocable covenant with Abraham: "I will bless those who bless thee, and I will curse those who curse thee."

Then the time will be set for God to take his faithful from the coming trouble. (Thessalonians and Revelation) Then the Destroyer will come to power.

The Holy Spirit must first be removed, as written in 2 Thessalonians 2: 7-9. The Destroyer is restrained by the Holy Spirit of God because once unrestrained, God knows he will destroy all mankind within a decade. Since the Holy Spirit also resides in believers, they must be raptured away before the Destroyer can come to full power. This is real; it will happen, as it has been foretold, and all who do not believe it will have no excuse because God has given warning after warning to all mankind.

Evil is already empowered all around us, and even though their power is restrained, demons are behind murder and mayhem in the world. They are all around us and desire our suffering and tears. Those of us who have the Holy Spirit residing in us are safe from possession but are still in threat of demon affliction, harassment, and even control. Christians can still be harmed by others possessed by demons if we are not diligent. Those who are not sealed by the Holy

Spirit can be possessed by demons and under their total control. They may not even know they are possessed because not all possessions are like the movies. In fact, most possessions do not even become violent towards the victim until they fight back or cease to be of use to the demon. I believe Serial killers are a perfect example of someone in complete control of a demon, giving all will over to them and wallowing in the darkness most of humanity cannot even fathom. That is a taste of the mind of a demon.

Stephen, your mother came to us either possessed or afflicted, at the very least, by demons. We found Hannah hiding in our church one morning when we came to set up for a luncheon. She was beaten and bruised, hiding under a pew, a terrified woman eight months pregnant. She cried that the devil was after her and her unborn child, so your father and I knelt down next to her and prayed for a long time. Others came and helped set up and allowed William and me to care for Hannah.

Stephen looked up from the journal to see the first rays of light peeking in the windows. The sky was becoming a beautiful light blue. He tasted his coffee, which was cold, and then grabbed both books and left Heather's office. He went to the kitchen and poured himself a fresh cup of coffee, then sat down at the island and continued to read. Betty and her husband, William, were the pastoral couple at their church. They were able to calm his mother enough to sit with the congregation, who showered her with love and kindness. Stephen read on for a while in his mother's journal.

I want you children to understand that the principalities and powers that Paul warned about are very real, and they hate all humanity.

Stephen, your mother was at the point of the greatest despair I have ever seen in another human being. We could never get her to answer any questions about where she was from or who your father was. We welcomed Hannah into our home and helped her prepare for the birth of her first child. You girls were so excited when he was brought home and fought over whose turn it was to hold him.

Between the help you girls gave and my time with Hannah, she was able to recover. Both her health and spirit seemed to brighten. I was able to be a part of helping her choose your name too, which gave me much joy. She wanted the name of a faithful character in the Bible, and I first recommended Samuel after the story of Hannah and her miracle son. Nevertheless, when she heard the story of Stephen, her eyes lit up, and she told me that was it.

After a few months, she started to regress and withdraw again. She said she was afflicted by evil and would wake in the middle of the night screaming from nightmares. She claimed the devil was after her child and begged me to promise her that I would protect you, Stephen, if anything happened to her. Her behavior became so erratic that William and I became concerned for the well-being of all you children. As a result, we convinced her to check herself into a hospital. A couple of days before she was scheduled to leave, we taught about the faith of Hannah and the dedication of her son Samuel. This had Hannah in the most excited state. She would not relax until we agreed to allow her to dedicate Stephen to God right there in front of the church. We did, and the congregation all prayed together for God's will to be accomplished.

That night was an amazing night in more than one way. We had several people come and rededicated themselves to their marriages and to God. As well several came to Christ that night too. She changed that night as if a light had filled her. She was joyful and smiled all night. She was no longer afraid. I didn't understand what was really going on in her mind or heart, but I was happy that God was working in all of our lives. We were even considering canceling her trip to the hospital, but she agreed that talking with someone there would probably help her to move on from it all. I used to feel guilty for sending her away, but then I think maybe that you children would have suffered if she had stayed.

A week after she left, we received a call from the hospital. Hannah had died under mysterious circumstances. They could not determine the cause of death. The staff was brokenhearted and said she was a bright light to all the others around her. She was scheduled for release and was interested in what she would need to do to be able to come back and help. Hannah was afflicted by demons; however, she was introduced to God, and in the end, had him as her comforter—"

Felix hissed and jumped off the counter. Stephen looked in the direction Felix fled from and saw a shadow in the sidelight of the front door. He set the journal down and walked to the door. As he reached out for the handle, the shadow vanished to the left of the frosted glass. Stephen quickly opened the door and looked down the hall, first left, then right. There was no one there, and there was no way anyone would have had time to get to the end of the hall. Stephen shut the door and leaned against it.

"Hey there, you're up early," Lucy said from the guest door.

Stephen was startled. Lucy just stood in the doorway, rubbing the sleep from her eyes.

"You okay? You look like you've just seen a ghost."

"I'm fine, just tired. I thought someone was at the door." He replied.

Lucy walked past him as they both entered the kitchen. Stephen sat back down at the island where he had been reading, closed the journal, and tasted his coffee.

cold again.

He watched Lucy as she grabbed a cup and poured herself some.

"You want me to heat you up?" she asked him, holding the coffee pot in her hand.

"What? Oh ... yeah, sure."

Stephen held out his cup, and Lucy poured. She took a sip, looking at him over the rim. She smiled, then, without another word, left, shutting the door to the guest area behind her.

Heather came into the room shortly after this.

“Hey, baby.” She leaned in and kissed his cheek on her way to the kitchen counter. She poured herself a cup of coffee and leaned against the counter facing him.

“Lucy and I were going to go shopping for her house today. Would you like to come?”

Stephen shook his head. “No thanks, I’m going to stop by Shelly’s for a visit. She has been bugging me about coming over.”

Heather gave him a surprised look. “Maybe I can cancel with Lucy and go with you. Would you like me to join you?”

“No, that’s okay Honey, go have fun. I will send your love and make a plan for us all to get together later this month. Plus, I may stop a few places for work, boring stuff really, love.”

“Okay, Babe,” she said, “If you’re sure?” Heather came around the island to where he sat. She put an arm around his waist and leaned her chin on his shoulder.

“What’s that, research?” She asked him, peering down at the books.

Stephen shifted the journal so she could get a better look.

“Your mom’s journal. Where did you find it? I’ve been looking for that Hun.”

“You have? Why?”

“Well, after you gave me the ring, I remembered your mother saying she had wise words for me there, for when the time came for our starting a family.”

Stephen slid it over, revealing the Bible underneath.

“Where did you find it?” Heather moved to the chair next to him and put a hand on it.

“Your office; actually, Felix found it. He was acting strange, so I followed him to your office, where he jumped up and sat on them.”

“He has been acting peculiar lately,” Heather admitted.

“I’m sure he’ll be fine,” Stephen reassured her. “Things have been exciting around here lately. He'll adjust to all of it soon."

Heather gave him a half smile as she looked over at her cat.

"You're probably right. How about you… you doing okay? You look tired," she said as she ran her fingers through his hair.

"Yeah, I'm fine. I just had a strange dream that woke me early."

"You want to share?"

"Maybe later. It's not a big deal, really."

"Are you having issues with us, Babe? I mean, taking the next step?"

"Not at all." He took her into his arms. "Marrying you is what I am most sure of."

He leaned down to her upturned face, so beautiful and sweet. They kissed and then held each other for a few moments. Heather opened the journal and thumbed through it with one arm still wrapped around her man.

"I love you, Heather," he whispered as he gave her a squeeze. He walked around to the sink and rinsed his cup. "And I, you Lover," Heather responded.

A Visit Home

Stephen drove east on the Interstate 8 to see his sister Shelly. He had always been close to his sisters, though their lives went in different directions. Still, he loved them very much and was always glad to see them. Shelly was Stephen's oldest sister and the one he depended on the most when he was a boy. She was mom when mom was away.

Stephen pulled into the driveway. He was lost in memories of childhood, seeing the old front door. Shelly had dedicated her life to church ministry. She put so much of her time into the teen groups and working in other departments that she never got around to starting her own family. Whenever Stephen asked about it, she would smile and say, 'I have 380 children and 16 grandchildren that fill my life.' This was referring to the years of teens that flowed through her ministry. Stephen got out of his car and was greeted in the driveway by Shelly.

"Hey, little brother!" She said as she hugged him. "I can't believe you actually came."

Stephen kissed her on the cheek. "I know, Shell. I'm sorry it's been so long. Things have been crazy lately."

She took his hand and led him inside. "Yeah, that's what I hear." She gave him half a smile.

"Come on. I'm baking cookies for church. You can help."

"Mom's recipe?"

The two spent the next couple of hours baking cookies and catching up on life. Shelly was a dark-haired woman of average height. She was wearing blue jeans and a tee shirt that begged the question: 'What would Jesus do?'

"I'm so happy for you and Heather, Stephen." Shelly sat down at the dining table with a plate of freshly baked cookies. He joined her, grabbing two of them off the plate.

"Thanks. Heather wanted to come, but I told her I would plan a longer visit in the next few weeks."

"That sounds wonderful. I'll call her and plan it." Shelly said.

Stephen took another bite. It was warm and soft, the way he loved them. The entire house smelled of cookie dough and melted chocolate. Cookies, baking in the oven, filled the kitchen with sweet smells. This reminded Stephen of his mother.

"I miss mom, Shell. I wish she was going to be here to see us get married."

Shelly stretched a hand across the table, touching the top of his. "I know me too. But she is watching from above, Stephen, and I know she's glad you two are doing things right."

"Do you really believe she is watching, Shell?"

"Yes, I know it." She smiled and took a bite of a cookie. "What's going on with you, hun? I mean, besides the new book and the wedding, is there something else?"

"No, I have my hands full with both, and that's enough for me right now."

Liar

"Well, I'm available if you need help, just remember that."

"I know," Stephen paused and looked into the kitchen. He could see his mother there baking in his memory. "Have you ever doubted, Shell, I mean your belief?"

"In God?" She asked.

He nodded.

"Not in God Honey, in myself, in his plan, or in what he wanted me to do, stuff like that, many times. But not Him."

"What about when everything around you is ugly, like murder, rape, war, and disease? How can there be a God—"

"With all the evil around?" She finished for him.

"Yeah," Stephen said. "How could He exist and not stop it?"

"Stephen, in all of those situations, He shines the brightest. God allows us to be free and hopes our choices will be good. Humanity has created the evil that so many blame God for. You need to realize that if humanity would have simply obeyed God's rules and allowed him to lead, there would be no crime, no suffering, no hunger, and no death. None of the ugliness that is in the world today would exist."

He picked up another cookie and ate it. "These are really good. Like Mom's."

Shelly smiled, "I'll put some in a bag for you to take home."

"That would be great. Heather loves 'em too. Hey, do you have Leroy's phone number? The number I have is disconnected."

"Sure, I'll write it down. I can do you one better, though. You should stop and see him. He is teaching at The College; in fact, if I'm right, his class will be getting out within the hour. He would love to see you."

"That sounds good. What part of campus is he on?"

"Do you remember Freedom Hall?"

Stephen nodded; mouth full of cookie.

"Room 107, I think."

Stephen got up, putting a hand on Shelly's shoulder. He bent and kissed her cheek, leaving a tiny touch of melted chocolate. "I will come back by here for the cookies around dinner time. Is that cool?"

"That's fine, tell Leroy I send my love. Shall I set you a place to eat?"

Stephen was already to the kitchen when she asked. He turned, "Yeah, set me a place," then walked out the door. Shelly listened to the front door close and Stephen's car start and leave. She looked up at the ceiling and sighed. "Thank you,"

Eschatology 101

The College looked different from the last time Stephen had visited, but he soon found Freedom Hall. As he approached the class, he had a sudden shooting pain up his spine into his head. It was sharp and almost dropped him to his knees. He stopped where he was and held his head in his hands.

"Are you okay?" a soft voice spoke from beside him. He felt a gentle touch on the back of his neck, and as he looked up, the pain passed as quickly as it had come. There, beside him, was a beautiful young woman. She had blonde hair and loving eyes. She smiled at him, and he felt warmth cover him. He smiled back, feeling a little foolish.

"I'm fine, just a headache. I'm looking for Eschatology."

The young woman smiled. "That is my class. I was just going back in now."

She gave the hall behind them a guarded look, then smiled as they approached the door. The two slipped into the lecture room and sat in the back row. Leroy was at the bottom of a large theater, speaking. He had a pointer towards a projector screen with the image of an archeological dig site. A man was knelt before an uncovered body holding out a measuring rod in the image. The skull and rib cage were all that were uncovered. The unearthed skull looked huge compared to the man beside it. Leroy squinted as he watched Stephen take his seat, then continued.

"This is a dig near Damascus in Syria. As you can see by the size of the skull near the archeologist, this individual was much larger than an average human. Using the proportions of the Scientist in the photo, we can determine that its stature was more than 10 feet tall."

Stephen looked at the young woman who led him and gave her a quizzical look. She smiled and then turned her attention to Leroy.

"Giants ladies and gentlemen, unfortunately, moments after this photo was taken, local authorities revoked their permits to be there and detained the entire team.

All research was confiscated except for the film, which was saved only through the quick thinking of a young intern. I know all this because the man in the photo was me."

Leroy looked at Stephen and put a hand up in acknowledgment. Several students looked back at him briefly as Leroy continued to speak.

Outside in the hall, shadows from the windows grew across the floors and walls in unnatural ways. One, in particular, left its natural place and fell on the doors to room 107. It rose up the door, forming into a humanoid shape. A moment later, it exploded, without a sound, into all directions, vanishing from the hall. All the shadows recoiled in revolution until they were once again the natural shadows cast from the windows. The hallway grew brighter as the sun came out from behind the clouds.

Leroy spoke about fallen angels and what he liked to call hybrids in the classroom, and Stephen listened attentively.

"They are genetic mutations of humans, who are birthed by human mothers, who mated with fallen angels. Nephilim, offspring of the sons of God and the daughters of men. Genesis 6: 1-6 'And it came to pass when men began to multiply upon the earth, and daughters were born to them. [2] that the sons of God saw the daughters of men, that they were fair; and they took them wives all which they chose.'

"The Hebrew word: 'Bene Ha Elohim' in the old testament always refers to angels. For instance, in Job 1, 2, and again in chapter 38. Also, in the New Testament, particularly in Luke 20:36. The first translation of the Old Testament was the Greek, 'Septuagint,' meaning '70.' The Greek language, being very precise, always translates it as' angles.' 'Daughters of men,' Hebrew word:

'Benoth Adam,' means daughters of Adam, not daughters of Seth, as some miss translate.

"Genesis 6:4 says, 'There were Nephilim in the earth in those days, and also, after that, when the sons of God came unto the daughters of men, and they bear children to them. The same became mighty men, which were of old, men of renown.'

"Nephilim means 'The fallen ones.' It comes from the verb, 'To fall away,' 'To cast down.' These hybrids resulted from the mischief between the fallen angels and human women. In this scripture, 'The mighty ones,' or 'The Ha Gibborim,' is written here. It was translated into Greek as 'Gigantes,' which does not mean 'Giant.' Feel free to look it up for your selves. It means 'Earthborn,' from the Greek' Gigas.' Although the word is translated into English as 'Giants,' some, but not all, of them were giants. Goliath was a famous one. However, it is not true to the original text, which meant 'Earthborn.'

"Genesis 6 says that Noah was a just man, perfect in all his generations. The word 'Perfect' means 'Without blemish,' 'Sound,' 'Healthful,' 'Without spot,' and 'Unimpaired.' The word was always used with regard to physical defects. The scripture clearly states Noah's genealogy was untainted and without blemish. The New Testament confirms this in Jude 6-7:

'And the angels who kept not their first estate, but left their own habitation, He hath reserved in everlasting chains under darkness, into the judgment of the great day. Even as Sodom and Gomorrah and the cities about them, in like manner, giving themselves to fornication, and going after strange flesh, are set forth as an example, suffering the vengeance of the eternal fire.'

"2nd Peter 2:4-5 says, 'For if God spared not the angels that sinned but cast them down to hell, and delivered them into the chains of darkness, to be reserved unto judgment, and spared not the old world, but saved Noah . . .' This clearly speaks of an event in time, were angels sinned and God punished them while saving Noah.

"Therefore, students, in plain English, This means?"

Several students raised their hands. Leroy chose one from the front of the class, and she answered.

"Angels bread with humans, creating a blasphemous, hybrid race, enemies of Israel and God. This was also an attempt to destroy the bloodline of man, so Jesus could not be born."

"Yes, very good, and?" Leroy prodded, and another student answered.

"God cleaned up the entire mess, saving only the genetically sound humans."

"Yes, fine, good answer. I know it may seem difficult to digest, but this idea has been embraced for centuries. It is found in legends of virtually every ancient culture: Sumner, Assyria, Egypt, the Incas, the Mayans, The Gilgamesh Epic of Babylon, the Persians, Greece, India, Bolivia, South Sea Islands, and even the Sioux Indians. They all have stories of Star people or gods producing offspring on earth.

"In Greek mythology, the Titans were partly celestial, partly terrestrial. They rebelled against their father, Uranus, and after a prolonged contest, they were defeated by Zeus and commended into 'Tartarus,' the pit of darkness.

"Atlas and Hercules were also Nephilim." Leroy looked at his watch, then cleared his throat. "Okay, class, that will have to do for today. We will pick up where we left off tomorrow. Be sure to finish chapter 3 in your textbooks."

The class started to gather their books and leave. Stephen got up and made his way down to Leroy. He remembered the girl and looked back to say goodbye, but she was gone. Leroy had three students around him asking him questions, so Stephen gave him space. Leroy answered their questions, then wished them a good day before looking at Stephen with a big smile.

"Hey, Leroy," Stephen said as he put out a hand to shake. Leroy looked at it as if a bug, then grabbed Stephen by both shoulders.

"My boy."

He looked Stephen over, then gave him a big hug.

"I'm glad to see you, Son. It's been too long."

"I know. I'm sorry. Heather and I have had so much going on, and my work is starting to take off. Actually, that is partly the reason I've come. I'm doing research and thought of you."

Leroy started packing up his things and gestured for Stephen to hand him a book.

"Well, of course, I'm available in any way I can be of assistance. I read your article on the occults in the Tribune. It was good, though a couple of points I did not completely agree with; all in all, it was a great read."

"I would love your feedback on it, Leroy. I would have scheduled an interview with you while I was writing it, but I thought you were in Israel or some other place at the time. I just found out yesterday that you were back."

Leroy and Stephen made their way up the steps to the exit.

"I think that was my last trip overseas. I'm getting too old for that stuff." Leroy held the door for Stephen.

"I'm sure you still got the juice, Leroy." Stephen patted him on the back as he walked into the hall. Leroy turned off the lights and shut the door.

"I don't know; that last trip really took it out of me. Besides, I have plenty going on here to keep me busy for the duration."

The two exited Freedom Hall and walked towards the cafeteria as they talked. They came to the doors of the cafeteria, and Stephen opened the door for his friend. Leroy smiled and entered.

"I was pleasantly surprised to see you come in and sit in my class. At first glimpse, I thought you were a late student that I was going to have to make an example of."

"I was going to wait outside your class, but I met one of your students who led me in."

Leroy stopped and looked at Stephen, "I thought I saw you come in alone?"

"No, your student, Sarah led me in. we sat together in the back."

"I'm sure I saw you sitting back there alone, Stephen." Leroy scratched his head.

"See, I'm getting nutty in my old age, Boy."

Stephen smiled, "It was dark, Leroy, and you were leading a class at the time. I wouldn't be too hard on yourself."

The two sat in the cafeteria and enjoyed lunch together. Stephen filled Leroy in on His and Heather's wedding plans and his book deals, and Leroy caught him up on family, friends, and church gossip. Stephen ordered a Latte and Leroy a cup of tea. Stephen brought their conversation back to Leroy's class.

"So, Leroy, You're telling me all those mythological heroes are real?"

Leroy sipped his tea and then responded. "All mythology is built on some truth. Often exaggerated but with some factual basis. Do you know how many civilizations have similar stories of a great flood?"

Stephen nodded. "So what you're saying is there were many great men of strength and power walking around in ancient times, and they were the source of the mythological legends we know today?"

"That's precisely what I'm saying, Stephen. I am not saying they rode lightning, as some stories say. That is an example of how humanity sees an event from different perspectives and forms a story.

"Imagine when Elijah was being picked up by the fiery chariot and taken to heaven. We know that story from a first-hand account. However, what if you were an Assyrian miles away from the event seeing a man riding what looked like fire or lightning? How would your version of the story be told? That story would become renown, and viola, a mythical legend is born."

"So what's this have to do with today, if God wiped them off the face of the earth in the flood?" Stephen asked him.

"That is a good question. Remember Jude stated that the offending angels were put in chains, as an example?"

Stephen nodded.

"Not all fallen angels were cast into that pit, only the ones who fornicated with humanity. Do not forget Genesis 6:4 says, 'there were Nephilim in the earth in those days, and also after that.' This clearly shows that other fallen angels did not heed the warning. Do you remember when Joshua first led the Israelites into Canaan?

"God commanded they completely eradicate certain peoples who occupied the land, including women and children. Now, why would God want them to annihilate women and children too unless He knew they were tainted again?"

Stephen had a notebook open, taking notes as Leroy spoke.

"Look at David and Goliath. Goliath was a giant man of renowned strength who caused the Israelite army to tremble. In addition, the ten scouts sent out by Moses before they entered Canaan. All but two came back trembling in fear, reporting that the land was full of giants so large they felt like bugs in their presence."

"I remember some of those stories from childhood, but I guess I never took them as reality," Stephen commented.

"Now look here in Matthew 24, Jesus speaks of the end-time being like the 'Days of Noah.' Many believe this is just a reference to him coming without warning, but Noah did warn people and was laughed at, so that cannot be the case. Either way, it is obvious Nephilim were around again after the flood, and I believe they are alive and walking around again today. Remember, not all of them were giants. Many had different strengths or powers. Satan is still breading his evil army, only restrained by God's Spirit. The scripture says that God will remove this restraining power when he takes away his faithful, and even now, His Holy Spirit is slowly giving over power to the god of this world because of the growing evil.

"Humanity has been slowly rejecting God and turning its back on Him, and the result is evil growing in power. 2nd Thessalonians 2:5-8 says that the one restraining must be removed before the 'Lawless One' can be revealed. This is another reason our church believes faithful Christians will be taken up before the tribulation. Because The Holy Spirit resides in Christians, and that spirit must be removed before Satan will be able to take full power over the world. Therefore, this cannot happen without first removing the church."

Stephen took a deep breath and looked up from his notebook.

"So, back to Nephilim. Angels have once again—"

"Fallen angels." Leroy corrected.

"Yes, the fallen ones have once again been up to mischief, taking on human form and breeding with humans. However, God is allowing this because it is all a part of his plan for the redemption of humanity?" Stephen asked.

"Well, his plan was to allow man to do things his own way for 6 days, or

6,000 years, and He has only been restraining Satan because He knew that Satan would completely destroy all of humanity within the space of a single decade once unrestrained. The 7th day, or Millennium, will be God's day to reign and right all the wrongs, to set everything right again."

Stephen tapped his pencil against his lips for a moment in thought, then made another entry in his notebook. He looked up as if to ask another question, but Leroy beat him to it. "I know what you're thinking. Why not just eliminate Satan and live in peace?"

Stephen nodded. "Yeah, why not?"

"Well, I am not here to figure out God in His wisdom. He is a just, loving God, and this is where my faith comes in, but if pressed to give answer, I would have to respond with: 'Free will.' God wants us to choose Him and that peaceful life. He wants our free choice to do what is right and learn from our mistakes, as any parent would want their own children to grow. You cannot have free will to choose what is right, to choose goodness, if the darker choice does not exist. You can't choose goodness if evil does not exist."

"Hmm, well, what does this mean for all of us here and now?" Stephen asked.

"That is, relative to where one is in all of this, I guess. It does mean that the principalities and powers that Paul warns about are gaining in power as we speak and that the end of days is near."

"Do these Nephilim, or hybrids, know what they are, Leroy?"

"I believe, and remember much of this is speculation, that some *do* know and actively serve Lucifer, but many may have no idea of whom they are or how he intends to use them in his schemes."

Stephen made another note and then looked up at Leroy. "So, you believe as God's Holy Spirit is quenched by humanity's sin, He withdraws, enabling Lucifer's power to increase in the world. This intern strengthens his fallen ones and their offspring, his hidden army here on earth?"

Leroy thought for a moment and then answered, "Well, to the first part of what you said, yes. However, the latter, I really do not know. I believe in the end, yes, this will be the case. I mean, if they were powerful men of renown then, why would they be less now?"

"Thanks, Leroy, this has been insightful. I do have another question a little off topic, though."

"I'll do my best to answer if I can," Leroy replied.

"What do you think about the theory, that Jehovah—Yahweh if you prefer—and Lucifer, are brothers, or that they could be two gods, locked in an eternal battle for a throne; and that we were created as a wager between them to settle this never-ending war?"

"Haaa," Leroy laughed. "That is a new one for me, but one I can easily answer. For one, Lucifer is the father of lies; it is his M.O. Secondly, it does not fit; there are too many holes. Yahweh has staked his claim to the entire universe as God. What has Lucifer done? Sure, he has a minority of people who worship him, but so does the NFL. Satanism is more of an occult than religion and is hidden amongst shadows. No, Lucifer hides behind other false religions. Baal and other pagan religions were his first attempt at being secretly worshipped. The great tribulation will be the first time he openly defies Yahweh, and the good book says that day will not end well for him.

"He is behind hundreds of other false religions and secular beliefs presented to humanity for the sole purpose of stealing souls away from God. Even when he makes his claim on earth, it will be as a counterfeit messiah. Not very original. Another reason, he is also not omniscient. If he were, he would have known Joseph and Marry fled to Egypt to protect Jesus from his attempt at killing the child. If he were like God, he would not have plotted to kill Jesus on the cross, thus fulfilling God's plan to redeem all humanity through that pure sacrifice. In killing Jesus, he gave mankind a chance to choose salvation and proved God's judgment over him before our time began."

Stephen sat there looking at him quietly. "I never thought about it like that. He *is* flawed. Making many mistakes."

"Stephen, you can't choose light without being aware of darkness. You cannot choose good without being aware of evil. Furthermore, you cannot choose God if there is no other choice to make. People blame God whenever tragedy strikes, but it is not His fault. Humanity, with our free will, chooses darkness. We allow immoral behavior, greed, and corruption to thrive in this world. This darkness is responsible for the death and destruction on this planet. Our evil choices have bred murder, rape, and robbery. They do not come from some unloving God. They are the product of a humanity that has rejected God. All the pain and suffering in the world is from a lack of God."

"Leroy, you can really wax eloquent when you choose to."

"Let me tell you something else, son," Leroy leaned forward and looked at him closely. "Two nations were founded under God's leadership, Israel and America. That is one reason America has prospered so much. However, as we remove support for Israel and turn our backs on God, His blessings will cease to fall upon us. Instead, He will deal with us as he did his children in the Old Testament. He punished His children and sent warnings in the hope that they would repent. Following this removal of blessing our nation will fall apart. I believe America is the linchpin that will set the end times into play."

"So did mom," Stephen said.

"Yes, your mother had a good grasp on the word and what it meant for her family. America must be removed as a superpower before all the pieces can fall into place in the Middle East."

Stephen sat there quietly, sipping his coffee for a moment. "Leroy, do you believe God would still communicate to man through dreams or visions?"

Leroy analyzed Stephens's expression for a little while before answering him. He could see that Stephen was trying to be careful in how he asked this question, as well as fear of the answer.

"Yes, I do, simply because the scripture foretells that in the last days, these things would again begin to happen. Look up Joe 2:28 and again in Acts chapter 2. Why do you ask?"

"No, reason, I was just wondering," Stephen answered.

"What about non-believers, and on that subject, what do you think about demons possessing them?"

Leroy sat back in his chair, tea in hand. He decided not to push Stephen for an answer.

"Son, for the first question, I believe you mean, would God visit non-believers in dreams, yes?"

Stephen nodded.

"Yes," Leroy answered and then remained quiet. It was obvious Stephen wanted more, so he continued. "Every Christian, who has ever been born again, has only come to the truth because the Holy Spirit came to them and removed the veil of deceit covering their eyes. Satan has blinded humanity to the truth. Scripture says that salvation will be as foolishness to a dying world. Only when God opens their eyes can they believe. We can be used by God to deliver the truth, but until the spirit of God comes upon them, they will remain blind. That is why we are taught to pray for those we are trying to save. As your mother and family have prayed for you and Heather."

"I'm confused; how does that explain non-believers having dreams or visions from God?"

Leroy smiled and sipped his tea. "Stephen, it is God who saves us all; He does not avoid the lost as if they are diseased. His spirit is still available to them if they will seek the truth. Many non-believers were led by God and used by God in history. Nebuchadnezzar had dreams of both his future and our upcoming future that God's prophet Daniel translated for him. Yet again, warning him that if he did not change his ways, he would be stuck dumb like an animal for seven years. When this happened, the King believed. He was the author of part of the book of Daniel. A once pagan King."

Stephen looked surprised. "Really?"

Leroy nodded. "I'm going to answer your other question about demons, but I am not finished talking about dreams, and I don't think you're finished talking about dreams either, are you?"

Stephen gave him a knowing look, then nodded.

A Dark Flock

A group of men clothed in robes sat in a circle around a large wooden table in the basement of a New York estate. Candles lit the room all around, and pentagrams and other pagan symbols were all over the walls. It was damp and musty within this chamber, and the walls revealed its age. One of the men was reading from a book as they worshiped Lucifer.

"We call on you, Dark lord, to imbue us with power. We dedicate our lives to your service. The riches we seek will also bless your plans for rule here on earth. Today we offer you this woman as payment for your blessings."

In the corner of the room was a young woman chained to the wall. Her tears had long made dirty trails down her face. Her face revealed the misery and cruelty she had endured at the hands of these men. She had streaks of dried blood all over her. The one speaking nodded to another, who got up and unchained the girl. She screamed a tired scream, one that said she had cried out so many times before this and was barely hanging on to the hope of freedom. He grabbed her by her hair and yanked her up and over onto the table.

She cried, "monsters, all of you are monsters."

She shivered, shock taking over her limbs. "I want my mom."

The cloaked man bent her over the table, smashing her face into it. She cried out. He pinned her over on the table with his body against her, one hand holding the side of her face against the table. The leader closed the book and walked over to her. He bent down and looked at her, speaking softly.

"My Dear, your time has come. You should feel honored, for you will be a gift to god. He pulled out a long knife and held it over the side of her throat.

"Lucifer, we give you this woman for your pleasure and amusement." He shoved the knife down. Her blood pumped out onto the table, and all the men in the circle put their hands out to feel its warmth. She twitched once, eyes wide in terror, then was gone.

"Funny! You should think your master would want your leavings," a commanding voice spoke from a doorway.

All the men jumped, startled by the unexpected intrusion. One turned and charged toward the voice in the shadow, knife out.

"You don't belong—"

He was cut short by a hand grabbing his own throat, crushing it, and snapping his neck.

He dropped to the floor, lifeless. The leader backed around the table, facing their intruder.

"Who...are you?" he shuddered.

The rest of the men followed him, backing out of their seats and away from that side of the room. The intruder simply stood in the doorway, mostly in shadow.

"Well, from what I heard, I am a brother in arms, though my service carries a much higher standard. Who are you?" the stranger answered.

"I am brother Smith," the leader said hesitantly, "I am a captain in Lucifer's army."

The man in the doorway cackled, "A captain, no less. Hilarious," The intruder shouted and then lowered his voice, "He never mentioned you."

All the cloaked men in the room fell on their knees, shaking in fear, their leader the only one standing. He sat in his seat with both hands on the table, one still holding the bloody knife, which he dropped.

"Whose idea was the girl?" the intruder asked.

They all pointed to their leader, brother Smith.

The intruder walked into the room, shadows still following him as he entered. He was clothed in a dark suit that much could be seen, that and his cold eyes that pierced their own. However, the rest of him seemed just out of sight.

"This is an insult to your master. That you dare offer him used goods. Do you think he wants your rubbish? DO! YOU?"

He shouted with a depth and volume that shook them in their cloaks.

"No… Sir, we only did as Smith instructed. He said—" Another man hit the speaker in the arm.

The intruder put a hand out, then tightened it into a fist. That man clenched from pain and grabbed for his groin, falling over.

"Continue, the truth is your only hope."

"He...He...Said we were sharing in her pleasure with Lucifer this way."

"Amusing! So very amusing. Do you think your lord likes to share? No…you may have what *he* is finished with if you please him in service, which is how this army is governed. Believe me, the reward for his faithful warriors will be far greater than some teenage brat.

"There must be penance for this insult. You may choose your sacrifice from amongst yourselves."

The men all looked at each other in confusion.

"Hurry, I do not have all day. Well…actually…I do. Nevertheless, I am not a patient man."

They all started pushing at each other and arguing in low voices, then the one who spoke up before looked at the intruder and spoke again.

"brother Smith led us to insult Lucifer. He should be the one to face the penalty."

There were protests from a couple of men, and brother Smith stood with an astonished look on his face.

"I have led you all well. You would not be here if—" He was cut off, grabbing his throat and falling to the ground. All the others backed away from him.

"Your choice has been accepted," said the dark intruder.

Another man started to speak but was stopped by the man next to him.

"We did not make a—"

The dark man smiled. "There is hope for some of you yet."

He pointed to the one who first spoke and finally condemned their leader. "You."

The man put a hand up in fear and backed into those behind him. Mr. Smith lay on the ground choking but still alive.

"You are promoted, Mr. Richardson."

The man started to speak, then held his tongue.

"You have shown me the leadership this group needs. If you fail, you will deal with me. If any of you disobey him, you will deal with the master, understood?"

They all nodded with half smiles.

"Good, good, now you need to bring your numbers up; the time of hiding in basements is at an end. Money will not be an issue. You will have an estate with plenty of room for future expansion, and your numbers will grow, or I will be displeased."

***

"Okay, demon possession." Leroy stirred his cup of tea and continued. "No one is sure without a doubt who or what demons are. Most believe they are fallen angels, and this may be true. Nevertheless, some reputable Christian research points in a different direction. Because demons always seem to be limited to having no bodily form, and angels-both heavenly and fallen-are able to take on form, there is an apparent difference. I am one of those who believe the latter."

Leroy paused for a response and continued, seeing Stephen writing busily in his notebook.

"When the fallen ones came down to procreate with humans, their resulting offspring were an abomination to God, maybe even soulless, though no one knows for sure. We know God wanted to wipe them out and made a point of it being an example to all in the process.

"My question Son is this, why warn the other angels if He was going to take away their ability to take on human form and mate with humanity?"

Stephen shook his head. "All of this is news to me, Leroy."

"The scriptures references to angels in heaven not marrying or being given in marriage does not mean their ability to choose differently was removed. David and goliath is the most famous story revealing the fact that angels were once again ignoring the warning and taking human wives."

"Forgive my interruption Leroy, but how's this going to explain demons to me?"

"I'm coming to that, Son. Now imagine how many people a thriving nation could grow to in a thousand years. My point is, the hybrid nations that died in the flood, and again in the invasion of Canaan by Joshua, as well, for the centuries since must be in the hundreds of millions."

"But they were wiped out, Leroy. Dead." Stephen interjected.

"Correct, I believe demons are the condemned spirits of those dead. Ghosts of the abominations bred from fallen angels and humanity. They have no bodies, nor do their spirits have a natural place to go."

"Paul speaks of different ranks of powers we must fight against: 'Principalities,' Lucifer's Commanders, or higher ranking devils.

'Powers,' perhaps Lucifer's power over creatures or other earthly things.

'Rulers of the darkness of this age;' this could be human rulers under satanic control or planted vessels of his evil army.

As well, Paul finishes this list, 'Against spiritual hosts of wickedness,' these being demons. The point I am making is that different types of beings work against humanity in this hidden war. There are different ranks of fallen ones, and possibly even different levels of demons, based on factors we can only speculate. This means we are up against a well-organized army hell-bent on the destruction of humanity."

"Well put," Stephen said. "I like the 'hell-bent' part; I'd like to use that."

Leroy chuckled. "Now, I believe demons cannot possess and control the body of a true Christian, and I emphasize 'true Christian' because many simply profess Christ but do not really possess him. A discussion for another time."

"Then why do I read so many stories about Christians harassed and even killed by demonic forces?" Stephen asked.

"We are on our way there, Stephen," Leroy answered. "There are ways to control someone without possessing them. Imagine an intoxicated person coaxed into a car, taken home, walked to their room and put to bed; this all without memory of any of it the next morning. That faithful friend manipulated and coerced the drunk person along, even guiding where they walked. Demons can effectively oppress, influence, and manipulate one's behavior, especially if alcohol or drugs are in play. They do not call them spirits for nothing." Leroy bounced his thick eyebrows and smiled.

"So you're saying demons, if allowed to enter a believer's world through drugs, alcohol, or other doorways, can control that believer?"

"Yes, some examples include God's anointed King Saul. After God rejected him, a demon oppressed him in 1st Samuel 16. This demon would sometimes cause him great bouts of depression and anxiety. Young David, God's anointed successor, was sent in to soothe the king with music. Saul had no knowledge that David was his replacement, nor had reason to hate him, yet Saul's demon probably knew David's line would be the line of Jesus and used Saul to attempt killing him. David's son, Solomon, allowed demon influences to enter his life through pagan wives. In the end, he allowed pagan rituals such as child sacrifice to be performed under his rule."

Leroy got up and pointed to Stephen's cup. Stephen nodded and continued writing in his notebook. Leroy returned, handed Stephen a fresh cup of Coffee, and sat with his tea in hand.

Leroy closed his eyes and was quiet for a moment. Stephen was going to ask him if he was okay but decided to hold his peace. The sun broke through the clouds outside, revealing bright rays of light in the cafeteria. It lit their table and warmed Stephen's hand. The sun brightened and filled the entire cafeteria. Leroy opened his eyes and took a sip of his tea.

"Not all demon possessions are head twisters; that would make for bad business in satanic goals. Many are seduced and may not even know they are being oppressed or possessed by demons, at least while they are needed."

Stephen looked up from his notebook. "What happens when they are no longer needed?"

"They are hung out to dry, my boy, left to face the consequences all their own."

Leroy opened his Bible and thumbed to a passage. "Let's read an example of how Satan leaves his pawns when finished with them. Matthew 27:3-5: 'Then Judas, His betrayer, seeing that He had been condemned, was remorseful and brought back the thirty pieces of silver to the chief priests and elders saying, 'I have sinned by betraying innocent blood.' And they said, 'What is that to us? You see to it!' Then he threw down the pieces of silver in the temple and departed and hanged himself.'

"Humans are like livestock to demons, and all that fall prey to their evil suffer."

"Do you believe you are safe from demons, Leroy?" Stephen asked him as he closed his notebook and leaned back.

Leroy interlaced his fingers, relaxing in his seat. "I can only put my hope in the Lord. I believe I am relatively safe as long as I walk in His will and give no place to evil."

"Relatively?" Stephen asked.

"Well, I am attacked all the time because I am a threat to lucifer's plans. Everyone stumbles, and that is when evil pounces. Christians are the enemies of Lucifer, so to say one is completely safe from demon attack is erroneous."

"With war comes death," Stephen said thoughtfully.

"Something else comes," Leroy added.

Stephen let out a deep breath. "This is a lot to take in. All I can say is if that is all true, it's a scary thought to go to sleep with."

"Yet faithful Christians are not overcome by fear but are excited about the future." Leroy leaned forward at the end of what he said and gave Stephen a penetrating smile. Have you been sleeping okay, Stephen?"

***

The dark man brushed some dust from his coat. “I have a small inconvenience in California that needs removing; you will see to it, yes?”

“Yes,” the robed men all said in unison.

He pointed to the girl. “This was messy and served no purpose. In the future, I require you to be more professional in handling problems.”

They all nodded again.

“You may draw all the blood you like and inflict all the pain you need on your time, but if the master calls you to perform, it is for his planning you will complete your tasks.”

“We understand, Sir, and will follow instructions. May we ask who you are, Sir?” Mr. Richardson asked.

“The Intruder smiled at him, obviously pleased.

“You may. I am your master’s helper. I am his ambassador. You may call me Charles.”

They bowed and nodded, “Thank you, Charles, for giving us this chance.” Their new leader said.

They all circled their demoted leader, Mr. Smith. He was now quiet, lying on the floor. He looked up at them with an expression that pleaded mercy.

“Now to Mr. Smith’s penalty. Kill him. I want to see how good you are with your hands.”

“No! No! Please!” Smith pleaded as they came upon him. His screams soon turned to mangled moans as they tore him apart. Charles stood at the doorway with a smile on his face as he watched. When they were finished, they all looked to Charles for approval, and he gave it. They knelt in a line before him with their heads down. They were covered in the blood of two victims.

“The cloaks have to go, my boys; a nice suit will be fine from now on.”

They all stood and removed their cloaks, throwing them on the table.

"I would recommend we take this mess to a furnace, save for the fact this entire house insults my taste. We shall burn it all to the ground and start anew."

One of the other men spoke up, "There is fuel in the garden shed. I'll retrieve it."

"Thank you, Mr. Henry," Charles responded.

Mr. Henry and another man left the cellar and went up the stairs. Charles looked at the rest of the men, who were piling up the bodies and all the cloaks together to make a bonfire. They broke up all the chairs save for two that Mr. Richardson pulled away for him and Charles to sit in. Charles sat in one, and Mr. Richardson claimed the second.

"Mr. Richardson, Craig, I have big plans for you and others like you in other cities. We must get organized and prepared for the master's plan. Your division is important because you are all men of power and influence in this country."

Craig nodded. Charles pulled out a piece of paper and handed it to him.

"These individuals are others I want drafted into our ranks."

Craig looked at the list. It had names of very powerful people: Senators, Bankers, and high-ranking military personnel. As well an address printed at the bottom.

"May I ask, Sir, What if—"

"They are already with us, son," Charles interrupted. "They just need to be informed of where to go."

Craig nodded and placed the paper in his pocket.

"You will have all the resources you need and the resources of many of the men and women on that list. I want you to delegate someone to form an outside faction of lower lings. Do you understand what I mean?"

Craig nodded. "A group of soldiers, expendable and not connected to us."

"Yes. Many returning veterans do not know what to do with themselves and others like them who need a family like ours. You will fund them and reward them but tolerate no mistakes. Your hand should be a firm extension of my own.

"I understand," Craig answered. "There is one group that simply needs leadership that I have in mind for a start, and I will have other for you soon."

"Good, this pleases. Follow my example and use the authority I have given you. You will be empowered to accomplish all I give you."

"I will, Sir, I swear to it."

Charles got up and went to the door, looking at all of the men. "Finish cleaning up this mess, and ensure all that is left are ashes. Mr. Richardson has the address of your new headquarters. Follow his instructions as if I gave them myself."

The group nodded and bowed as Mr. Henry and the other man returned with gasoline. Charles looked at them for a moment, then over at Craig.

"Mr. Henry will head up my California assignment. Walk me out, Mr. Richardson so that we can talk about it."

Craig Richardson followed Charles out the door. Mr. Henry handed containers to other men, and they all started dousing the fuel all around.

Charles and Craig walked out of the house to where a limousine waited. A huge man got out and opened the door for them. Craig could not help but stare up at the colossal man towering over him, having to be close to seven feet tall and twice his girth. Both men got into the car. The driver closed it and stood by. After about ten minutes, the door opened again, and Craig Richardson got out. Charles leaned out the door held by his giant driver.

"No collateral damage in California; all surrounding players are key to our plan. Look at me and tell me you comprehend."

Craig looked at him and nodded. "The inconvenience will be removed clean and carefully, with no mess. It will be a surgical procedure, sir."

"No collateral damage," Charles repeated.

"Yes, Sir, the others will not have any harm come to them," Craig assured him.

Charles smiled and nodded, now satisfied. His phone rang, and he answered it as his driver closed his door. "Hello, princes; how is California?"

Craig turned to go back into the house as the limo drove away. Mr. Henry was at the door.

"We are ready to fire the house when you are."

"Good, tell everyone to leave, then when we are all gone, you start it and get out. I will see you downtown."

"What's next?" Mr. Henry questioned.

"I will send word of where we are to meet next week. Until then, everyone needs to go on as usual. You and I need to talk, though. Meet me at the office, and I'll bring you up to speed."

Mr. Henry went downstairs, and Richardson stood watching the limo disappear down the road. *That man scares me even more than the giant.*

***

Heather and Lucy arrived at Lucy's new home in the hills above Ocean Beach. As Heather turned onto the street, she was amazed at the sight of the house. It was a three-story home of pillars and glass set high on a slender plot. The second level protruded out almost to the road, with a large patio in the center.

"It's beautiful, Lucy," Heather said as she pulled into the driveway.

"Yes, I love it, though father was not as excited as me. He wanted something with land that he could secure from nosey neighbors, like our homes in Italy and the Middle East. They are complexes, not homes, in my opinion. I plan on getting to know my neighbors."

Lucy gave Heather a rebellious smile, and both girls giggled as they got out of the car. Lucy punched in a code at the garage door, and it began to open.

"Well, I'm impressed, girl," Heather said. "You are loaded, aren't you?"

Lucy blushed a little, "I have a bit of money, but I am by no means spoiled by it." Heather slapped her on the rear as they walked in, "I know, Sweetie, there's nothing wrong with being blessed."

"Does this house scream spoiled girl?" Lucy questioned.

"No, not at all. I kinda figured you were loaded when I saw your Park Avenue address on the package your dad sent Stephen. The San Remo isn't a slum, Honey."

"Daddy used that address? He usually insists on his PO Box for all correspondence." Lucy punched in another code at the door leading in from the garage, and the two girls entered the first floor. This floor was mostly below ground, so there were no windows. Heather followed Lucy in as she turned on the lights.

"The lower levels will be daddy's dungeon and West Coast office. There is a street-level entrance at the other side of the property he will use for business."

She led them down a hall with a little theater and several closed doors.

"This will be his office." She pointed to each door: "Wine room, temperature-controlled storage, and here we plan on installing a vault because it is set deepest underground."

She turned and led Heather toward a large rectangular room at the end.

"This will be Daddy's showroom for pieces he is displaying. He really has too many pieces in New York, so I thought it would be nice to set up a small showroom here and make some room." Lucy's eyes were bright and full of excitement.

"It sounds like it will be nice. I can't wait to see it. Stephen said your dad has some of the nicest pieces he's ever seen outside a museum."

"He has, and they are, but I refuse to decorate this house with any of them. I want modern designs on the upper levels. This is where you come in."

She took Heather's hand and quickly led her back the way they came.

"Come on, I'll show you the rest. I'm so excited to hear your ideas."

The two girls returned to the front of the house, where a circular staircase led them to the upper levels. At the top of the stairs, Lucy let go of Heather's hand and pulled out her phone. Heather looked around as Lucy entered the kitchen and sat at the bar. In front of Heather was a floating wall that separated the living room from the open kitchen and lounge area. Set in this wall was a large fireplace that could be enjoyed from either side.

"Daddy, we're here. I'm showing Heather around now."

Heather walked around exploring. There were high ceilings and beautiful marble tile throughout. On both sides were giant sliding glass doors that led out to the floating patio. It had a short guardrail, and privacy screen stretched between its rungs. She looked over at Lucy, who was talking to her father on the phone. Lucy gave her a wink and waved at her.

Heather walked towards the back of the house, where she discovered a guestroom and lavatory. To her right was a staircase. It ascended behind the kitchen wall to the third level. At the top of the staircase was a long hall with doors on the left. The first two were average-sized bedrooms, with a bathroom in between, and farther down the hall was the master bedroom. The master bedroom was gorgeous and had its own deck with a guardrail and privacy screen. As Heather entered, she saw a 90-degree view out the glass façade. She could see the ocean and pier below. To her left was a large bathroom and giant shower. Beyond the bathroom was a large walk-in closet.

This is amazing. I could have fun setting this place up.

"Do you like it?" Lucy said from behind, startling her.

"I love it, Lucy. You scored."

Lucy gave her a one-armed hug as they looked out at the Pacific Ocean.

"I'm glad you like it."

The two girls walked around talking about design ideas. They finished in the kitchen and sat down at the island with wine.

"Heather, I want you to blow my mind, okay?"

"I will, Honey, I promise."

The two clanked glasses and made their way out to the main patio. Lucy sat cross-legged on the deck, leaning against the guardrail. Heather came and sat near her, looking out at Ocean Beach below.

Lucy's phone rang, "My father, I will be just a minute."

Heather nodded and took a sip of wine. She watched Lucy play with her hair as she caught her father up on all their ideas, then felt overwhelmingly sick. She pointed to the house, giving Lucy a sign that she would be right back. Lucy barely noticed her, listening intently to her father. She finished her glass of wine and handed it to Heather for a refill.

"Daddy, you can do whatever you want downstairs."

Heather made it to the restroom just in time to give her expensive lunch over to the porcelain god. She flushed the toilet and cleaned herself up. She felt dizzy as all the blood left her face, and she grabbed hold of the sink to keep from falling as her legs began to shake. The feeling started to subside, and she sat on the lid of the toilet until she felt better. When she came into the kitchen she refilled Lucy's glass. She looked at her glass with a little wine left in it, then poured it down the sink and filled it with water before returning to the patio.

"Daddy says hello, and extends his gratitude."

Heather gave a gracious smile, "It was nothing, really," as she handed Lucy her glass. Lucy winked at her as she took it.

"I will tell them, Daddy, and we will see you next week." Lucy sipped her wine as she listened to her father speak. "He's doing research today. I will, of course, and thank you for pulling strings with the escrow. Heather and I are working on all the rest… You also."

Lucy ended her call and set the phone between her legs. She noticed that Heather switched to water.

"Are you okay," she questioned, "you look a little flush. Is it the wine?" She rolled her wine around in its glass, examining it.

"I'm fine, I just felt woozy for a minute, but I feel much better now."

"You sure?" Lucy pushed.

"Yes, I'm fine, really. So what would you like to do for patio furniture? I was think—" Heather grabbed her stomach and wrenched over again. Her glass overturned and spilled on the deck as she rolled onto her knees. She tried to get up, but it was too late. Heather vomited right where she knelt. Lucy grabbed her long hair, pulling her own hair tie out, and used it to tie Heather's back.

"Honey, it is okay; get it out." She reassured.

"Ugh...oh my, god...I..'m so sorry." Heather managed as she finished heaving. "I don't know what's come over me. I...I'll...clean it up."

"Nonsense, Sweetheart, I will pull out the hose, and it will be gone. Let's move you to the restroom. Do you feel well enough to make it?"

Heather nodded, holding her stomach. Lucy lifted her up, and they walked into the house. After a few more minutes in the bathroom and a fresh glass of water, Heather's color returned, and she started to feel human again. Lucy left her sitting at the island and went outside to hose off the deck.

What is this all about? Surprise grew on her face as she thought of reasons for being sick. *You're late and now feeling sick in the morning; what else could it be?*

Lucy came back into the house and sat down next to Heather.

"All done, not a trace it ever happened, Honey. How are you feeling?"

"I feel much better now, really. I think that will be the last of it, for today anyway."

Lucy grabbed her wine glass, rinsed it out in the sink, then picked up Heather's and filled it back up. Well, good, I don't want you dying on me now. Why do you say for today, have you been feeling this way long?"

Lucy gave Heather an astonished look as she realized what Heather was about to say.

"I think I'm pregnant," Heather said softly. Lucy started to tear up as she hugged her.

"Oh, Heather, I am so happy for you. Are you late?"

"Just days, but somehow I know."

The two girls hugged. Lucy sat down next to her and put a hand on Heather's. "So, have you told Stephen?"

"Well, I kinda just figured it out for myself. I think I will wait until I know for sure."

"We could go get a pregnancy test if you want," Lucy offered.

"Yeah, maybe that would be a good idea."

The two girls finished what they were doing at the house and locked it up. On the way to Heather's loft, they stopped at a drugstore and picked up a test kit. When they got home, Heather went straight to the bathroom.

Lucy turned on some music in the lounge, dropped her shopping bags in her room, and lay on her bed. Felix jumped on her bed and cuddled up to her. Lucy picked him up and laid him on her stomach, where he purred as she stroked his back.

"Your family is about to get a little bigger, Felix." She said in a melancholy voice. She looked out the window and closed her eyes.

"Knock, knock," came from the door.

"Come in, Darling," Lucy responded.

Heather came in and lay down next to her. Felix came over for affection from his mother and then jumped off the bed. Heather put her hand on Lucy's, and Lucy looked at her. Her eyes looked moist and beautiful.

"What's wrong? Heather asked.

"Nothing at all. I am just overwhelmed with joy for you and Stephen. I want so bad to be where you are one day."

"Oh Honey, you will be. You are as amazing a person as you are beautiful. It's only a matter of time before you find someone worthy."

They hugged, and then Lucy kissed Heather's cheek. "I am happy for you, Heather. You are such a beautiful person, and I know you will be an amazing mother as well."

"Thanks, I hope I can be. I want to be a good wife and mother more than anything in the world."

She held up her test stick, and it showed + positive. She smiled, elated.

"We need to celebrate Heather. I want to take you and Stephen out to dinner tonight. Maybe we could invite Peter as well."

"That sounds like fun, Honey. I'11 call Stephen and find out when he will be home. How are you and Peter getting along, by the way?"

"Heather, Peter is the sweetest guy and an all-around catch, but we're just too different for anything romantic to develop."

Heather smiled at her and combed Lucy's hair with her fingers. "That's what Stephen said."

"He did? Well, you have nothing to worry about regarding bad feelings between Peter and Me. We already talked about it. He agreed and is content with being my friend."

Heather sat up and walked to the door. "I'm going call them then, okay?"

Lucy nodded.

***

Stephen spent the next hour explaining to Leroy about the dreams that he had been having and the conversation he had with Peter about them. Leroy listened attentively and did not seem concerned by what he was hearing.

"Stephen, one, you're simply having dreams because a lot is happening in your life, and this is your mind's normal response to getting engaged and taking a major step in your career. Or two, God is trying to reach out to you and show you something." Leroy sipped his tea with a simple smile on his face.

"Or three; I'm going crazy and should be locked up," Stephen added.

"Or that," Leroy agreed.

Stephen put his notebook in his bag and rested it on his lap.

"What do you think, Leroy, really?"

"Son, you know I was very close to your mother. I happen to know that not one but two mothers dedicated you to God. I also believe God takes these things very seriously. You are not going to get away from your maker. Be glad he's taking this approach and not turning you into a drooling animal like he did King Nebuchadnezzar."

"So why. What's He trying to show me then, in your opinion?"

"Well, if I were having these dreams, I would expect that He was preparing me for something involving his end plans. On the other hand, he could wish you to share the dreams with someone who will act on His behalf. Didn't you tell me that he had said something about you being shown a future you would pass on?"

"Yes, he told me the future I saw was my son's, That I was to pass something on. We were cut off."

"Stephen, I think you should embrace this. If God is contacting you, you are blessed. Just relax and see where this goes. Promise me you will keep an open mind until you have had a chance to learn more. Write down what you are dreaming. Maybe God just wants you to write all these things down and give your work to your future son."

"You're taking this too well, Leroy. This is insane. What am I supposed to do the next time one of those beasts tries to rip my head off?"

"You said yourself it is a dream. If that is the case, laugh in their face because they cannot hurt you. If it is not a dream, then you know God is involved, and he will protect you. What is insane is that so many people do not believe these things are real."

"I just want to focus on my life."

"Do that. Do just that, but if a dream comes to you, do not fight it. Realize where you are and investigate. Research this as if your dreams are your next big story. I will look into some of the other things you described to me, and then we will sit down again. We'll figure this out together."

Stephen nodded,

"God loves you, Son. The sooner you accept this, the sooner your life will return to peace."

Stephen's phone rang.

"Hey, Love, how's your day going?"

Celebration

Stephen walked in the door shortly before eight that night. He could hear the girls talking in the master bedroom as he walked past the kitchen. He set his satchel on the island and stroked Felix's back as the cat came up and nudged him. He entered the room and saw the girls lying on the bed with their feet up on the wall over the headboard. They had cotton stuffed between their freshly painted toenails.

"Hey, Baby," Heather said, looking back at him.

Lucy looked back as well and then swung her feet around and sat up on the edge of the bed. "I'm going to go get ready; I'll leave you to talk."

"I like the new color," he said, motioning towards her bright-colored toenails. She smiled and wiggled her feet back and forth on the wall.

"Me too, Lucy bought it, and we did each other's nails when we got back."

Heather was wearing soft cotton shorts and a tank top and had her hair down with tiny braids of hair in a couple of places on both sides. It was different, but Stephen liked it. He kissed her, and she pulled him back when he tried to sit up. The kiss lasted several minutes, and he pulled her into his lap as they finished.

"So what's this news you have that we need to celebrate?"

Heather pulled him tight, and rested her chin on his shoulder.

"So Shelly isn't coming?"

"She had too many things going on to jump and go like that, Love, but said to tell you she would like to get together soon if you two can make a plan."

"We will, I promise; I will call her tomorrow and make a plan."

Heather pulled back and smiled at him, searching his eyes. Then put her chin back on his shoulder, holding him tightly. He squeezed her and caressed her back, waiting for her to talk.

"Honey, do you think I will be a good wife?"

He kissed her neck. "I think you're going to be an amazing wife; you already are, as far as I'm concerned."

"I feel the same way, Babe, like we've been married for years."

They sat quiet for a few moments longer, and then she turned her head to the side, resting her cheek on his shoulder. She kissed his neck and caressed his chest.

"Do you think we'll be good parents?"

"I know we'll be good parents. Why do you ask?"

She leaned back and looked into his eyes again. She was radiant and had a glow. At that moment, Stephen knew. She looked complete as if every hope and dream was fulfilled in her life.

"Are you—" was all he got out before tears welled in her eyes, and she nodded with a smile.

"You're sure?"

She nodded again.

I'm going to be a father...

"I was late, and after feeling sick the last few mornings, decided to take a test. Lucy took me to get one on our way home. Are you happy, Stephen?"

He looked at her and wiped a tear off her cheek. "Heather starting a family with you was always the plan. Of course, I'm happy."

They kissed, falling back on the bed.

Daddy!

Mitch rushed out of the shared men's room and back to his room, where he quickly dressed for work. He grabbed his smokes from the dresser and finished buttoning his shirt, looking at himself in the mirror. Behind him was his dead daughter bouncing on the bed. He flashed her a scowl, and she flipped him off in return. Mitch finished getting ready and lit a cigarette.

"Daddy?"

He ignored her, went over to his desk, picked up a bottle of aspirin, and swallowed two, followed by two big pulls on a bottle of Jameson whiskey.

"DADDY!" the little girl screamed in anger.

He ignored her, taking two long drags from his smoke before flicking it with force at the dead girl standing on his bed. She dodged it as it flew by her head and out the open window. She glared at him, standing there with her little fists on her waist.

He slammed the door behind him. Mitch heard the muffled yell of his dead daughter as she cursed him from within the room.

Mitch was beginning to realize that these ghosts, or whatever they were, in no way were his family, no matter how much they looked and sounded like them. This gave him comfort that they were somewhere better, maybe waiting for him. Mitch hit the door and was soon back in the stock room down the street. Brandy was at the employee sink, stuffing her nose with cocaine.

"You better take it easy with that stuff."

"Oh, Mitchy, you do care. I knew you did. I'm just getting my groove on, that's all. I can stop whenever I want to." She said as she finished wiping her nose.

"Please don't call me that, Brandy." He pulled his bottle out of its hiding spot, took a big swig, then returned it.

"Oh yeah, I'm sorry, Mitch, I forgot. You know I didn't mean to. I keep forgetting." She watched him take another swig off the bottle.

"Hey, you too, Doll. You eat anything today, or just the liquid lunch?"

She went over to him, fixed his hair, then looked him in the eyes.

"Oh Mitch, what am I going to do with you?"

She smiled at him and then slapped him on the butt as she walked out. He puffed on his smoke and yelled out to her as she left. "Where am I tonight, bar or door?"

"Bar back, Baby. I may need you to back me up a little tonight, though. I have five VIP tables," she called back.

Imaginary Friend

Lucy walked into her room and pulled open the doors to her closet. She turned to the mirror on the back of one and undressed. She grabbed some underwear and a t-shirt putting them on, modeling in the mirror for a moment and then walked over to the other side of her bed and sat on the edge, looking out the window.

"You're beautiful, Sister."

It was the voice of a sweet little girl.

Lucy turned, startled to see her imaginary friend from childhood.

"You're not real, Ariel, but thank you." She continued to stare out the window.

Traveling all the time with her father made it hard for her to develop real friendships, and Ariel appeared when Lucy was six and living in the Middle East. She filled the void that was Lucy's loneliness after her mother vanished. Lucy had long since forgotten her.

"Why are you being mean, Luce? That hurts my feelings."

Lucy turned back to her. She was still the young girl of seven or eight who had played with Lucy and shared all her innermost feelings. Tears welled up in her eyes, and Lucy's heart broke. She put out both arms inviting the little girl to come to her, and she did. Ariel flew to her, falling into her arms, hugging her.

"I'm sorry, Sister," Lucy said as she hugged the little girl. "It has been so long since you were in my life."

"I missed you, Luce, but you stopped needing me, so I had to go," said little Ariel.

They finished their embrace, and Ariel sat on the bed next to her, looking Lucy up and down. "You've grown up, Sister." She said, caressing her back. "You are so beautiful, Sister; don't be sad because he loves her."

"Who? Stephen?" Lucy snapped with an offended look. "As if, sis, he's just a friend, and so is Heather. They are my friends. I'm happy for them."

Ariel just smiled up at her as Lucy got up and walked back to the closet.

"You're wrong this time, Sister. I am happy for them. I just long for what they have." Lucy adjusted the back of her underwear and pulled a short dress off its hanger. She held it up to herself in the mirror and looked over at Ariel.

"Honey, I'm glad to see you, but you're not real. I made you up. They are my real friends, and I cannot do this with you. It isn't healthy."

Ariel stood by the bed, looking at her. "I know you, Sister, better than anyone, and I see your heart. I just want you to be happy. Can't you—"

"Stop it!" Lucy cut in. "Stop it right now. You're not real!" She pulled the dress over her head, adjusted it in the mirror, then turned around. Ariel was gone.

"Oh, Ariel, I'm sorry, this is how it must be." She whispered to the empty room.

The doorbell rang, and she left the room, looking back one more time, expecting her friend to be there, but the room was empty.

Lucy came into the main loft. "I got it."

She opened the door. It was Peter.

"Hey, Hun. Good to see you." She hugged him.

"You too, Lucy, so what's the big celebration about?"

"You'll have to wait for Heather and Stephen to find that out," Lucy replied as she shut the door behind him.

"Okay, we're ready," Heather said, coming out in a sexy dress. She was followed by Stephen, wearing slacks and a dress shirt.

"Glass of wine, anyone?" Lucy called from the counter, where she filled a glass.

"Sure, I'll have one," said Peter.

"Really?" Stephen asked, perplexed by the idea of peter drinking.

"One is not a big deal, buddy. It is moderation that matters, right?"

Heather gave him a hug and kissed him on the cheek, then looked at him. "Thanks for coming, Pete." She said as she adjusted his shirt.

"Not a problem, Sis, so what's the big news" Peter's words trailed off as Stephen rubbed Heather's stomach.

Peter took her by the shoulders and looked at her. “Am I going to be an uncle?”

Heather nodded, floating on her toes. Peter hugged her and picked her up in his arms, twirling her around. He put her down just as Lucy was coming up with his glass of wine. He took it and hugged Stephen with his free arm. “I’m so happy for you both.”

“Thanks, Brother,” Stephen said.

“I set us up for bottle service downtown. We have a car on the way,” Lucy said, taking a large drink of her wine. Stephen looked at Heather, then to Lucy with a questioning look, but before he could ask, Heather ran her fingers through his hair, tussling it.

“There, that’s better, Hun. I like it like this.”

He took her by the waist and looked into her eyes. “Do you think it—”

“Baby, don’t worry. I’ll have a glass of champagne and switch to juice afterward.”

Stephen looked relieved and kissed her lightly on her glossy lips.

“You sure you want to go out like that if you aren’t going to drink?”

“Lucy came around and put her arm around Heather’s waist, and the two smiled.

“We want to dance, Babe,” Heather said as she looked at her friend.

“Something I may not be doing again for a while, considering my condition.”

“Okay, then, if that’s where you want to go, I’m in. You in Pete?”

Peter nodded, “I’m in; let’s do this.”

“What about Kimberly and the girls? Do they know yet?” Stephen asked.

“They are on their way to the club now, but they don’t know what we are celebrating yet,” Heather answered.

Onyx

The owner of The Onyx Room walked into the back room. "You're late, Falcone. Where's Brandy? I heard her voice."

"She just walked out front. Do you want me on bar-back tonight? Brandy said something about needing my help."

"Yeah, stay behind the bar tonight, but watch Ronnie; that guy is one slip away from gone. I want you to keep one eye on him at all times. If I find out, he let one more minor in my club he's gone. You got me?"

Mitch nodded, "What about VIP? You got someone to back up the girls?"

"You let me worry about the management of my club. If they get backed up, do what you can, but watch Ronnie tonight."

"10-4 Curtis," Mitch said.

"Call me Curt, Mitchel. You know I don't like Curtis. Oh, and you make sure you keep your focus on your job and not my girlfriend's ass so much. You two are getting a little too chummy, in my opinion."

"I'm not sniffing up anyone else's tree, Curtis."

Curtis shot him a look.

"Curt," Mitch corrected.

"Good, good, that's what I want to hear. I see who really busts ass around here, don't think I don't. You keep it up, and you may be the one managing things when I'm not around. You get me?"

"Yep," Mitch replied.

Curtis was soon out front chopping his gums in Brandy's ear next.

"Douchebag," Mitch mumbled as he put out his smoke. *I don't see how she puts up with that guy's claptrap.*

He adjusted his clothes and returned his bottle to its hiding place when

Brandy came to the door. "Honey, I need you to cover my number five, they just walked in, and all they want is Champagne. A group of seven; can you handle them?"

Mitch nodded, "What do they want?"

"Cristal," Brandy answered and was gone.

Mitch went to the walk-in, grabbed the Champagne, put it in a stainless-steel bucket, and filled it with ice. He threw a serving towel over his forearm and grabbed some glasses on his way out. The VIP area was just off the upper-level dance floor. Several low booths were set in two curves around the back wall, cordoned off, and guarded by security. Table five was the last one in the back and the best one, in Mitch's opinion. It offered the most privacy because it was turned in such a way that offered the most concealment from the rest of the club. He always had to keep an extra eye on it when certain guests reserved it because they would try just about anything they could get away with back there, including having sex. They were told to turn a blind eye to the drugs and as much of the other stuff as possible without leaving the club liable if someone was hurt.

Mitch gave Big T a nod as he passed him at the security barrier and walked up the three steps into the VIP area. He noticed the Lamborghini dealers in the first booth and nodded to them as he passed them.

Schmucks.

They always tried stealing the booze from other VIP guests while they were dancing and were very cheap for guys who acted like they had money. Mitch disliked these guys and felt sorry for whoever had their table. He proceeded to the back, passing three more full booths of customers enjoying themselves. As he approached the last booth, he heard someone call his name from behind and looked back to see Brandy give him the thumbs up. In the same instant, as he was turning around, he smashed into the back of a woman who had gotten up and was grabbing her purse. The glasses chimed, and one dropped but was caught by her as she turned and looked up at him. She was beautiful, and Mitch was frozen in place for a moment. She stood up and smiled. Something about this woman had caught him off guard.

Annie?

She looked just like his dead wife, except for the green eyes. Annie had hazel eyes, and this woman's smile was bigger, but other than that, she looked just like her. She said something that he did not hear, but then he broke free from the trance he was in.

"I am sorry, Miss. I didn't see you get up."

She smiled again, a forgiving smile that took command of Mitch's heart and soul.

"It was my bad, don't worry about it." She said as she set the glass on their small table and walked around him.

He turned, still holding the mess of glasses and Champagne against his chest.

"The lady's room is on this side of the bar, yes?" she asked him.

He nodded then gathered himself and placed the champagne bucket and glasses on the table.

"How is everyone tonight? I'm sorry about bumping into your friend. It gets crazy in here at times."

Annie's date nodded and lined up the glasses for him. "It's all good, man, no harm, no foul."

Mitch pulled out the bottle of Cristal and showed it to them. The first man nodded in acceptance, and the other two smiled. He was sharing the booth with another younger guy in his 20s and a blonde who stood and grabbed a glass.

"I'm Lucy, Sweetie, would you happen to have anything stronger?"

Mitch smiled, *a woman after my own heart.* "We have whatever you want. Should I take back the Cristal?"

Annie's date shook his head. "No, that's what we requested. My fiancé and I will stick to the Champagne, thanks."

His fiancé... read that loud and clear.

It was getting louder as a new mix came on, and the club livened up. They were practically yelling as they spoke to one another. Mitch popped the cork and started to pour. He stopped after the first two glasses were full and then looked at the blonde and her date. They nodded, and he poured. He pushed three other glasses back and looked at Lucy.

"They are on the dance floor." She answered.

He nodded, "So what else would you like me to bring? I'm Mitch, by the way. I'll be you host tonight."

Lucy gave him a mischievous smile, "Something manly, Honey. What do you suggest?"

Mitch looked at the two guys, who just smiled and then back to Lucy.

"Well, I'm partial to whiskey myself, and I'd say that's the manliest drink around."

"You have any Single Barrel?" the beautiful woman asked him. She was now sitting back down with her legs pointing towards him, showing just a glimpse of what was in between. Mitch looked her in the eyes and smiled.

"I'll grab you a glass."

She gave him a penetrating look, then broke away and patted her date on the leg.

"Would you sip some whiskey with me, Peter?" He looked at his friend a little nervously, then put on a look of confidence when he replied.

"Sure, I could have one, Sweetheart." He gave Mitch a confident look, which told Mitch he had no confidence in anything he was saying.

Mitch set the bottle of Champagne back in the bucket. "I'll be right back with your whiskeys."

As he came back down the steps of the VIP area, he saw the brunette coming out of the lady's room. Mitch stopped where he was and just stared at her.

Annie.

"What's up, Babe?" Brandy said from his right.

He turned to see her coming out with an empty bottle and some glasses. He gave her a distracted smile as he followed her gaze past him to the brunette.

"She's a hottie," Brandy said. "You know her?"

Mitch nodded, then shook his head, confused by thoughts. "Um, no, she's my... She's one of the customers you just gave me."

Brandy smiled at him. "Nice, Baby." She walked past him towards the bar and turned back as she crossed paths with the brunette. She looked the girl up and down and winked at him.

Mitch started moving towards the bar and met the brunette in the crowd.

"Hi again, I'm... Mitch, your—"

"What?" she said, leaning in to hear him better.

Mitch spoke up, "Hi again. I'm Mitch. Your friends ordered another bottle. I'll be right back with it. You have Champagne waiting."

"Oh, thank you, Mitch. I'm Heather."

She started to pass him when he spoke again, stopping her. "Be sure, and let me know if you need anything at all."

"Thank you, Mitch, I'll do that." she walked back to the steps of the VIP area as Mitch headed back to the bar. He walked into the storeroom and sat down, lighting a smoke. He took a deep drag and exhaled. Brandy peeked in, "You okay, Romeo?"

"I'm fine; she just reminds me of someone, that's all. I didn't expect that."

"You're turning red, wow! I never saw you like this." She came in and messed up his hair. "It's good, I mean, I'm glad to see some life in your eyes."

Someone called her name, and she caressed his cheek before leaving. Mitch got up, went to the sink, and then splashed cold water on his face.

She's not Annie.

Mitch looked at himself in the mirror for a moment and then left the back room. Lucy and her date both had two fingers of the whiskey, and eventually, so did the other man. However, Heather just sipped on her glass of Champagne and then requested juice. Her date had eyes for Mitch, so he was careful not to be caught looking at her too much while he was there. The other girls were obviously single, and the blonde was especially intriguing. It was clear her date was not her boyfriend, and she flirted with Mitch whenever he came around. She was a knock-out, and Mitch liked her, but this brunette, Heather, had him feeling sideways. It was as if Annie was there again, alive, and that all their history had never happened. The fire, she and his daughter dying, all of it gone. If he kept her in his peripheral vision, it was as if his wife was alive. She sounded different, but it was easy for

Mitch to imagine all the differences gone. To him, her eyes were hazel, and her voice was Annie's. He spent most of the night watching her from afar, and a few times when he was noticed, the other girls would wave, thinking he was looking at them. He used this and flirted back with them to get a chance to be close to Annie or not Annie. A few hours later, he found himself back in the storeroom wondering what they were celebrating and talking about, trying to remember her smell. She smelled good.

Porcia came in the back and leaned against the wall for a moment looking at him.

"You got a smoke?" She sat on a chair next to the employee lockers and crossed her legs. Mitch threw her his pack. She pulled out a smoke and threw the pack back at him.

"Light, Tough Guy?" She gave him a sexy sneer.

Mitch still said nothing. He threw her his Zippo, and she caught the healthy toss with a snap in her tiny hand. She flinched a bit but liked it. Mitch had a feeling that just turned her on. She lit the smoke and puffed for a minute, putting his lighter somewhere in her bra. Mitch took a long drag off his smoke and put it out on the floor. He looked over to Porcia and put out his hand.

"What?" giving him a quizzical look.

"My lighter, Sweet Tits"

She smiled, "Come get it."

Mitch walked up to her as she stood, looking at him with a bit of apprehension. He backed her up against the wall. Putting his hand in her shirt and gave her breast a long squeeze.

The club was pumping, and the dance floor was full of young bodies moving to the beat. The place was full of the pungent musk of lecherous people. Perfume and cologne overpowered the senses.

Mitch was soon behind the bar helping the bartenders catch up on glassware. He loaded several glasses into the little dishwasher behind the bar and then pulled out a rack of steaming ones from the other. As he stacked them, he noticed Ronnie flirting with a young woman by the door. She could not have been more than 18, and it was obvious she intended on getting in. At the same time, he noticed Brandy talking with table five as they were getting up. It looked like they were getting ready to leave. He scrambled over, trying to get in between them and the other exit, but saw the young girl kiss Ronnie on the cheek and enter the bar. Two other young women followed her, obviously underage as well.

"Damned you, Ronnie." *What a good-for-nothing shit!* He had to intervene, which would blow his last chance to interact with Annie's doppelganger. He changed directions and intercepted the three girls.

"Woe, ladies, I need to see your IDs."

They all groaned and complained that they had already shown them at the door, but Mitch wasn't listening, he watched in frustration as the mysterious brunette left the club and his life. As she left, he turned back to the girls and caught one by the arm as she tried to slip past him.

"Honey, if you're 21, I'm 80."

"You're acting 80." She snapped.

"IDs ladies."

Mitch walked them back to the door as they complained, then begged and finished at the door with a couple of insults. After they left, he looked at Ronnie, who gave him a devastated look of defeat.

"Why? You know you're already on thin ice, and that shit could get the club closed down. Why are you sabotaging my job?"

Ronnie gave him a stupid look and shrugged. "They were hot, and I folded, Man. Are you going to tell Curt?"

"I don't want to be stuck doing your job if I fire you, but I am hiring someone to back you up. If it happens again, if I find another minor in this bar again, you're gone whether you let her in or not. And believe me when I tell you, no club in this city will hire a liability like you if we fire you. Think it through. You piss me off."

Ronnie nodded, obviously worried. Mitch walked back to the back, deeply disappointed. He felt like all the air was let out of him by this woman leaving.

Heather...her name floating in his memory.

The crowd in the club started to die down a bit, and last call was soon called over the loudspeaker. Mitch spent the next hour cleaning up and restocking. After the last of the customers were gone and the front bar was restocked, Mitch sat in a chair in the back. He was swigging on an unfinished bottle of Champagne from table five, puffing on a cigarette. He let out a sigh as Brandy and Porcia came in.

"Hi Honey, you doing okay?" asked Brandy.

"Another day in paradise, Sweets."

Porcia shot him a knowing look as she walked over to the sink and checked her hair. Brandy joined her, and the two did a line.

"Few of us are going to an after-party. Want to come?" Brandy asked.

Mitch and Porcia looked at each other with guilty looks on their faces.

"Oh, I see…I take it you have plans." Brandy said with a smile. "Well, don't hurt your selves." She checked her nose in the mirror, then walked over to Mitch, bending down. She gave him a peck on the cheek and whispered in his ear.

"She acts tough, Honey, but she's still a girl, remember that."

Mitch smiled as she stood up and began to leave.

"Maybe you should join us then and give her a hand."

She gave him a shocked look and then waved him off.

"Don't do anything I wouldn't do, you two." She gave Mitch one last look from out in the hall, then was gone. Mitch turned to see Porcia leaning on the sink, looking at him. He finished his smoke and the bottle of Cristal and then got up and threw it in the trash. He walked towards the door to leave, and Porcia cleared her throat.

"My car is in the parking garage. Want me to drive?"

Mitch nodded, "sounds good. I'll be ready in ten minutes," and walked out the door without looking back.

Out at the bar, Brandy was counting her tips, and the two bartenders were leaving. Mitch nodded to them as they shut the door. Brandy had a smoke hanging from her lip as she finished a stack of ones and picked up a stack of tens.

"So you have fun with table five tonight?" she asked, giving him a brief look.

"She looks just like her; it's uncanny."

Brandy stopped counting and gave him a stunned look.

"Anne?"

Mitch nodded a tired nod.

"Oh Mitch, I'm sorry, you should have told me, I could have-t"

"Told you what," Porcia cut in as she walked out.

"Don't worry about it, just go get ready, I'll be waiting right here."

She smiled and then put her thick fold of tip money in her purse.

"I am ready."

"Okay, well, why don't you go warm up the car? I'll be right behind you."

Porcia gave him an icy look.

"Why don't you play with yourself tonight, prick," and walked out the front door.

Mitch was indifferent; He looked over at Brandy. "It's okay, it was nice. I mean ... It felt good to be around her."

Brandy put a hand on his shoulder, "But it's not her doll."

"I know, but it was nice." He got up to leave. "The offer still stands if you want to come have some fun." He smiled at her and walked to the door.

"What makes you think you even have a date anymore, Romeo?"

"She'll be there, she likes the game."

"You're bad, Mitch, really. Be good."

"Will do, mom, I always am."

Mitch put a hand up as he opened the door to leave.

"I know where she works," Brandy added just as the door was closing. Mitch froze in place and looked back. "Who?" He questioned as he walked back in the door.

"Your mystery woman; she has an interior design firm near 10th avenue. I think her company built this place, to be honest. I'm not sure about this, but I know someone who would know."

"Will you ask Curtis for me?"

Brandy nodded, not taking her eyes off the money she was counting.

"Thanks," Mitch said.

She turned and looked up at him. "It's no biggy. Be good tonight; remember the saying about not shitting where you sleep."

"What, Porcia? We're just passing the time." Mitch hollered as he left.

He turned to walk up the street when Porcia pulled up in a silver Porsche 964 Turbo. He opened the door and looked at her, "Really?" With an arched eyebrow.

"Really what?" she snapped, waving him to get in. He got in and shut the door as she hit the gas.

"You don't think it is a little cliché to be named Porcia and driving one?"

"Um, I didn't pick you up to get advice from you on fashion or my choice in cars, Mr. Bar-back, and it was a gift. What do you want me to do, turn down an eighty thousand dollar car because of the name?"

Mitch shook his head. He looked over at her and smiled. "Got any booze on daddy's boat?"

"Yeah, but the *yacht* is a Hatteras, just in case you need to roll your eyes some more, Slick."

"Hatteras is fine ... That's not your last name, is it?"

She glared at him, then cracked a half smile.

High Places

A bright flash came down from the clear night and vanished near a monument in the hills north of downtown San Diego. The floodlights, pointing up onto the giant, white cross on Mount Soledad, flickered and went out just as another falling star flashed overhead. They soon came back on, however, very dimly lit. Two beings now stood at the edge of the memorial with the giant cross behind them. They were brilliant-looking angels, one more magnificent than the other. They both had enormous wings that stretched out twice their length before folding behind their backs. The One who appeared first was bigger and brighter; He was beautiful. Everything about him was the purest white-hot platinum. His pearlescent skin danced with tiny pulses of living energy within. His clothing was majestic and powerful. Lightning was trapped within every thread. He had a breastplate of the purist gold and platinum that shimmered like a liquid, decorated with dangerous looking settings of diamonds in brilliant patterns throughout. His arms and lower legs had armor that matched. His eyes were mesmerizing. They looked like deep blue jewels, yet fire seemed to rage from deep within their centers. His wings also were different. As they folded behind him a second set unfolded briefly to accommodate the fist as all four closed behind him.

Both beings looked down upon the sleeping city and ocean beyond. The second angel looked over his massive shoulder at the cross.

"Of all the places I could find, you lord, his monument was not an expected one."

Lucifer looked at the cross behind him and smiled.

"It will not stand for long, and soon after I pull this cross down, the one who hung there will fall as well."

"They are fools to worship his defeat, my lord."

"I killed the beggar once; I'll do it again, only this time for good."

An osprey flew in front of them, and Lucifer put out his hand. The bird tumbled through the air for a moment, then stabilized and flew to him. He looked at it for a moment and then waved his hand, causing the bird to take flight.

"Samyazal, I am not confident in how things are transpiring with my vessels or that Asbeel has covered every possible avenue of attack from our enemies."

"My lord, has Asbeel failed you in this mission thus far?"

"Not entirely, though; it was never my plan for the boy to fall into the hands of my enemies to be raised, nor was it my plan for him to be in love with someone other than his intended mate."

Lucifer's skin fluctuated with shimmers of darkness as his anger was roused.

"My lord, how could we have known his mother would run to a church for protection?"

Lucifer glared at Samyazal with hell burning in his eyes. His skin cracked with rage, and blackness spewed briefly before receding. Samyazal faced the ground and knelt.

"I beg your pardon, my lord. We should have guessed our enemy was lurking about when his mother started to fight us. This is a mistake we will not make again."

Lucifer looked back out to the ocean. "This is what I want: Care in what you do. Our enemies surround us and are interwoven in my vessel's life. I want these threats removed."

"My lord, we are taking steps now, only limited by our inability to intervene directly."

"Those restraints will soon be gone, and then there will be no more mercy," Lucifer said. Even now I sense the power his host has over our armies is weakening, but be careful as they are still more power than you. We must keep our losses to a minimum until his seal is broken and we are on equal ground in battle."

Samyazal stood back up, “Asbeel has organized your following in the east, as you requested, and I am organizing here as well. He has sent us loyal men who will intervene soon, lord.”

“Watch the boy, Samyazal, he is not to be witness to anything that would steer him away from plan.”

“I will, my lord, though it is difficult when he is surrounded by our enemies.”

“And my dear daughter, who keeps her on track?”

“My lord, Asbeel has watch over Lucy and has his demons watching her while he is in the east.”

“Don’t count on them; they are cowardly and unpredictable,” Lucifer responded.

“Yes, my lord, she is near him most of the time, so I have eyes on her as well, though Asbeel’s servant, Ariel, has been close to the girl since childhood and assures me everything’s well in hand.”

“What about this, Peter? I do not like what I have seen in her behavior with him around. She is to remain pure. Remove him as well as the old man.”

“Yes, my lord, though this will take all my resources as His watchers have eyes on them both. What of the other woman? What plan have you for her?”

Lucifer smiled at his captain, “That is why I sent Asbeel to organize in the east. We cannot touch her ourselves, but I have one who can be pushed to do what is needed.”

Lucifer looked at Samyazal with a thoughtful gaze,

“Remember the importance of not allowing this to become a tragedy; otherwise, the boy may break down and change tack.”

“My lord, may I ask then, why don’t we move forward with the earthborn? He has shown great interest in her, and her infidelity would drive your vessel into Lucy’s arms.”

Lucifer folded his arms and looked out to the west. “This one is unruly. He struggles against me, and even now that we have him, he still fights for control; something smells of my enemy’s trickery within him. I will leave nothing to chance. We keep him pointed on his path to her and the men from the east theirs; if one fails, the other will succeed."

"My lord, we will provide you an heir, and he will be magnificent, I swear to it."

Lucifer turned to him, becoming more brilliant, his wings unsettling. "He will be magnificent once he is ready for my taking, and I will hold you to your oath."

Samyazal bowed and nodded in agreement.

"I expect perfection from her loins. My enemy's runt had the planets align for his birth, and I will have nothing less. She must carry his child soon. I want this to be complete on the day the mothers die. That blood is to flow in honor of my son."

"She is more than ready, my lord, and Ariel assures me that she desires him."

"And what of the boy? Does he desire her?"

"My lord, Ariel tells me he finds her desirable but that the other woman holds his heart. Once she is removed, all should fall into place."

"On with it then."

Samyazal spread his wings and exploded into the sky, vanishing into a flash of light. Lucifer turned and looked up at the giant cross. "This is my time, my world, not yours. I will sit above the stars, your head my footstool."

Four mighty wings exploded open, and he took to flight. As he approached the cross, he spat upon it and then vanished.

Daddy's Yacht

Porcia sat up on the end of the bed, naked and covered in sweat. They were both still breathing heavily.

She looked back at Mitch, "You scared me."

"You were a little scary yourself there for a minute." He returned.

"I mean it; what was that?" she stood and faced him. He adjusted a pillow behind his head, "wild sex."

She turned and walked through the main cabin and into the galley. Porcia opened the refrigerator and pulled out a water bottle, rolling it across her forehead. Her sweaty body shimmered in the moonlight, flooding in the windows, and the cold bottle brought her some clarity.

"Can you bring me a drink when you come back?" Mitch called from the room.

"Get it yourself; I'm off the clock."

Porcia went into the bathroom and looked at herself in the mirror. She had red marks on her neck from where he had been choking her. There were bite marks on her breasts and also on her inner thigh. She felt shame wash over her. Her life was playing out in her mind, and all the choices she had made that brought her to this place.

Life? ... It's not even a life. She thought to herself.

She pulled her hair back and grabbed a scrunchie from the shelf to tie it off. Porcia grabbed a towel and started wiping off the sweat from her body.

How did I get here?

She looked back in the mirror, disgusted with herself, and threw the towel on the ground.

All you do is degrade yourself more and more, and it's never enough, is it? No matter how extreme an act, the need is never met.

She opened the shower and turned the hot water on, and the room soon filled with steam. She caressed the places he had bitten her.

You did this to yourself.

Tears filled her eyes as she realized she had wasted so much of her life on meaningless pleasures, which always left her empty. She climbed into the shower and eased into the scolding hot rain.

Mitch got up, pulled on his pants, and went out onto the back deck of the master cabin, lighting a cigarette. He looked out onto the bay, thinking about the brunette from the club.

She looked just like you, Annie ... Where are you? The further I drift into darkness, the further away you feel.

Mitch turned to go back into the master cabin and stopped. He could hear the sound of a crying woman. He leaned over the side rail, looking in the direction the sound was coming from and realized it was coming from the boat.

"Oh man, Brandy warned you. Now, look what you did."

Mitch searched the forward part of the boat until he found the bathroom and opened the door. Her sobs stopped immediately as he startled her.

"Get out!" she barked in a cracking voice.

"No. I'm not leaving," He snapped back.

She jumped, frightened by his response. "Please, Mitch, I am not up for more." Her voice was pleading. This made Mitch feel even worse.

"Listen, I'm not here for that. Why are you crying?"

She was quiet for a minute, then in a low voice, "No, it's me, or yes, it's what we both did in there and what I have become over the last couple of years."

Mitch sat on the toilet, "Porcia, you wanted all that. I wouldn't have done any of it if I thought it would upset you."

The water turned off. "I know, somehow I knew a long time ago that you're not the cold creep you act like you are; maybe that's why I felt safe bringing you here."

"I'm sorry if I hurt you." He stood and put a hand on the shower door.

"Can you hand me a towel?"

Mitch grabbed one off the rack and held it over the glass door. She took it, blotted her face and hair, and stood there holding it against her chest.

"You didn't do anything I didn't ask for or do myself, Mitch. You did scare me for a minute, though."

"How?" he questioned.

"Your eyes...They changed...Like you became something else."

Mitch did not know how to respond. He sat back on the toilet.

"Not just that, but after I bit you, I felt like something evil was all over me, and inside me, it scared me to death. I couldn't scream or anything."

"Porcia, come out, please."

The door opened, and she stood there, a shy wet girl holding a bawled-up towel against her breasts. She no longer looked like the woman who brought him to the boat for sex. She looked like a young woman who wanted love.

"I understand, I'm…I have no heart anymore, so I didn't see you."

She sobbed for a few minutes until Mitch picked her up and carried the naked girl, still dripping, back to the bedroom. He laid her down, pulled a sheet up, and kissed her forehead. "You are much more beautiful than I thought you were. Why do you pretend?"

She looked at him with brokenness. "I live in denial, and that's how I cope. I guess."

"I like this side of you much better."

"What sobbing and heartbroken?"

"No sweet-cheeks, real. A woman with depth."

She noticed a little bit of dried blood on his neck from one of her bites and winced.

"Did I do that?"

He smiled and nodded.

"I'm sorry."

"I'm sorry too...I think we both have been hiding from hurt in all the wrong ways. Maybe it's time for a change. What do you think?"

She nodded, still holding the towel against her like a favorite teddy bear.

"I want to go home."

"Where's home?" he asked.

"Colorado."

"Do you have people there?"

She nodded again. She looked younger and younger to Mitch as they spoke. He saw the disillusioned teen leaving home hurt and angry at the world and trying to mask it with a hard heart and wild living.

"You're young still. You could go to college and be anything you want. How old are you, by the way?"

"Twenty four."

They both sat quiet for a moment, and then she pulled herself up against the pillows. She dried her upper body and wrapped her hair in the towel, looking at him intently the entire time.

"What about you, Mitch? Do you have family near?"

Mitch felt his chest tighten, "My family is gone, and I have been trying to bury them in a bottle and meaningless sex ever since."

She winced a bit at the last part of what he was saying.

"I don't mean you, Por—"

"Yes, you did," she interrupted. "It's okay. I understand, really."

"Actually, this time ... tonight? With you? It *is* different. You are special, and I see you now. Who you really are."

She reached forward and kissed him on the cheek, then hugged him. They sat there silent for a few minutes. It was very quiet, except for the jingling halyards against their masts and other rigging in the marina.

She took a deep breath, "Something else touched us tonight, didn't it?"

He sighed and was quiet for a moment before answering her.

"Yeah, but you're going to be okay." She looked at him with concern.

"And you?"

"Don't worry about me."

She was looking out the window now. "Mitch?"

"Yeah?"

"Do you believe in God?"

"I am starting to wonder."

"My parents believe in God. I never did. I made my mom cry because I thought it was ridiculous."

"And?"

"I don't know ... something scared me. I'm scared for you."

"Don't be."

"I was out of control, Mitch. I wanted to draw your blood, or whatever touched me did. At my worst, I don't think like that."

He leaned forward, and at first, she flinched. He smiled and brushed the hair out of her eyes.

"I'm leaving Mitch. I'm going home."

"Good."

He followed her gaze out the sliding glass doors. The yacht swayed as a wake touched its hull.

"I wish Brandy would do the same. You're both better than all that."

She turned and smiled at him.

"You do care. Brandy always says that. I think it's funny. I think she has a thing for you, though she won't admit it."

Mitch's face saddened. And silence filled the cabin for what felt like hours for Porcia.

"I lost my wife and child in a fire and have turned my back on love or anything that resembles it ever since. I don't want to talk about it…can't. I guess I'm afraid that if I face it, I will go insane."

"I'm so sorry Mitch, I didn't kn—"

"Stop, don't do that ..."

She knew it was better to drop it, so she did not pry any further.

"I'm glad I got to do this, Mitch. I'm glad you came tonight."

He was silent still.

"I know you're broken, and now I understand better why you are the way you are. I hope someday you can let go of that pain and allow yourself to feel love with someone again."

She smiled at him and then lay back down. He lay down behind her and stared out the window, talking with her until she fell asleep.

***

The four arrived back at the loft around four in the morning after a walk on the beach. Heather filled a glass of water and drank it as Lucy and Stephen, both very intoxicated, collapsed on the couches laughing uncontrollably. Lucy reached for the remote and turned on the radio, and the room filled with music. Peter got up from a lounge chair, and Lucy caught his hand and squeezed it as he walked by. He gave her a brief smile, went to the island, and accepted a glass of water from Heather.

Lucy rolled off the couch onto the floor, and the two started laughing again. Peter and Heather gave each other a smirk and watched the others for a few minutes. Peter leaned and clanked his glass with Heather's

"Did you have fun tonight?"

"Oh, I did, Pete, thanks. I am worn out from dancing, though."

"You girls were grooving out there. I still can't believe Angie fell."

Heather laughed, "Yeah, that was so funny. She's going to be embarrassed tomorrow."

Stephen was now quiet, and Lucy was zoning out to the music. Peter got up and put his glass in the sink.

"Pete, you know you're welcome to stay the night, Dear." Heather offered.

"Thanks, but I am going to go soon."

"Well, it's up to you. I'm wiped out. I'm going to go to sleep." Heather walked over to Stephen and sat beside him on the edge of the couch. She touched his cheek, but he did not respond, so she pulled off his shoes and left him to sleep it off.

She stopped near Lucy, who was woo-whoing to the music. Lucy put her hand on Heather's rear, then let it slide down to her thigh, where she gave it a squeeze.

"You're so beautiful, Darling," Lucy slurred, "I'm glad you're my friend."

Heather smiled and bent down to Lucy's level,

"You are too, Babe." She walked to the bedroom. "Night, you two," Heather finished.

"Night Prego." Lucy blurted.

"Goodnight," Peter whispered as she hugged him.

Lucy sat up and put her arms in the air looking at Peter. "Put me to bed, Doll."

Peter came over, picked her up, and carried her into the guestroom. He laid her down and sat on the edge of the bed next to her. She gave him a girlish smile,

"Will you stay with me for a while?"

Peter nodded, "Until you fall asleep."

The room was dark. Lucy sat up and awkwardly managed to shuffle her dress up to her waist. She gave him a helpless look,

"A li'l help, Handsome?"

She put her hands in the air, and Peter pulled her dress over her head and arms. He laid it over a chair next to the bed as Lucy climbed under the covers. Peter struggled, trying not to stare at the gorgeous woman half-naked as he sat back down next to her. She patted the bed behind her, and Peter hesitated. Instead of crawling next to her, something every cell in his body was begging him to do, he leaned against the headboard and caressed her head.

"I am not going to wait anymore, Peter. I am afraid of my future."

"What are you talking about?" he asked.

She turned her head and just looked at him with a severe look.

"Sister, what do you think you are doing?"

Lucy looked over at the corner of the room where Ariel was standing. Peter followed her eyes to the same place and saw nothing but the curtain.

"Why are you afraid of your future?" he asked.

"Not him, Sister; remember, you are saving yourself for the one you love."

"Love could follow later," Lucy rejoined, looking at the empty corner. She looked back at Peter, who looked confused.

"NO! It will not," barked Ariel.

Lucy ignored her and kept her gaze on Peter. She grabbed his neck, gently pulled him closer to her, and then kissed him. For a moment, he was captivated by the amazing woman and kissed her back but then pulled back.

"Lucy, you know how attracted to you I-"

"Shhh. Peter, please. I am offering myself to you right now."

Peter stood up, a war raging within him.

"Sister, stop this; he is not the one." Ariel's voice was full of alarm.

Lucy shot her a defiant look. "The one? What do you know?"

Peter looked in the direction she was speaking, perplexed. "Who are you talking to?"

She looked at him, startled by the fact she had allowed the slip.

"Never mind, Peter, Listen to me. I want you right now. We can learn to love each other, I think."

"Lucy, I wish it was that simple."

"Why! What has God ever done for you? I mean, look around Peter; where is He? I'm right here, now, willing to be yours." Her veins began to come out in her neck.

"Lucy, He is all around. He has held me up through every hard time I have ever had. He has never let me down or betrayed me, nor has he ever done anything to hurt me. 'For I know the plans I have for you, says the LORD; plans to prosper you, and not to harm you. Plans to give you hope and a future.'"

"What is that?" she accused.

"Jeremiah 29:11, a verse I hold dear."

"You are quoting the Bible to me! Really?" Her voice was loud and hurt.

She pulled off her covers and stood on the bed, anger and hurt in her eyes.

"I offer you this, and you quote scripture?"

Peter looked at her, and He was torn.

"What...are you a homosexual or something? She jumped off the bed and walked up to his face.

"No, Lucy, Let me show you God and see if a relationship is possible—"

"Peter," Lucy pleaded, "don't you want me? I could have chosen any guy I wanted and offered myself to you."

"I do want you, I ju—"

"No, Peter, I do not want to hear about God. That is foolishness."

She sat back on the bed, shock and frustration on her face.

"I told you, Sister, he is not the on-"

"Shut up bitch!" Lucy snapped at the empty corner before looking back at Peter.

"The truth of the gospel is foolishness to the perishing." Peter quoted.

"Not another verse, Peter."

"I care about you, Lucy, and do want—"

"Get out! Right now!" she stared at him with disdain.

"Good sister, he is not good enough for you," Ariel called from the corner.

Peter walked to the door and stopped, "I care, Lu—"

"Shut up ... Get out!"

Lucy threw a shoe at him, hitting him in the chest. Peter walked out of the room and closed the doors behind him. Lucy broke down in tears. She lay down facing the window.

"I'm sorry, Peter," she whispered.

Ariel came to her and caressed her face,

Peter put on his shoes and then went to the door to leave. He stopped and looked back, wanting badly to go to her. He walked out the door and closed it softly behind him.

Lucy opened her bedroom door, "Peter, don't go ... I'm sorry."

There was no answer; Peter was gone. She returned to her bed and hugged a pillow.

I'm sorry, Peter.

***

Stephen was flying through space and came down to the sky above his city. He flew around, looking at all the familiar places until something pulled him down to a rooftop. He did not recognize the house as he looked down, but he was sure he was in the hills over Ocean Beach. He looked to his left and noticed his spirit guide had appeared next to him.

Oh no, not again.

"Stephen, something is about to happen."

"Enough, Man." Stephen interrupted. "You're not real; this is my mind dealing with anxiety about my future. I don't want to hear it. I have a life and want to enjoy my dream in peace."

"We are trying to help—"

"Oh, stop! I mean it. Just leave me alone." Stephen tried to take flight but was still anchored by some unseen force. He looked over at Gabe. "You going to let go or what?"

Gabe looked into the sky for a moment, then back at Stephen, "Very well, Stephen, I am sorry you feel this way."

He put out his hand, and Stephen was free from the force holding him. He took to the air and looked down, and his spirit guide was gone. He started to fly away when he noticed a Mercedes turn into the driveway of the house. It looked like Heather's car, but he was unsure, so he hovered there. At the same time, he heard someone crying and woke up.

He was now on the couch, and the crying was coming from the guest area. As he got up, something fell to the floor with a clang. It was the gold coin that Charles had given him. He picked it up and immediately felt the anger rush into him that he felt on the rooftop.

He followed the sobbing sounds into the guest room. As he opened the bedroom door, a shadow darted across the room towards the curtain. Lucy looked back up at him and then turned back to the window, silent.

"Are you okay?" he asked.

She wiped at her eyes. "I'm okay, Stephen. I'm sorry if I woke you."

He came to her side of the bed and sat next to her, brushing her hair back from her eyes. "You want to talk about it?"

Lucy shot up and hugged him. She sobbed and trembled in his arms.

"Sweetheart, what's wrong?" he asked her.

"I don't want to be alone anymore," she sobbed.

"Oh Honey, you're not alone ... You know that Heather and I are here ..." He said. "And everywhere you go, people want to know you. You commanded that club tonight, Princess—"

She pulled back, astonishment in her eyes. "My father calls me that," her voice soft. Stephen smiled, "I'm sure it's because he sees what I see."

"What do you see, Stephen?"

"I see a gorgeous young woman with a dazzling personality who walks into a place like the sun. That's what I see."

Her eyes glistened, and he could feel her heart beating harder. His kind words touched her where it hurt the most, and she was utterly vulnerable to him. Lucy's defenses were down; only the real girl before him, making her even more beautiful. She kissed his lower lip and breathed him in. Her smell intoxicated him, and he kissed her back. Once the dam gave, a flood of passion filled them both. They were soon lying down, enthralled in each other's arms. They rolled over, and she straddled him, looking down on him with deep want in her eyes. He caressed her and pulled her to him, their breathing heavy. She sat up and quickly removed her bra, then kissed him again, their bodies tight against each other.

"Stephen," she cried out in ecstasy. "I need you."

Stephen Jumped, feet flailing from an impact on his stomach and opened his eyes. The hit came from the cat, leaping onto him from the top of the couch. A twang resounded as something metal hit the floor, and he looked to his right just in time to see the gold coin roll under one of the couches. Stephen sat up, out of breath. He looked around the room in confusion, still half of his mind in the guest room with her.

A dream…

Felix meowed as he got up and walked into the kitchen. He topped off the cat's water dish looking at the double doors that lead into the guest area. He approached the doors and leaned close, listening for any sound, but heard nothing but dead silence. Stephen went straight to his room, undressed, and got into bed next to Heather. She cuddled up to him, and he kissed her neck.

"I love you." He whispered before closing his eyes. Guilt wreaked havoc on his thoughts. *I would never do that.* He argued within himself. He finally fell into a dreamless sleep.

Inside the darkness of Lucy's room, little Ariel was quietly smiling. She was perched like a predator upon the top of the curtain rod. Her eyes were inhuman and glowed like an animal's as she snickered, pleased with herself. Her arms and legs were abnormally thin and long now, and her face that of a devil.

She crawled down the wall and along the floor like a spider, vanishing under Lucy's bed. Lucy lay there, eyes wide, out of breath, staring at the ceiling. She held the covers against her chest. She touched her neck, then ran her hands down her body, letting out a frustrated groan.

What is happening to me?

She looked at that empty corner and then around the room in confusion. passion still raced through her, and she could still smell his scent. She sat up, letting the cover fall; the thought made her shiver and then cry. She reached to the floor, picked up her bra, and then lay back down facing the window. Tears rolled down her cheeks, and she sobbed as quietly as she could.

Felix came in, jumped onto the bed, and then hissed at the floor beneath. He walked around the bed, keeping a vigilant eye on the floor as he patrolled, then curled up in front of her. She pulled him close, and Felix let her hold him like a teddy bear.

"Felix, I'm going crazy, kitty." She wept.

Teeth

Mitch could not escape the misery inside him; only keep it at bay moment by moment.

Out on the deck, his dead daughter appeared doing cartwheels. She was beautiful this time and showed no sign of the horrible death she suffered. She stopped and walked up to the glass door and put her mouth on it, blowing. Sharp teeth showed through the glass.

"You finished with the whore?" She gave him a wide grin. "You were supposed to choke the bitch to death, Daddy, her and the other whore."

Mitch ignored her and got up. He went to the bar, found some whiskey, and chugged. As he let the booze run down his throat and numb him, he noticed a shadow dart in front of the doorway. He dropped the bottle on the floor and ran to the room. Standing there on the bed was his dead little girl, only now her eyes belonged to something evil. A knife dangling from the tip of its handle in her hand between two fingers. It pointed at Porcia's neck.

"Leave her alone, you little bitch!" he screamed.

She lifted her free hand to flip him off and dropped the knife. He jumped forward to stop her and managed to deflect it before it plunged into Porcia's neck. She awoke, startled to see Mitch leaning on her with a knife in his hand.

"What are you doing?"

"You're leaving… now." He pulled her up and sat her on the edge of the bed.

"What are you talking about? What is all of this?" still half asleep.

The little girl was standing outside the glass again with her head cocked to one side. She smiled at him and pointed behind him. There on the wall, a shadow was forming and crawling up to the ceiling. It was taking on form and solidifying.

"Please trust me, Porcia. You need to pack your stuff and leave now. Remember what we talked about?"

She nodded, eyes wide.

"You have a good life in front of you, but you have to leave now to grab it. I'm afraid if you wait, you may never be free of all of this."

She just looked at him with confusion on her face, yet down deep, she had the same fear: that if she did not act, it would be too late.

Mitch yelled at the ceiling in a commanding voice that scared Porcia,

"Get away!"

It seemed to stop whatever it was from moving, and the little girl at the window grew a scowl on her face. Mitch looked at his dead daughter,

"You too, you little bitch!

He threw the knife as hard as he could at the window, and the butt of it struck right in front of his dead daughter's face. It shattered, and the demon shattered with it. Trails of blackness swirled around where it had been standing.

Mitch was gathering up her clothes and throwing them at her. She looked at the broken glass and then up at the ceiling, "Mitch?" her voice nervous.

"What?" he answered as calm as possible as he gathered her things.

"Do you know what I was dreaming?"

"No, what were you dreaming?"

"I was dreaming I was on a road trip. The music, the smells, it all seemed so real. Then I stopped because a large wolf was blocking the road. As I was getting out of my car, a beautiful woman whispered in my ear, and you woke me."

Mitch looked at her with concern in his eyes. "That's why you're leaving right now." "It's because of them, isn't it ... the ones that touched us?"

He nodded without noticing as he pulled out some luggage from her closet and stuffed them with everything he could find.

"What are they, Mitch?"

Mitch looked out the window and saw the sky start to lighten. "I don't know, but they follow me wherever I go and don't like me being close to anyone. I think that's why you need to go."

Porcia pulled her shirt over her head and stood up, pulling on her underwear. She looked at him nervously. "You're scaring me, Mitch."

"I know. I'm sorry, but I won't lose anyone else." He stopped what he was doing and touched her cheek. He smiled, "I'm glad we met. I'm glad I met you both."

"Us both?"

"You and Brandy have helped me in a way I can't explain." Alarm passed over his face.

"Brandy! Hey Porcia, you need to promise me something, okay?"

She nodded, eyes wide. "Pack everything you need, nothing more, and leave right now. I'm not saying you can never come back, but right now, you can't be here. Go see your parents, okay?"

She nodded again and started looking around for some pants in the pile of clothes. Mitch walked to the door and looked back.

"I mean it, Porcia; you are better than all of this." He smiled, and she ran over to him, hugging him around the neck. "I'm afraid for you, Mitch."

"I'll be okay as long as those I care for are far away. That is the only way they can hurt me. I think. If you two are safe, I can beat them." He looked at her one last time, then kissed her and left. She stood there holding a pair of pants for a moment, experiencing what had just been their first kiss. The spell broke, and she rushed out to the aft deck then yelled, "Mitch, don't kill her…If you kill her, they will have you forever."

He stopped. He looked across the dock at her with confusion in his eyes. "Brandy? Do you think I would hurt Brandy?"

"Not Brandy…." Puzzlement on her own face at what she was saying.

"Leave San Diego, Sweet cheeks, okay?"

Porcia put up a hand, and he was gone.

Mitch's only other worry was Brandy. He ran down the dock and was soon on his way home. Something in his gut told him that was where she would be.

True Feelings

Brandy was rehearsing what she was going to say in her head as she got to the double doors which led upstairs to Mitch's place.

"Oh, this is crazy. What am I doing?" She turned to walk away, then stopped.

She took a deep breath, turned around, and walked back to the doors. The anxious young woman entered the code Mitch had given her and climbed the stairs.

***

Mitch hailed a taxi and headed to his place. He had an overwhelming feeling that Brandy would be there and that she was in danger. He started to talk to whatever God was out there in his head. *I don't know if you exist, but my wife believed you did, and I would like to believe they are with you. If you are real, please show me. I'm not asking for me...I deserve whatever I get, but these girls...*

He pointed, "Here."

He threw a twenty up front and had the door open before the car rolled to a stop. Mitch ran in front of the car and across the street.

***

Brandy knocked on the door, and it opened. "Mitch, are you here?" She pushed the door open a little farther, worried she would be walking in on him in bed with Porcia and embarrass herself.

"I'm sorry for coming over like this, but it's important."

"Come in," came from the dark room. The voice was Mitch's, and he sounded calm, so she stepped into the room. There in the darkness was Mitch's silhouette sitting in a chair facing the window.

"Are you alone?" she asked.

"Not anymore; you're here." He replied.

"I need to tell you something, Mitch, and it couldn't wait."

She walked up to him and stood at his back. He was smoking a cigarette.

"I'm sorry for barging in like this, Mitch, but I realized something tonight when you left with Porcia."

He was quiet, so she continued, "I realized I was jealous and more than that... I have feelings for you." Her voice trembled.

He stood and pulled her into his arms. She held on tightly.

"And I, you Brandy… Dear."

At that moment, Brandy heard a subtle difference in his voice that made her nervous. Was this Mitch? He held her tightly as she tried to back up and get a look at him.

"I'm so glad you finally shared your feelings with me." He said.

This isn't Mitch! Her heart screamed.

There was a commotion out in the hall, and she heard someone running down the hall. She was frozen by fear,

"Where is Mi—"

***

"Brandy!" The shout came from the hallway. It was Mitch, and she pulled away enough to see Mitch stop at the door, out of breath.

The door slammed shut in his face, and she screamed.

Sunrise Highway

The sun was beginning to crest the mountains in the east, and the sky was changing from a deep purple to a beautiful baby blue outside. Birds began singing, and cars started all over the city as their drivers began their commutes. The city was slowly coming to life for another fast-paced race for the things people must have. A flock of small birds scrambled for some food found on the rooftop of the loft and then took to flight, headed in the direction of the bay.

***

The marinas were also a bustle as anglers started boats and dockworkers rolled carts. A seventy-foot yacht swayed in its slip as boats cruised by, its back deck strewn with the glass from the broken sliding door. The ship had no signs of life within.

***

Dawn had changed to day on a lone highway pointing east. A silver sports car flew down the four-lane highway doing 75, music pumping within. A song had caught Porcia's attention, and it brought her to a better place.

'You felt my pain—and not once have you left me,
You held me close and blessed me;
Protected me every day!
I've tried—everything just kept going wrong,
I let go; you kept holding on; that's how you loved me!
You cried—when my heart cried a broken song,
Because of you, I'm now growing strong;
That's how you love me.'

Porcia had been crying as she drove, dawning her sunglasses as the sun pierced through her windshield. It seemed to impale her pain as well, warming her with its rays and calming her heart. The song touched her deeply as if written for her alone.

Who am I? That you are mindful of me?

That you keep thinking of me?

You're…unconditional.

Who am I? That you would still love me?

That you would even want me? You're…unconditional.

The tears stopped, and hope filled her. She smiled as she drove down the highway listening to the song. Her cell phone rang.

"Hi, Dad!"

"Hey, Sweetheart, have you left yet?"

"Yeah, I left right after calling you."

"Sweetheart, you should have gotten some sleep first."

"I know, Dad, but I wasn't going to sleep anyway, and I wanted to get home in time for church tomorrow. You and Mom are still going, right?"

"Well, yeah," her father stammered. "You want to go to church? Are you sure you're okay, Honey?"

"I am now, Dad." There was silence on the line for a moment, and she could hear him whispering in the background.

"Well, your mother is happy to hear you want to go to church, but please drive safe, Dear. If you're late, we can always go to the late service… Your mother says we will go to the late service, so don't speed."

"Okay, Dad. I'll see you soon ... Hey, Dad?"

"Yes, Dear?"

"I love you ... I'm sorry for how I left things."

"Oh, Sweetie, we love you too." It was her mother on the phone now. "We understood that you were upset when you left. Please drive safe. We're so happy you're coming home."

"I will, Mom. See you soon."

She hung up and turned the music up as the car soared down the road.

Papacy ~ Puppetry

Cardinal Leonardo Delgado sat at his large desk alone in his office. He looked out his window at a beautiful view of the ocean below him. He sighed.

"Not what you expected, is it?" A commanding voice spoke from a part of the office that lay in shadow.

The Cardinal stumbled out of his chair, startled by the unexpected intrusion.

"H—how did you get in here...Who are y—"

"Quiet yourself, Leo," the stranger in shadow cut in.

He stepped out from near a bookshelf on the other side of the room, revealing himself to the Cardinal. He was a well-dressed man in his thirties, with dark hair that fell to his shoulders. His dark mustache and beard that ran along his jawline to his sideburns were perfectly trimmed. His suit was of the highest quality and tailored. The stranger carried a silver crested cane that was obviously for show.

"Sit down, Leo, that is, unless you would prefer we invite the authorities in to discuss the money you embezzled from the church."

Leonardo sat, stunned. "How do you know a—"

"I know many things, but you need not worry. I am not here to blackmail you. I like an enterprising man; that is why I put you here."

"Who are you?" Leonardo quivered.

"I am the prince of this world, soon to be king."

The Cardinal grabbed for his crucifix, stumbling out of his chair. He backed away and around the room, towards the window. The stranger calmly sat in one of the guest chairs in front of the desk and inspected his fingernails. As Leonardo made his way around the room, he reached a table with a vial of holy water sitting on it.

He picked it up, trying to conceal it behind his back as his other hand clutched the crucifix hanging around his neck.

"Your talisman will change nothing; it is actually somewhat of a trophy of mine. See, I have one myself."

The stranger pulled a beautiful silver crucifix out from his jacket. It shimmered, ending in a razor-sharp blade at its bottom. He embedded it in the top of the desk, causing Leonardo to jump, dropping the holy water. He fumbled to pick it up without taking his eyes off the intruder. The stranger got up and walked over to the trembling Cardinal as he tried to remove the cap from the vial. He managed to send out one sprinkle of holy water toward the intruder, two drops hitting the man's face. One ran down his cheek, and the other rested on the bridge of his nose.

The man grabbed Leonardo's wrist, removed the vial from his hand, and gave him a perfect smile. The Cardinal froze in fear, well aware he was facing a being, not of terrestrial birth. The man's face was attractive and symmetrical, without blemish. He had beautiful blue eyes that seemed to draw him in and comfort; at the same time, a horrible darkness was there as well. He felt a pinch of pain as the dark man squeezed his wrist, holding up the vial between them. The dark man's eyes moved to the vial.

"This? I invented. Hell, I invented most of your rituals."

The dark man drank the vial's contents and then tossed it to the floor.

"Let us end the unpleasantness before you anger me, and I remove your skin, aye?"

The Cardinal nodded, and the dark man let go. He returned to his seat, pointing to the Cardinal's chair as he went. Leonardo obeyed without another word.

"Nothing on this earth can harm me, not garlic, silver, or your silly holy water; your churches are my entertainment. I can do much more than you think, and I am growing stronger by the day ... Do you know why I grow stronger, Leonardo?" The Devil drawled.

The Cardinal shook his head, still in disbelief at what was being said.

"It is you, my son ... All of you ... You embrace the pleasures I have given you, all the while rejecting your once beloved god. Humanity is empowering me. It is as if, in action, you have made your choice for king."

Leonardo tried to speak. "I am a—"

"Your hate gives me pleasure. Your lust! Oh, I shall not speak of that, or I may need to have a moment with your secretary to sate myself. Your greed is a beautiful thing."

The dark man kissed the silver top of his cane and smiled.

"You reject my enemy and embrace my kingdom, and because of this, that bastard son grows weaker; the chains that once held me back cracking and failing. I've never been stronger or held more power over this world than I do today. HELL, Man, if I were as strong as I am now, Hitler would have wiped this planet of your god's filthy brats. His failure was my last. Next time I will not empower one man, but ten to do my bidding, and young brother Andrews will be my speaker, my prophet, my John the Baptist, so to speak."

The dark man let out a long exhale. "You were going to be there, Leo." The two men sat quietly, looking at each other for a few minutes, though Leonard avoided Lucifer's eyes as much as possible.

Lucifer removed the crucifix from the desk, returned it to his pocket, and started rolling his cane about in his hand. The top of the cane changed form as it moved. It appeared to be alive as it transformed into a wolf.

"Okay, back to your boo-boo. Let me start by saying that I have been looking after you for some time now."

Leonardo remained quiet-his entire reality shattered.

"You are in the position you are because I wanted you here. I nurtured your every desire and fulfilled all your perverted dreams. Hell, your drive for power and money? I fed that to you like a mother gives the teat."

Leonardo's nails dug into the arms of his chair, but he remained silent.

"It was I who gave you your seat, not him." He pointed up at a painting of Christ.

"That bastard son had nothing to do with it. I groomed you to ascend to the papacy and lead my new world order. Nevertheless, you took your eyes off the prize, and now you are tainted. Your sick hobby will come to light, and this will become a political nightmare."

"There is no way to prove I took the money. I was careful." Leonardo disputed.

"Not the money, Worm. That, I rather enjoyed watching you bring about, and you are right, no one will blame you. In fact, I have it on good authority that your only competition for the papacy will be blamed for it, which falls perfectly in line with my plans. However, your moment of weakness with the girl is going to come back to haunt you, and I will not take the chance."

"Girl?" Leonardo asked, flustered.

The Devil's eyes burned with rings of fire, and his face grew hideous for a moment.

"Do not play the fool with me," he snapped. "Save your deceit for the church."

The Cardinal looked down at his desk in shame.

"Man...You are all so sick and depraved. I love it!" He cheered. "I give you pleasures, and you act like animals. No, that would lay insult on the animal kingdom."

The Devil's face grew serious, "You jeopardized your position and my plan for a moment with a young girl."

"I tried to—"

"Shut it, Fool!"

His face again disfiguring, with eyes like hell. The devil calmed himself, regaining his attractiveness.

"I understand the desire for young flesh, hell, my motto is: The fresher the fruit, the sweeter the taste. As soon as they claim their place, they seem to become more a pain than pleasure. Nonetheless, self-control was required, and you failed in this."

"I made a mistake, but no one knows." The Cardinal pleaded.

"No one knows yet...She talked...Others saw you with her."

"I could ha—"

"What, Leo, have her killed?"

"Well..."

"She is already dead." The devil said with indifference. "She talked, and to people difficult to reach out and touch. No, it will surface...these things always do in political arenas. So, the only question left is: Can you still be of use to me?"

"I am a servant of Christ. I made a-mis—"

"You serve yourself, don't be obtuse! You pray your cookie-cutter prayers to a dead woman, who hears none of them, and you act the part."

"You may have power here, but I do not serve you," the Cardinal said as he got up and marched to the door.

Lucifer was up like lightning and grabbed him by the throat, lifting him off the ground. His face cracked with rage, and fire boiled under his skin. His eyes were terrifying, and his teeth grew sharp as he growled at the Cardinal, choking in his grasp. Lucifer walked him to the window and slammed his face against the reinforced glass. Leonardo prayed a fruitless prayer and then began to weep.

"You will sit down and do what I say, or today you leap to your death, a discovered pedophile."

The devil let him down and returned to his seat, pointing to the Cardinal's chair without looking back. The Cardinal sat, pulled out a handkerchief, and blotted at the blood on his temple.

"You will step down from your position after making several changes in staff appointments. As well, Leonardo, You will see to it that your recommendation for replacement will be upheld."

"Who ..."

"Bishop Andrews," the devil answered, his face now a perfect radiance again.

"Andrews? He is much too young. No one will endorse that appointment."

"Yes, they will after you point out some important facts you know about their own closets, my friend... He will sit in your seat."

"What will happen to me?"

"You will retire, enjoying your ill-gotten gain, and not become a headline."

"I'll do this because I have no choice, but not out of allegiance."

Lucifer leaned forward, causing Leonardo to jump in his seat.

"You will worship me, all of you wretched worms. He chose you weak-willed pigs over true beauty and perfection, and that will be his undoing. I see you for what you are: Cattle. You are born screaming and die gasping and do nothing of value in between." The Devil stood and walked to the window. He gestured for the Cardinal to come, and he obeyed.

Engagement

The marina on Mission Bay was still alive, with boaters coming in from a day of fun out on the water and other festivities around the bay. Heather and Stephen's engagement party was set up in one of the buildings overlooking the boats parked neatly in their slips. Music resonated from the double doors opened up to the bay, and there were sounds of laughter bursting from within. Charles walked out to the patio that circled the marina. It was peaceful out here. He looked back inside and caught a watchful look from Leroy as the man passed by. Lucy appeared at the door, intent on following him out. She held two drinks in her hands.

"Daddy, here's your scotch," handing it to him. "Are you enjoying yourself?"

He gave her a reticent smile. "It's lovely, Dear. I am happy for your new friends."

"Me too, Daddy." She tried her drink, and they both looked out at the water. "That is the boat they will hold the ceremony on."

Lucy pointed at a 75-foot yacht with Ocean Romance painted on her stern.

"It is a Yacht, my Dear. You have grown lax in your eloquence, Princess."

"Of course, Daddy, excuse me. She's beautiful, though, yes?"

"Yes Honey, very elegant. You have grown rather close to Heather over the last couple of months, haven't you?"

Lucy looked at her father as if searching for an answer. "I have, Father. She is the best friend I have ever had."

"So quickly? You barely know each other."

"Yes, Father, it has been a short time since we met, but still, she is the closest friend I have ever made. We talk about everything, and she treats me like family."

"Just be careful, Dear. I do not want you to be hurt."

"Hurt? How could I be hurt?"

"I don't know, my Dear, I—"

"There you are," called a voice from behind them. Heather's hair was up with curled locks delicately hanging down on both sides of her face. She was wearing a beautiful sundress and looked amazing. Lucy embraced her as she walked up.

"Father and I were just talking about how lovely this party is and how happy we are for you and Stephen."

"Well, thank you, both of you. I am so glad you were able to come, Mr. Rutherford."

"Charles, Dear, please. Mr. Rutherford sounds so formal, and you are more like family to my daughter. In fact, we had just finished discussing how close you two have become."

Lucy and Heather gave each other loving smiles, and Heather put her arm around Lucy's waist. "We have. Your daughter is amazing and already so very dear to me."

"So, will you hold the ceremony on the open ocean or the bay?" He gestured over at Ocean Romance.

"We are going to start here; however, the actual ceremony will take place in San Diego Bay. Mission Bay is too shallow, and the bridges too low for Ocean Romance. We will board here and then have drinks and appetizers on the way."

"That sounds unique. Usually, the drinks are served after the ceremony." Charles said.

"They want it to be a relaxed ceremony," Lucy added, looking for Heather's confirmation.

"Yes, that's the plan," Heather added. "Afterwards, we'll return to Mission Bay for the dinner reception anchored in Mariners Cove."

Lucy had an excited look and burst out, "And a wonderful fireworks show will complete the reception." She was as excited as Heather. "Isn't that romantic,

Daddy?"

"Yes, Princess, it sounds wonderful." He looked into the crowd of people dancing and talking to each other. "It sounds extravagant."

Heather followed his gaze inside, spotted Stephen, and waved. He found her and headed towards them.

"Well, As Stephen probably told you, Mr. Ruth— Charles. We have most of our savings in our home and my business startup. We are fortunate, though, because we have many friends who have stepped in. My company covered all of this tonight as a gift, and Ocean Romance is a client's Yacht. They agreed to take us around, and all we had to cover was the fuel and reception costs."

Stephen walked up and put his arm around Heather. "What are we talking about?"

"Heather is telling us all about the wedding plans; they sound wonderful," Charles answered.

"Oh yes, we are very excited and glad you and Lucy can be there."

Stephen gave Lucy a brief glance, then smiled at Charles.

"I was just explaining how blessed we have been by friends helping us put it together, Honey," Heather added.

"Oh yeah, wow...It has been amazing. We had planned something much simpler until people stepped up and offered to help."

The two kissed and looked at each other very much in love.

"Fireworks even, that must have been a feat to get arranged," Charles added.

Heather and Stephen smiled at each other again. "No, that would be the cunning of my talented wife-to-be. We moved the wedding up to accomplish that. See, every year, the Mission Bay Yacht Club puts on a firework show the day before the Fourth of July. It is rather extravagant, and most of the crazies don't show up until the next morning. So we are simply anchoring our party in a prime spot to see it."

"Isn't that wonderful, Daddy? I hope my wedding is as wonderful, Heather."

Heather reached out a hand to Lucy, grabbing hers. "It will be, Baby. I'll help you plan it."

The two girls stepped away from Stephen and Charles, still holding hands.

"Pardon us, gentlemen," Heather said, "We have little girl things to do." She winked at Stephen, and they disappeared into the party.

Stephen looked at Charles and shrugged. "You see why I love her?"

"I do indeed, my friend. I'm very happy for you."

The two men looked silently out on the bay where the sun was beginning to set. There was a scream of girls' voices, followed by giggles from inside. They both looked back and then at each other.

"Stephen, I am wondering if you will have time to take a short trip with me next week to start some research for our book."

"Next week? Well, sure, I can make that work. How long of a trip?"

"I think we could accomplish what we need to in a matter of days, say a week?"

"Um, sure, I'll just double-check with Heather, but I am sure that will be fine. She and Lucy will be getting started with work on the OB house by then."

"OB?" Charles asked.

"Sorry, Charles, Ocean Beach. Locals call it OB, force of habit."

Charles nodded, "Great, then let me know. I would like to leave Tuesday if that will work for you."

"I'm sure it will be fine, Charles; where are we going?"

"Well, first to Jordan, I have a home there, and then to Israel. Your passport is up to date, yes?"

"Um ... yeah, it is ... Israel? Wow, you're not messing around, are you?"

"I rarely do when it comes to things I am passionate about."

Stephen was wide-eyed. "Well, I am excited. I have never been near that region of the world. Will I have time to get visas?"

"I will take care of everything. If you give me your passport, I'll send it overnight to my agent."

Stephen looked at Charles and then back into the party. Heather and a crowd of girls were dancing and laughing. She waved at him, and he waved back.

"Great, I'll give it to you tomorrow. What do you say we rejoin this party,

Charles?"

"That sounds fine, Stephen; though, I think I may say my goodbyes and get back to my room. I am a little tired from travel. That is if you would not be offended?"

"Oh, no, Charles, not at all. I am glad you took the time to come, really."

"Splendid then," Charles patted him on the shoulder and finished his drink, and the two went back in. Charles walked towards his daughter to say goodnight but was headed off by Leroy.

"Hello again, Mr. Rutherford. I was hoping to finish talking with you. We were interrupted. You were explaining—"

"I am terribly sorry, Leroy, but our talk will have to be postponed to another time. I am just leaving. I only wanted to offer my congratulations and see my daughter. Perhaps anoth—"

"I was leaving myself. Why don't I walk you to your car? We can chat along the way."

Charles gave him a polite smile, though irritation was clearly in his eyes. "That would be fine; I'll just say my goodbyes first."

"I'll join you." Leroy returned.

Charles kissed his daughter's cheek and said goodbye to Heather before vanishing into the crowd. Leroy waved to Stephen as he followed. Stephen found his fiancé, and they danced, trading partners with the many guests who were there with them.

At one point, Lucy and Stephen were put together, and Stephen awkwardly stepped off the dance floor, leaving Lucy standing there. Heather caught it and motioned for Lucy to join her and two other girls dancing, and she did.

Stephen got another drink and returned to the walkway to look at the calming marina. He listened to its sounds. The clangs of halyards beating against their masts were like wind chimes to him. He loved it here; this place was his sanctuary, a place he could always come and relax, be closer to nature or maybe God? *God ...* he thought ... *If you are out there ... thank you for creating her. Thank you for this.*

He turned to go in and saw Heather leaning against a pillar supporting the walkway roof. "You okay, Handsome?" she asked, eyes full of love.

He pulled her into his embrace. "I am. I was just thanking God for you."

"God? That's interesting. I think I like this side of you. Speaking of God, Leroy left and wanted me to tell you to please call him. He said you would understand."

"Yeah, I will tomorrow. It looked like he and Charles were hitting it off." Stephen offered.

"They both stayed much longer than I'd expected, this crowd being so young and all."

"Leroy has some pep still left in him, Darling."

"I love him ... he's been so good to us, hasn't he?"

"He has. I always wondered if Mom ever considered getting remarried to him after Dad died."

"Those two were very close. I wondered the same thing there for a while when they were going out to eat all the time. They would have been a cute couple."

"You're cute." He said, looking into her eyes.

"No, we're cute," she finished. She kissed him, and the two looked out at the bay.

"You would tell me if there was anything wrong, right Babe?"

"Honey, you are my closest friend and the love of my life. You know I would. Why do you think something is wrong?"

"You go off to another world a lot lately, and I've noticed you act very cold, or maybe a better word is indifferent towards Lucy lately, too. I don't know, Babe, I just want to be sure your happy."

"I am, Love, you make me happy, and I'm excited about our future."

The girls came to the door calling Heather, and she put a hand up, warning them away.

"Can you tell me where it is you go when I see you look like that?"

"Now, Love?"

"Now. We are celebrating our love for each other; what better place for us to express that love than here, sharing our feelings."

Stephen smiled at her and held her tightly. "You are so amazing. How did I ever win your heart?"

"Those beautiful blue eyes and this nice bum." She gave it a squeeze, then kissed him.. "Stephen, *you're* amazing. You are gentle yet strong. You listen and know my needs. You remember every detail of what pleases me and surprise me with it. I am always amazed at your wit and how you see the world."

They held each other for a while, enjoying the music and view. Heather pulled back from his embrace and gave him a demanding look. Stephen knew that look very well, and it always ended with Heather getting what she wanted.

He did not want to get into everything, especially the dreams. Tonight was too perfect to infect with the fact he may be going insane.

"What?" he defended as she continued to pierce him with her eyes. "Okay, okay…I've just been thinking about life and ... What it all means. I mean ... with all the research I've been doing ...." He trailed off.

"You're wondering if God is really out there looking down on us," She finished for him.

"Okay, that's one question on my mind. I see people like Pete, who are always content, full of peace, and it sounds right, but then I see everything else, and that door just slams shut."

"I know what you mean, Babe, me too. I have been reading your mom's journal, and it has me thinking, too… a lot. I know there's a God; I always have. My hang-up was whether my parents had Him right or not. Starting a family has really made me think, not just for my husband and me but for our child. I want to raise our children sure of the truth."

"And?"

"And what?"

"What's the truth?"

"I don't know, Baby, but I'm going to find out. I've decided to go to church tomorrow with your sister, why don't you come with us? It won't kill you."

"Not yet, Love. If you find something you feel is true, share it with me, and

I'll do the same, okay?"

"Okay, Babe." She rested her head on his chest, and the two rocked back and forth to the music playing in the hall.

"So what about Lucy? Why have you been being so cold to her? Did she do something?"

"No, not at all, it's hard to explain, but she did nothing to deserve me acting cold towards her, and I'll be friendlier okay?"

"Not okay," Heather objected, looking back up at him. "I want to know what is bothering you. I am getting ready to commit my life to you. I want to know when something's wrong." Her voice peaked as the last words came out.

"Honey, it's noth—"

"Stephen!" She rebuked.

"I had a dream about her," he finally blurted out. Heather looked at him intently.

"A sexual dream?" her eyes examining his.

"Um ... a little, not really ... Listen, Heather, I would never do anything."

"Shhhh," her voice soft, as she put a finger against his lips.

"Before you go on, listen to me. I know who you are. Better than you know yourself, I think. I would not be giving you my hand in marriage if you were capable of cheating, Stephen."

He relaxed a bit. "Thank you. I have no idea where it came from. I don't look at her like that, or…."

"Honey, don't overthink things; it's normal. Hell, I dreamt about being with Peter once, and I am in no way attracted to him, really, he's like my brother." She scrunched her face in revulsion, "Dreams are funny things."

"You dreamt of sleeping with Pete?"

"Babe, it wasn't a porno. It was just a moment in a dream that made no sense."

"That bothers me, somehow."

"Please don't let it. You trust me, right?"

"Yes, without a doubt."

"Then believe me when I say that I have never looked at Peter and wanted him or even thought about what it would be like. That's my point; it was a crazy dream."

"I don't want anyone but you, Heather, and I just felt guilty about the dream. I want to be loyal to you in every way."

Heather caressed his face and kissed him. "I love you, and I trust you."

They held each other for a while until the girls returned, calling for Heather. She kissed him and left, her hand lingering in his.

She stopped by the door and looked back. "Can you stop alienating her now? She is important to me, Babe."

He smiled at her and nodded in acquiescence. Heather blew him a kiss and returned to the party. Stephen went back inside, got another drink, and found Peter and a few of his other friends. Peter and Lucy had not said a single word to each other since the night she told him to leave, and when prodded, Peter gave up nothing.

Stephen and Lucy crossed paths a couple of times during the night, and both times, she was shy and polite. Stephen was kind but still very distant; it made him feel bad, but he was still uncomfortable with her. The woman frazzled him. He was madly in love with Heather and loyal, but this woman threw him off-kilter. She had this sexual energy that reached out and grabbed him by the throat and threatened to devour him. He knew it was not her fault and felt even worse for the way he had been treating her.

tomorrow.

Tonight was Heather's night, and that was all he wanted to focus on. The night drew to a close, and most of their guests left, saying their goodbyes and sharing their excitement for the upcoming wedding. It was a fantastic night, and Stephen's fiancé was radiant. She commanded the center of attention just by being the woman for whom he had fallen so deeply. It filled him with joy seeing her like this, on her night. As they packed up to leave, Heather sent him to retrieve her makeup bag from the lady's room. When he entered, Lucy was there at the mirror. She looked so alone, and it broke his heart. *You're a jerk, Man.*

He felt terrible for having any part in making her feel the way she did now. He walked over to her and pulled her into his arms. She let him and hugged him tightly.

"You are already an important part of Heather's life, you know that?"

She nodded in his arms.

"And mine."

She pulled back wide-eyed. "I thought you hated me." Her voice yielding.

"I in no way hate you. I...I've been trying to keep my focus on my marriage to Heather, and ... I've felt a little distracted by you," He finally divulged.

"Distracted?"

"It's nothing, Lucy. What I'm saying is I've been cold towards you, and it was wrong. You did nothing to deserve it, and I am sorry."

She hugged him again and then stepped back, trying to be appropriate.

"I forgive you." She said in a formal tone and then smiled at him. "I have Heather's makeup bag. She asked me to find it."

"Oh, really?" Stephen smirked,

"I'll take it. Do you want to drive back with us?"

"No, I have a car here. I'll be back after we finish cleaning up."

"Lucy, we hired people to do that; you don't need to."

"I know, but there are some things here I would like to collect as souvenirs for Heather. I thought I would put them, along with some photos of tonight, into a scrapbook for her as a gift."

She smiled at him, looking brighter now, a stunning woman.

"That's awesome, Lucy; thank you for thinking of it. I can see why Heather adores you so much."

As Stephen left the hall, she called him from the bathroom door. "Stephen!"

He stopped and turned.

"Do you know if Peter is still around?"

"I do. He is saying goodbye to Heather."

"Could you ask him to wait for me? I need to talk to him. Tell him I will be right out?"

"Will do."

Stephen returned to the car, where he found Heather and Peter talking. Heather gave him a sly smile, and he returned it with a playful sneer. "What are you two love birds talking about?"

Heather shot him a scornful look.

"Love birds?" Peter asked.

"It's an inside joke Pete, don't read into it."

Heather pinched the edge of skin behind his arm as he leaned against the car next to her. It hurt, but he ignored it and kissed her neck.

"Is there anyone else inside?" Heather asked with a mocking grin.

"Um, yeah, smart ass, there is. I ran into Lucy, helping with the clean-up."

"Clean up? Why is she bothering?" Heather started towards the hall, and Stephen grabbed her arm. "It's fine, love, I told her. Pete, she wanted me to ask you to please wait for her. I guess she needs to talk to you."

Peter looked surprised but happy to hear the news.

"Yeah, that's fine. I'll make sure she gets home okay. You two go home."

They hugged, and Stephen and Heather got into her Mercedes and drove off. Peter waited out in the parking lot for a few minutes and then got impatient and walked back to the hall. When he turned the corner, Lucy was coming out, and they almost ran into each other. She had a bag full of party decorations and other stuff in her hand, and she almost let them drop.

"Hey…" Pete said.

"Hey, there, Peter." She said, her voice timid, looking at the ground more than at him.

"Do you need a ride home?" he asked.

"No, I bought a car this afternoon." She pointed at a new Mercedes S500.

"That's yours?"

She nodded, unsure of herself, "Too much?"

"Oh, no, not at all. I like it. It's a newer version of Heather's, right?"

She nodded, "same series."

"…It's nice."

"I loved driving Heather's so..." Lucy trailed off.

"Well, yeah...they are nice cars, great workmanship. I heard they are going to be merging with Chrysler soon, though."

"Yeah, I heard that too. I thought it was just a rumor, though..." Silence invaded the moment again. She looked at him resolute. "Listen, Peter."

"Lucy, I'm sorr—"

"No, let me speak." She demanded.

He submitted.

"I want to apologize for the way I treated you that night." Peter put up a hand to cut in, but she pointed a finger, and his resolve faltered.

"I am sorry for yelling at you and for throwing my shoe at you. You did not deserve it, and I felt terrible after you left."

"I forgive you, Lucy, and I am sorry for hurting you. It was not what I was trying to—"

"You do not have to say it. I get it; God and all that. I understand that you were not rejecting me, and you're right; it was wrong for both of us, at least not our first time. I felt trapped on a track I could not change and wanted to break free. I felt like that would accomplish it, but I was wrong."

"I am very attracted to you, Lucy. You are amazing, and If I thought we—"

"We don't, Peter, and we probably never would have. I know this now. I just pictured myself with someone loving and kind and thought, 'why couldn't we.' But the truth is it's not there between us, and you did the wise thing."

"Well, if you think so, I guess you're right."

"Please don't stop being my friend, Peter." She almost whispered.

"I have no plans on it, Lucy." Peter grabbed her bags and walked her to her car, handing them to her after she got in and shut her door. She smiled at him and waved, then started her car.

Peter walked back to his car, got in, and started it up. He leaned his head back, closing his eyes.

A horn honked, and he jumped. Lucy had pulled up next to his car and rolled down her window. Peter rolled down his.

"You okay, Doll?"

"Oh, yes, I was just resting my eyes while my car warmed up."

"Oh, yeah, they told me that at the dealership; something about breaking it in and warm ups? I don't remember. Anyway, would you like to spend the day with me tomorrow? I was going to work on a special gift for Heather, and I know she will be gone."

"I would love to, but can it wait until, say, eleven? I have church but could be back out here by then."

"That will be fine. I will be at the loft. You can help me, maybe get lunch too?"

"Yeah, that sounds good. I would love to."

"Great, see you then, Peter." She waved and was gone.

Peter sighed.

At the edge of the parking lot, in some bushes, stood a man in the shadows. A glimmer came from his eyes as Lucy's headlights swung past him. As soon as the light was gone, he backed away and was gone.

Standing

Leroy's teakettle started to whistle. He got up from his armchair, stepping into his slippers as he went to the kitchen. It was dark here. The only light on in the house came from the living room lamp, like an amber minor's lantern lighting the way. Leroy knew his home well, though; most of it not changed since Jimmy Carter was in office. He poured the steaming water into his cup and inhaled the fragrance.

"Thank you, Lord, for your bountiful blessings."

He returned to his chair, setting his tea on the table next to him. He opened his Bible and then looked into the kitchen once more. His focus was on the phone mounted on the wall.

Maybe I should try again.

Something darted in front of his kitchen window, which looked out to his side yard. Leroy ignored it, imagining the neighbor's cat running along the fence. He closed his eyes and prayed quietly for a while, that is, until the teakettle started to whistle again. Leroy opened his eyes in confusion. He was sure that he not only turned off the stove but that he had also placed the teakettle in the sink. This was something he had done a thousand times before, a ritual burned into his mind by his late wife, who always worried about fires. He got up, turned off the stove, and then placed the kettle in the sink, staring at it.

"Stay."

Lord, something is afoot; I smell it and feel it on my skin.

"Jesus, give me the strength to bring you glory."

He returned to his chair and sat, this time just listening. He grabbed his tea and drank, enjoying it, knowing in some way it was his last. The kettle started to whistle again, and Leroy's heart rattled and began to beat fast.

"Get behind me, unclean spirit. You have no place here. This is a house of GOD!" Shouting the last three words powerfully.

Glass broke in the back of the house somewhere, and Leroy stood up, startled.

"I am your vessel Lord, take my fear and make it strength."

He grabbed a pen from the end table and stood at guard. Another shadow darted by the kitchen window, and more glass broke in the back of the house. He stalked to the kitchen and pulled the kettle off the stove, this time holding it as a weapon. He looked at the phone, then down at his hands. One held the pen, and the other the steaming hot kettle. Somehow, he could not bear to release either to use the phone; instead, he turned and faced the living room, ready for whatever came.

Two shadowy characters emerged from the hallway. Leroy could smell booze and body odor.

"Get out of my house, you cowards!" He rebuked.

The two laughed and stepped forward, hands out to catch a stray. They were dirty looking homeless men, but their eyes were not human in any way. They reflected the low light as animals' eyes do, and their smiles gaped wide.

"Oh ... I see, you fools of the abyss think you can stop God by bothering an old man?"

The homeless man to his left charged, and to his detriment because this was the hand that held the steaming hot kettle. Leroy swung with all his might and caught the homeless man across the face. The force sent them both to the ground, the evil man screaming in rage, and Leroy off balance, into his water cooler, and then to the floor.

The other grabbed him and assaulted him all over. Face, arms, and ribs, like a crazed ape attacking him. Leroy covered his face as best he could. Someone else entered the living room behind his attackers. The first bum, still raging from his boiling assault, joined in pummeling him.

"I REBUKE YOU IN THE NAME OF JESUS! I BIND YOU FROM THIS HOUSE IN THE NAME OF YESHUA, THE SAVIOUR OF THIS WORLD!!" Leroy's voice was powerful now.

He stood as they fell backward, writhing in pain.

"Jesus commands you to leave these poor lost souls and return to the pit from which you came!"

Leroy now stood defiantly, staring in the direction of the third being in shadow. The living room light was now out, and the only light came from outside. He could not see the third well enough to make out features, but...

"I can smell the ugly on you." Leroy rebuked.

The two homeless men shook on the floor as the demons within struggled and left them. Leroy could not see anything leaving them but knew that it was happening. The third took a step forward, then hesitated, revealing only his eyes. They were glowing, horrible orbs full of an evil Leroy had never before imagined. Its eyes were hate and rage. Leroy saw centuries of life in these eyes.

The two homeless men on the floor scrambled to their knees, confused and scared. The being in shadow looked down on them and put hands over their heads. The Devil twisted his hands in the air, and both men's necks snapped simultaneously. They fell back twisted.

"This is my Lord's house. You are not welcome here, Destroyer." Leroy proclaimed.

The being motioned toward him, and Leroy flew, landing in the kitchen sink, grimacing in pain as his old body took the hit. He fell back down to the floor on his face.

"Your faith is strong, Old Man, but not that strong."

Leroy threw the pen at the Devil, and he caught it.

"Is this a joke?" he said to the old man who was now leaning against the cabinet on the kitchen floor.

"Are you throwing your inkwell at the Devil, Son? You know it did Martin no good."

"I look forward to the day that Michael chains you like the disobedient dog you ar—"

Leroy was cut short by a hand picking him up and launching him from the kitchen into the living room, where he hit the mantle, bones breaking, and then to the floor. Leroy's breathing rasped, and he coughed, blood coming from his mouth. He stayed down, this time face on the floor.

"Lord, I thank you for this opportunity to stand." Only faint whispers could be heard from Leroy.

"Pray all you want, old man; he will not deliver you out from my hand. This is my time now, and his power is weak."

"I...was...n't...asking for deliverance from you." Leroy said through pain. "I... asked for the strength to give you this." Leroy got up on his knees as if bowing, head still hanging to the floor, and he raised one hand and flipped the devil the bird.

Forgive me, Lord.

He was kicked in the face and hit the wall. He lay there gasping, drowning in his own blood. He coughed it up and fell back on his face.

"Stephen is mine, and you can do nothing to change that. I want you to know that before you die. I also want you to know I will visit his whore next."

Leroy's muscles clenched in anger, and he used all of his strength to get up on all fours, his head still hanging low, blood dripping on the floor below him.

"He won't get the message you left for him either. That is being taken care of at this very moment. He will never hear your warning, and neither will she. She will die, and he will father my vessel."

"No.....They both will be saved...." Leroy spit the blood from his mouth.

The devil walked back into the kitchen and picked up the homeless men, like dolls, placing them in positions that made the scene look like a robbery.

Starting in a low voice, Leroy began to speak. "And though this world with devils filled, should...threat...undo us..." He spit up more blood, taking pained breaths. "We will not fear, for God hath willed, His truth to triumph through us."

He looked up at the devil, blood on his mouth, and smiled, somehow stronger. Lucifer made no attempt to hide his hideousness. His hands and feet sharp and far from human, like his skin. Dark wings of blackness behind him, his only covering. A true monster, this one the worst a man could imagine.

"The prince of darkness grim..." Spitting more blood defiantly on the floor at the devil, who smiled fixedly at the dying man, allowing him continue.

"Come now, old man, finish your nursery rhyme." The devil mocked.

"We tremble not for him;" Leroy was up on one foot, stabilizing his broken body.

“His rage we can endure, for low his doom, is sure...” Leroy was now up though shaking. His hands were on his knees for support, but still keeping the devil’s stare. The devil walked to him and grabbed his collar, lifting him straight. Moonlight hit his face revealing two black holes spinning where his pupils should be so dark that Leroy could see light being sucked in, illuminating them.

“Finish it, Worm!”

“One little word shall fell him.” Leroy finished, then braced for his flight back into the kitchen, breaking the table with his fall. He lay there broken.

A fallen angel entered the house and looked around in confusion. “My lord, I thought...” His words fell silent at one look from his master.

“Where is the other?”

“Outside, my lord.”

Leroy started mumbling something, at first incoherent, then clearer and louder. Lucifer and his captain turned in the doorway.

“How you are fallen from heaven, Oh Lucifer, son of the morning.”

The dark angel looked at his master, astonished. Lucifer’s raging eyes burned.

“How you are cut down to the ground. You who weakened the nations For you have said in your heart: ‘I will ascend into heaven, I will exalt my throne above the stars of God.’”

Leroy’s voice grew stronger, louder, and full of renewed strength. Lucifer looked at his captain and nodded, “Finish him.”

The dark angel went after Leroy but was stopped by an unseen force as if stuck in thick mud. His movement was slowed even though he raged with all his strength to attack the old man. Lucifer looked up to the sky, enraged.

“Your time is done!” This is mine!” he screamed.

Leroy was up on his knees, resting back on his haunches. “Yet you shall be brought down to Sheol, to the lowest depths of the PIT!”

Lucifer tried to reach the old man on the ground but was also locked in some un-giving embrace, which slowed his movement to a crawl, his claws outstretched to shred the old man.

“Those who see you will gaze at you and consider you saying: ‘Is this the man that made the earth tremble?' You will be trodden like a corpse."

He smiled at the evil creatures in his home, then looked around at all the memories and love that once filled it. "You think God has abandoned me, but I tell you truly, this is the Father granting my last wish, which was to look you in your ugly mug and laugh."

He did laugh loudly for a moment. Leroy's strength gave, and he fell over to the floor again. The two dark beings were nearly on top of him, still slowed by God.

"Into your arms, I entrust my spirit, Lord."

Leroy closed his eyes and breathed his last. At that moment, the unseen force holding back the devil and his captain vanished, and they exploded forward. Lucifer howled in rage, looking down at the dead man.

"I will torture your loved ones; none of them will escape. I will be the one who will pave my streets with their corpses!"

Watchers

The loft was dark and very quiet, save for the faint noises of downtown. Felix was napping on Heather's bed when a noise from the kitchen woke him. He got up, stalked to the cracked bedroom door, and peered out. A shadowy figure was standing in the kitchen, near the telephone, fidgeting with something. The figure removed a tape from the answering machine and then placed a new one in its place. There was a click as the answering machine came to life, playing the outgoing message. The figure threw something in the trash and walked out the front door, locking it behind. Felix clamored up to the counter, sniffing around. He went over to the edge of the counter near the trashcan and looked down.

It was not long before Heather and Stephen came home, and Felix greeted them as they entered the door.

"Felix... Honey, must you make such a mess. Stephen can you feed him, please," Heather said as she picked up the fallen trashcan and loose garbage on the floor.

"Love, I fed him before we left. See, he still has food." He pointed to the cat's dish.

"He has been acting so strange lately, Babe. I'm a little worried about him."

"He's okay, Honey; it's just been exciting around here lately. He'll be fine." Stephen stroked Felix as Heather picked him up.

"Has mommy been neglecting you, Honey?" she kissed the cat and carried him into their room.

On the roof of a neighboring building, a pair of eyes in shadow watched the open windows of the loft. He stood there for several hours, as he had done for many nights. He watched Heather come out from her bath and climb into bed. He watched Lucy when she came home. She liked to undress and stare out the window, and he watched intently until she vanished under her covers without noticing him. Tonight, he noticed someone else in Lucy's room, someone small, maybe a child. The figure moved about the room and then vanished behind the curtains. The stalker ducked low and then peeked back out. Two glowing eyes were peering back at him from the curtain. He figured this was their cat and left his hiding place for the evening. The night was clear, and moon shown down with bright elegance upon the city.

Stephen and Heather were in each other's arms, fast asleep, and Felix was at their feet. In the guest room, Lucy lay in bed quiet. The room empty, save for a shadowy figure perched on the top of the curtain rod. It was Ariel, watching her ward carefully. An angel of God descended to the rooftop and was soon inside. He approached the master bedroom and entered without opening the door. He stopped at the foot of the bed and caressed Felix's back. The cat purred, content with his presence in the room. Concern dwelt on the angel's face for the sleeping couple.

Another angel descended and joined the first as he returned to the great room. They spoke in an unknown tongue.

"Le almano Da terro seraph," one said to the other.

The two angels entered Lucy's room, and immediately Ariel squealed in terror, losing her perch and falling stiff to the floor with a thud. The demon scrambled under the bed and then back out behind the curtain like a terrified mouse bouncing around for cover. Lucy stirred but was calmed by the angel's outstretched hand. The demon froze in terror, looking at them, and exploded into a cloud of blackness that reformed outside the window. The first angel raised a hand, and the smoky entity shot away in fear.

The two angels looked down on the sleeping girl, "This one's will is still her own," said the second angel.

"Yes, for now," answered the first.

"It saddens me that we cannot save them all."

"As it does our Father, Arphax, as it does our Father."

"Phanuel, Is there no chance for us to save her?"

"Father would save any who would allow Him," Phanuel replied. "His wisdom is beyond ours, and we must remember our interventions may not disrupt the free will of any unwilling to give it."

“The darkness that deludes is growing stronger, and the prayers that empower us weaker, brother.” Arphax continued, “Darkness encroaches this entire house and threatens their well-being.”

“We will do all we are able. My hope is that he will see the danger in rejecting our help in time to save her. For now, keep watch, but do not interfere.”

“Yes, Phanuel, Father’s will is my will.”

The two angels left the loft, and the night grew quieter still as darkness gave in to early dawn. Stephen’s sleep was sound, empty, without event, but Heather’s was a nightmare of screams and dying. She sat up and went to the kitchen, shaken from the dream. She drew herself some water and sat looking out the window of the great room. She thought about the dream. In it, she was dying, and the ones she loved were crying. She went to the shelf where she had put Betty’s journal, and Bible, grabbing them both. She sat on one of the couches and started to read. As she did, she caressed her belly, looking forward to the time when it grew with their love.

Other Side of the World

On the other side of the world, two Jordanian men were working to finish preparing for the arrival of their employer. They were employees of the Rutherford estate near Amman, Jordan. One was the head groundskeeper, and the other a new hire.

"ta'ala ela hona," the manager called. He was looking over supplies in the storage building. His name was Marwan, and he had worked for the Rutherfords since he was a very young man, working his way to a position of authority. The second man joined him, out of breath. It was a very hot day, and their clothes were stained with sweat.

"Merhaba, Marwan, Kayfa haluka?" said the new hire.

"Ana Mapsut, 'I am good.' Now listen to me, Omar. You must be diligent about keeping track of all supplies. We are not permitted to run out; it is forbidden. We must keep six months of supplies stocked at all times. Mr, Rutherford is unyielding in this. Everything, even gardening supplies. Do you understand me?"

"Yes, Marwan, I do. I will be more careful in the future. I have the list of what we need in my pocket, I was going to order yesterday, but we worked so late, I forgot."

"You must remember this, or you will not last long here. This is a good job and better pay than most. Mr. Rutherford is very generous to his employees but will tolerate no mistakes."

"Is it true what they say about him, Marwan?"

"What do they say? This isn't about him being the devil, is it, because I have important things to do, more important than that foolishness."

Omar hesitated, "Well ... they say he is over 100 years old but stopped aging."

"That is ridiculous talk from Bedouins who lack knowledge. Would you work for the devil?"

"For the pay, I was offered, yes, I would," answered Omar with a smile.

"Well, I would not, so do not waste my time with this craziness. He is a man, and he ages. Though I would not test his patients, I've seen him angry."

"Really? Marwan tell me ... what did you see?"

Marwan sat on a box and rolled a cigarette beside Omar. "Well, once, when I was delivering supplies in the evening, I happened upon Mr. Rutherford and another man in an argument. This other man towered over him and was tough looking. I remember fearing for Mr. Rutherford's life as the two got angrier. Mr. Rutherford grew furious, and I froze where I was, afraid to make a sound. Then Mr. Rutherford slammed the man against a wall, speaking in a voice I could not hear clearly. When the man walked away, I could see the fear in his eyes. Whatever Mr. Rutherford said to him must have terrified the man. I was troubled by seeing such a large man so afraid of an old man half his size. I was also surprised at the power Mr. Rutherford showed when he slammed the large man against the wall. Powerful Yes, surprisingly strong and dangerous to those who cross him, yes, my friend, yet this does not make him a devil. The rest of those rumors are foolishness. Remember, Mr. Rutherford treats his own well and crushes those against him. Just do a good job and not cross him, and you will prosper here."

Omar looked uneasy, "What happened to the large man?"

"I do not know. I never saw him again," Marwan responded.

The two men worked quietly after that, getting the property ready. The property was more like a compound, with high walls all around and several buildings within. There was an enclosed pool and garden at the rear of the compound and staff apartments just inside the front gates. The main house was very large and impressively built, with a helipad set on a platform on the roof. The compound had 24-hour security, staying on even when the owners were away.

This security group looked more like special forces than private security and trained all the time. All security personnel wore full military gear and carried assault rifles, and the building security dressed in suits, though they were also heavily armed. There were security cameras everywhere one looked and a high-tech security building that monitored a ten-mile radius somewhere on the compound. Men would enter a small storage shed and not come out for hours, and this shed was off limits to all but top security and Mr. Rutherford.

After years of working here, Marwan figured out that the shed was the entrance to an underground bunker where this security headquarters was located. As Marwan and Omar finished their work for the day, two large cargo trucks pulled into the motor pool, followed by two armored Humvees with machine guns on the roofs.

Omar started to speak, and Marwan cut him off. “Do not ask. It is not part of our job or any of our business.”

The two men packed their things and got in a jeep to leave. Marwan started the engine and put it in gear. He waved to security as he drove out the gate and down a dusty road. “We will need you back here on Monday morning. Be prepared to stay for the week. I will have a room ready for you when you come.”

Omar nodded without another word.

***

The following morning Stephen woke late and rushed to get ready. He had minutes to leave to make it to the meeting with the publishers on time. He showered, shaved, and was drying off when Heather came in and asked if he had checked the messages.

"Babe, I am running so late. I don't think I did. Why?"

"Well, Sandy said she left me a message to remind me about our appointment with a new client, and I was sure I saved a message for Lucy that came in yesterday ... You know what, Babe, it's no big deal, I probably erased it by mistake. I'll call Sandy back, and Lucy and I will see her realtor anyway."

"Good. Love, I am gone." He kissed her on the corner of her mouth, and she stopped him and gave him a proper kiss.

"I love you." She said.

"Love you too, Honey."

She followed him out as he filled his coffee cup.

"Have a good day, Babe."

He nodded, taking a drink from his coffee at the same time, and was out the door. Heather rounded the corner of the island and poured herself a cup of coffee. She opened the fridge, pulled out some creamer, and topped off her cup before returning to the couch by the window. As she sat down, she caught a glimpse of a man darting behind an air conditioning unit on the roof of the neighboring building. Heather put down her cup and walked up to the window. She stood off to the side near the open curtains and peeked out. She could see the shadow of someone squatting down behind the AC unit. She backed away and pulled the curtain halfway shut. Feeling self-conscious about being in her underwear, she snuck around the back of the couches and scurried into Lucy's room.

"Lucy, you awake?" she whispered as she entered. The bed was empty, and Lucy peeked around the corner of her open closet.

"Yes, I'm just looking for something to wear. Why?"

Heather darted over to her bed and sat low on the floor. She motioned for Lucy to join her. "I think we have a peeping tom on the roof across the street."

Lucy walked over to the window, still in her underwear, and stood there with her hands on her hips. "Where?"

Heather came around, pulling a blanket off Lucy's bed around her waist. She stood at the edge of the window, peeking out.

"There." She pointed to the large air conditioning unit. "See the shadow? I saw him dart behind it when I looked out the window."

"Maybe it's a technician." Lucy offered.

"Then why did he jump behind the unit when I caught him looking over here?"

Heather was still whispering.

"Dear, I doubt he could hear us from here." She smiled mockingly at Heather, and they both started laughing. Heather stepped out and looked. The shadow was gone.

"Where'd he go?"

Lucy looked back at the rooftop. "Yep, look there, someone just shut the rooftop door. Do you think he can see all the way in our rooms? That building looks like it's much lower than ours."

"It's only a three-story, but from that far back, I bet he could see at least to our beds." Heather lay down on the bed and looked out the window. "Yeah, I can see the entire AC unit from here. So he could at least see to the bed. That creeps me out. Stephen and I must have been putting on a show for him."

"It's probably nothing, Heather. You said he was at the AC unit. Maybe he is a technician and just looked over at the same time and felt embarrassed."

"Yeah? You think? I'm getting privacy tint for the windows. I don't want to feel insecure if I walk around in my underwear."

"Don't be; let them look. It's not like they're doing anything. If you got it, flaunt, Baby."

"You're bad, Lucy, I flaunt it all the time, but for Stephen, that's all the show I plan on giving."

Heather pulled the curtain and threw Lucy's blanket back on her bed as she walked out of the room. "Hey, did you erase the messages on the machine?" She called from the hall.

Lucy followed her out and sat at the bar. "No, why?"

"No reason, I was just wondering. I guess I did by mistake. Your realtor left you a message, and I saved it, or thought I did."

"My father called and told me already. It was nothing important. So what time do you want to get started?"

Heather picked up her coffee and took a drink as she walked back to her room. She sat down on her bed and pulled on some thigh highs. "I have a meeting downstairs in an hour. It shouldn't be too long, say 10:30?"

"Perfect," Lucy answered. She came into the room and sprawled out on the bed. "Wow, your bed smells like sex, Rock Star. You and Stephen *are* putting on shows in here."

Heather turned red and smelled her blankets. "It does? Is it bad?" I don't smell anything."

"Honey, it's not a bad smell; it's nice; it just smells like you and Stephen."

Heather smirked at Lucy as she got up and went to her closet.

"So, this is where all the magic happens." Lucy was laying on her back, looking out the window. "Um, yeah, I guess you could say that," Heather answered, pulling on a professional skirt and zipping it up. She peeked out the door at Lucy, who smiled back as she got up. Heather was buttoning up a silk dress shirt. Lucy picked up Heather's Coffee and took a sip.

"So, are you and Stephen on better terms now?" Heather asked.

"Yes, we talked. He said he was sorry. Heather, he is so adorable. He told me it was because he didn't want anything distracting him from you."

"You *are* a bit of a distraction too, Dear."

"Never in a million years Heather, not my style."

"I know. I was just pointing out the obvious."

"You really are lucky, though. He worships you."

"I know. I am blessed."

"I hope I find that someday, something that makes me smile like you."

"You will, Babe, I promise," Heather reassured her. "How does this look?" She modeled her attire. Lucy walked around, looking her over, and handed Heather her coffee.

"Like a sexy CEO." She slapped Heather's rear and went into the kitchen. Heather sat down at her mirror and started putting her hair up. Lucy poured herself a cup of coffee and came back to Heather's door. "I'm going to go take a shower. I'll see you back up here at 10, then?"

"Ten-ten thirty-ish," Heather answered.

***

Stephen and Charles were sitting at a café downtown. Charles ordered tea, and Stephen an espresso.

"So with things wrapping up on my book, editing and cover design in the safe hands of the publisher, I feel free to fully focus on our project," Stephen said.

"Well, all that is left is for us to get to work. Did you get a chance to talk to Heather about our trip?"

"Yes, and she is fine with it. She said the next two weeks will be her busiest, between her job and helping Lucy with the house."

"Great, great, now one more surprise."

Stephen's breath hitched.

"I am of the hope that you would not mind leaving today instead of tomorrow. I have an essential client I must meet there, and it would make my life so much easier if we could leave today."

"Um…sure…I guess like I said, Heather's swamped. What about the Visa?"

"They will meet us in New York. I need to stop there for a meeting, and then we will fly to Jordan. Will that work?"

"Sure, I just need to get home and pack. When will we leave?"

"I can have a car pick you up in an hour if that will be enough time?"

"That's fine, Charles. I'll be fast. I'm honestly not sure what to pack."

"Just pack the personal things you cannot do without. I will send you out with a consultant while I am in the meeting In New York."

"Oh, Charles, I cannot—"

"Now, Stephen, please. We have been through this, and you know how it is going to end. I spend more on uniforms for all my staff than some people make in a year. It is not about me doing for you but making things easier for us both."

"I'm not going to argue, Charles. I'll pack a bag, and if I am short anything, I'll graciously accept your offer as an expense towards the book?"

Charles nodded.

Stephen drove Charles to his hotel, dropped him off, then went home. When he got there, Heather had just returned from her meeting downstairs. She was changing when he came in.

"Hun, I have to leave today instead of tomorrow. I hope you're okay with that."

Heather turned and looked at their open door. She walked over to it and shut it by backing against it. "How much time do we have?"

"Minutes." he responded, removing his shirt. Heather came to him, and they both fell on the bed.

Lucy came out of her room, ready to leave. She was pulling her hair into a ponytail as she walked over to the master bedroom. She stopped, hearing the passionate sounds coming from within. She walked over to the radio and turned it on. The music seemed to be in perfect timing with the lovemaking coming from the other room, and she turned it up before going into her room.

"You want him, do you not, Sister?" asked Ariel.

Lucy looked over at her imaginary friend. "I want that. I'm tired of waiting for what she has. That is all. It's not about him."

"Yes, it is. He makes you tingle, I can see, Sister."

"Shut up. You don't know a thing. I'm just ready, and I am not waiting anymore. I will find the next attractive guy I meet and experience whatever I want with him. Maybe tonight." Lucy said with a rebellious tone.

"Sister, be patient, you have saved yourself this long, and soon the love you have waited for will be in front of you. I have seen it."

The doorbell rang, and Lucy jumped. She went out into the great room and answered the door. It was the driver.

"I am here to pick up Mr. Meyers for his flight?" he asked.

She smirked and turned, leaving the door open behind her. "He might be a few minutes. Come in."

The driver followed her in and stopped at the island.

"Stephen," She shouted. "Your driver is here."

A moment later, he emerged, frazzled, buttoning up his shirt. Heather followed him in a robe, carrying his bag. "I'm sorry I am running a little late," Stephen said to the driver, who nodded.

"I can take your bag down to the car and wait for you, Sir."

Heather set it on the counter, finished zipping it closed, and handed it to him. She was red in the face as she kissed Stephen. He pulled her tighter, and the two kissed hard. The driver walked out with the bag, looking at Lucy with a smile on the way.

"I love you so much, Honey," Stephen said, looking into her eyes.

"I love you too. Be safe, Babe. Promise you'll call me."

"I will Love, I promise." He kissed her again and picked up his writing bag, giving Lucy a wink as he went out the door.

Lucy looked over at Heather and smirked,

"Go get dressed, Tramp." Heather laughed and went into her room.

***

Stephen met Charles on the tarmac, and the two boarded a Learjet 60, which a moment later was taxiing on the runway. Inside, a beautiful flight attendant brought out Champaign for the two men, and they touched glasses.

"To the beginning of our new adventure," Charles said.

"New beginnings," Stephen replied.

The jet was soon in the air, and Stephen looked down on San Diego. His love now far below. Charles had his eyes closed and a set of headphones on. Stephen pulled out his wallet, and the gold coin fell into his lap. He picked it up and rolled it between his fingers before placing it behind a credit card. He thumbed through his pictures stopping on one of him with Heather early in dating. He could still smell her on him and imagined her on the plane with him. He flipped to the last photo, which was a picture of his mother and Leroy. The image made his heart hurt, missing her. He wished she could see how things were going in his life. She had always encouraged him to follow his dreams and read all of his stories, loving even the bad ones. Leroy had his arm around her, and the two looked happy. Stephen looked at Leroy intently and then remembered the forgotten call.

I'll call him from New York. He promised himself.

In New York, they were quickly guided to a car and driven into the city, where they arrived at Charles' Park Avenue address. In the lobby, Charles introduced Stephen to a woman named Kathrin, who escorted him into a lounge to talk about what he packed for the trip to the Middle East. Charles disappeared into an elevator with two administrative assistants. He was soon back in a car and shopping for the things he would need. The next hour and a half was fast-paced, planning and repacking as he prepared to leave.

Afterward, they met Charles at a posh restaurant for a meal and then rushed back to the airport. Once they were back in the sky, the attendant served them Turkish coffee. Stephen enjoyed his cup, looking out the window at the ocean below.

***

Heather and Lucy finished their work for the day, leaving Lucy's new home.

"Let's go get a fish taco." Heather proposed.

"Okay, sounds good; I'm starving."

The girls jumped into Heather's car, drove down to the South Beach Bar and Grill, and grabbed seats with a view of the beach and pier. They ordered fish tacos and calamari.

"This place has the best calamari in San Diego," Heather said. "The owner is also a fisherman and brings in his own catch fresh for the menu."

"Hey, handsome, may I get a pint of Blue Moon and an ice tea for my friend?" Lucy looked at Heather, and she nodded. The bartender picked up a pint glass and pulled the dispenser, filling it with beer, as he looked Lucy over.

"He's cute," Heather said. Lucy looked at him and smiled at Heather.

"Yeah, not bad, huh? Maybe I'll have one of those too."

The two girls laughed and then continued to eat their dinner. After they finished and Lucy allowed the bartender to get her number, they went for a walk on the beach. The sun was setting, and the two found a great spot to sit and talk. Heather shared about losing her family when she was young, and Lucy told Heather about all the traveling she did with her father. Heather tried to imagine growing up going from one private school to another as they moved around and felt sorry for Lucy.

"I can't imagine what it must have been like growing up without a mother."

"Well, you cannot miss what you have never known, right?" Lucy tried.

"You have no memories of your mother at all?" Heather asked.

"I was an infant when she died, and my father adopted me."

"What about your fraternal father?"

Lucy shrugged, "I never found out who he was. My father said that information died with my mother. I think he knew him, though... Things he has said over time. I never pushed him on the subject."

"I'm so sorry, Lucy," Heather said.

"Maybe that's why Stephen and I feel so close to you because we are orphans too." She hugged Lucy, and they sat there talking for another hour about life, love, first kisses, and other things. When they got home, Lucy went straight to the shower to get all the sand off, and Heather sat at the bar, letting the long day sink in. She thought about Stephen, wondering where in the world he was at this moment. She pictured him over the ocean, flying to the Middle East. He promised to call her when he arrived; remembering this, she got up to check the answering machine.

She was excited at seeing the blinking red light and hit play. There was only one message, and it came from Shelly.

Hey, kids, I hate to be the one to bring you this news, but I know you would want to know. Leroy passed away last night. We don't have too many details yet, but Randy, his grandson, told me it looked like he disturbed a robbery and was killed. We won't know anything for some time because of the police investigation, but they want to hold a funeral for him in two weeks. This will allow time to get the body released by the police department and for relatives to arrive. I know this will be a couple weeks before your wedding, and I don't want it to... well, you know what I am saying." It was apparent she was crying as she spoke. "Call me if you need anything or want to talk. Remember, he lived a full life and was so happy when he heard the news about your engagement. He would want you to have a happy wedding... I love you both very much... Bye.

The machine clicked off, and Heather stood there stunned. Her heart hurt deeply. Leroy was always so special to her and the entire Meyer family. Tears started to flow, and she broke down right there, squatting on the floor in the kitchen. Lucy came out with a towel wrapped around her and ran over to her.

"Honey, what is wrong?"

"It's Leroy; they killed him," she wept.

"Who killed him?" Lucy asked.

"I don't know…but they killed sweet Leroy. Who would be so evil?"

Heather sobbed in Lucy's arms.

Lucy got her up and walked her to the room, where she laid her down. She pulled a cover over her and lay down, holding her in her arms.

"Oh, Sweetheart, I am so sorry. He seemed like such a wonderful man."

The two girls lay there for a couple hours, mostly quiet. Heather would say something nice about him every once and a while and then start crying again. Lucy just listened and held her, caressing her head. The two fell asleep.

Later the phone rang, and Lucy jumped, pulling her towel back around her as she got up to answer it. As she rounded the island into the kitchen, Heather called from the room in a broken voice.

"Don't tell Stephen if it's him."

Lucy got it just as the answering machine picked up. "Hey, hang on," she said as she tried to stop the outgoing message. "Hello?"

"Hey, Lucy, is Heather there?" Stephen's voice sounded a little crackly.

"Um... yeah... Let me see." She said, dropping the phone.

Heather was up and in her bathroom, splashing water on her face. She wiped her face and looked over at Lucy with her raccoon eyes. "I will be right there. I just need to get myself together. I don't want him to know. Not now, maybe not until he comes back, okay?"

Lucy nodded, concern on her face, as she returned to the phone. "She is going to be a minute, so what's up, Rock Star? You having fun?"

"I am. We just arrived and are getting ready to drive to your dad's place."

"Cool, make sure he takes you to the caves near our house; they are amazing."

Heather was walking up as she said this. "Here's your darling." Lucy handed the phone to Heather.

"Hi, Babe," Heather said in a stuffy voice.

"Hey, Love, are you okay?"

"Yes, Babe, my sinuses are just acting up. I'm fine. How was your flight?"

Lucy got a bottle of wine from the pantry and opened it. She poured herself a full glass and Heather a small one. Heather waved a hand, rejecting hers, but Lucy gave her a stern look, nudging it forward. It was only a couple swallows, so

Heather did not fight it. She took a sip and listened to Stephen's excited voice on the phone. Hearing him so happy made her feel better. She could not bear to ruin this time, Stephen's moment to shine, with the news of losing Leroy. Though he kept talking about everything that was going on and their plans, Heather absorbed very little; her heart was broken. She did her best to hide it from him, though. She was happy for him. She could not help but be happy when he was happy, but it was mixed with the sorrow of her loss.

"I am so proud of you. I knew your writing would finally take you places."

"Thank you, Love, that means the world to me. I will get you something nice. Charles is already talking about having you and Lucy come out with us next time."

"That sounds amazing, Babe. I can't wait. Promise me you will be careful over there, though, okay?"

"I will, Honey. Charles has security like the president over here. I doubt anyone is going to mess with us. I love you. I have to go."

"I love you too. Call me when you can."

"I will." There was silence on the line for a moment, and Heather almost thought the call had ended. She was going to hang up when he spoke again. "Heather, are you sure you're okay? You sound…I don't know... sad."

"I'm fine, Babe, I just took some allergy medicine, and it's making me drowsy. I am sure I'll be fine by tomorrow."

"Okay Honey, if you're sure. I love you, Heather."

"I love you too." She finished.

They hung up, and Heather turned to Lucy, tears back in her eyes. "I couldn't tell him. I hated lying to him."

Lucy hugged her. "I know. You did what was best. There is nothing he can do from there, anyway, and he will be back in time for the funeral, so don't worry about that now."

She handed Heather her glass of wine and sat at the bar, holding her hand. The two looked out the window at the city lights. On the rooftop of the building across from them, a man leaned against a rooftop door with a bottle in his hand. He remained in shadow. He stared across at the two girls sitting at the island.

Jordan

Stephen came out of the airport offices and climbed into a black SUV, where Charles was waiting.

"Everything okay back home?" Charles asked.

Stephen had a bewildered look on his face but smiled. "Yeah, everything's fine, I guess. Heather seemed down but said she was okay."

"She's probably missing you a little,' you being so far away. Did you tell her about our planning a trip over with her next time?"

Yes, and she sounded excited about it. I'm sure you're right."

Their car was rolling down a dusty road into the afternoon, escorted by two hummers in front and two in the rear. They drove into the city of Amman, ate a big meal, enjoying some friends of Charles.' The food was amazing, and the drinks intoxicating. It was the first time he saw Charles with a buzz, and he somehow felt more comfortable with the man after this. They eventually made it back to Charles' home. He was shown to his room, which had a view of the pool behind the main house. The room was opulent and comfortable looking.

Stephen settled himself and lay back on the bed. He was almost falling asleep when he heard giggling outside by the pool. He sat up and looked out the window, where he saw three girls at the pool. One took off her robe and jumped in completely naked. The other girls, wearing skimpy bikinis, sat at the pool's edge with their feet in the water. The women were gorgeous. Dark hair, olive skin, and perfect bodies. Stephen looked away and went to his bag. He unpacked his things, trying not to listen to the sounds below. Soon there were more voices, some of them male, and Stephen returned to the window to look. There was a man close to his age and another, maybe forty. They were handsome looking as well. The men both had beautiful women at their sides as they arrived. Seven of them were having a little party down there, and Stephen looked over at his open bag, the board shorts on top.

I could just go for a dip.

He thought about Heather as he stared down at the sensual feast below.

"I don't think so."

He went downstairs and found Charles looking over some papers at a desk set off in a study. "You have guests, I believe ..."

Charles looked at him quizzically.

"The pool? Young naked models running around?"

Charles' eyes lit. "Oh, yes, we have some friends that visit from time to time." I forgot that they were going to be here. You should go join them. They are very friendly."

"Yeah, I feel that Heather wouldn't love the idea of me skinny-dipping with Middle Eastern models."

Charles smiled at him and looked back down at his paperwork. "I understand." He closed the folder and got up, walking out of the room and into a huge great room with a bar at the back. He poured a scotch and offered the glass to Stephen. Charles poured another.

"I am going to go have some fun, and I'll be keeping my short pants on, so come relax if you like. I promise to keep the naked models off of you if you need my help." He smiled at Stephen and went down the hall.

Stephen downed his drink and went up to his room, and changed. He was standing at his window wearing the new board shorts he bought in New York, looking down on the soiree.

I'll just go get wet and relax for a bit before bed. Stephen was soon downstairs, being introduced to everyone. The two men were relatives of the king of Jordan. The girls were daughters of some other important family.

***

Heather was looking at a blueprint of Lucy's living room and talking with a contractor.

"It's not a retaining wall, so I want you to take it out: we will have a large marble pillar brought in to add support next week."

Lucy came downstairs with bright eyes and smiled at Heather, who winked at her as the contractor made a mark on the blueprint.

"So this wall stays, and this one goes, right?" he asked.

"Yes, and before I forget, please be careful moving things around downstairs. There are valuable pieces in those crates."

The man nodded and walked away.

"Lunch?" Lucy asked, "I'm starving."

"Sure, that sounds good. Where do you want to go?"

"I was thinking Harney Sushi?"

"They're not open yet. Why don't we go to Pacific Beach? I know a place there."

Lucy nodded, and the two girls left.

Heather turned on the radio in the car and was quiet for most of the ride. Lucy noticed that she was listening to a new station; this one was Christian.

"You doing okay, Honey," Lucy asked.

"I *am*, Sweetie. Why do you ask?

"You seem to be quiet much of the time lately. I also have noticed you stealing away every couple of days. You would tell me if you needed space, right?"

Heather looked at her and then back at the road.

"I love being around you, Lucy. You are such a blessing. I don't need space from you. I'm glad you're here with me, especially with Stephen so far away."

She patted Lucy's leg and then turned onto Mission Bay Drive. Lucy laid her head back, listened to the music for a minute, then looked over at Heather.

"This music reminds me of Peter. . .I should call him."

"I still wonder about you two. There is a dynamic between you both I'm not sure you are recognizing."

"He grows on ya. He makes me feel like a better person when he's around."

"You should call him. Maybe you two can grab dinner tonight. I'11 be out again."

"Yeah, maybe I'll do that, Lucy said, looking at Heather intently. "So where do you go when you vanish on me, if you don't mind I ask ... You know, it really isn't my business," she finished.

"It's no mystery. I don't mind sharing. I've been spending time with the baby, sometimes on the beach or someplace with a view of the sunset, just talking to him."

"Him? How do you know it's a boy?" Lucy asked.

"I'm not sure, but something tells me it is; in fact, I think I already have a name picked out, that is, if Stephen likes it too."

"Oh really, I want to name my first child—If it is a boy—David; I've always loved that name. What is the name you came up with?"

"Samuel," Heather answered.

She pulled into a small sushi restaurant's parking lot and parked the car. Heather looked over at Lucy with a soft smile. Lucy smiled back, a little confused by the look. "What?"

"I like David, that's a nice one. She grabbed her purse and tapped Lucy's arm. "Let's go inside, this place has good sushi.

After grabbing a couple plates Lucy clanked Heather's glass with her own. "To Samuel and David." Heather repeated the toast.

"So, one-on-one time with your baby, huh?"

"Well, not always. I have been meeting up with Stephen's sister Shelly, also. She has been helping me to understand some things that I wanted clarity on."

"You mean about God, right? She's the one you have been going to church with?"

"Yeah, she's great. You should come sometime."

"I would, but I don't go for the whole church thing," Lucy responded. "No offense to you, and Peter, though. I respect other people's beliefs."

"I know, Lucy, I understand. I used to be like that, and part of me still is, but being pregnant has opened some doors in my thinking. It's a miracle in itself and... Well...I want to be sure of what's real before bringing a child into this world."

"You make me want to be pregnant, Heather," Lucy whined, closing her eyes. "I can't wait to feel those things."

"About God?" Heather asked.

"No, just… I don't know... To have my mind go to those deep places, planning my future and the future of my child."

Heather did not respond. She felt as if Lucy had no idea what she was feeling or experiencing: Her questions, concerns, or hopes for her family.

"I am more than ready. I feel I've wasted so much time being educated in subjects that give me no joy, traveling the world instead of meeting that special someone, and... well… becoming a mom. It is the one thing I think I was made for." Lucy said, picking up her beer and downing it. "Can I get another Asahi, please?"

Heather examined Lucy. She saw her clearer somehow. She saw the girl she had already gotten to know, but she saw someone else at that moment too. She could not put her finger on it, but something loomed over Lucy, and it felt like pain and darkness. Heather wasn't sure if it was Lucy's future or her past, but it made her skin tingle.

Lucy looked back at her after getting her beer, and her expression changed to concern, or was it fear? Heather tried a smile, still chilled by the feeling of doom, and managed a half-hearted one. Lucy smiled back, but they both seemed to be withholding now.

After lunch, Heather drove Lucy back to her place to pick up her car and waved goodbye. She headed home and was soon on the couch—drapes pulled—reading Betty's Journal.

***

Lucy didn't stay home long. She headed to a bar, the fire inside her insatiable; she wanted to pick up a man. She went to the Onyx Room to see if the cute VIP host was working.

What was his name, Mike? No... Mitch, that's it!

She repeated the name in her mind, trying it on. Mitch seemed to fit; she thought the time had come to pop it and get it over with. When she got there, they had just opened, and the club began filling up. She went up to the bar and ordered a Patron and a Modelo. The bartender was falling all over himself, eyeing her while serving others.

I could, but no... Mitch will be my first. She smiled at the thought of taking control of her destiny, choosing the man to first bed her. When the bartender returned, she ordered another shot and beer and asked him where Mitch was.

"He quit, Baby, but I'm here." He said.

She ignored it, wanting to get information from the guy. "Quit, really? We were just in here, and he served us." She pushed, not convinced Romeo was giving up the goods.

"All I know is after the Brandy thing, he and the owner brawled in the back. They smashed up the place too. It took us six hours to clean up the mess. Curt started it, the cops said after watching the video, so Mitch wasn't arrested, but he should have been for what he did to Curt."

"What did he do, and what thing with Brandy? I think she was our server also: Cute redhead, right?" Lucy asked the man.

"I'd love to fill you in, but I've got to serve drinks; maybe later we could—"

"I'll wait. She cut in sharply. And if you satisfy my curiosity, maybe I'll satisfy yours."

The bartender, Brad, as Lucy would find out later, smiled. As the night went on, Brad came and filled in the rest between serving other customers.

Supposedly, Brandy ended it with the owner telling him she was in love with someone else. However, she never came home that night to get her things as she said she would do, and the following morning the police were at the club asking questions about her and Mitch. Curt flew off the handle once he realized Mitch was involved and told them he lived on the corner of Fifth and Market in a motel room. They left, and soon Mitch arrived, and all hell broke loose. Curt started by throwing bottles at the guy until one struck home, and then it was on. Mitch threw him around the back room like a rag doll. One of the other servers said she saw the video while the police were viewing it: Curt flying across the room, smashing into racks full of booze, knocking them over. Mitch took off, yelling, 'I quit.'

When Lucy pushed about Brandy, the bartender's expression grew dark. "They found her body in the ally next to his motel, right below his room. Her neck was broken."

After hearing this, Lucy thought giving up her virginity to the man a bad idea.

I don't want it that bad.

She finished her drink and started to leave but was caught by the bartender near the door.

"Hey, Baby, where you going? I thought you were going to take care of me too."

Lucy grabbed him low and squeezed, "Take your hands off me."

He complied, turning red with pain. She did not let go. "Are you satisfied, Baby?"

He nodded vigorously.

"You sure, Baby? I want to be sure and give you the entire experience."

He nodded again, "please." He groaned, and she let go.

She left the club with the bartender gasping and waddling away.

I cannot stand arrogant fools, she thought as she walked down to the corner of Market Street. She had not realized she was doing it when she left, but now that she was here, she decided to check it out. Lucy found the entrance and followed another lustful fan up the stairs, refusing his invite into his room. As he retreated, she stopped him. "Hey, Bud, maybe I could come in for a minute." She stopped at his door, though unwilling to enter.

He looked back at her with disappointment. "Are you coming in?"

"Maybe, first, I have a question for you."

He nodded. "Do you know a guy by the name of Mitch that lives here?"

He nodded again.

"Is it true he killed some girl?" He smiled and shook his head at the same time,

"No, they thought he did and arrested him, but Terry in 20 vouched for him. Come on in, I…" He turned, and she was gone.

Lucy was soon knocking on room 20, and an elderly man answered.

Much safer.

She entered when he invited. Inside, he told her how he heard screams and opened his door in time to see Mitch run to his door as it slammed in his face and that he smashed at the door while the girl was screaming inside.

"So there's no way he could have been the one who killed her?" Lucy asked.

"No. I was there when he broke through. The room was empty. I called the police and went back to my room, but later, when they came around asking questions, I found out they had arrested him, so I went down stairs and made a statement backing up his story. I guess whoever killed her threw her out the window and then went out the same way. All I know is she was alive and screaming when Mitchel was beating on the door trying to help her, and she was gone when he broke through."

"Wow," Lucy said, mouth open. "I just saw them both not long ago, and everything seemed so normal, almost boring. Do the police have any leads?"

"Well, I overheard one talking about a jealous boyfriend. I guess she had just broken up with him to be with Mitch."

"Wow!" She sat there wide-eyed for a moment, looking at the sweet old man.

"Mitch was a troubled man but very kind, in my opinion. He left a couple days later; I'm not sure where."

Lucy thanked the man and left. Back home she took a long shower and went to her room, where she sprawled out on her bed.

"I'm glad you waited, Sister. It's for the best. Do you want to play a game?"

"No, turn on my Stereo, something mellow." She was starting to wonder how she ever got along with the brat. She rolled over, looking out the window, then remembered the man on the roof, and pulled a comforter over her. A moment later, she bolted up, flipping the cover away, and stomped over to the window. She stared out the window; their stalker was nowhere to be found.

She went to her closet and looked at herself in the mirror for a moment. She turned sideways and rubbed her nonexistent pooch, wishing it were there. When Lucy came back out to the great room, she noticed that Heather was asleep on the couch. She had fallen asleep with the journal in her hands, and it was about to fall to the floor. Lucy picked it up and thumbed through it for a moment, then shut it and pulled Heather's blanket over her. Felix climbed up on top of Heather, and Lucy picked him up in her arms and returned to her room. Felix hissed and clawed out of her arms as soon as she entered it.

"Ouch! Cat, what was that for?"

She got into bed. Ariel was still there standing in the corner, and it started to freak Lucy out a little bit.

"What are you doing there? You're being a weirdo."

"I'm a weirdo? I am not the one who talks to imaginary friends."

Lucy picked up a pillow and threw it at her, but Ariel moved to the right, dogging it.

"Then why don't you leave! You little shit?"

"Once you find your love, I may."

Lucy threw another pillow and yelled at her, "Leave. I don't need you. I have friends."

She was startled by Heather standing in the doorway.

"Oh…shit. Heather, I'm sorry."

"Who were you yelling at?" Heather asked.

"Please don't think I'm crazy. I was having a bad dream and woke up still in it. I was arguing with a childhood friend."

"Oh, okay, well, I was wondering if it was my throw pillows; Stephen didn't like them either."

The two girls looked at each other, then started to laugh. Lucy looked at the corner of the room to see if Ariel was still there, but she was gone. Heather sat on the bed and noticed Felix come to the door and stop. He looked at Ariel, now perched up on the top of the curtain rod, like a hideous predator, with a smile bigger than her face. The demon snickered. Another hideous creature crawled into the room from behind Heather's legs and slid under the bed; it peeked out on the other side and smiled up at Ariel.

"Come here, Buddy," Heather called, but the cat turned and left. "So I thought you were going out tonight." She asked.

"I did, and you would never guess what I heard."

"What?"

"Do you remember the cute host at the Onyx room?"

Heather nodded.

"Well, supposedly, the girl who was serving us was dating the owner, but she dumped him for Mitch, the host."

"You mean Brandy?" Heather asked.

"Yeah, but the freaky thing is, they found her dead in his alley that night, and the next day Mitch and the owner destroyed the bar in a fight."

"Really, that's terrible. How did she die?" Heather asked.

"I don't know, but I guess a witness cleared Mitch," Lucy said.

"Then, who…the ex?" Heather proposed.

Lucy nodded, "Looks like it. Isn't that insane? We just saw them, and now she's dead, and he's missing."

"Whose missing, Curtis?"

"No, Mitch, they released him, and then two days later, he cleared out. No one knows where he is."

"That's bizarre," Heather said.

Angelic Standoff

On the rooftop of the loft, a lone angel descended and stood. It was Arphax. Two fallen angels descended on the other side of the roof and glared at him.

"You have no place here. There are none of His followers here."

They circled Arphax but kept their distance. These two lieutenants were lesser angels and knew Arphax was a more formidable opponent.

"You would be wise to keep your distance, little ones; I am in no mood for your treachery." He rebuked.

"Why are you here? You have no business here, and you are outnumbered."

"By who... You?" Arphax laughed loudly. "You are no threat."

At that exact moment, Samyazal came and hovered above his lieutenants before dropping right in front of Arphax. He circled Arphax, his wings half-charged still, making himself larger. He looked him over, sniffing at him. Arphax's expression remained calm, though Samyazal was his size and strength.

"I smell your master on you, or is that fear and submission I smell? You weaken yourself by surrendering your will to Him, brother."

Arphax kept his gaze upon the two smaller angles. "I am here because she searches for the truth, and until that decision is made, you are forbidden to harass her."

"*I* am forbidden?" asked Samyazal, still pacing around him, his wings now folded behind his back.

The other two grew closer, "This is our house. You have no—"

The dark lieutenant was quieted with one look from Samyazal.

He stopped in front of Arphax, his two lieutenants standing at his side. "They are right, brother; this is not your territory. We have it. No one has called your master here."

Arphax and Samyazal stood face to face; Arphax, a brilliant angel in contrast to Samyazal's countenance.

"You're wrong, Fallen one; many have called us, though they all do not live; Father has heard their prayers for their young, and we have answered."

"We?" Samyazal snorted.

BOOM.

BOOM.

BOOM.

Three angels of the heavenly host came down to the rooftop. Two of them, massive angels, landed behind the fallen and the other beside Arphax.

"We!" finished Phanuel from behind Samyazal's lieutenants. They turned to face Phanuel, and Raphael, the other great angel.

The one that landed beside Arphax was smaller than he but just as brilliant and more feminine looking. A great sword took shape in her hand, as did her shield. "Lucifer has taken my ward, so Phanuel asked that I join you. Would you like me to remove these gnats, Arphax?"

Samyazal looked behind him at the other two angles, giving them a nod, before turning his gaze back on Sarakiel.

"Maybe you should have done a better job of watching over him, Little one," teased Samyazal.

She pulled back her sword, ready to strike, but Arphax touched her shoulder. Her eyes burned like brilliant Amethysts as she walked up to Samyazal, who was far greater in size.

"He chose to stand up to your master, not calling for help. A weak old man stood, defiant to your great god. Things would have been very different if I had not been restrained."

Samyazal kept his eyes on Arphax, not giving her the respect she deserved.

"And how did that all work out for him?"

Phanuel came around, joining Arphax and Sarakiel, and Samyazal gave him a brief look before returning his gaze to Arphax. "brother, you settle for weakness when you could join us and experience your full power, unrestrained by Him." His arm thrust to the starry sky as a sword formed in his hand. "He only limits you;

how is that love?"

"You would not know true power if it struck you in the face. Would you like me to demonstrate?" Arphax rebuked, his own sword at the ready.

All the angel's swords were out now, shields forming in their hands. Phanuel stepped between the two, "You both know what will happen if we start this. We are not interfering, and you will not interfere either."

Raphael walked over to where Lucy's room was and vanished into the loft, coming back up with two squealing demons in his grasp. They screeched in pain as their necks burned where he held them. He threw them to the rooftop, and they darted back and forth, looking for an escape from all the angels. Ariel vanished into a cloud of back dust and blew away, but the second scampered into the aim of Sarakiel, who pierced it like a bug with her great sword. It screamed in agony and burned to ash.

Samyazal walked toward the edge of the roof and looked down. Two more fallen descended to the rooftop; one of them was Asbeel, another Captain of Lucifer's legions. He looked over the scene, then over to Samyazal. "Not now, we have control here, and they know it."

He nodded to the two lesser angels, and they took flight, vanishing into the sky above. Asbeel gave Phanuel a deadly look. "You know you have no power here. I need not prove it to you...." He gave Samyazal a signal and took flight, exploding into the sky, followed by the fallen that came with him. Samyazal came closer to Arphax, ignoring and almost stepping on Sarakiel.
"brother, I wish you could see that you're on the wrong side. I fight for our kind, for you. When we are victorious, it will be ours. Humanity is a horrid species that only destroys. This world would not miss them if they were extinct; it would again flourish like it did before they came and defiled it."

Arphax stared into Samyazal's deadly eyes. They were still brilliant jewels but lined in damnations fire like his master's. "I see your final destination burning within you, Fallen one. I am no longer your brother; you do not fight for me. You fight for a lie."

Samyazal walked away but turned back, looking at the four angels of God. "You have no place here ... Look and pity them as you please, then leave." He exploded in the sky and was gone.

Sarakiel looked up at Arphax and put a hand on his shoulder. Phanuel and Raphael joined them. “This does not show promise for the girl,” Raphael said.

Arphax looked at Phanuel, then back to Raphael. “Father is doing all He can for her; we must trust His plan.”

Phanuel nodded and took flight. Raphael looked at Sarakiel. “You are a superb protector, and I know how much you wanted to step in for Leroy. Do not let his death crush your resolve; we all know where he is.”

“I know, Raphael, but it still saddens me when any of our own must suffer.”

“Arphax, I wish you well in this mission Father has given you. Your restraint may be as vigorous a challenge as your proven skill in battle. Father’s peace guide you, brother.”

Arphax nodded. “Father’s will is mine.”

After Raphael left, Arphax looked at Sarakiel. “I am glad to have great company joining me.”

She smiled up at him, “let us go see our charge”

He nodded, and the two descended into Heather’s room.

Ariel reappeared on the building across the street, hunkered on the top of a vent like a bird trying to stay warm. Her yellow eyes peered across the dark at Lucy’s room, contempt on her hideous face.

A man came out onto the rooftop but did not see her. He sat on a bucket and opened a bottle of booze, swigging from it and looking over at the same building. He spotted Ariel out of the corner of his vision, and his eyes flickered with a yellow glow.

“I see you.” she spat.

He smiled, “*We* see you.” He answered.

***

When Stephen woke in the morning, he was alarmed. He vaguely remembered being put to bed; however, not much else as he went downstairs. He found Charles sipping some tea and reading a newspaper.

"Last night...." He started.

Charles looked over at him and then back at his paper. "You had a fabulous time. The girls loved you, by the way."

"The girls... Did I—"

"Relax, Stephen, your purity is intact. You passed out when your head hit the pillow, and they returned to their guest rooms."

"Guest rooms? So, they are going to be staying here?"

"Well, yes, I offered when I found out they would be here for the week. I thought it would be nice to have some more company here to enjoy the evenings with when we are not working."

"So why wouldn't we ask Heather and Lucy to join us?"

"Well, if you must know Stephen, they are both very busy, for one, and to be honest, I did not think of it until last night. It really should not be a problem. They are nice people, and I enjoy being surrounded by beauty."

"There's no problem, but I just don't want to do anything that would hurt Heather; you understand that, right?"

Charles smiled at him but still showed signs of irritation. "I am very aware of what it is you are referring to, and I respect whatever choices you make regarding monogamy in your relationship. They are not prostitutes, my friend, and I do not require you to partake in their delicacies to have a good time. Though, the two that put you to bed definitely took a liking to you." Charles finished.

"I appreciate everything, Charles, and plan on enjoying myself here, but those delicacies cannot be on my menu."

"I understand. All that I am saying is enjoy yourself. I am not judging you."

"Well, I am going to get cleaned up. Do we have a plan for today?" Stephen asked as he started back up the stairs.

"I do. I have a short meeting. *Try* and enjoy yourself a little while I am away. Breakfast will be served out in the atrium in an hour."

Stephen showered and got dressed. He sat on his bed, looking at the picture of Heather. Something was wrong; he could feel it in his gut. He calculated what time it was and realized that she might still be awake. He went downstairs and asked a servant if there was a phone he could use. The woman pointed into the study. He sat at the large desk.

Country codes...

He looked at Charles' Rolodex and noticed the added digits to his New York home. Stephen added those numbers to his own and made the call. A busy signal came across the phone. It wasn't the normal tone he was used to, but he figured that was because he was overseas. He noticed some documents under a folder labeled investments. One of them revealed a letterhead: LSC Life Systems Corporation. His curiosity won over, and he lifted the top corner to see what else was there. A robotics corporation and a computer manufacturing company were among the ones he recognized. The lounge area flooded with the sound of young women as five girls came flooding in. Stephen tried to reset the documents as they were and walked out of the office.

"Hollo, Estephan," said one, with a sharp accent. The others giggled. All but one spoke English though not fluently. They were all dressed in tight shorts and sports tops and looked like they had just come from the gym.

"Will you join our breakfast?" another asked him, smiling.

Stephen nodded, walked out into the main lounge, and sat on one of the couches. The servant brought him water on a silver platter. He took it and nodded.

"You are much fun last night." The first said as she sat.

"I overdid it last night..."

The girls looked confused.

"Drunk." He explained.

They all smiled, nodding in understanding. "You are fun." They all agreed.

Stephen pounded his water and got up.

"I will see you at Breakfast."

They all nodded, then spoke in Arabic. Stephen went upstairs and lay on his bed. *Oh, boy, this is going to be an interesting week.*

Breakfast was served in a large, enclosed Atrium with open French-style doors on all sides. Diaphanous drapes fluttered away from their openings as servants brought in tray after tray of food. After breakfast, Stephen went out and lay in the sun by the pool, and the girls soon followed. They came out and chose lounge chairs all around him, asking him all kinds of questions. It was hard not to look at such beautiful women, and he got up and jumped into the pool. A few laps later and he was feeling good again. He missed the ocean and thought about surfing with Heather. The rest of the day was uneventful, save for when the girls decided to join him in the pool. They wanted to play some kind of game with a ball that included tackling, and that lasted all of ten minutes before Stephen retreated to his room, claiming a headache.

"Too much drink last night." He complained as he tried to get out of the pool. The two girls who had taken him to bed coddled him before he got out, rubbing his temples, trying to help.

"Thank you very much. You are very kind," He managed as he climbed out. Stephen went and took a long shower and then a nap. After being woke for an afternoon meal, which he declined, he thumbed through his writing bag. Inside was a note from Heather. He lay there, sleep still in his eyes, and read.

Hi Dear, I just want you to know how excited I am for my future with you. I want you to know that no matter what happens in our life, be it success or troubled times, that I am happy because it will be with you; my closest friend and precious lover. I touch my belly, and my heart leaps in my chest with the joy that our love is growing within me.

Be safe while you're far from me, and have fun. This is your time, a time you will always look back on with fondness. You worked hard to get to this place and deserve to be happy. I love you, baby, with every bit of me.

We will be waiting faithfully for your return.

We (our child and I)

Yours forever,

Heather Leigh—Meyers.

H.

Stephen reread the note three more times before putting it back where he found it. Everything in his life was perfect; the woman he was about to marry, his friends, his career—everything. He freshened up in his bathroom before going downstairs. He was greeted by Charles, who was standing next to another man, and the girls, who were all dressed to go out.

"Stephen, there you are, my friend. Khalil here wants us to join him for a banquet tonight."

Stephen's two fans danced on their tiptoes, hoping he would join them.

"Let's do it," he said, followed by the girls cheering and bouncing some more.

As they were getting ready to leave, Stephen pulled Charles aside. "I tried to call home earlier but got a busy signal. I'm not sure if dialed right."

Charles put a hand on his shoulder. "I'll help you make the call later when we get home. It is the middle of the night there now. Will this do?"

"Yes, Charles, thank you."

That night was a re-run of the night before, with elaborate dinner courses coming out, some Stephen enjoyed, and others he passed on, afraid to ask. The girls seemed to be on a permanent joy ride laughing constantly and very lively. Stephen wished Lucy and Heather were here. He pictured their expressions and reactions to the fun they were having. Drinks came around several times, and Stephen joined in. It was Charles that had to be carried back to the car this time, though. Stephen was ripe for the wagon himself when they finally left. It was lucky that Charles' security knew how to handle things when they left, or they never would have made it home.

When they arrived, the staff helped Charles to his room, but he came back out twice, demanding he be able to hear the party from his window or he would not go to sleep.

Hairy Ones

Peter was driving home from visiting a friend, exhausted. There was a light fog on the mountain road, but only in patches. He was on a road that would bring him from the mountains of Jamul, east of the city. His radio stopped working, and he tried adjusting the station when something huge ran in front of his car. He hit the brakes, sliding sideways and almost off the road. Peter looked out his window and saw a long drop down a ravine.

I'm awake now.

He backed away from the road's edge and looked into his rear-view mirror. There, in the middle of the road, was the biggest wolf he had ever seen or was it a buffalo? *There is a Buffalo farm near here,* he thought.

It stared at him, unmoving and fierce like an ancient statue left to guard the way. Peter pulled back onto the road and noticed the thing was running after him. He increased his speed and started to leave it slowly behind when he hit another patch of fog and had to slow.

He drove as fast as he felt safe, glancing in the rear-view mirror constantly to see if the animal was still there.

About a half a mile later, the road grew clear again, and Peter sped up a little. He made little progress because here, in the middle of the road, was another one. This one was facing him. Peter stopped his car, staring at the thing. It just stood there. He looked in his rear-view mirror and saw the fog coming up the road.

Peter flashed his brights at the animal. No effect. It did not flinch. It just stood there, its teeth bared in a fierce snarl that begged for blood. Peter hit the horn, and still, the beast did not move.

He put the car back in gear and floored the accelerator, flying at the wolf, the car's motor screaming. It did not move, and Peter was approaching fast. When Peter was only feet away, it darted into the darkness and fog. He slammed on his brakes because of a sharp corner just beyond where the beast was standing and then took a deep breath before driving on.

A bad feeling overtook him. He knew this was an evil attack and started to pray. As he came around another bend, the fog was back and much thicker. He had no choice but to slow down as he strained to see the road through the dense fog. About a half a mile farther, it became paralyzing. Peter considered pulling over but, remembering the wolves, chose to move on. His radio started to show signs of life and came on for a second. He shut it off, flinching at the same moment, as something ran in front of his car again. This time he clipped whatever it was, and the car spun sideways to a stop.

Peter's heart was pounding, and his car stalled in the road. He tried to start the car and got nothing, not even a click of the starter.

Something snarled behind the vehicle, and he turned, but all he could see was the white blanket of fog.

Another jumped on the hood with a bang as it climbed onto the roof. It was big enough to cave in his roof, and Peter could hear it breathing up there.

Another slammed into the passenger's side of the car, buckling the door panel on the inside. The entire vehicle moved with the impact, and the car felt unstable, as though it were no longer on level ground.

He looked out his window and saw the shoulder of the road but could not see more than a foot beyond. He had no idea whether it was a two-foot ditch beyond or the sheer cliff he had seen a mile back. The snarling continued, and whatever was on the roof clambered down the back of the car and was gone. All Peter saw was a blur of dark fur through the back window.

"Lord, I need your help."

Peter tried to start the car again, and it cranked but did not start. He could hear growling and snarling all around him. The fog was beginning to thin out, and he could see several feet around the car. Dark flashes were darting back and forth outside, about ten feet away from the car. Peter looked out his driver's window and saw a deep ravine below; his car was inches from going over.

The growling became louder. He looked out his passenger's window and saw a giant wolf, black as night, eyes yellow moons. It stepped out into the middle of the road, posturing to charge at him.

Sweet Jesus, now might be good.

The beast exploded towards him at a full charge, intent on ramming the car. Peter looked out his driver's window at the deep ravine below and knew that one more impact, like the last, and he and the car were going over.

He looked back at the charging monster just in time to see it smash headfirst into nothing. That animal fell to the ground, only feet from Peter's car, dazed. There were yelps of pain all around him in the dense fog and then silence. Peter sat still, waiting for something to happen, and nothing did. The giant wolf started to get up and looked over at Peter, then something near scared it, and it cowered. The wolf, now low, scurried away, crying with its tail between its legs, and vanished into the darkness.

Peter sat there in the dead quiet for almost ten minutes before moving. He tried the ignition again, and it started on the first try. He pulled the car back into the road, then pulled over to the opposite shoulder and got out. The fog was lifting, and it was still quiet out on this desolate stretch of mountain road, not even the sound of crickets. He could feel the cool mist touching his face and tickling his lungs as he breathed the moist air. An overwhelming sense of nature began to fill his nostrils as if life was returning to this mountain. Plant life, soils, and mountain fragrances filled the air again.

As the fog rolled out, the natural sounds of nature returned, and Peter found no sign of the pack of wolves that had been there. He returned to his car but stopped before opening the door. Something or someone was there at the side of the road. He saw the fog move as if something moved through it.

"I know you're here." He called out, "Whoever you are....Thank you."

Something down deep in his soul whispered to him. Peter stood there in the dark of the road and listened.

Transcendentiam

ENGASTRIMUTHOS - (GK: "ventriloquist")
Demons associated with séances, fortune telling, and necromancy. Connected to mediums in the Bible and other ancient texts.

"Behold there is a woman that hath a familiar spirit at En-dor."
I Samuel, 28: 7, b.

En-Dor
The road to En-dor is easy to tread
For Mother or yearning Wife.
There, it is sure, we shall meet our Dead
As they were even in life.
Earth has not dreamed of the blessing in store
For desolate hearts on the road to En-dor.
Whispers shall comfort us out of the dark—
Hands—ah God!—that we knew!
Visions and voices—look and hark!—
Shall prove that the tale is true,
And that those who have passed to the further shore
May be hailed—at a price—on the road to En-dor.

But they are so deep in their new eclipse

Nothing they say can reach,
Unless it be uttered by alien lips
And framed in a stranger's speech.
The son must send word to the mother that bore,
Through an hireling's mouth. 'Tis the rule of En-dor.

And not for nothing these gifts are shown
By such as delight our dead.
They must twitch and stiffen and slaver and groan
Ere the eyes are set in the head,
And the voice from the belly begins. Therefore,
We pay them a wage where they ply at En-dor.

Even so, we have need off faith
And patience to follow the clue.
Often, at first, what the dear one saith
Is babble, or jest, or untrue.
(Lying spirits perplex us sore
Till our loves—and their lives—are well-known at En-dor . . . .

Oh the road to En-dor is the oldest road
And the craziest road of all!
Straight it runs to the Witch's abode,
As it did in the days of Saul,
And nothing has changed of the sorrow in store
For such as go down on the road to En-dor!

—by Rudyard Kipling 1916

***

Mankind knows very little about demons. I will only reveal as much as needed to finish this story, though, in the end, all will be revealed to humanity. Some glorious, much of it horrifying; yet, each of you has the choice to remain guarded.

Engastrimyth demons can do far more than control human vocal cords; they can also control the body. They are perfect mimics of the dead, often portraying someone they possessed over a thousand years ago or a lost loved one who passed away within days. There are several different kinds of demons, just as there are different ranks of Angels, though I would not have you confuse demons with we bright ones. All demons are determined to deceive and harm humanity. Some haunt and torment. Others pretended to be lost loved ones in order to manipulate the living. Some demons act like poltergeists, causing much harm. As well, there are also others even more deadly. All of them hate you and seek your demise. Some, if allowed in, can manifest and kill. I have witnessed a many stubborn, and strong peoples fall prey to demons. They are what hides behind most of the unexplained. 'The Hairy Ones,' 'The Greys,' and 'The Reptilians' are just a few of the names given them by humanity. The living ones are mutated blasphemies of terrestrial and heavenly consummation. Defiance to the Father in life and damned as demons in death. Those fooling with technology in attempt to advance the race, only open doors, which empower and release demons. This story is as much about the strengthening power of evil as it is the unfailing love of our Father and maker. As scary as the darkness surrounding you may be, it does not come close to the beautiful light which will destroy every shadow we see.

***

At a research facility hidden deep in the mountains of the Western United States, a lab tech by the name of Albert Redding was logging in the night's results. They were promising. Albert Redding's expression revealed his excitement as he typed his final report. Albert was a pudgy man in his thirties with curly hair that was usually disheveled. The few times he made an effort to remedy this, his combed hair would resemble a wet water buffalo's helmet. His talents lay in source code. Computer language and science. A man dedicated to research, taking very little notice of his own reflection. Mirrors were, for Albert, places to scribe formulas. His mind ran circles around most others when it came to mathematics and computer systems but was impaired when it came to social life.

Tonight's success was astronomical regarding the research they were doing. The lab was built for the sole purpose of human immortality. The research facility had several divisions and was privately funded by billionaires, who spent as much money on secrecy and security as they did on research. Albert was given whatever he wanted as long as he produced results. Tonight he had. His department was in charge of the sequencing and transferring of digital consciousness. There was a significant breakthrough in artificial intelligence, which his lab quietly siphoned over to another lab owned by LSC (Live Systems Corporation) for commercial applications. However, this technology seemed to be hitting a wall. They had failed to create an independent thinking intelligence. The technology could go no further.

They had now successfully transferred the consciousness of a rat into a computer system that controlled a robotic arm and head, and the results were amazing. The arm worked feverishly to feel around the Plexiglas box it was mounted in, its head moving back and forth. The robot would even stop to look at its arm for hours at a time as if analyzing itself. The arm worked frantically for an escape, and when food was introduced, it attacked with fervor, cramming the food into the robotic mouth, which only ended in a tube to a trash can. The robot did not know this, though, and would continue feeding itself with as much food as available, cleaning up every last crumb its hand could pick up. After feeding, it would go back to attempting escape, stopping every hour or so to reexamine its arm meticulously.

The optics were innovative technology that Albert barely understood: his expertise was software. The data medium had been formatted with a basic OS, a backbone that could only receive commands. Albert's custom software was innovatively designed to recognize and mimic brain impulses. It would then translate them into code that could be used by the system. This system was also designed to learn, by trial and error, which codes successfully accomplished what the mind desired, and correct mistakes. A basic version of his software was being used in amputee prosthetics, in which the patient was able to control the movement of an arm or leg. Bios software controlled the robotic functions, but no system was programmed to tell the robotics when or why. This required the digital mind to connect between bios and OS. Albert could type in code and execute, and the hand would clench into a fist; but once the command was completed, there would be nothing.

Upon downloading the digital equivalent of a rat's mind, the system went haywire. All kinds of code started flooding the screen. Though simple, one-line data strings, it was still amazing to watch. Albert called his administrators with the news, and soon the entire team came to watch the new mind find its way around inside the system. There were several erratic attempts to take possession of the robotic arm, eyes, and head, which looked more like the twitches of a dying animal than controlled movement. Still, the team was cheering with every attempt.

48 hours later, the AR (Artificial Rat) took possession of the arm and started sweeping it around the box. Another 48 hours, and it was using its eyes and mouth, trying to bite down and looking all around. The moment that everyone was in awe over was when it discovered its hand. At this point, code overflowed the system as it realized what it was. System fans were whining, trying to alleviate the overheating CPU's as the system ran beyond its abilities. That day, it stared at its

hand for six hours, moving it slowly around, flexing each joint as if teaching itself.

Tonight was another leap forward. Albert had successfully downloaded the data, or AR, into another system, which controlled a small robotic mouse. It had wheels instead of feet, but it could stand up on the rear wheels and move an elongated head around as it moved. It did not have a mouth, which became problematic when the AR discovered food again. It seemed to go into shock because it did not know how to reach out or devour the food.

The AR became violent and flew around the test floor, slamming into the borders of its little world until damaging the body it was given. Albert uploaded the software back to the arm and head and put food in the box, and moments later, it was back in control, stuffing its mouth with everything it could find. Another thing he noticed was that when he tried to copy the software or consciousness, it would simply crash, doing nothing. This would be another avenue of research, which he slotted for another team to investigate.

Can we duplicate a consciousness?

He finished his report and packed up for the night. It was now almost dawn, and he was exhausted. His staff apartment was on site and only a 10-minute walk from the lab, so he grabbed a Zippy Cake from the vending machine and ate it as he left. As Albert entered the last hall of the sublevel labs, he heard a clamor from a restricted area and stopped. He looked down a corridor and saw a fully humanoid robot fumble into the hall, smashing at walls. It looked at him and then charged the other way, followed by two staff Albert did not recognize.

The robot stopped and destroyed a water fountain mounted on the wall with several blows, then beat its own head, sparks and electronic shorts flaring, until it was still. Two more white-coated men came out of the lab and joined the others, picking it up.

Albert leaned back against the wall out in the hall, not wanting to be seen. A moment later, he took two steps backward and started whistling as he walked passed the scene as if hearing nothing. He went through the security doors with his key card, not looking back, and was soon in the elevator going up. When he reached ground level, he was met by two security-personal, who informed him that he was needed back downstairs. Albert complied and went back. The two white-coated lab techs greeted him when he got back down to level eight.

"Albert, right?" said the bigger one, a blonde-haired, blue-eyed man with a slight German accent. The other, also blonde but smaller, only smiled.

"Um ... Yeah, may I be of some help?"

"The smaller man took him by the elbow, still smiling, "Yes, we hope you can."

Albert complied.

Two hours later, Albert made it back to his apartment and poured himself a large chocolate milk. He should be happy. He was now promoted and in charge of two testing labs. His work with the AR had opened the door to the next stage, which was human trials. They showed him the damaged robot and explained that they had used his software to transfer the consciousness of a dying cancer patient into the system. The problems arose when they tried transferring it to the working robot. It seemed to have control of only one side of its body at a time and then went insane at the point of realization. Albert had already spent many hours theorizing about all of this, and his notes on stepping into the body were invaluable. At first he was surprised that they had taken his software without him realizing it and pushing past him in its use annoyed him. He was the lead, he was its creator. Of course they failed he thought.

He criticized their entire track of implementing *his* software. Demanding that they re-write the software so that the mind only gathered control over one extremity at a time. Like slowly waking and feeling one's feet. This would allow them, or it, to come to terms with everything. He also thought that the original source code created by the mind was probably corrupt and that they would need either to go back to the original code or find a new volunteer.

He gathered these theories from watching and studying the first moments of realization. This realization was when the consciousness took hold of the software platform and new code written. Albert believed that this was like repopulating a brain, redesigning its nodes and pathways. He was designing a circuit board that mimicked the billions of individual neurons in a brain. Albert told them that the software needed to facilitate this implantation or marriage of mind and tech would be complex. They told him that the software was priority one. He was also told that he would have seven more volunteers to work with.

Albert's first task upon returning to the lab would be to analyze the AI that they had already tried implanting and determine if it was still viable or too corrupt to save. He believed this would answer more questions for him than anything else. Before he left, they had given him two instructions. The first he expected, which was that this project was restricted to him and his team only. The other was that there was to be no auditory ability allowed in the test subjects until they approved it. This last restriction tugged at his mind as he sat on the couch watching the sun break over the mountains.

Why would they care? He kept asking himself. What would these volunteers be saying that they did not want spoken?

Back in the lab, the damaged robot lay on an exam table. The lights were all off, save for one light, in the far corner of the lab. Something dark was squatting over the robot. It had elongated arms and legs and a skinny body. Its head was almost all mouth, filled with sharp teeth. On top of the head were two small yellow eyes. It was an Engastrimuthos.

The demon touched the robot, sticking its long clawed finger into the hole in the crushed head, feeling its own at the same time. Three more demons showed and climbed up, looking down at the robot on the table. A Fallen-One entered the room and approached the table, moving the head of the robot, examining it. The demons fumbled backward and to the floor but stayed near. They kept themselves on the opposite side of the exam table, looking up at their commander. They spoke in odd and faint sounds before vanishing into black clouds.

The dark angel went to Albert's apartment, stood over the man's table, looking at his notes. It took on the form of Albert, picked up his pencil, and wrote down a mathematical equation, followed by some code.

Wide Awake

The following week was a blur for Heather, and she looked forward to the weekend, so she could take a day off for herself and do nothing. She oversaw the remodel at Lucy's new place, shopping with her for interior decor, and managed to stay on top of a new project her office assigned her in the downtown area.

Each day after work, she would steal away to walk on the beach or sit on the pier and enjoy the last rays of sunshine for the day. She was going to take another trip east to visit Shelly, but Stephen had left a message on the machine, promising to call today, so she rushed straight home to be there when the phone rang. Heather arrived home to an empty house. Lucy was out on a date, and Felix was her only company. She took a shower and put on comfortable clothes before setting down with Betty's journal and Bible. About twenty minutes into her reading, she fell asleep. The phone rang, waking her disorientated and confused. Heather jumped up and ran over to the phone, picking it up just before the machine got it.

"Hello?"

Static. Crackling.

"Hello?" she repeated.

More static, but in the background, she heard a faint voice trying to talk to her.

"Stephen, is that you? I can barely hear you."

The phone went dead, and she returned to the couch with it still in her hand. She clicked the remote to the stereo. Heather sat there quiet for a moment, just listening to the sounds and staring out the window. When the radio began to lose reception, the speakers put out only audio fuzz. Heather clicked it off and lay back on the couch. She suddenly felt a chill and grabbed a folded blanket to cover her bare legs. The house started to shake, and glass was breaking all around her. She jumped up and looked around, panicked.

This is a big one.

She ran to the front door, grabbing Felix as she fled the loft. She thought going outside might be the best place to go. The building was shaking violently now, and Heather started to get really scared as she ran to the staircase. This was the biggest earthquake she had ever felt before. Alarms were going off as she hit the stairwell. Felix jumped out of her arms and vanished as she made it to the parking garage and out to the street. She crossed the street and watched her building shake. Something came crashing down to her right, and she looked to see a building falling into the road. However, that was not what she was focusing on.

A man, a familiar man, was standing in the middle of the street staring at her. He had a gun in his hand and a demented look on his face. She let her instincts take over and ran back to her building, which was beginning to calm. She made it in the door, bolting it behind her, and ran up the first flight of stairs. Two shots rang out from behind her. She screamed as she made her way up the stairs. As soon as she was on her floor, she heard a violent yell, "Whore! Come here."

Whoever this man was, he was inside her building now and coming after her. She darted for her door, still wide open, and closed it behind her, bolting the lock. She ran to the phone, but could not find it. It was on the couch, so she ran over there just as he started beating on the door. Loud booms were coming from him, kicking it and slamming into it, and the door began to crack. She grabbed the phone and ran into the other loft, trying frantically to dial 911. The phone gave a busy signal. She clicked it off as she ran into Stephen's office and hid underneath his desk.

Heather peeked out at the window, wondering if she should climb out and take her chances getting over to the trees on the side of the building. She was angry with herself for not putting on shoes when she left the house. He was in the house now, destroying the place, looking for her. Heather crawled to the door to her office, realizing it would be closer to the trees.

She quietly closed the door, joining her office to Stephen's, and tried the phone. It was nothing but static.

"Damned!" she cursed it in a low voice. Her heart was pounding. She was terrified. The place grew silent now, and this made her feel worse. She made her way over to the window and opened the side light, which led to a four-inch lip, not even a ledge. She looked to the left and could see the corner of the building, about three feet away.

I could make that.

She started climbing out, swinging one leg out the window and holding onto the window frame. Her right foot found purchase, and she began to distribute her weight over to bring her other leg out when he came crashing into the office.

She screamed as loud as she could and started to fall when he grabbed her by her hair and pulled her violently in. She scraped her leg on the window frame as she flew through it, and her thigh began to bleed.

She forgot about it the moment she landed hard on the floor. All her breath was knocked out of her, and she saw stars.

He picked her up by her hair and threw her against the wall. She cried out in pain and was blacking out.

"Please, my baby...Please," she managed as he dragged her by her hair out of the office and all the way to the guest area. She managed to get free, losing a chunk of hair, and ran for the double doors leading out into the main loft.

He caught her, and threw her backward, sending her through Lucy's doors and into that room. She turned, trying to get up, when he came in and straddled her. His eyes were different; these were the eyes of an animal. Something evil held her gaze, and she looked away. He grabbed her by the face squeezing tightly, hurting her, and she cried out. His voice sounded as though it was two voices, which were not human.

"We've been looking forward to this, Whore," they said.

"Please, I'm pregn—"

He slapped her so hard she lost her breath.

"What is that to us, Whore?" He looked down on her, his face changing. This was no man, or if it was, he had some serious problems. For a brief moment, his eyes changed and showed fear. There was someone else inside, someone fighting for control. She was too terrified to think, but she was sure of what she saw.

"I think we should eat her eyes...." One voice began, this one smaller, more distant.

This man is possessed.

Heather struggled to get free, but he was faster and stronger. Her tank top ripped in half as she pulled away.

No, please, God.

The man started choking her. *God, please help me, Please protect my baby.*

She kicked, and managed to get free long enough to back herself up to the bed and covering her naked chest with her crossed arms.

"Jesus, help me!" she screamed at the top of her lungs.

The man stopped, and looked at her, puzzled. He jumped forward, intent on finishing what he started, but couldn't move. Something was holding him back. Rage filled his eyes, then fear, and two creatures withdrew from him, first appearing as clouds of black smoke, then forming into hideous things, which scampered around the room for escape. The man's face changed, and Heather almost felt sorry for him. He looked mortified and worried. His eyes were now human looking, and his face though stricken with fear, more benevolent. Heather pulled a pillow over her naked chest and moved to the edge of the bed. The man's mouth was open, and he looked as if he was trying to speak but could not. The two demons screeched and exploded into flames in the air and were gone.

Heather tried to get to her feet, but she was shaking too badly to stand, so she leaned back, not taking her eyes off the troubled man. A bright light filled the room, and she shaded her eyes with her free arm, seeing the man fall to the ground before she passed out.

A moment later, she opened her eyes, and everything was cloudy. Her vision felt like looking through a fish-eyed lens. A dazzling man was standing over her attacker, looking at her. He was the most beautiful man she had ever seen. Not in the general way of judging handsomeness or beauty, but in a new way, somehow. Heather did not know how to describe his beauty.

He was… "wonderful," she whispered.

Her vision was still clouded over like a satin finish of frosted glass, but his brilliance was unhindered by it. She looked at him, eyes and mouth wide. Looking at this man brought tears to her eyes. She was both sad and overwhelmingly happy at the same time. His beautiful face held so much love for her; it pierced her heart, and the tears flowed.

"Wonderful..." she repeated inarticulately.

"Thank you, Heather; you are special to me also." He responded. His voice was like the most beautiful melody ever played. Like a full orchestra playing the most beautiful score ever composed, it pierced deep into her soul, seeing and knowing her.

…Loving me.

He touched the man on the floor and then came closer to her.

"Heather, I love you so very much, and I am so glad your heart is ready. This man is troubled, but he, too, I want to save. He was made to destroy, but I want to use him for good. I made you for good, and I have been waiting for you."

As the being of light came closer, Heather saw his scars. Across his face and on his neck were jagged-looking lines where his flesh had been torn open.

"Are you ..." She could not finish, but she knew who he was.

Jesus…

She started to sob, tears still flowing, but not for her. For Him. She knew his love for her and saw his suffering, suffering that he took on for her. It all made sense, and it all was clear to her at this moment. He came closer, looking deeply into her eyes.

"Oh, Dear, your beard," She cried as she looked at the part of his beard that would never grow back again, ripped out by a Roman soldier.

She fell forward to the floor, ashamed of herself for being the cause of his pain—this wonderful being of love and light.

"Your heart sees the truth; now follow it."

She did not get up. She was afraid to. She just wept on the floor. "I will be with you always, even when the darkness comes."

She sat back on her feet, afraid to look up at him, and he put a hand on her chin and lifted her gaze to His own. His smile filled her with a buzz like no drug or pleasure could touch, and she quivered. He touched her forehead, brushing her hair out of her eyes.

"Go to her, and let her lead you to the truth and trust in me."

"And Stephen?" She asked.

His smile grew. "I have been watching him all of his life and want nothing but goodness for you both."

"I'll do anything for him..." She stammered.

"And that love is what I seek. I will fight for him."

Her vision was clouding over and panic set in. she stumbled, trying to get up, feeling around.

"Lord?" she cried.

"You are safe," his voice fading.

The phone rang, startling her, and she opened her eyes. Her vision was clearer now but still cloudy from the tears in her eyes. She sat up and realized she was back on the couch, Felix looking over at her from the coffee table. The phone rang again, and she jumped up to get it. She looked down at herself as she ran over to the phone and saw that her top was not torn. As she picked up the phone, she looked around the house. Everything was in its place; nothing fallen from the earthquake.

A dream?

"Hello, Heather. You there?" Stephen called into her ear.

"Yes, Baby. I'm sorry, I just woke up. How are you?" her voice brightening at the end.

Stephen filled her in on everything and told her that they were leaving the next day to go to some dig. He had been to many historic sites that were in the Bible and discussed historical information with both Jewish and secular historians. Stephen's notebooks were full, and he sounded excited about all the ideas they had come up with for the story. Charles had taken him to a very secret dig, which penetrated hidden tunnels under the city of Jerusalem, and were hoped to lead to the chamber that held the 'Ark of the Covenant.' The archeologist leading the search was following a story about Jeremiah hiding it in secret tunnels before Israel was invaded thousands of years ago. This project seemed to be Charles' biggest passion. He was spending significant amounts of money on bribes and other expenses to be able to be there, digging. They were going out again in the morning and would not be back until the day before he was flying back. Heather encouraged him and was genuinely excited about everything he had told her. Part of her was even able to let go of the dream in which he had pulled her from, though her other half was still there, still shaken by the events that had unfolded. She filled him in on how things were going at home and discussed plans for the wedding. This made her feel happier as they finished talking.

"I miss you, Love," he said.

"I miss you too, Baby. I'll see you Wednesday then?"

"Yes, Honey."

They hung up the phone. Heather got up, changed, and left. She was not sure what to think of the dream. The man was familiar, but who? She could not place the face, but she knew she had met this person in real life. That much of the dream had been real.

How much more of it was? The thought of that really happening made her tremble, and she had to shrug it off. Jesus appearing was more real than any memory in her mind. She believed he was real and that he was trying to reach out to her. Seeing him opened her eyes somehow. She saw her life through His eyes, all the wrong she allowed to thrive in it, and she saw His grace. Tears filled her eyes again, and she turned on the radio. She drove east to Shelly's.

20 minutes later, Heather got out of her car and knocked on Shelly's door. Tears were rolling down her cheeks, but there was also a sense of peace and imminent joy inside her; this was where she was supposed to be, as if she was on the right track again. Shelly opened the door, and worry fell over her face at the sight of Heather. Her first thought was the baby, and she put out her arms. Heather

embraced her, sobbing.

"Oh, Honey, what's wrong?" Shelly asked.

"I've been such a fool," Heather muttered, still holding onto the woman who had become her big sister in her teens. Shelly walked her into the house, where they both sat on the couch.

"Honey, tell me. What is it?" Shelly pushed.

"I've been a simpleton, so naive. Stephen and I both." She took a tissue from Shelly and dried her eyes.

"Heather, you've got me worried." Shelly pleaded.

"Oh, Shelly, Everything is great with Stephen and me." She followed Shelly's eyes to her belly, "The Baby too." She rubbed her tiny belly and pulled Betty's journal out of her bag, handing it over to her.

Shelly eased at the sight of it and smiled. "Oh…OH!, this is about God?"

Heather nodded. "I get it now...It's all true, every bit of it." Tears began to fill her eyes again, "And I realize for the first time in my life how special the work my parents were doing was."

Shelly took her hand, "I'm so glad to hear this. Your parents prayed for this day."

"I know, and I wanted to share it with someone who would understand. That's yours now, by the way." She finished, pointing to the journal. "She knew...or He knew...I'd read that when the time was right for me to see the truth."

Shelly thumbed through it, "They both knew it." Shelly muttered her own voice breaking.

The two women hugged. Heather stayed at Shelly's house that night, and they spent hours talking. She didn't want to be alone, and this home held power for her, peace. Shelly made up a bed in her old room, and they made popcorn and watched movies until late into the night.

***

Heather and Lucy were very busy over the next several days, trying to finish Lucy's house before the wedding. As well, Heather was wrapping up her projects at work in preparation for the time she would be taking off for her Honeymoon. The girls spent time together in the evenings when Lucy did not go out, and many of Heather's other friends were around most days with all the excitement of the upcoming wedding. Heather saw things in a different light now. It was as if blinders had been removed. She could see pettiness and other things she had never noticed before in her friends. She still adored them and did not think less of them, but she could see hidden miseries and insecurities. There was something missing in their eyes. She noticed how most of them drew their happiness from the tangible. Be it clothing, jewelry, or a new car, these things seemed to have no hold on her anymore, and she found it harder to relate to some of the conversations. Heather watched them whenever they spent time together and realized that not one of these girls was spiritual. She had no Christian friends save for Peter. She found herself surrounded by people who were unable to relate to her newfound joy. They did not see the beauty all around them as she now did.

Views were more breathtaking, and the act of kindness noticed on the street filled her with joy. She found herself thinking about more profound things, more important things, all the time, and the few times she would bring these to the other's attention, they would all smile and sigh, attributing it to the fact she was pregnant. Though that added to her emotions, it did not touch what God had placed in her heart. Her eyes were open for the first time in her life to the good and the bad, and she knew everything would change.

Lucy seemed to enjoy the other girls, though Heather could see she never really opened up. She never revealed who she was deep down around them; Lucy saved that for when they were alone. Heather liked the real Lucy much more than the one she put forward around strangers. That side of her was sharp and funny but also dangerous in some way. The night before Stephen arrived home, Heather went to bed early. Lucy was on another date with the bartender from the bar in OB they had been frequenting. She took a long bath, listening to music. Candles burned around the tub as she prayed. After her soak, she got out of the bath and climbed into bed. She prayed for Stephen's safety and for his eyes to be opened. While talking with Shelly, she decided not to be aggressive with him about her newfound belief.

Heather closed her eyes and was soon asleep. She could smell the ocean and other fragrant smells. She opened her eyes to a beautiful light. Everything was bright and clean. She felt sand beneath her feet now, soft and cool. As well, the sun shone down golden. It was like no light she had ever seen. As she breathed in, the air filling her lungs was pure energy, filling her with power and joy. The feeling she could fly overwhelmed her like a new sense.

A beautiful young woman was now standing beside her. She had blonde hair and impressive eyes. The place was so bright that everything seemed to have a truer color, like walking out of an office with poor lighting and seeing the color of her dress more radiant in the sunlight. The girl smiled at her and touched her shoulder. Heather looked down, and now she was wearing a beautiful white dress, almost like the one she bought for her wedding, light and soft. Heather looked to her right and saw that she was on the edge of a beach, though she did not hear waves crashing. There was water, though, and the white sand under her feet felt like beach sand. Off in the distance, about one hundred yards away, was a towering waterfall. The next moment she was beneath it, its flow plunging into a beautiful lake that led toward the beach. The water was breathing its gentle waves on the sands. There was a man next to the young woman now. He looked at the woman, who nodded and then walked away.

Heather smiled at the woman and then turned to see the man was gone.

I like this dream a lot better than my last.

"I don't blame you," the young blonde said. Heather was startled by this.

"Did I say that aloud?"

"No, but your thoughts are just like speaking to me," answered the girl.

"Who... are you…where am I?" asked Heather.

The young woman's eyes were gentle. "My name is Sarakiel, but you may call me Sarah if you like."

I thought angels were male….

Sarakiel smiled again. "We do not have such divisions in heaven, though some are of greater stature than others. I accepted a female role to complement humanity's expectations. That and human females are inspiring to me."

Heather looked at the angel. She was clearly female though her features left room for anything. "You are beautiful." She finally said.

"Thank you. I am blessed by our Father." The angel answered.

"Is this Heaven?" Heather asked.

"This is as much of heaven as you can touch in your present state. The rest is much more spectacular."

"My state?" Heather asked.

"Yes, your fallen state. In this body." She pinched Heather's arm, giving her another perfect smile. A beautiful boy was playing at the edge of the water now with two other children, and he turned and waved.

"Hi, Mommy," he called before running down the beach with his friends.

"Is that your child?" Heather asked.

"No, Sweetie, he is yours."

Heather followed the child running down the beach. He was beautiful and happy.

"But I am not ye—"

"Heather, time is only relative to you, not Father or to any of us here."

Heather was trying to add up what all this meant, knowing there was something important about what she had just seen, but it was all too overwhelming for her, so she sat.

She looked around and found herself in her loft, only whiter, brighter, softer. She found Sarakiel standing beside her again. "In this place, your only limit is in your mind, as is the case in your own world also, to be honest. But here, it is much easier to control."

"Are you telling me that I am controlling all of this?" Heather asked.

Sarakiel nodded, still smiling. "I love this part most of all."

"What part is that?" Heather asked.

"Introducing people to paradise."

Heather's mouth was wide. "Am I dead?" she said, her voice peaking.

"No, but I want you to realize that the world you live in, the place you believe to be reality, is not. Your life will not truly begin until you pass from that place, and now, you are guaranteed a place here with us."

"What about Stephen? Where is he? Why can't I sense him like I do the boy?"

Sarakiel's expression betrayed her own concern, and this quickened Heather's heart.

"His future is still uncertain."

"But you said time is not relative here. Why do I see my unborn son and not him?" her voice lifting in panic.

"Heather, because he may not ever come here... Father wants him to come to us, but he is caught in darkness and in the hands of the destroyer. I am afraid that only through great loss will he be willing to turn to God, and even then, he may still reject the truth."

Great loss.... Heather pondered the words. "Is there anything I can do?"

"Seek God's guidance. He loves him and wants to help too."

"I know in my heart that if I push him too hard, he will only reject it more. I don't know how I know this, but I do."

"That is the wisdom of our Father's spirit in you. Many things will begin to be opened to you now. It is different for everyone. Father pays special attention to those who will have a major impact on His plans for humanity, which is why you are here."

"I will have an impact on humanity... How?"

"I do not know the answer to that question, but I know Father uses little things in big ways. You may only affect one person, but that person may play a major role in the future of millions."

Heather looked at her intently. “I seem to recall that those God pays special attention to also have short life spans.”

“This is true, but remember, this life you hold so dear... It is not real.”

“I don’t feel comforted by those words, Sarah.”

“Think of your life, now on earth, as being in the womb. You are alive but not really living yet; you are being prepared in the womb for a better one once you are born.” Sarakiel smiled and took her hand. “You will see, trust me. For now, just focus on enjoying the new life that you now share with Father, and know you have a future.”

They were now on another beach, this one loud with crashing waves, and Heather looked all around. All kinds of people were around; some waded into the water, and others lay on the sand. Everyone was happy. She looked up and saw a cliff over the beach. It was green and beautiful. There were opulent buildings built all across it, and they looked like they were made of Pearl and other fantastic building materials she could not describe.

She had never imagined structures so impressive in her wildest dreams as an architect. Her heart started pounding, and she felt overwhelmed by it all. Heather looked back to Sarakiel, but she was gone. The beach was gone too. She turned back to the cliff, but it was now a white wall. Everything was now whiteness. She called out but only heard her own voice echo back to her. She closed her eyes and thought of the beach and opened them again, but still, she was in a white space. She tried again, thinking of home, and the light diminished outside her closed eyelids.

When she opened them, she was looking at her bedroom ceiling. She was home. She looked around her room, which was just beginning to come to life with the first rays of sunlight from outside. She was warm under her covers and felt rested. Felix was asleep on the foot of her bed. Heather sat up and sighed. There was so much running through her mind, but she had to set it aside and begin her day.

After eating some breakfast, she sat by the window in the great room and read for a few minutes. She finished her cup of coffee, took a shower, and got ready for work. Still, the words continued to roll around in her mind.

Lucy had not come out to greet her as she usually did, and Heather peeked into the hall of the guest area. Her door was open, so Heather looked in. Lucy was sprawled out facedown, in her underwear. She closed the door and wrote Lucy a note before leaving for work. All day, she was overwhelmed by the dreams, trying to make sense of them, and figure out what everything meant. Seeing her son pulled at her the most, why did this cause her alarm?

'Your only limit is your mind.' 'His future is still uncertain.'

Heather was alone in her office and went to her door and shut it. She sat in her chair and prayed until there was a knock.

"Come in," she called.

The door opened, and Peter walked in. She smiled, so glad to see him, getting up and hugging him.

"I was hoping to catch you for lunch," he said.

"Um ... sure, that would be great; I'll call Lucy and let her know you'll be joining us." Peter looked at her uncomfortably, and she recognized his dilemma.

"Oh, yeah, sure...I'll let her know I have other plans. It's no biggy."

The two went out to lunch and talked, Peter, telling his story about the road and Heather hers. Peter came over and hugged her when she told him about her change of mind; however, their moods darkened when the subject turned to her dreams and his brush with the beasts on the road.

"I honestly believe God saved me on that road, Heather."

"It sounds as terrifying as my dream."

The two discussed the possibilities for what was going on and agreed that something evil was surrounding them.

"The damage to my car is very real, and clearly, dreams and reality are thinly veiled."

"And Leroy? That death was no dream," She replied.

Heather began to cry. Peter got the check and drove them both down to the docks. They made a plan to keep what they thought between the two of them until they knew more. Peter thought it dangerous to share everything with Shelly, not wanting to involve her. He believed that Leroy died because of something he found out. After hearing Heather's account of the angel talking about Stephen, he shared what he knew about Stephen's dreams.

"It is clear they are God's attempt to help him. Maybe you should share your dreams with him too."

Heather looked at him with concern, her brow tightening as she sat on the dock box next to her boat. "I am going to tell him I found God, but not push. I'll let him lead that conversation, but I don't know if I should share the rest."

Peter thought about this for a moment. He leaned against the bow of Serenity, then his expression sharpened. "Let God lead you in that, too, though. I think your sharing might make him feel better about his own dreams. Maybe he will feel safe to let you in. He doesn't want to worry you, but if he knows you are having them, too, there will be no reason to hold back."

"Good point, Hun. I'll consider it," she said.

"I only have one other question." He looked at her tentatively.

"What, Peter? We can't keep anything from each other."

He nodded, letting go of what ever held his tongue, "Have to ask... Do you think Charles or Lucy have anything to do with all of this?"

Heather was surprised by the question but thought hard. "I really don't know, Peter. I mean, Lucy has become a close friend, and I can't see her wanting to hurt either of us..."

Heather was silent for a moment, looking at the dock. Peter said nothing more.

She looked up, an idea in her eyes. "I do feel there is something dark looming around Lucy, but I don't think she is a knowing participant."

Peter looked out at the marina, pondering everything. He walked to the end of the slip and turned around. "I agree... I get the same feeling about her, but what about Charles?"

***

Stephen arrived in San Diego around sunset and was dropped off at home. When he got in the door, it was quiet, most of the lights were off, and the reddening light outside was filling the loft. He could hear music playing in his bedroom and followed it into their bathroom, where she was getting ready to take a bath. Candles were lit, and the tub was filling with bubbly water. Heather had her back to him. He came in and kissed her on the neck. She stood there looking at them both in the mirror, her arms crossed over her naked chest.

"Hey, Sexy," he said, kissing his way down her neck to her shoulder.

"Hey, Stranger." She loved him with her eyes. They were full of emotion."

"You okay, Love?"

"Never better, Baby." She looked down at her naked belly putting her hand there, and his followed. "You want me to join you?" he whispered.

"That's okay, Honey. I'm going to soak for a while, okay?"

"Okay, I'll go unpack."

She turned, embracing him. Her hold was iron. She released him, putting both her hands on his face, and kissed him. "I love you." She said, looking deep into the man.

"And I you." Stephen left the bathroom and started to go through his baggage, stealing looks at her as she got into the tub. He threw his laundry in the hamper and went to the great room. Lucy was coming in as he sat down at the bar with a beer.

"Well, hey there, Rock star, I didn't know you were back." She stopped at the island, looking at him with a buzzed look.

"You look like you've been having some fun," he said.

"Yeah, a little. Nothing too exciting. How was your trip?"

"Amazing. I can't wait to go again with you and Heather."

"Heather and *me,* huh? You're inviting me to take a trip to my home?" She winked at him and sauntered over to the pool table. "Want to play a game of pool? I've gotten much better since we last played."

Stephen got up, taking a swig of his beer. "Sure."

Heather let everything go, just melting away in the hot water. The music was soothing and made her tired. After a long soak, she got out and toweled off. She returned to the bedroom, drying her hair. The stereo was on in the great room, and she could hear laughter. She pulled on some shorts and a shirt and then sat at her dressing table, brushing her hair. Lucy let out a scream of laughter in the other room, and Heather went to the door, opening it. Stephen was chasing Lucy around the table. He tackled and pinned her to the floor. Lucy laughed hysterically, holding on to the cue ball for dear life.

"I GET A RE-DO!" she screamed as he pried the ball from her hand.

"No do-overs. You took your turn." Stephen answered, getting up.

"NO!" she shrieked as he placed it on the table, shooting before she could reach him. At that moment, they both realized Heather was there.

"I'm sorry, Heather; I didn't mean to be so loud." Lucy apologized.

Stephen just shrugged and smiled at her. "I win." He finished as he laid the cue stick on the table. He walked to Heather and pulled her against him, kissing her.

"What—ever, d-u-d-e." Lucy Drawled.

The doorbell rang, and Lucy got up. "That's for me. You two go have fun." She strutted to the door and answered it. It was the bartender she had been seeing. Lucy looked back at the couple and gave them a drunken smile, head tilted to one side and eyes closed.

"I'm going to bed, Luce. I'll see you in the morning?" Heather said.

Lucy put a hand, up her gestures exaggerated, and waved. "Yep."

Heather and Stephen closed their door and looked at each other.

"She's a happy drunk, isn't she?" he asked.

"She is, and she's been a comfort to me while you were away. I missed you."

Heather put her arms around his waist and hugged him. He held her there for a moment enjoying the presence of his lover. "I've missed you too. I never sleep well when we're apart."

Heather pulled away and went to the bed, sitting on the edge. She looked at him with a content look. "I'm going to take a quick shower. Will you wait for me?"

She nodded, keeping his eyes as he walked towards the door. Stephen was in and out and soon climbing into bed next to her. He pulled her close and started to kiss her neck. She wanted to talk to him about everything but was waiting for him to ask. It was obvious he didn't want to talk, so she rolled over and straddled him. They made love, this time more intimate for her. She put all of her love into being with him. Really loving him.

Afterward, they lay there quiet. He caressed her and held onto her. She rolled over and looked into his eyes.

"So, how was your time with Shelly?" He finally asked.

"It was great. She's really helped me understand things."

There it is. The door opened. He has to ask now.

He smiled at her and closed his eyes.

Really? She was frustrated but kept her cool. She kissed him on the nose and rolled over.

"So that's it? You're giving up that easy?" he asked.

She rolled back over and looked at him with irritation. "What do you mean?"

"Love, I can tell when you have something important on your mind, and I saw it the moment I walked into the bathroom. Talk to me."

She was so annoyed with him. She closed her eyes and ignored him.

"Okay... What are the things you have come to realize?" he asked softly, kissing her neck.

"You obviously are not interested, and I'm not playing games with you."

"Honey, I wasn't playing a game; I just know it's best to let you share when you're ready."

She was silent. "I'm sorry. I really want to hear about whatever's on your heart."

"Really?" she asked, looking back at him.

"Yes, really, tell me all about it. I love when you share important things with me."

She smiled. "Okay."

***

The next several weeks flew by like a storm, not slowing until just days before the wedding rehearsal. Leroy's funeral the only break in the fast pace for them all. And pushed Stephen further away from the topic of God.

Stephen had been traveling off and on with Charles and ideas Charles had always leaned in one direction, which bothered Stephen, but he did not voice his concern as much as make an effort to seek other perspectives on materials they discovered. What was so remarkable to him was that as they researched ancient stories and mythological lore, one idea began to take shape in his mind: Everything was connected.

Every ancient story about gods riding lightning, great catastrophes, superhumans, star people, devils, or angels was all connected. They all had a root, or beginning, in the Dead Sea Scrolls, Greek Septuagint, or other supporting documents. Even writings not considered the inspired word of God, like the book of Enoch, and Josephus, either supported Biblical roots or were derived from them. There was nothing that Stephen explored that could not be explained by Biblical texts. He found that the evidence pointed to the same story being told by many civilizations, and all pointed in one direction.

Moreover, they honored either Lucifer or Yahweh. Although the names were often different, the individual was always the same. Like a criminal profiler searching for his killer, Stephen discovered that the beings being feared, honored, or worshiped always seemed to be either one or the other. Everything led back to them. The Zodiac was originally Hebrew signs for their holy days and events like the birth of Christ. Virgo being the sign for the virgin, which was the constellation in the sky in September when Jesus was born.

Stephen was astonished to find modern science verifying that there was a supernova viewable in the sky at that time, which some think might have been what prompted the wise men that the messiah was born. Stephen flew to Idaho to meet with Chuck Missler and two PHDs who had a plethora of information for him to analyze. He realized it would take him months to work through his notes and probably years before he fully understood most of it. They talked about Mars being in a different orbit, which carried it much closer to earth in those days, and showed him other ancient civilizations who worshiped Mars as a god they could see in the sky. This kind of data only supporting events in the Bible involving extreme gravitational forces in Joshua's and Hezekiah's time.

He was shown text in the Bible where the lineage of Noah was listed and where one of the sons was born during the time of the 'great movement.' This being the separation of the continents from Pangea to what we know today. He was overwhelmed and excited about all the information he had gathered. He knew with it, he had the makings of not one book but maybe four.

Stephen had closure in one aspect of his questioning mind. It is either Yahweh, the Jehovah of Christianity, or Lucifer the son of the morning. They are real, and all the other ideas out there are images of these two. He could rest in the fact that he believed there were higher powers, and this was a step in the right direction. He felt he was ready to consider that the God of his father and mother was the true god, but something stopped him from taking the next step in that direction. A stubbornness refused he accept and anger at any power that would allow Leroy's murder.

Stephen had hours of notes and microcassettes to review, as well as mounds of photos piled high on his desk. He had set it aside once home, but his mind was swimming in all of it, even as he helped his future bride choose table décor.

Heather finished her projects with her architectural firm and was wrapping up Lucy's remodel. Things were so hectic that the couple could barely catch up on anything intimate between them. There was always something keeping them from true closeness. They both felt it and longed for some time alone, so they ran away from everything, vowing at least 24 hours of intimacy to catch their breath. The couple ended up renting a hotel room just a few miles from home, leaving all avenues of outside communication behind.

There was a simple note on the countertop in the loft stating that they were gone until the upcoming Monday, with no reason why. Everyone understood, and

Lucy even took charge when pressing matters came up.

Heather and Stephen lay in their hotel room bed, looking out at San Diego Bay.

"I needed this, Babe," she whispered.

"Me too, Love," he said in her ear before giving it a tender kiss.

"I don't care if the cake comes from Von—"

He placed a finger on her lips, hushing her. "Rules, Love."

She smiled. "We have to check out in a few hours. What should we do?"

He rolled her over with a mischievous smile and tickled her. She screamed and then giggled. He stopped and looked into her eyes. These moments lasted forever, memorizing each other, absorbing every detail of the other. The two preparing for a future together. She finally broke his stare by smiling.

"What?" he asked.

She didn't answer. The smile implied, 'I know something you don't know.'

"What," he repeated.

His fingertips pressing against her ribs, causing her to tighten in defense. She relented, not wanting what his fingers promised.

"Don't! You'll make me pee, Stephen."

"We have ways of making you talk." He said in a mock-Nazi-officer accent. "Talk, Fräulein."

"I know what you meant to say is Frau, Dearest."

"Yes, apologies, Frau Swan. What were you going to say?"

"Well, Mr. Fritz, I was just thinking that you may have set yourself up for failure by taking me away like this." One side of her mouth climbed slyly.

"Oh, yeah. How is that, princess?" He laid down beside her.

"Well, how do you plan on topping this on our Honeymoon?"

He laughed. "Don't worry, Heather. I still have some tricks in my bag, have faith."

He pulled her close to him, kissing her behind the ear. She closed her eyes, relaxing in his embrace. His last word echoing in her mind.

Faith.

As they got ready to leave, Heather looked at him in the mirror and caught his gaze. He smiled as he closed their luggage.

"I do, you know," not taking her eyes from his.

"You do what?" he asked, walking over to her and pulling her against him.

She looked down at his hands, now resting on her stomach, placing hers upon them.

"Have faith."

"Good, I'm glad," he responded.

"No, not that Babe…I mean, yes, I *do* have faith in you, in us, but that's not what I am talking about. I found Him. I have faith in God."

Their eyes met again in the mirror. "Is this something you need to talk about before the wedding?" He asked, calm on his face, though she thought there was something else there too. *Irritation?*

Maybe not, but she was sure he didn't want to have this conversation, just like the last attempt, which was politely accepted but not considered.

"We can if you need to, Love," he finished. Her eyes fell once again to their interlaced hands on her belly.

"No, not if it doesn't interest you."

"If it's important to you, it interests me, Love," he answered. She looked back at him, her eyes full, her expression revealing her love for him.

"I just want you to know He is real, and I accepted Him into my life."

"Who, God?" he asked.

She nodded. "Yes. Jesus. It's all real, Babe, and I want you to see the truth…when you're ready."

"After Leroy, I'm not feeling wonderful about any god right now…I'll consider it. I already promised you that."

"Okay."

Rehearsals

Heather was running around, getting ready for the rehearsal dinner. The group of girlfriends had commandeered the master bedroom, and Stephen was sitting at the bar with a glass of wine when Peter arrived. The two men sat quietly, looking out the window at the city now splashed in orange and purple hues from the setting sun.

"You've been scarce as of late. Everything okay, Pete?" Stephen asked.

"I've had some things going on, but I'm good. You know me, Man. God always has my back."

"Well, I'm glad Lucy has you as her date tonight. I couldn't stand that bartender she was toying with."

Peter's surprise was not well hidden, though he made great effort not to show it. Stephen caught it. "I thought you knew…..I don't think it was anything serious."

"Lucy is free to see whomever she pleases, Bro. We're just friends," Peter answered with more emotion than he intended.

"I'm just say'n, Bro."

"Saying what, boys?" came Lucy's voice as she entered the lounge. She was devastatingly gorgeous, and both men froze, jaws unhinged. Lucy smiled, pleased with their reaction. She was wearing a diaphanous silk dress, which was so light it almost floated with her rather than hanging on to her well-sculpted figure. She bore minimal makeup as usual. Both girls rarely wore much makeup. Tonight though, she did have a light shading of peach around her eyes, which complimented the dress. Lucy's lips were also luscious, and her hair was drawn in small braids along the sides of her face, which rolled up and vanished into the long flow of hair down her back.

Princess Leah's got nothing on you, girl. Stephen thought.

Her dress ended a few inches above her knees, dancing there as she moved, revealing a little thigh with each stride. As the two men finished their assessment, a second set of heels joined Lucy's. These ones a baby blue. Stephen followed them up his fiancé's legs, which ended with her million-dollar smile.

"I see they approve," Heather said.

Lucy replied, but Stephen didn't hear it because he was imprisoned in the sight of Heather.

She was made up just like Lucy, Heather, a baby blue version of Lucy. Her hair was the same also, save for little white flowers throughout hers. She broke his heart. A vision that he would carry in his mind until the day he died.

"I love you," Stephen said in a dreamer's voice.

The two girls laughed, which helped break the spell which robbed him of all eloquence. Heather walked up to Stephen, and he reached for her hand.

"You look amazing." He managed.

Lucy was greeting Peter, who himself was at a loss. The other girls came out and joined them. Peter took Lucy's hand and looked at her with a smile. She looked at his hand holding hers, a little foreign to the idea of him doing so, but was pleased with his fortitude, all the same. The group of friends got into two cars and left for the rehearsal, which was held at the same place as the engagement party. The place was full of the beautiful and wealthy. Heather had massed many influential friends in her business dealings. Most of southern California's finer restaurants and nightclubs bore her artistic touch.

Charles was there for most of the evening and graciously agreed to stand in for Leroy, giving away the bride. Heather made a shocking announcement, trying gently to replace her maid of honor, Kimberly, for Lucy. This became an emotional moment that most of the men tried to back away from. In the end, she compromised and made them both maids of honor, though Lucy stood closest to the bride and would walk first with Stephen's best man, Peter, as her escort. Heather had tried to explain that it was more about the flow of the wedding, wanting Peter and Lucy to come together. Still, a small rumor floated from table to table, consisting of details about Kimberly stepping over the line with Stephen a few times at the engagement party. Stephen was oblivious to all of it by choice and stayed out of girl business as often as possible.

He noticed how well Heather took the situation in hand and calmly brought it to a peaceful resolution. She was amazing like that. Such a peaceful creature, always a blessing, rarely the problem. He pictured her as the mother of their children dealing with difficulties and smiled.

"You're going to be a wonderful mother." He whispered to her when it was finished.

Music came to life, and people mingled after the meal. He watched her move about the room, pleased. She was like an angel. His brow furloughed as he noticed something. Tonight, he saw more. She had an even greater radiance, somehow. Something new. She was pregnant, and this a significant moment in her life, but there was even more. A grace which carried wisdom as well as beauty. She caught his gaze, and he smiled.

There is more to you, isn't there? He thought. *You have found something. I can almost—"*

"She is beautiful, isn't she?" Lucy said, giving him a start.

"It's faith," he blurted out before thinking.

Lucy gave him a funny look. "Faith?" She asked.

"I'm sorry, you caught me in mid-thought…Yes, she looks amazing…You both do."

She blushed slightly. "Thank you, Stephen. She was the one who wanted us to dress alike tonight."

She gave him a probing look, wondering if he was following her, knowing he was not. She pulled up on the edge of her dress and touched one of her braids.

"Oh, yes, of course," he offered, still half in his last thoughts. A moment passed with them both silent, watching the crowd.

"I think it was a sweet thought. You both look lovely." He said.

"She asked me if she could consider me her sister today…" Lucy's voice fought emotion. It was clear what this declaration from Heather meant to her.

He held one of her hands in his own, looked at her for a moment, and then leaned over and kissed her on the cheek. She tried to hide the shock and inner joy this gesture brought her, moving her eyes forward. He pondered the beautiful woman sitting next to him, so much a mystery and, in other ways, an open book. She held so much strength and fierceness, which could be focused on defeating the strongest of foes, yet a delicate girl seemed to have grown up within her with a great need. He put his arm around her and pulled her closer.

"We're both glad you are in our lives. We love our own deeply, and you will always feel this with us as your family."

He turned from Lucy in time to see Heather approaching, her smile large. She was in her element. She touched Lucy's elbow as she passed on her way to her place at Stephen's other side.

"It's perfect, Hun." She kissed him.

"I'm glad you're happy, Love."

Lucy squeezed his hand as she got up and faced them both. "Tonight is perfect. I am going to mingle. Do you need anything?"

The couple looked at each other and then shook their heads. Lucy left them to enjoy the evening.

"You ready for the real thing, Sweetheart?" he asked.

She leaned against him. "More than ready."

A new song came on that was an obvious favorite among most of the women because they flooded the dance floor, some pulling their dates out of chairs or away from conversations.

Stephen looked at Heather, who gave him a half shake of her head, still against him. He could see the mother growing in her. "So… faith…huh?" he said, looking at her.

She smiled, still clinging to him, so beautiful. "Yep."

"Well, I want to know what gave you this new faith."

"Really?" she answered, brightening.

"Yep," he said, "tell me about Him."

She turned and faced him, her arms around him. "Love," she said, looking into his eyes.

"Love?" he asked.

"Yeah, He is love. Love like you, and I have, but far greater."

"Hey, Heather," one of the girls called. She was holding a phone.

"I'll be right back; hold that thought, Babe."

"Okay," Stephen said.

As Heather walked away, he noticed Charles leaving and stop by the door. The man waved. Stephen waved back. Lucy caught up with her father and appeared to argue with him about something for a moment, but then nodded and gave him a hug goodbye. She came up to Stephen and stopped. "I have to go. Daddy has a business friend at the airport I must go meet to pick up a package, and he can't go. Will you still be around in, say, an hour, or should I just head home?"

"I'm ready to go now, so I'd say go home."

"What about cleanup. Do you need any help?" Lucy asked.

"No, we have people to do that, and Peter and I can handle the rest."

"Okay. Tell Heather I'm sorry, and I'll see her at home."

"I will," Stephen answered.

Lucy grabbed her purse and pulled a shawl over her as she walked out the door.

A few moments later, Heather returned with a stressed look.

"What's wrong," Stephen asked.

"I told you we should have just settled for a store cake, Babe. Have you seen Lucy?"

"She just left for the airport." He answered.

"Damn," she said. "I have to run, Babe. I'll be back in 30 tops, okay?"

Stephen grew worried, "what's wrong?"

"It's the cake. Listen, if Lucy comes back before me, tell her I'm going to borrow her walk-in cooler, okay?"

He nodded, still a little confused. She grabbed her keys and shawl, kissed him on the corner of his mouth, and wiped the lipstick off his mouth.

"I'll go with you," he demanded.

No. no, Babe, it's no big deal. Keep everyone happy. I'll be back in time for our goodbyes."

"You sure?" He asked, uncertain.

"Yeah, Hun, all I have to do is open the door at Lucy's. I'll be back in a flash."

Stephen started to follow her, not wanting her to leave.

"Babe," she said, looking back from the door. He stopped, almost as if her tone implied the command.

"I love you," she said, blowing him a kiss.

A loud sound came from the crowd, 'oohing' the night's first fallen soldier. One of his college buddies took a spill, the booze shuffle failing him. Stephen went to intervene.

He helped the poor guy off the dance floor, grabbing a bottle of water from a waitress as he escorted him to the tables. He spotted Heather's other maid of honor, Kimberly, at one of the tables and smiled. "Hey, Rob, have I introduced you to Heather's maid of honor, Kimberly?"

As his friend was safely sitting, he handed him the water bottle. Rob looked at it, bemused as if he had never seen one before. Stephen looked back at the door. "Kimberly, this is Rob. Rob, Kimberly."

As Rob opened his mouth to say something stupid to the girl, Stephen left them and headed for the door. His phone rang, and he answered.

"Baby, hey, I caught Lucy in the parking lot. Her car's acting strange. Lights come on, but it won't start. Can you or Peter check it out? The keys are in the ignition. We're going to run to her house, then she'll drop me off and take my car to meet her dad's friend, okay?"

"Okay, I'll go check it out. Be safe."

"I will, Baby. Love you."

"I Love you too, Honey." Stephen returned the phone to his pocket and walked out to the parking lot. The black Mercedes was sitting there, dome light still on. He got in and tried the ignition.

Nothing.

Peter came up to the car, giving him a start.

"What's going on? Where's Lucy?" He asked. Stephen climbed out of the car. "With Heather, dealing with the cake."

He leaned against the back quarter panel. "Lucy's car won't start."

Peter sat in the driver's seat and tried it again, nothing.

"It has power; the lights aren't dim at all," Peter said. He moved the shifter back and forth, making sure it was in park, and tried once more. The engine turned over and purred like a precision machine. Peter looked out at Stephen and then shut it back off. He got out of the car and pocketed the keys. The two men walked back to the hall.

"You want to help me get Rob into a cab?" Stephen asked.

"Sure, and people say I'm the party pooper. At least you don't have to worry me about me vomiting all over the place."

Stephen put his arm around his shoulder as they walked back. "True dat, Bro, true dat."

"That and you have some other qualities that make you worth keeping around."

Peter tried to pull away, but Stephen turned his hug into a headlock as the two horsed around, sparring in front of the dining hall.

Angels in Waiting

In the shadows surrounding the parking lot, surreal shapes landed all around. One stepped out, placing its hand on the hood of Lucy's Mercedes. Two others joined it. They were fallen ones. Three heavenly host descended, facing them. Arphax and Sarakiel among them. Two more fallen ones emerge from the other end of the parking lot, followed by six more. It was becoming crowded.

"Your treachery tonight seems obvious, but there will be none here," said Phanuel emerging from behind the first fallen with four more holy Angels at his side.

"You are outnumbered, brother. How would you stop us if harm was our intent?" said Samyazal.

BOOM, BOOM, BOOM. Angels, both dark and light, slammed to the ground all around. Time seemed to freeze in a one-mile area around them. Leaves on trees froze in place, no longer swaying in the coastal breeze and the sounds of the party and marina began first to slow like a record player on the wrong speed to total silence. With such a large gathering of the angelic, a static seemed to rise in the atmosphere, and the marine layer fell away in a clearing circle as if God himself was gazing down. Swords appeared, and all stood ready, save for Arphax and Samyazal, who only stared at one another.

"Your posturing wastes my time and Father's, for you know He will not allow—"

"He is not my father," Samyazal interrupted.

Arphax smiled. "This is clear. Enough games; what chaos are you trying to accomplish here?"

Samyazal's expression now content. "What makes you think the action is here, brother?"

Arphax looked at Sarakiel, who turned to take flight.

"Enough!" said Michael as he appeared from nowhere, surprising them all.

"This is a distraction Arphax," he finished, walking too close to Samyazal, who was forced to retreat a step. There was anxiety in his face and also rage. These two had stood toe-to-toe before, and it was apparent Samyazal fared the worst in that experience. Sarakiel took flight but returned on Michael's command. "No, they are not alone." He called to her.

She returned, "They?"

"The Lord is with Heather and the other," Michael answered.

All the fallen had fear cross their faces.

"This matter, tonight, is being decided by other hands. There will be no angelic touch. It is Father's will." He stared at Samyazal with deadly exactness, locking him in place with it as he circled the evil leader. Michael was towering over them all; the greatest Angel present. He looked at Arphax and Sarakiel. "You have done all that you can." He looked back at the fallen, now gathered together.

"These dark ones would have the life of Peter as soon as you took flight, and that is not Father's will. Not here. Not tonight."

Sarakiel approached Michael. "Will Father protect her from harm?"

"One of them is meant to do much. The other, I have no answer. I know that all she loves or prays for is here in this place. Her prayers are for him, not herself."

íroas

"I do not fear Satan half so much as I fear those who fear him."
—Saint Teresa of Avila

Heather pulled into the driveway of Lucy's new home as Lucy clicked her garage door opener. Heather put the car in park and got out. "I'll just be a minute."

Lucy climbed over to the driver's seat and then turned the radio to a rock station. Metallica came blasting through the open window, and Heather looked back. Lucy gave her a mock-head-bang, and Heather laughed as she entered the code at the door going into the house.

Charles had commissioned a large walk-in cooler for 'sensitives,' he had called them. And though its intended use was for cold storage, it was capable of temperatures as low as 32°F. Heather's plan was to lower its temperature setting so it would be cold enough to store their wedding cake, which needed a new home because of an equipment malfunction at the cake shop.

She adjusted the gauge and opened the door to see inside just as the fans spun to life. She pulled a table into the walk-in for the cake company to set it on when they arrived. As she shut the door, she felt the presence of someone else nearby, but her eyes were still adjusting to the darkness after closing the walk-in door.

Why didn't I turn on a light?

There were two others in this place with her. She could hear their breathing, and one sounded charged.

Heather turned for the hall and her only exit, but it was too late; he grabbed her. A hand covered her mouth, the other around her chest and arms, now rising to free her mouth to scream. His breath was hot on her neck.

"You're a looker now, aren't you, Bitch?" He said with lust in his voice.

Metallica still belched into the doorway from outside.

"Why would anyone want to do in such a fine piece?"

She struggled and stomped his foot, but the other presence caught her second kick. The heavy breather now had one ankle and finally caught her other, holding her legs out as she squirmed.

A muffled cry came out as they carried her toward the back of the dark storage area. Heather was terrified; they were too strong for her. She tried to get free but couldn't.

Heather screamed under her powerful assailant's hand, then bit hard, causing his release for a moment.

"Please don't. Please. I'm pregn—" SLAP!

The one she had bitten caught her across the mouth.

"Hold her," the one holding her ankles said.

She was crying now. *Not like this God, please.*

The breather put his hands around her neck and squeezed, things turning red in her vision.

A loud clang reverberated as Heather felt her assailant's fingers loosen, then release.

"You want some too, Tough Guy!," Lucy screamed as she swung the fire extinguisher again, this time at the face of the other. It clipped him in the nose, breaking it, and sent him falling.

Heather had opened her tear-filled eyes just after the sound of the canister hitting heavy breather in the head. He was laid out but still conscious. Heather scrambled backward, pulling her dress down as she gained a view of the situation.

Lucy was at the end of a full swing, and both men were floored but moving. She clambered to her knees as Lucy screamed, "RUN! Heather, now!"

Heather got to her feet and started to run as Lucy delivered a roundhouse kick to the head of bloody nose. If it had connected, it would have been lights out; instead, he had gotten up, taking the brunt of the kick in his neck and shoulder.

"Run," she screamed again.

Heather obeyed, thinking about her phone in the car. As she reached the door, she looked back to see the breather clamp onto Lucy from behind and squeeze. Bloody nose was coming at her with a fist aimed for her head.

Heather froze, not able to leave her friend. Lucy kicked up, sending her and the breather backward into a wall, and at the same time, pulled the pin and trigger on the fire extinguisher. The cloud enveloped bloody nose first and then the room in a choking cloud. Heather looked at the door and remembered the alarm mounted there. She hit the panic button, but there was no siren sound. The bleeder connected a hook to the side of Lucy's temple, sending her and the breather down. He yelled, "Get the other one!"

Lucy rolled away from him, but he kicked her in the ribs, causing shooting pain. Breather got to his feet and ran after Heather, who had vanished into the garage.

Lucy let loose an uppercut, aiming for the bleeder's precious place, unfortunately, landing it in his gut with less effect. Her side hurt with this action, but before she could plan her next move, he swung her in a half circle towards another wall. Her head made first contact, sending stars before her eyes, followed by blackness.

***

Heather ran for her car and was about a foot from her open door. Time also seemed to slow as she saw him, her killer from the dream.

At first, his eyes appeared evil, like the dream. She also thought she heard him say, "where you think you're going, Bitch?" She froze as he raised the gun just like he did in her dream. The next moment orange flame surrounded by a black cloud erupted from the barrel.

This is it.

Time seemed to slowly come back to life as the gun fired, and she saw his face clearly. It wasn't evil; she saw benevolence in his worn expression now. It was also fatigue as if he had just run the longest marathon of his life. And he had not spoken at all. Those words came from behind her.

She felt the air change near her left ear as the bullet shot by her at impossible speed. She turned to see the heavy breather spin around violently from the impacting round. She remembered the dream. Where God said he wanted to help the man, the one he removed the demons from, and it seemed He really had. She turned, falling, but he caught her in his arms.

"You're okay," he said.

He brought her to her car and sat her in the driver's seat.

"Lucy!" Heather whispered there is another—"

POP.POP.POP.

Three shots rang out from the garage, their flashes lighting up the darkness. Mitch ducked, the first shot hitting him in his upper chest, and red blossomed near his left clavicle. The second and third shots hit the driver's door and window, sending shattered glass all over the ground and on Heather. Mitch looked at Heather for a split second, but in that moment, she knew him, a battered soul who had made it through the dark. He darted to his left into the open yard, drawing fire away from the car and Heather.

The bleeder, now immerged from the dark garage, looked at his fallen partner and fired two more shots as Heather darted out, and around the back of her car, one bullet pierced the windshield and driver's seat just as she vacated it. She fell hard and felt darkness cloud her mind as her head hit the driveway.

Mitch landed on his back in a bush and unloaded his revolver. Every shot flew wildly at the second shooter, still targeting the fallen girl now sprawled out helpless in the driveway.

His gun lifted in line with her head and fired. At the same time, one of Mitch's shots hit his gun, sending the shot off course. The man seemed possessed by only one objective and now charged at her with the gun, inoperable but held up as a bludgeoning weapon. Mitch's last shot made it home, striking the man in his neck, blood erupting from the mortal wound. He dropped the gun, putting one hand to his gushing throat.

"Who are you?"

The man dropped to his knees and then on his face.

Mitch got up and was on his way to Heather when another pop came from the garage. It was the breather up again. He looked horrible, his eyes huge and visceral.

***

Stephen and Peter were talking with some of the guests who were asking about Heather when they both felt a tingle of anxiety fall over them. Peter excused them, pulling Stephen to the side. "Where did you say the girls were going?"

Stephen's face was grim. You feel it too, don't you?"

Peter nodded. "Something's wrong."

Stephen and Peter scrambled for the parking lot, sure that something was very wrong and the girls were in trouble. They jumped into Lucy's car, which again would not start. Stephen screamed in frustration when Peter spotted a couple coming out to their car and got out. They commandeered the couple's Lincoln Town Car and told them to call the police. After running two red lights and nearly taking out a taxicab on Mission Bay Drive, they crossed the San Diego River screaming into Ocean Beach.

Neither spoke. Peter prayed. Stephen ripped the car to the left and onto Nimitz Boulevard to avoid traffic. The car's tires sang as it drifted onto its new course.

He gave Peter brief glances. Stephen slammed the gas pedal even further to the floor, side swiping a parked car as the Lincoln screamed across the next corner. They were now flying up the hill to Lucy's. Stephan's grip on the wheel a vice, and Peter's the same holding the door handle, ready to spring the moment they arrived.

***

Mitch froze, looking over at Heather, who had pulled herself up against the back of her car, her legs pulled under her. She had one arm behind her, bracing herself up, and the other hand rested against her side. She looked down and then at Mitch. A red rose was forming just under her ribs. Mitch's heart cried out.

Failed.

He gave her a look to calm, and she acknowledged it. He turned to the man now directly above him on the driveway. He looked confused and angry. One arm was useless; the other held the gun. He swung it over to Heather in a gesture saying 'stay,' then back to Mitch. He aimed point-blank at Mitch's face, only 6 feet away now. He wouldn't miss. The man half smiled.

You firs—"

A loud "Clang" resounded from the impact of the fire extinguisher against the side of his head. Lucy had thrown it from the garage with everything she had left in her. It had spun upon her releasing it, and she almost cried out when it looked as if it was going to fly right past him.

She flinched as the base of the red tank came around just in time, striking the man on the jaw, breaking it. He and the extinguisher seemed to take the same flight past Heather, landing at the end of the driveway. Lucy didn't hesitate. She was on him and pummeling him with the fire extinguisher. Three good swings ended the bastard. Lucy would not have stopped if it weren't for Heather's cry for her friend. Lucy ran to her and held her in her arms.

"Oh, Honey, your hurt," She cried; the rage fading into tears.

"I'll be okay, I think," Heather said softly, holding Lucy as tight as she could. Lucy looked over at Mitch, who had just dropped, exhausted and in pain.

"Who's he," she asked, warily watching him, also eyeing the nine-millimeter that rested only a foot from her grasp. He saw this and put his hands up, letting his empty revolver hang on his finger and then fall to the lawn. Still breathing heavily, he lay back in the grass.

"He saved me, Luce. That's our host."

Lucy looked back at him again. He lifted a hand and gave an exhausted wave before letting it drop.

Lucy tried lifting Heather and winced with pain and then knelt down and just held her.

"You going to live there, Mitch?" She called over to him as she brushed some hair out of Heather's eyes.

He put up an okay sign, then. "Her?" He asked, worry in his voice.

Lucy leaned Heather against her and pulled her dress up. There was a dark wound in her side near the edge of her ribs. Blood had drenched that side of her. Lucy felt her hand around Heather's back and felt a relatively small exit wound which gave her some hope the damage may be minimal.

"I don't know. It went through, but she's lost a lot of blood."

Sirens were close now.

"Pressure on it..." Mitch mumbled before passing out.

***

The large silver Lincoln slid sideways onto the street, bouncing onto the curb—both doors flying open at once. Stephen and Peter ran to the girls. Seeing them was the last straw holding Lucy's strength, and she broke down crying, kissing Heather's quiet face. Her eyes were closed, but she squeezed Lucy in response. Her hair was wet upon her face, makeup soured a little, but she was still so beautiful. Lucy started bawling as the men reached them. Stephen and Peter were both in shock at the scene. Stephen knelt next to Heather, holding both girls, trying to see who all the blood was from. Peter came to the other side, and Lucy put out an arm, sobbing uncontrollably.

"They shot her, Peter."

Stephen pulled Heather into his lap, resting on the ground next to Lucy, who took turns sobbing to him and then Peter. At the sound of Stephen's voice, Heather's eyes opened. "Hi Babe," she said, almost like a dream.

"Hi, My Love," he said, tears in his eyes.

"I should've gone with you," he said. She put a bloody hand on his cheek, looking up at him. "It's not your fault, Honey... "Her voice small. "I'll be okay," she finished.

Lucy cried harder in Peter's arms, looking back at her.

"I tried to protect her. I tried my best." She was inconsolable.

Stephen looked at the wound and then at Peter, who looked devastated. Heather could see her reddening underwear and frowned. "Maybe I should go to the doctor, Babe," she said calmly.

"She's in shock. I'll call 911."Peter said, going to the open door.

Two police cars arrived, followed by an ambulance and a fire truck. When they were putting Heather on the stretcher, she pointed at Mitch being lifted onto his own. "He saved me, Babe."

Stephen looked at the unconscious man.

"God brought him to save you." She said, delirious now.

Stephen kissed her "to save *you* Honey, and he could've done a better job."

He looked at the man as he passed and then back at his fiancé. "You're going to be okay. Just hold on, okay?"

She nodded.

At the hospital, Lucy refused treatment, demanding to be near Heather. The three of them were allowed to go see her before her surgery. She asked for one at a time, starting with Peter and then finally with Stephen.

"You know why I'm the happiest woman in the world, Stephen?" She asked.

No, why, My Love," he said, tears falling down his cheeks.

"Because I found you, and then I found God."

Stephen kissed her.

"Take care of her, okay? She's all alone again."

"Honey, don't talk like that." He responded.

"She needs us, Babe. All she could say was, please don't leave me."

Heather's eyes were full of concern. "Listen to him also," she said, eyes focusing on his for a brief moment. Stephen couldn't understand what she meant but nodded.

"It's okay, Babe. I'm happy. I only have one more hope." She said softly.

Stephen could hear Lucy burst into new anguished sobs in the hallway as the doctor spoke to her and Peter. He knew what he was telling them. He knew the reason why they were able to visit her was that she was going to die. Stephen's eyes swelled with the misery of loss he was being forced to accept.

"What is it, Heather, Love of my life?"

"Follow me, Baby. Please… find me. Jesus wants you..." She trailed off.

Those were her last words, though she remained for a moment longer. Her beautiful eyes staring into his.

"I will follow you. I promise you this, I will follow you... and I will find you."

As his words fell out in tears, Peter and Lucy were at his side again.

Heather's lips turned up in a smile, and joy seemed to fill her eyes. This moment for his lover was without fear, and he could not fathom why. Heather's sight moved beyond him. She seemed to be looking past him, at something wondrous, until her eyes were no longer possessed by life.

Stephen fell on her sobbing, and Peter and Lucy joined him. The hospital staff left them alone for a long time. Peter prayed over his lost sister and grieving friends. Lucy was given a sedative after losing control and screaming, "Don't leave me. Please don't leave me." After that, they took her in to get checked out. The x-ray showed two fractured ribs, and the doctor treated her for a concussion.

Peter visited the room of Mitchel Falcone before returning to Lucy. The man seemed as devastated by the loss as he was but did not explain why. The only thing he told Peter was, "I failed. He wanted me to save her, and I failed."

Peter asked the injured man how he knew God wanted him to save her, but he didn't say another word after that. Lucy was released, and Peter took her to the loft and put her to bed. He offered to come back for Stephen but was refused.

"Go be with her, Pete, please. She needs someone close. Will you stay over tonight with us? Stephen asked.

Peter nodded, and they hugged. Stephen shook in his embrace, keening, dying in his friend's arms. The time finally came when Stephen had to let go of his fiancé's hand. It was the most difficult thing he ever had to do. He kissed her now cold lips, sobbing. "I'll find you…"

Stephen walked away from the room and the love of his life.

"Treat her with respect," he said to the doctor. After gathering himself, he entered Mitch's room. He stared at the man for a while before speaking.

"She died thinking you saved her; that God sent you, and you saved her..."

Silence filled the room, choking both men.

Mitch just looked back at him, disappointment on his face. Stephen could see that somehow this man had really wanted to and his own self-condemnation for failing, so he left it alone and walked back to the door.

"Maybe God could have told you sooner…"

Mitch looked at him, but before he could respond, Stephen left. It was silent again in Mitch's room. No words surfaced for him to yell back to the grieving man. He closed his eyes.

"Thank you for what you did for her," Came Stephen's voice from the doorway again. "She left this world at peace and with a smile on her precious face. You had some part in that."

Stephen turned back to the hall but stopped when the man spoke in a broken voice.

"My wife and child burned to death in our home."

Stephen leaned against the door and remained silent.

"I died when they died. Their ghosts tormenting me day and night…until meeting Heather. She awoke something bright within me."

Stephen knew the goodness Heather conveyed everywhere they went. His heart was cracking in two, robbed of such light. He held his emotions tightly now. Cold chains forming.

"Evil took hold of me and was carrying me to oblivion. I tell you this because the darkness that had me wanted me to kill her. He freed me though, and sent me to save her."

"But you failed."

"Yes…I failed."

"I don't know what you expect me to say," Stephen finally said after a moment of silence.

"Nothing…"

"You've been shot. Lost a lot of blood. You need rest, Thank—"

"No…Here." He put out a hand.

Stephen walked over to him without thinking and grabbed it.

A bright light pierced him, dropping him to his knees. His eyes were tightly shut, face strained by the pain of revelation—of another's sight.

Something From Ashes

Stephen took a taxi to the marina and got into Lucy's car. It started right away. He cried loudly. The engine purred its loyal reconcile as he wept. The fogged windows enclosed the sorrow inside. He would not survive this. He did not want to. Nothing in the world held any desire for him anymore.

"It all means nothing now," he said aloud.

"It all means nothing without you."

Follow me……….

Outside, Sarakiel descended; her eyes were sorrowful, feeling the young man's grief. Her presence there seemed to go unnoticed by him. She laid a hand on the driver's window. She was joined by Arphax next, who also placed a hand on the car in loving counsel. Soon a dozen angels surrounded the car with the broken man inside, all with hands out in prayer. God's love surrounded Stephen as he died inside the Mercedes-Benz.

Lucy and Peter were asleep on the couches in the great room by the time Stephen came in. He thought how one might not call these first few hours for the grieved sleep. Nor did he feel they would sleep soundly for a long time to come. The sky was a beautiful blue when he came in, and the others woke upon his keys hitting the counter. Lucy ran to him, falling on him, fresh tears flowing again. Her touch seemed to be all that was needed to ignite fresh flow of his own, holding her in the entryway. Peter joined them, putting his arms about them both. After a few minutes, he calmly coaxed them into Lucy's bedroom and then to the bed.

Stephen, still in his bloodied, shirt and slacks, faced the window; his stare fixated on the blue morning that seemed to merge with images of Heather in her baby blue dress. Lucy cuddled behind him, one arm under Stephen and wrapped around his chest, holding him tight. Lucy's other arm, draped behind her, held desperately to Peter to enclose her other side. Eventually, the three fell asleep, tears drying on their faces.

Stephen dreamt of Heather all morning, all the memories that were the dearest at first. The last was different, though, like a new memory. He had awoken someplace strange but beautiful, and she had found him. She was wearing the same blue dress, her hair the same as well. She was even more beautiful than he ever remembered; her skin more flawless and full of light—of joy. Her voice was hers, only it held more resonance, as if music was embedded within each syllable. He remembered holding her and spinning with her in his arms. There was a little boy there too, but Stephen wasn't sure who he was. He knew he was connected to Heather somehow. Things were cloudy, time strange. Days were passing with them together. When he awoke from this dream, only fragments remained. All but two phrases faded from their days of conversation.

Follow me, baby.... Listen to him.

That afternoon, as he got up, everything was soundless, as if God had removed his ability to hear. He went to their room only after Peter and Lucy agreed to come with him. He had stood by the door waiting for something, and the others knew without a word said. Peter placed a hand on Stephen's shoulder before cracking the door. The three entered together, still silent, not a word yet spoken between them. It was still. Too quiet and cold. A warmth that once charged the room was now gone. He was afraid of the room and the lost love inside. He packed a bag and asked Lucy to pick out some of Heather's clothes for her funeral.

After they finished, Lucy and he stared into the master bedroom from the doorway. The bed untouched since the last time they slept in it. Her smell was still everywhere. Stephen closed the door.

"Can we go someplace else, Luce?" He asked, sounding almost childlike.

"My home is..." She trailed off, knowing he knew. It was going to be a crime scene for a while.

He looked at her, broken.

"We could go to New York if you like… or even farther," Lucy offered.

New York might be okay... After..."

Lucy nodded. "I know. We'll see to her, then go, okay?"

He nodded, then looked at her. "She asked me to take care of you, and I can't take care of myself."

Lucy hugged him. "She asked me the same thing. It's okay..."

They hugged for a few minutes standing there in front of the closed door, him holding his travel bag and her Heather's last outfit.

Peter took care of them over the next few days; Stephen's sister Shelly also came with food. Charles had come by, grief sick on his face, and offered to handle all the logistics of the upcoming business, as well as funeral arrangements if Stephen wished. Stephen had gratefully accepted, only saying, 'she's important.'

Charles offered an arm around him and promised that Heather would be provided the best of goodbyes. He also asked Stephen if there was any desire regarding Heather's business or if that was already taken care of.

"I have no idea what to do with it. I know things should be able to run as they are for a while, as Heather had planned to be away..." He sat, looking towards the doors leading into her workspace, with fresh tears forming. "We'll leave it in the capable hands of her employees for now," Charles comforted.

"No," Stephen said. "She would want them to have it."

"I'll see to that as well then," Charles finished.

The funeral was as spectacular as Stephen pictured their wedding would be and other than Charles asking for his signature a couple of times, he was left alone. Peter and Shelly were around daily, and Stephen often talked one or the other into staying the night, always sleeping in Lucy's room. Stephen had not seen his bedroom door open since he closed it.

Lucy arranged for them to fly to New York and stay for an indeterminate amount of time, and Charles came by one last time to send them off.

"Go rest, my friend, take care of each other, and grieve your precious loss. All will be fine here. Your friends and I will see to everything."

Charles showed Stephen some paperwork regarding Heather's business for him to sign. Charles had purchased the small company for almost twice its worth and then given all but a 15% interest to her employees. It was now theirs, as

Heather would have wanted. A large sum of money was deposited into Stephen's account, and he did not have to worry about anything.

Stephen and Lucy said goodbye to Peter and Shelly, Lucy giving Peter the first kiss right on his lips. "I love you, Peter. Thank you for your goodness to us both."

He declined an invitation to join them but promised a visit as soon as work permitted.

They were gone, San Diego behind them, and all affairs in good hands. New York would hopefully be enough distance for healing. The Park Avenue home was spacious and opulent, and New York was full of distraction. This still changed nothing for Stephen; Heather was everywhere: in the colors, the smells. She always would be. He had good and bad days but tried to hold it together and move on.

Sometimes he would catch Lucy hidden someplace, crying. She, too, was trying. He supposed, honoring Heather's wish that she take care of him. One day he caught her hiding in their adjoining bathroom in tears. She had turned on the radio and the shower to conceal her sobbing, but he had heard. He came in and shut off the radio before climbing into the shower fully clothed and pulling her out weeping in his arms. She sat wet as he held her.

"Why did she leave me, Steve? Why?" She sobbed.

"I don't have the answers, Honey, but I know she didn't want to. We must remember that she loved us and would never have abandoned us if she could've helped it." Tears came again to his eyes, and they sat on the toilet seat, Lucy in his lap, arms around him.

"I miss her so much," she cried.

"I do too."

Stephen carried her to her bedroom, laid her down, and pulled her cover over her. She caught his hand, looking at him in agony.

"Please stay. I don't want to be alone."

Stephen pulled off his wet shirt and slacks and then hung them in the shower. He wrapped a towel around himself and lay down next to her.

That evening they got up, changed, and went out for dinner. It was a silent meal, though neither felt uncomfortable in the silence because they both understood where it came from.

Their lives were shattered by their loss. They were like ghosts in a world that moved at light speed around them. Stephen drank heavily that night, and Lucy followed suit.

"Save the strong drink for those in sorrow," he said, receiving his fifth Scotch. "I guess I understand that proverb now."

Here he was, in another world, another man, with another woman. The one before now gone. This was the dream now. Sleep was waking back in her arms. Sleep was real, life was not. He realized all the time that had passed since Heather last looked into his eyes was a blur of nothingness.

I'm not really here. This isn't real.

Lucy smiled at him and waved to their server. "I'll have what he's having." She pointed to Stephen's glass. "A double."

The booze numbed the pain and made it possible to close the cellar door in their innermost place, sealing away what seemed impossible to withstand.

This night was the first time either of them laughed. Though drunk, it felt okay for a moment. He remembered dancing someplace vulgar before staggering home at the break of dawn. They were now vampires. Light brought pain with its reality, and it was only a matter of time before all the pieces were in the right place. He opened his eyes and found himself still dressed, though red stains dotted his white shirt. One shoe was still on, and Lucy was asleep next to him. He kicked off the other shoe and closed his eyes, wanting to return Heather.

Colorado Springs

It was a beautiful late summer evening. The last rays of sunshine were now behind the forest of trees that surrounded her family home set from a small lake in Colorado Springs. A young strawberry blonde in her twenties was returning from the lake. She had her hair pulled into a ponytail and was still wet from swimming. She had a tiny pooch, betraying the life growing within her. Swimming always cleared her mind and helped her think. The signs of her condition were beginning to show in her face and her bikini top, which was already beginning to feel snug. Her body was becoming something amazing, transforming inside and out.

She pulled a shirt over her head as she walked up the boardwalk from their dock and looked back, remembering her blue jean cut-offs she had left hanging. She paused to return for them, looked down at her swollen belly, and then waved the idea off.

She caressed it, standing still, now halfway between the glassy lake and her family home. She often found herself in these moments of reverie. Life looked different now through the eyes of this soon-to-be mother. Her body sang to her all the time as her breasts were changing into life-giving islands for her unborn child.

They tingled sometimes, arousing her remembrance of the pleasure that started it all. Other times they gave little bits of disgruntled complaint, as did her transforming womb. She felt like a butterfly with all the changes happening to her. She was thankful because her emotions didn't really wreak havoc on her as her mother warned they might. It was all joy. She loved every moment of it. This was not planned, but she didn't care; God had her, and she trusted the plan.

Finding God and then finding out she was going to be a mother happened in quick succession. Both brought forward a great strength she never knew she had. She was prepared to sacrifice for this child and felt no regrets. She ran her fingers across the tan skin of her stomach, the fine blonde hairs tickled as goosebumps rose.

She thought about him, her last lover. The father of the one within. They were pleasant thoughts. There was no bitterness. He had no idea. They were never close, only a brief moment between them, but somehow, now, there was a bond, and her love for him grew with his child. She pictured one day seeing him again, but for now, something very dangerous loomed between them.

"Porcia," a voice called.

She broke from her dream world, both hands on her belly, and looked up to the house. It was her mother standing on a large wrap-around porch. She was smiling in understanding.

Porcia smiled back, "Yes, Mother," she called, now walking towards her.

"We are going to watch the movie that Dad rented. You want to join us?"

Porcia gave a wave as she grew closer. "No, thank you. You and Daddy enjoy. I'm going to take a bath and relax with a book.

"Okay, Honey, I just thought I'd offer. I know how you love the action films, like your father." She paused… her mother's expression filled.

Porcia stopped, now only feet away. "What?"

Her mother smiled.

"What?" She repeated, now looking down at herself for whatever anomaly had grabbed her mother's attention.

"You look so beautiful, Dear," her mother said as she opened the French door for her daughter. Porcia smiled, a little embarrassed because she *felt* beautiful.

Love surrounded her. She gave her mom a peck on the cheek on the way by.

"Love on your father on your way, okay?"

Porcia entered a large sitting room and crossed through an opulent kitchen where her father was shaking a bowl of popcorn.

"Hey, Daddy."

Hey Beautiful, you joining us for the movie? It's the new 'Die Hard.'"

Porcia hugged him, forcing him to set down the bowl of popcorn. "I love you, dad. I'll catch the second showing in the morning. I know you and Bruce Willis all too well."

They smiled at each other.

"Okay, Dear, coffee and McCain mañana," he said.

"It's a date," she said, leaving him.

She went upstairs and was soon undressing while a bubble bath filled next to her. She looked herself over in the mirror for new changes to her body's profile and gave her belly another caress. She was almost asleep in the tub about twenty minutes later when a boom rocked her calm. She pictured Bruce swinging on some impossible rope or steel beam as the whole world exploded behind him.

She got out, dried herself, wrapping a towel around her. The upstairs had two wings set in opposite directions from a central staircase in the main entryway of the house. Her father had designed and overseen the construction of the home himself. There were many hidden places and high-tech gadgets all about, but the design was natural, with lots of wood throughout.

Near Porcia's room was a beautiful tree trunk that appeared to be supporting the upstairs landing. Hidden behind it was a spiral staircase that led to a false wall into her father's study, where a panic room was secreted behind a wall with all the bells and whistles. These things were essential to a worried father who used to be into prepping when the house was built, now a long-lost hobby. Porcia loved playing in the walls and hidden passages as a child and would use them to play hide and seek with friends. Some, but not all, of the secrets were known by her friends growing up; however, Porcia knew them all.

She entered her room and let her towel drop as she went to her closet. She pulled on some comfortable underwear, a tank top and jumped on her bed. Two pages into her reading resulted in heavy eyes and then sleep.

She was awoken later by a loud bang, sounding like something had fallen over. She grabbed out at her sides as if to catch herself from falling and then sat up, realizing she was in bed. She heard voices, men's voices, in the hall.

Something is wrong.

It wasn't the TV that woke her but some kind of trouble going on outside her room. She jumped up and peeked out her cracked door and saw two people dressed in black. One looked female in shape though they both were wearing Halloween masks. Her heart began to pound, fear jumping up from within. One was Bugs Bunny, and the female was Miss Piggy. They were looking in the other rooms. Porcia looked down at herself barefoot and in her underwear. Before she could make a plan, Miss Piggy turned and headed her way. Porcia jumped back and looked around.

Home invasion, home invasion, what do we do?

She thought of her parents, and her heart stopped.

The panic room, get to the panic room!

That's where they were supposed to meet in this situation. She hoped her parents would be there waiting for her.

Miss Piggy was almost to her door. She could hear the woman calling.

"Her room's here at the end."

Porcia was agile, even with her swollen belly. She put one leg out her bedroom window and then her other just as the door opened. She had just cleared her curtain when the voices entered the room.

She used toe holds to keep herself on the tiny ledge holding onto a copper gutter moving around the outside of that same great tree trunk protruding from the house. The other window was closed, so she held on as long as she could. She felt silly with her rear exposed to the world hanging out here, but fear soon again overrode any embarrassment.

"She's not in her room. DAMMIT." The woman spat.

She could hear the two now enter the other room on her left, so she moved back. Her first attempt at reentry almost ended in a fall as she lost her footing.

She clung sharply to the lower fascia below the window, one leg hanging down, the other heal on the ledge. Her hands burned with pain in holding on with only her fingertips.

Porcia heard the voices enter her room again. Bugs Bunny looked out the window and to his right, where she had just been only moments before.

Her grip was failing, her heart pounding. The drop would be survivable but would result in probable injury and the alert to her location, as the copper-clad awning was ten feet below her precarious position.

The baby too.

Right as she resigned herself to call out to the invaders for help, they retreated. Porcia used every last bit of her strength to lift herself up and reached her fingers around the windowsill. She pulled herself up and into the bedroom, carefully rolling into the room and breathing heavily.

She heard someone yelling downstairs.

"Where is she?" Screamed an angry-sounding man.

"Check the other wing," he yelled up to the Pig and Hair.

Porcia again felt terror fill her. Her parents would never help anyone cause her harm. Tears began to rise but not flow. "God," she said, closing her eyes. "Please be with mom and dad."

She opened her eyes, and they were again full of determination, pain, and now, anger. She opened her door and waited for the precise moment to act; her years of playing hide and seek came to surface. Bugs and the Pig came out of a room just as the false wall in the tree trunk came to rest back in its place, never wiser to the fact that their target had once again been within reach.

She made her way down the spiral staircase and out another false wall into the den, where the panic room was hidden. After checking it and finding no parent inside, the girl, still clad in only her underwear, snuck out of the den and tiptoed to the kitchen, where she crawled up on the counter and peeked over a high pass-through wall looking into the living room where her parents had been watching TV.

The site almost floored her, but she held back the scream now welling up. The sight was of her parents tied down on the floor, arms pulled painfully out at their sides. They were side-by-side. Her mom was praying quietly. Porcia could see her lips moving.

"Oh, Mommy." She whispered. *What do I do?*

There are two more in this room. Kermit the Frog and Mickey Mouse. She wondered if Kermit and Miss Piggy were actually a couple.

"Where is she, pops? I'm not asking nicely again." Mickey Mouse had a sledgehammer held up over her father's head.

Dad's guns. That's our only chance. She thought, getting ready to back away and look in the den. However, the next few moments seized her, freezing her in place.

"You're wasting your breath praying. God is dead. He won't save you." The man said, looking down at her mother, still praying with closed eyes.

"He has already saved us. It's you who is dying and doesn't know—"

CRUNCH. The sound of the sledgehammer crushing her father's face cut short his final words.

Porcia was frozen in horror and didn't even notice that she was screaming a bloodcurdling scream until she heard the voice of her mother.

Kermit and Mickey spotted her. The scream becoming something of the most profound anguish ending with a murderous rage.

"Run! Baby, run. You know wher—"

CRUNCH. Another swing ended her mother's life. Kermit nodded to Mickey, who charged after Porcia. "Downstairs! She's downstairs!

Porcia fell backward, sprawling to the floor on her back, legs in the air, but then quickly regained her feet. Tears flowed down her cheeks as she turned and ran. Still screaming a horrific death howl as if from an injured panther, her anguish and rage forming within her, fusing into something new. Footfalls were on the stairs, and she knew two of three avenues were closed to her.

Mickey had crashed through the kitchen door and collided with a fallen trashcan. She made it into her father's den, slamming the solid oak door and locking it. This would give her only moments.

There was an enormous standing-safe next to the door where her father kept guns, but she had no idea what the combination was. She jumped as they slammed into the door the first time. Her scream was fading into coherent thoughts.

Boom! Came from outside the door again. There were no windows in the room. She was trapped. There was a safe room, but she was not sure how well-stocked it was anymore. Porcia jumped up and jammed herself between the safe and another wall, crawling her way up for leverage.

Boom!

The door jamb was giving.

Porcia pushed with every ounce of her strength, worrying deep within about the baby. Finally, the safe was tipping. Her face was red, veins protruding, as if in early labor.

Blam! The safe crashed to the floor, blocking the door.

Boom! Came another crash from outside the door. This time the jam gave, but the safe held, only allowing about a one-inch gap. An eye tried to spy through the opening, and then they began kicking and struggling to get in.

"Outside. Cover all sides of the house in case she tries to get out!" Kermit yelled.

The sledge was crashing away at the hardwood door, but it was holding. Porcia spotted a lone shotgun leaning where the safe once stood. She grabbed it and chambered a round but stumbled coming back around, and the gun went off early. This put a hole in another wall. She cocked the shotgun again and pointed it. There was silence outside the door. They were listening. The stillness remained for another moment until she pulled the trigger again.

Click. The gun was empty.

She cursed herself and threw it to the floor. The demolition resumed.

Porcia, now done crying, had cold calculation on her face. She was up and looking around for another weapon. She opened the false wall to the panic room, but the power went out as she did. Backup lights clicked on in the room as she searched. Her father had stopped taking the room so serious years ago, but she knew she could lock herself in and be okay if she needed. She tried the phone, but there was no tone. Finally, the beating at the door stopped, and she eased over to the door. She caught part of what was being said.

"At every window, Man."

She heard the sound of splashing water, but it wasn't water at all. The smell of fuel filled the room.

They're going to burn the house with me in it.

That's when she remembered the other escape. A false wall that opened into a slim gap between the walls throughout the downstairs. This one would lead to the back of the house, but not out. However, from there, she could escape behind the laundry wall, which would open to a tunnel leading to the detached garage. If they were there, she was screwed, or if the garage was lit, she would fry, but it was her only chance.

She went into the safe room, looked for a flashlight, and found her dad's go-bag full of a large amount of cash and some documents. She grabbed the flashlight, leaving the bag, and was in the passage to the back of the house by the time the fire was blazing. Smoke crept in from who knows where, but she pulled her tank top up and over her mouth to help her breathe. She made it out of the passage and into the hall, near the laundry room, when she saw stars and hit the floor.

It was Kermit, a shotgun of his own in hand. He put a boot on her throat, pinning the dazed girl to the floor.

"That's an abomination growing inside you, Girl, don't you know that?" He lifted the Kermit mask. A normal-looking guy in his 30's was beneath. Someone she could picture at her church. He bent closer.

"The only earth-born allowed around here are his; now tell me... where's the daddy?"

All of this had Porcia confused. It made no sense. She wanted to hurt this murdering sack of shit but couldn't move. Fire was raging now, and he noticed this. He didn't plan on being around to cook.

"Time's up. We'll find him. We may not be able to see him now, but he'll make a mistake."

Kermit pointed the shotgun at Porcia's face, and she screamed in rage for the wrong being done her and her unborn child. It wasn't fear but animalistic condemnation. He pulled the trigger, fire erupted from the barrel, then darkness.

Outside several people in dark clothes and masks watched the house become engulfed in flames. When it was clear no one could make it out, they dispersed.

Kermit and Miss Piggy giving each other a fatal kiss before jumping in a black SUV that drove off.

The house began to collapse in on itself, but there was water. First, only a trickle, like someplace in the darkness, a small creek was flowing. Soon the sounds of the conflagration were muted by roaring floodwaters and then a great waterfall that thundered. Porcia couldn't see but felt coolness and then, more specifically, mist on her face from the great waterfalls that seemed to surround her. That was when the feeling returned. First, the mist, then it was the sweat on her face.

I have a face? She thought and then felt her hands. Soon she could feel her entire body, but nothing around her; it was as if she was floating in... In... In between everything. Darkness still surrounded her, but there was no pain.

"Porcia?" spoke an incredible voice. She knew it without hesitation.

"Yes, Lord."

"You must die to the world."

"Have I died, Lord?"

"Your time has not yet come, but all who know you must believe you're gone. It's the only way to keep them safe."

"Who, Lord?"

"Your daughter and her father."

"My daughter, Lord… I'm having a...?"

"Yes, but you must keep them separate for now, or the fallen will be able to find them and hurt them both."

"I understand, Lord. I think I've known this since I found out I was going to be a mother."

"I will guide you, and your child will be my goodness in a dark future."

"Yes, Lord," Porcia said, now feeling something hard against her back. "And my parents Lord?"

"They are safe and at peace with me. Their only prayer was for you to get out. I am answering that prayer now. Remember, the world must think you're gone. And that I love you."

His voice was fading, and time was speeding up again. She came to a hard landing. Porcia was on her back again, feet in the air, just like before. The kitchen was the same, her scream rattling her own mind. She was up fast, pulling the trashcan over on her way to the den. Inside, the safe fell just as before, only this time she gathered herself and was clearheaded when she grabbed the leaning shotgun and had it pointed at the place the eye was about to appear.

Boom!

Parts of the doorjamb disintegrated as she pulled the trigger. So did most of Kermit's head from what Porcia could determine. She screamed at the top of her lungs as she went to the panic room and gathered things.

"Hey, Pig Piggy. How's it feel to have someone you love lose their face?"

She heard a retched scream and then kicking at the door increased.

"You Bitch! I'm gonna cut that rat out of you while you watch!"

Porcia grabbed the go-bag her father had hidden, still astonished at how much cash was inside. She added water and the flashlight before swinging it over her shoulder on her way out. There was a blast of a shotgun outside the room and then the smell of fuel like before. Porcia was already inside the walls.

She laid out a blanket dousing it with water, then wrapped it over herself and waited by the escape at the rear of the house. The smoke came, and she covered her mouth, breathing through the moist blanket while she waited. The voices soon ceased, and she knew it was now or never, the house consumed in flames. The heat was overwhelming already as she peeked out and then ran from the hidden access to the passage behind the laundry room. Fire was all around, and her blanket was beginning to dry.

Porcia yanked over the washer, breaking the water line as it fell. Water again sprayed its life-saving force over her and the burning doorway. Porcia climbed up on the dryer and removed the false wall piece, which gave her access to a crawl space. She was soon deep inside the tunnel, which came out in the garage.

"Please let it be safe."

Smoke was creeping along behind her, slowly stocking her as she went. She knew once she opened the other end, the airflow would suck all that smoke up to the garage, which was almost 10 feet higher than the house. When she made it, the smoke was all around her. She had no choice but to go through and hope for the best. When she pushed on the access, it was cool, and soon, she was on the floor of the garage, coughing and hacking. The garage was empty.

She peeked out a window and could see her family home collapsing in flames. Tears welled up in her, but so did her resolve. She watched them try to drag Miss Piggy into an SUV, but she wouldn't leave. They ended up leaving her behind. The Pig stood there guarding the burning house.

Porcia gathered herself and looked around for something to cover up with, not wanting to hike off in her underwear, but there was nothing. She looked out at the Pig, prancing around to make sure no one could get out alive. She spotted her cut-off shorts hanging on the end of the dock.

There was nothing she could find that would make a useful weapon, but she picked up a small pair of pruning scissors her mother must have left behind. The thought of her mom in her garden broke her heart, fresh tears flowed down her cheeks. Anger set back in, and the sight of a shovel leaning near the well-house gave her the plan.

Porcia timed the crazy Pig's pacing and ran for the shovel as her back was turned. Once there, everything seemed to happen like a dream.

Screaming was next, both women charging. One wielding a spade, the other a sledgehammer. Porcia was quicker, with less weight to swing, and panned the woman across the face.

The two ended up in a deadly grapple, rolling on the ground until water engulfed them as they fell into the lake. Porcia wasn't sure if it spanned 30 seconds or an hour, but she remembered standing in knee-high water looking at the woman floating face down. The rest was even fuzzier.

Her memory was shattered, but there were parts coming back to her. She remembered sirens as she darted away, pulling up her shorts as she entered the trees.

Then there was walking, late into the night, in absolute silence. Then the sun high above the trees. There were tears and yelling at a tree. Waking at dusk again, in great pain. Her left hand wrapped in torn fragments of her tank top. It was a red ball, her pinky finger missing. It took her an hour and a bottle of water before fragments of how the lost digit returned to her.

She saw the shears, remembered the pain as she lopped off the finger, and had an image of it smoldering in the burning embers at the edge of what used to be her front porch. She had stared at it as it blackened, only breaking away at the sound of sirens. Porcia also sensed pain in her mouth and felt with her tongue where a tooth had once been, now painfully tender and bloody. She had no memory of that loss. Beginning to think more coherently, she went through the pack. She found some food, tried to eat, but couldn't. Finished her water, then found passports for her parents and herself, staring at them tearfully for a while, then continued the inventory of the bag. There were some bonds and other monetary notes she wasn't too familiar with, along with a load of cash. It totaled around $230,000.00.

She couldn't fathom why her father would have prepared a bag like this. He was a legitimate businessman. The amount wasn't shocking because she knew he was worth over 30 million in assets and property; all of this hers now if she weren't supposed to be dead. "It must have been God," she whispered to herself as she repacked the bag and lay on it as a pillow. Cash wasn't as comfortable a stuffing as she'd imagined it might be.

He must've known I'd need it. Why else?

Porcia cried over her lost parents most of that night, not feeling the elements, too engrossed in her grief. She had walked for miles as she did, and ended up near a highway, where she was quickly picked up by a truck driver.

"I hope you left him," the chubby old man said, looking at the wretched girl.

She realized that he assumed she was fleeing an abusive mate and nodded. The story becoming more real as she told it to others who gave her rides. She had been a mess: dark smudges all over her, tracking black rivers of tear-led highways down her cheeks. The first night, in a small motel, she took a three-hour-shower. Sitting in the tub, she let the warm rain cover her weeping head. She bathed first in her clothes, then eventually removing them. Her white cotton panties were brown from dirt, mud, and ash. She threw them away, opting for just the shorts, and hitchhiked until reaching a new place. Some place unknown and comfortable because of its unfamiliar way. She bought some clothes that were designed for a woman twice her age, throwing the old away.

Colorado was soon behind her and South Dakota ahead. She settled in a small town near Mount Rushmore called Custer and got a job in a hole-in-the-wall bar with sawdust on the ground and lustful drunks on the stools.

That lasted only a month until she found a better job working in a grocery store down the road. She didn't need the money, but it passed the time. She knew she would soon be on the road again but was waiting on God to guide her. She wanted California, to see a sunset on the waves, but she knew that was the wrong way. Florida became the apparent goal, and soon she was on the road in a primer-grey Dodge Caravan that she bought for $800. As she drove, she missed her life, the old one. Peace soon washed over her though as she rubbed her swollen belly.

"Florida's where I'll have you, Sera," she said, driving down the highway with the sun on her face. They were going to be okay.

Seeds

"The will is a beast of burden. If God mounts it, it wishes and goes as God wills; if Satan mounts it, it wishes and goes as Satan wills; Nor can it choose its rider... the riders contend for its possession."

— Martin Luther

Stephen had let the booze be the agent of pain control and used it liberally. Lucy did much the same, though not to his extent. This continued for 3 months. One night they came back, and Stephen had to carry the drunk, giggling girl to her room. They entered the room her laughing at something. Stephen tripped and stumbled in the darkness, clunk.

Lucy's head hit the doorjamb, and the two exploded into laughter. They fell to her bed. The moonlight, coming in the window, shown across it, lighting the beautiful woman's eyes. At that moment, guilt seemed to form on both their faces as if realizing their laughter was insult to their grief. Lucy looked at Stephen intently, still in his arms from their fall. He looked back.

"I'm tired of crying."

"I know."

"I still miss her, but I don't want to die."

He said nothing. She closed her eyes for a moment and then opened them, tears again at their edges.

He caressed her cheek. "No... Not tonight... I don't want tears tonight."

He kissed her. There was a brief pause after he pulled back from the kiss.

That moment passed, and their mouths once again connected. All their pain and anger was released through the animalistic lust that enveloped them. They were soon undressed, clothing more torn than unbuttoned.

She lay before him naked, submitted. She took no initiative as he would have expected from her displays of wildness in the past. Not this night. At this moment, she seemed to take on the persona of innocence. Desire, fear, and uncertainty in her eyes. Her body obeyed his moves, following his lead entirely, and the moment he gave himself to her seemed full of anguish and pleasure in her expressions. After this, her lust surprised him. However, as she enveloped him within her, he fell into her dream. She became Heather though her name never made it to his lips.

At one moment, while she was a top of him looking down, he saw both women intermingled. Lucy's eyes grew darker, almost green. Her pleasure became Heather's; even her hair grew from a brilliant platinum to shimmering dark in the moonlight. He allowed his fantasy of Heather to take him and loved her through the flesh of another woman.

Afterward, they showered together. Lucy was like a fiend, never getting enough. They made love there, too, and fell asleep exhausted as the sun began to rise. He never noticed the crimson mark of her virginity given him because of the darkness both in bed and in the shower that followed. Maybe if he wasn't drunk, he would have at least seen the treasure she gave in that moment of pleasure and pain.

Lucy woke at 3 in the afternoon without him there. She sat up more rested than she could remember. She looked at the red mark on the sheets, marking the loss of her innocence. She lay back in bed, looking up as she caressed her entire body, reliving the event in her head.

Lucy showered and then came out to eat but did not find Stephen in the penthouse. A note was there waiting, and she opened it eagerly, a smile on her face.

Lucy,

I'm not sure what to say to you about last night.

I've spent the last few hours trying to understand what I feel, as well as find the words to convey these feelings to you.

At one point, I returned to your room and stood over you as you slept. I thought: you are so gorgeous and even more so asleep. My body craves yours already as I write, but my heart is screaming betrayal and so many other emotions I've yet to understand.

Where do we go from here? What is next? My heart is Heather's, and I don't know if I will ever be able to love like that again. Not for the possibilities that obviously lay between us. For I could see many more nights with you just the same. You pleased me, and you know you are dear to me, as you were dear to Heather. So, where do we go from here?

This is a question I cannot answer alone. Perhaps together, dear Lucy, we can answer this question. In your answer lies my hope.

I don't want to hurt you, and I fear I may already have, but if you can understand my loss, my still broken heart...maybe you understand. Yes, I believe you do. You loved her too.

So tell me, sweet Lucy, what do you want and need? Can you bear my limitation, accepting me as I am?

Will the limited love I can hand out be enough for you for now? Can we heal together and see how things turn out?

Your very pleased lover of last night

Stephen.

Lucy read the note several more times. Each time with a mixture of hurt and happiness.

He's being honest and not rejecting you, only asking for your patience. She sat back down and wrote.

Dearest friend and lover, Stephen

What can I say in rebuke? Your honesty and eloquence, considering your pain, honors me.

I know that last night was not planned, nor was it the wisest of choices for two in so much pain. However, I cannot change that now and will admit I wouldn't want to. No one understands my grief like you, and this may be part of why last night held so much healing and pleasure for me. Having you forced my grief to flee. Though it returns a new, but this only makes me want you to come to me soon and again fill its place.

I understand, I do, and feel many of the same feelings as you.

I would rather share what limited love you have left to give, with the hope for more with healing time, than let last night mean nothing.

For me, I know I can love you and love Heather through loving you. Maybe this is what she meant by telling us both to take care of each other???

I know this. I feel closer to her being near you. So, maybe for you, it could be the same... With me?

My answer is I'll be patient and understand just as long as you promise to never push me away.

Also — my body needs you too. Please come give me more of what you did last night.

Unconditionally yours

Lucy R.

Stephen spent a couple of hours in Central Park, walking and thinking. He spoke to Heather, but she did not answer his questions. He saw a little girl and her mother walking by. Her voice sounded just like Heather's as a child when he first met her in Sunday School. He fought back tears, not wanting to break down.

Not here.

So, he returned to the penthouse apartment. Inside, it was quiet. He could hear distant music from Lucy's bathroom. It was something classical, he thought, maybe Mozart. She was probably showering, and the thought excited him. Sex with her shut off the grief, at least for a time. He went to the lounge and found his note gone and another sitting in its place. A bottle of fine whiskey and two glasses rested on top.

This is a good sign.

He poured two fingers and then two more for Lucy as he began to read. Stephen set the note down and picked up both glasses. He moved to the bathroom, excited by the image of her wet skin. He entered, set the glasses on the counter, and undressed. She watched him, excited yet with a slight trepidation.

She seemed intimidated by him sexually yet hungry to overcome this fear. Her mouth was opened, her hands caressing her own body without being aware of it. He stepped in, and she took a deep breath as they touched.

The two spent the next couple of weeks doing nothing else. Drinking and screwing.

They still had times of tears, and sometimes the drinking would take them to this despair rather than block it out. Lucy was inexperienced in bed but seemed to pick it up fast; her appetite for him drove her in ways Stephen had never expected. It was all pleasure and highs.

The two traveled around Paris for a week, then to Greece, partying with elite strangers. Stephen could see how Lucy might feel lonely, surrounded by so much plasticity in the friends she had. None of the warmth he grew up with.

She surprised him with a brand-new Ducati motorcycle that they took on a ride upstate before having it shipped west.

Stephen was beginning to tire of being away; though it held memories he missed home, so they returned. It was not long after returning to California that Stephen began to withdraw. He grew quieter and quieter in between their drunken revelries. She noticed this but could not get him to talk about it. It was apparent she wanted to move on with letting go of the pain of losing Heather, and Stephen knew it was probably the mature thing to do; however, he could not let her go. He thought if she knew how many times he had really been making love to Heather while they were together, she wouldn't stick around.

He was also haunted by the vision, that moment alone with Falcone. The images came back to him when sober. They created too many questions for him to consider and were quickly put away.

He cared for Lucy and wanted to make her happy, but he was still haunted by a ghost. He stopped sharing his grief, noticing she no longer wanted to reopen wounds that, for her, were healing, and this broke much of the bond that had brought them together. He was soon alienating himself. It was now one glass he'd fill, not two.

The first time they saw Peter again was a month after their return from New York. Lucy had arranged for most of his things to be moved to her house, now with no sign of the tragedy that had transpired there. The loft was still the same save for Stephen's missing wardrobe and a few other items. Felix refused to be picked up, so he was left behind. The girls at Heather's design company promised to keep his food and water full.

Stephen had vanished for 24 hours and just returned to see Peter in their living room. A cup of coffee in front of him and a cup of tea in front of Lucy. They were sitting too close, but Stephen really didn't care. He did, but he didn't at the same time; after all, he pretty much stole her from Peter, anyway.

He had two days' growth on his face, disheveled hair, and smelled like stale beer. Lucy looked uncomfortable with them both in the same room.

"Don't mind me. I'm just popping in for a bite and a change of clothes." He cracked a beer, looked back at Peter, and nodded.

Peter raised a hand.

"Isn't it a little early for that, Stephen?" Lucy asked, looking at his beer with disdain.

He ignored her and pounded it, opening the fridge for another.

"You see what I mean?" She said to Peter in a low voice.

He put a hand up to calm her.

She ignored Peter's attempt. "Where have you been? I've been worried." She snapped, the pain in her voice pricked Stephen.

"Working on the boat."

She stood up, hands on her sides.

Oh no, Stephen thought, *here we go.*

"Where's your motorcycle? I saw you get dropped off by a taxi." She asked.

"I had a little accident, but I'm okay." He smiled. "Nothing's broken."

Tears threatened her eyes. "Why are you doing this to me? What did I do?"

Stephen looked at Peter and raised his eyebrows, indifferent. He felt terrible for hurting her, but feelings were killing him too. He couldn't afford emotions. Heather was there.

"You would never put Heather through this." She chipped.

"That's because my life would be perfect if she were here." He said, feeling the sting of her saying the name and his own stab.

I won't be able to take that one back....

"Steve, can I talk to you?" Peter asked.

Lucy sat down, tears now flowing down her face.

"Sure, Pete. I'm sorry we haven't had you over, Bro. Things have just been... Well, you know, and I wasn't sure you'd come considering..." He pointed to Peter, then Lucy, and finally himself with a mouthful of the sandwich. He swallowed. "Tangled web, or is it a triangle?"

"There is no love triangle here, Steveo," Peter said, defiant. "There's two friends of mine, one of which is acting like an ass right now."

He approached the kitchen counter where Stephen was standing with his lunch and second beer. Stephen's eyebrows rose again, surprised by Peter's effrontery. Another oversized mouthful of sandwich being chewed.

"What is wrong with you?"

Stephen didn't answer, only looked amused as he took another bite.

"Where's my friend? The guy I have known my entire life?" Peter pushed.

Stephen said nothing, chewing more dramatically, refusing to go anywhere real.

"Where's the guy that my sister Heather fell in love with?"

This sparked a hint of pain and emotion and Stephen's eyes. Peter saw this and went in for the kill.

"Because she would be ashamed of what I see. You hurt her friend, turn your back on those who love you?... I'm glad she's not alive to see you —"

Stephen moved fast, beer on the floor first swinging wide. He clipped Peter on the tip of the jaw. But Peter recovered quickly, using Stephen's momentum to push him into the living room. Stephen turned, surprised but not finished. He started to move, then stopped. He swallowed and then stared. Lucy was standing, hand to her mouth. Fear and devastation in her eyes.

Stephen put his hands on his side, swaying a little, and smiled.

"Well, Pete's showing a little backbone. I'm proud." He said with overdramatic movements of his head, finishing with his chin out, mocking Peter.

"You're drunk and making a fool —"

"Or is this about the girl who got away?" Stephen continued.

Jamming a thumb back towards Lucy. "Maybe if you showed a little of that manliness the night she offered herself to you, things would be diff —"

This time it was Peter who moved. He stepped wide, and Stephen saw this and swung again, this one with a force to do actual harm. Peter ducked and came up behind the man's back, shoving him into a wall. He slammed his elbow into Stephen's throat, getting a hold of one hand, and hyperextended the hold. He now had his friend pinned against the wall.

"Don't mistake my love for fear," he said, letting him go.

Stephen stood there, surprised by his friend's move. His eyes wide, a little joy for his friend still hidden in them. Stephen loved the man, and everything about this situation seemed wrong.

"I'm so sorry, Peter," Lucy pleaded, tears flowing.

"It's okay. I forgive you. He responded. He looked over at Stephen, "I'm really disappointed in you, Man. I've loved you as my brother most of our lives, and for all of it, until now, I respected you. The Steve I know wouldn't take a woman's virginity then treat her like you have Lucy."

She again covered her face in shock. Too many private things were being revealed in this room. Stephen's face was wider.

Virginity?

"You didn't know? How could you miss something like that?" Peter asked. He looked at Lucy. "Now I'm the one who must apologize, Lucy."

He looked back at Stephen. "Be a man, Steve. Find your integrity again. You're going to be a father."

Peter walked out the door without another word.

Lucy ran upstairs, bawling.

Stephen slid to the floor, dumbfounded. *Virginity?... Father?* "Leave the place for a couple days, and the young get restless."

He remained downstairs for an hour before going after Lucy. All of this was a load to consider. The fact he had so much wrong the biggest bite to take.

When he entered the room, she was lying face down across the bed.

"I'm sorry," he said.

She remained quiet.

"I didn't know it was your first time..."

She sniffled a little, listening.

"I do remember it being special, though; it was special for me." That may be part of why I have grown further and further away. "We stopped talking, that bond we —"

"YOU stopped talking." She interrupted. "I just kept falling in love."

He was silent, putting a hand on her leg. She allowed it to remain. "You seemed ready to stop grieving, and I wasn't."

"Wasn't — or are not?" She said, rolling over.

"I'm *not* ready to stop grieving... And... I didn't want to pull you down."

Her eyes were charged, and her face reddening. "I asked you one thing —

don't push me away."

He nodded.

"I told you I would be patient, and I never complained. Do you know what it is like to be in love with someone, in love with a ghost?"

He shook his head.

"It hurt, but I was okay with it because she was my ghost too. Someone we could share, and I was okay sharing you with her."

Stephen remained silent.

"You have to let me in or let me out, Stephen."

She rolled back over, but he caught her and pulled. She first fought but then allowed him to pull her up into his lap. She hugged him tightly. "I loved her too."

"I know you did."

I miss her too."

"I know you do."

"Then don't push me away... I was even willing to name my first child Samuel for her."

Stephen hugged her. "It's okay, Love. I'm sorry."

She pulled back, surprised by his choice of names, but then rested her chin back on his shoulder.

"So… a baby?" He asked as he rubbed her back.

A Displeased God

Craig Richardson sat at a large dining table with several other lawyers from his firm. The table erupted with laughter at the completion of a story about a congressman, his wife, and his mistress. "I think we should dig into the rumors about her college experimentation. We may hit pay-dirt there. We—"

"Hey, Tom, didn't your wife go to Smith College?" another man named Jason interrupted.

Tom shook his head. "I told you we met at Harvard."

Craig waited patiently for a moment to continue, then cleared his throat when a well-dressed man in his thirties came to the table. He was wearing a dark tailored suit and carried a brilliant silver-headed cane.

"Pardon my intrusion, Craig. Is this seat taken?" He sat before a response could be given.

Craig felt a cold wash over him as if stepping out into a frigid Arctic winter. He didn't know the man but knew from where he came. This man was darkness. Clean-cut, elegant dark hair and piercing eyes. He carried himself as one of the elite. A couple of the other attorneys at the table held the same expression of familiarity on their faces.

"Pardon me, Sir, but this is a private —"

"Shh," said the dark man. "Hello, Mr. Richardson."

Richardson nodded, not sure how to react.

"I regret to intrude on your discussion about the Congressman's trouble. I am an associate of Mr. Rutherford."

Three of the lawyers at the table knew the name.

"Yes," said Richardson. "How is Mr. Rutherford?"

"My friend, Charles…" The dark man said, speaking slowly and calculating as he waved for service.

"I'm sorry," Jason interrupted. "But we are in the —"

"Hush, Boy. You need to learn your place," said the dark man.

Jason looked irritated and was about to retaliate when Richardson caught him, probably saving his life. "Shut up, Jason." Giving the young attorney a sharp look. "Go on, Mr?"

"Mr. Reficul. My friends call me Louis."

The young attorney stood.

"Before you leave to go pop that fine-looking graduate student you've been daydreaming about. Can I give you a little advice?" said Louis.

Jason remained still, confusion on his face, looking at the others. Some looked interested and generally entertained. Others, confused, looking to Richardson as to whether to stay or go. He obviously recognized the stranger to be someone of importance. So, they did not move.

"I'll take your silence as a yes," the dark stranger finally spoke. His smile was beautiful, his attractiveness meeting deadliness in a perfect combination of elegance.

"Respect is something anyone in power has learned to both give and expect from his equals. It is simply a sign of ignorance and simplicity when one interrupts another who has the attention of a room. It says: I'm really not listening to what you are saying, and neither should anyone else. It is among these refinements that powerful men and women arise with."

Everyone concurred and nodded. "Well put, Mr. Reficul," said Richardson.

"Before you interrupted my new friend here," he put a hand out towards Richardson. "He was discussing the option of looking into the accuser's past for anything that might help our poor Congressman out of hot water."

Jason had heard enough and walked away.

"I will save you the time and trouble. That young man is going to be no good for this firm. As well, is fondling two of your wives, gentlemen." He looked at a balding man across from him, who seemed to be putting things together in his head. The stranger nodded at him, and the man got up. "I've got to go. I'll see you on Monday." He left in a hurry, a wife to confront.

And later murder with a golf club…

"Mr. Reficul, how may I help you?" said Richardson, attempting to be gracious.

The server came. Louis ordered. "A whiskey; something fine, or I'll send it back."

He gave the young server a wolfish grin; she smiled back. He watched her walk away, then turned back to Richardson.

"It is our friend in common, Mr. Rutherford."

Richardson looked around the table. "Can you gentlemen excuse us, please? This is in regard to one of our most esteemed clients. We'll continue Monday."

The men started to get up, two of them looked at Richardson for confirmation. He nodded, and they sat back down. The others said their goodbyes and gave the stranger polite nods as they left.

"Then there were four." the dark man said, enjoying the moment.

The other men moved closer as the server brought Louis his drink. "It's our finest," the girl said as she slipped him an extra napkin with her number on it. Louis' hand was someplace under her skirt for a moment. A couple looked offended near where Louis was seated, and he smiled at them, which made them turn away uneasily.

His expression seemed to hold more than an ordinary man's, as other animations in his eyes and face surfaced slightly. Richardson noticed a flicker of hideousness disappearing as he looked back at him.

"How's Mr. Rutherford, Sir? I hope well." Richardson asked.

"Not good, not good, I am afraid. It seems there was an incident in San Diego, and his lovely daughter Lucy was harmed."

Richardson looked at the others, all three men now alarmed. The blood could be seen leaving his face.

"The girl is a beauty, I tell you, and carries one hell of a punch. But some cretin beat her and kicked her while she lay on the ground. It is a complicated mess: Blood all over the place. Three dead, two injured."

"I assure you, Mr. Reficul, we authorized nothing even remotely like what you have described."

The man looked at them. The others nodding their affirmations.

He smiled. "Can I consider you a friend, Craig? As Charles is my loyal friend?"

Yes, Sir, you can."

"Then call me Louis, please, and let us be frank."

Richardson nodded.

"There was to be no collateral damage... This was entrusted to you to complete. Did you disregard your orders, or were you contravened?"

I was obviously disobeyed." Richardson answered.

"Very well, Mr. Henry's punishment will be more severe. Yours… Is a choice."

"A choice?" Richardson asked.

"Yes, whom will you choose to suffer tonight, your daughter or your wife?"

Richardson's throat became a dry desert. He could barely swallow. "My... Wife." He finally spoke.

The dark man looked at him sharply. "Man, no loyalty to the women who stood by you through two affairs and the rash?" His smile was still there but almost devouring now. Hidden anger behind it. "You should know Charles would like to remove your limbs by hand." The dark man stared at him. Richardson achieved one dry swallow.

"Next time, one of them dies. It is entirely your choice if you want to tell them your daughter's assault was her father's fault."

"But I chose my wife?"

Louis smiled. "Yes, your wife's punishment is having to watch. I would hurry, though; your daughter may not be enough to satisfy them long."

Richardson was up and running for the door, where he hailed a taxi and vanished.

The other man gave nervous smiles to their master. He finished his drink and got up.

"Lord, may we ask the punishment brother Henry was given?" One asked him.

Their dark Lord sat again, smiling. "Well, you two are sick little bastards."

They remained silent. He got up. "His was to brutalize his daughter himself. Pay the bill."

He vanished into the crowded restaurant like a fading dream.

***

Charles sat sipping a cup of tea as his stewards came with the in-flight phone, handing it to him. “There’s a call, Sir. From San Diego.”

He smiled, accepting the phone. “That will be all, Susan. Thank you, dear.”

She smiled and returned to the rear of the plane.

“Yes?” He answered.

“Good evening, Sir. You wanted to be kept up-to-date on the situation involving special attaché Henry?”

“Yes? What is it?” He responded, firmness and disgust in his eyes.

“Turn on the local news, and you will see.”

“Thank you, Robert. I will do that. Be sure and keep an eye on my daughter for me.”

“Will do, Sir. She’s having lunch with Mr. Meyers now. Nothing exciting here. She’ll be in good hands, Sir.”

“Great, I know I can count on you.”

Charles hung up his phone and found the news channel he wanted.

“Sources say Henry was on vacation with his wife and daughter. When asked for information about any signs of instability, Ambassador Campbell refused to comment on his assistant, only stating that they never worked very closely together.

“Once again, for those who have just joined us, we are viewing the scene in downtown San Diego, where it is confirmed that Special Attaché To Foreign Relations with Britain, Mr. Andrew Henry leaped to his death from his hotel balcony after having a mental breakdown. Police will not confirm or deny if he is the one suspected of the brutal assault on his own wife and daughter or if the suicide was from the shock of finding them.

One hotel employee said that the three were together and seemed happy when they entered the hotel lobby for their room around 6 PM. Witnesses say no one else was seen coming or going right up until Mr. Henry leaped to his death.”

Charles clicked off the television and finished his tea, satisfaction on his face.

Renewing Old Ties

Stephen and Lucy gathered their towels and surfboards after spending the day at the beach. He had decided to embrace the things he had shared with Heather rather than put them away, where they would only swell and fester. Lucy was excited when he offered to teach her how to surf and had caught on more quickly than expected. The afternoon's highlight was when Lucy discovered why Stephen so strongly recommended she wear something a little more durable rather than her skimpy bikini. She went in hard on a larger wave and came up missing most of her bottoms and all of her top. Stephen helped her find the top floating at the shore, and after that, Lucy put her shorts on. They spent the last few hours lying on the beach talking. It consisted of difficult things that needed to be said first, talking about their loss and how both expected life to continue.

They did not touch or make eye contact during the conversation, maybe it was out of respect for the dead.

Stephen held no hope for a love like he had before but found himself trying. Lucy's heroic attempt at saving Heather was pivotal in his decision to commit to the relationship. When he thought about this, she became acceptable, not a betrayal of his love for Heather. It was true; they both loved her.

They packed up and returned to Heather's VW van, a project she and Stephen took on early in their relationship. After loading up the boards and bags, Stephen took Lucy's hand for the first time and led her to a passenger seat. She sat and pulled his hand to her thigh. They looked at each other.

"Thank you, Stephen," she said, staring at him. Looking for a response before it was given. He smiled. She pulled him in, kissed him half on his lips, and then backed, remaining very close to him.

This was too intimate for him, and she noticed but did not relent. This was going to be her space now, and she had to claim it. Her smile broke the uncomfortable feeling between them and drew out his own. "It feels good to know you care for me."

He winked, avoiding a response, and gave her hand a squeeze as he pulled back to go around to his side of the van. "That's what we do…"

He brought them to Bareback Bar and grill for what Stephen said would be the best basket of fries she would ever have. They ordered big messy burgers and a basket of the famous fries. Lucy looked around the small bar from their high table in the center of it all. The place was full of beautiful people eating and drinking. She smiled at him, glad that he was allowing her into this world of Heather's and his own. He knew what she was feeling and felt bad for not enjoying it himself. He was forcing himself to let go, and *the best way out was always through*. Heather's memory reminded him of this.

Facing the pain instead of running and medicating it. This way was harder but more fulfilling. She was here. Not so much the bar, though she was everywhere, her memories anyway. No, Heather was in the places he made himself go. The difficult places. She existed where he faced his pain. Her presence lay where he showed courage and tried doing the right thing. Giving Lucy these moments, the shared things special to Heather, was a sacrifice that brought him closer to her ghost.

He smiled at Lucy and touched her hand. He thought about these feelings of being closer to Heather when pointed in a good direction, and it made him think about her words.

Follow me. She had said.

She found *Him*, that incomprehensible being which supposedly held all of it together, and somewhere inside, Stephen wanted to believe He was true. This went against every cell in his body, though. And there was the man from the bar, to consider. Flooding images like a fast-forwarded film blasting him when he touched Mitch. The brief moment of wonder between the man and what must have been God was overwhelming. He wondered if this was what Heather was trying to describe to him.

Lucy sensed his depth of thought. "She would be happy to see you here enjoying your life, Hun." She offered.

"She *is* happy." He looked at her, wondering how much to share. "Did she ever talk to you about her newfound faith?" he asked.

"A little, but I'm not down for all that. She respected that I wasn't." Lucy said, defiance in her expression.

Door shut.

"Yeah, she was not a pushy person." He decided to change the subject. "I never really thanked you for what you did that day….for Heather, I mean."

Lucy's expression crashed, and Stephen realized what he had done. "I'm sorry, I just …didn't want to ... never say it."

Lucy's eyes revealed the tears available if she did not stay in command. "I failed. Stephen. I have gone over it a million times."

"Lucy, you didn't fail. You were brave. What an amazing superhero you would make." He smiled, hoping to bring her back to the lighter side.

A small smile formed, flattered by his praise. "I tried with all my heart, Stephen. Can we not talk about this anymore? Can we just let all that lie? I would like to finish this night without crying."

He gave her hand another squeeze. "Yes, I am putting all the parts down and burying them. I want you to know you were my hero that day, and when I think about that, it makes caring….loving you okay."

Her eyes lit. *Loving?*

"I will leave it at that. I just needed that said. Thank you for putting your life on the line to save my… her. I want to move forward, somehow, some way, and live the life before me. I have no idea how I will do this and hope you can be patient with me as I figure it out."

"I told you how I feel and only ask that you not push me out." She said.

Stephen nodded, taking her other hand. He looked at her, seeing the hope for them in her eyes.

"I don't want my child to grow up with the pain we now feel. Heather would be scolding me for it. This much I know for certain. Let's get married, Luce….I can't bear much in regard to all of that, but… Want to do it right for the child." His expression became weary.

Lucy's eyes were the biggest he had ever seen. She looked happy.

"Don't worry, Doll. Daddy will probably do everything for us." Her posture even sprung up an inch. Any chance of tears flowing was gone. "You'll ask me tomorrow at dinner with Daddy, Yes?"

He nodded, smiling at her pleasure, the ache of what should have been deep inside him.

"May we go buy a ring in the morning, Stephen?"

This surprised him. "Yes, though the best places to shop are back east."

"No, I know just the place, right here…Unless you want to pick it out?" She waited for his response, and his smile was all the permission needed.

"Great, tomorrow breakfast, then off to get my ring." She was happy. He was happy, or as happy as he thought he should be. A pain weighed deep inside him that he thought would never leave, but he was going to step forward and try doing …..Well, living.

"What about Peter, Doll. You must fix that." She said matter-of-factly.

"I will. I already have a plan. I must do something, and I need his help to do it."

Her expression betrayed her worry.

"I need to say goodbye to Heather in one more way, and I need to do this without you. Can you understand that? Also, Pete and I must settle things, and some of that involves you."

She nodded submissively, then smiled. She leaned over the table and kissed him, nocking a saltshaker to the floor.

Peter will be coming over tomorrow afternoon to help me with some things after he finishes his meeting with the host." She said incidentally.

"The host?" Stephen asked.

"Yes, Mitch. The host from the bar. The one that day….." her expression again assaulted by the violence that occurred.

The Host….

"He was our host at the bar! That is what she meant…I thought she was—"

"What are you talking about?" Lucy asked.

"Nothing. I will call Peter when we get home. I'm sure he will talk with me. He would want to do this with me."

The two finished their meal, talking about the future, but Stephen's mind was swimming through explanations and theories about everything.

Mitchel Falcone....the host... has more answers.

The Science of Devils

Albert had become increasingly concerned about the technology to which he had opened the door. Even more so, its application. He had been trying to perfect the software for the transfer of consciousness, and though they had made great leaps, something always seemed to go wrong. Five subjects were lost, and another almost corrupted beyond saving. It was upon examination of this sixth that he noticed something irregular. Upon discovering it, he went back to the other files and found the anomaly within them as well. All strings had trails, and this string did not originate at the transcend-connection. It came from somewhere else. Albert was perplexed. Somehow another source of code was being introduced alongside the trans-code from the subjects. It acted more like a virus or worm in that it would migrate into the other strings and mimic them, and in doing this, destroy them. It was as if another consciousness was being uploaded and trying to assimilate the subjects.

At one point, he decided to go to his supervisor and reveal his findings. He gathered the documentation and was near the office of his senior manager when he overheard agitated voices. They were muffled but still loud. He made out enough to discern his manager was being reprimanded for failing to achieve some goal. His manager, Mr. Cranbourne, was a big harry man who often intimidated Albert with his presence alone. His voice carried with it an arrogant self-confidence, which dominated the room when he spoke, and this set Albert even more on edge. The other voice in the room, an equally powerful one, was not one he recognized.

"I have given you everything you need to take possession. I cannot control how your …those things will handle it. Maybe we should allow the subjects to assimilate the system and then attempt ownership of the completed product."

"NO. That will not do! The voice returned, followed by the slamming of something in the room. This startled Albert, causing him to drop his folders on the floor. He bent down, picking them up as the office door opened. It was Cranbourne.

"Albert, Hey, I was just thinking about you. How may I help you?"

Albert nervously walked closer, looking beyond his manager for the other voice. His manager opened the door wider, motioning his entry, and returned to his desk. The office was empty. "I don't want to interrupt." He said.

"You're not. I just finished a phone call and was going to come see you anyway. What can I do for you?"

"I…I, well, I think I found the problem with the transfer protocols."

As Albert explained the discovered lines of code, he saw his manager's face change from friendly and helpful to almost perturbed. Albert decided less was more and wrapped up his explanation. "I think if we set up a new protocol for transfer, this breach would not occur. I can investigate where it came from if you like…"

"No, no, Albert, I will put another team on the security of the servers, as I know how busy you are. Let's do this. Continue running system tests of the software as is, and alongside, you can work on a new protocol; that way, my bosses can see progress while we look at the changes you think necessary, okay?"

"Oh…Okay," Albert said. "I can have the new protocols up and running by end of month, though. What about our subjects? I have one left. Shouldn't we wait until I have—"

"No, we move forward as scheduled. I will have more subjects here by end of the week. I want to start processing seven this week."

Albert nodded and retreated from his boss's office. It was at this moment his trust in what he was doing and for whom broke down. He could not let the questions growing within go unanswered. It went against the grain of who he was. He began digging into some files, which were revealed early by mistake. When creating his own back door to the filing system on his server, he discovered another one already in place. By turning the doorway in on itself, he was able to trace its origin to a server in New York. There were names of prominent individuals and corporations. One name seemed to be referenced often as Albert searched through memos and other folders: Rutherford.

He found himself in a server full of folders with names he recognized. One which stood out to him was the Bilderberg Group. It seemed everyone was connected in one way or another with the powerful elite. His jaw dropped at some of the project names. Shortly after he started copying files from the server, his presence was discovered on the server. Albert was a proficient hacker because of his extensive knowledge of the core of software. He understood it at a level most could not. He opened another session on the computer next to him and executed his own code from it as his first session became compromised. He pulled the LAN cable and rebooted the first machine. With several keystrokes, the second system found its target and began running the protection client in circles. Albert reconnected to the New York server from the first computer and began the download again while the other system kept security busy. He chuckled at the basic defenses on the server. However, he had scarcely downloaded a few memos and documents he found interesting when computer two froze. He was astonished. They had beaten his program. *No one could beat it, not that fast?*

His neck grew cold, and fear grabbed ahold of his heart like an icy hand squeezing. He yanked the drive that was being loaded with files and pulled the power to both systems.

They know where I am then, he thought.

Albert got up, threw some things in his bag, and left the office. He was soon outside of the complex and in his car. He knew all of this was connected, and the powers behind all of it had caught him sniffing where he did not belong. The names of the files scared him even more. *Depopulation Projects...*

He started his car and drove away, throwing his cell phone out the window as he drove across a bridge. Albert drove on into the night until his eyes refused him service.

At this point, he looked for a truck route into the Colorado Mountains, so he could sleep. It was not more than a couple hours after falling asleep that Albert was shaken awake by a horrible howling sound. It was a mixture of bear moan and maybe a hyena's whine, though carrying the depth of something much bigger. He could not only hear but feel the footfalls as it ran around his parked car. Albert was too frightened to turn on any lights. He sat up, peering out the windows of his back seat as whatever it was circled, rebuking his presence in the forest. Once Albert thought, he caught a glimpse of it as it crossed a slash of moonlight, but his mind refused it as real. The thing was running around his car about ten yards away. Howling. Albert pulled on his shoes, looking around. When he looked to his right, it was a blur of massiveness charging him.

Hairy…was the only word that formed on his lips when it struck his car. He flew backward, hitting his head against the rear window support. Stars danced in his head. Something was pounding on the roof of the car, putting large dents the size of basketballs in the roof with each blow.

Whatever it was, it stood on two legs because that was all he could make out outside the window. Something huge and hairy stood over his car, pummeling it. The passenger windows shattered with the next blow, which also created a large U out of the passenger window frame. With the windows explosion came another blast, overpowering Albert's senses. It was a pungent smell of musk, which carried with it the orders of the homeless and finishing with wet dog, which repelled him back.

Albert wanted to scream but was unable to do anything. All his life, he loved watching documentaries about Bigfoot and other unexplained citing's in the forests around the world, but now, he was about to die at the hands of what he always thought fantasy.

A mammoth hand breached the back window, shattering the glass. It grabbed hold of the frame of the car and lifted. Albert, and his 1993 Saab-900, were now four feet off the ground and rising. He scrambled forward to the driver's seat, not sure how this would help but feeling safer being as far as possible from that hairy hand. It screamed now, sounding more like an ape this time, and the car tilted, sending him face first into his break peddle and floorboard. He tasted the dirt from the floor mat and then stars as the back of his head crashed back up into the steering wheel. Albert slammed back and forth, dazed. More windows were breaking as he bounced in every direction.

It's shaking me out. Like a coin stuck in a piggy bank!

He screamed in his mind, terrified. *I'm dead!*

His hand found the steering wheel, and he latched on. This helped him gather some stability while still shaking violently. This thing was holding a car out in front of it, shaking it like a pillow. Its legs were two oaks, and its fingers grasping the inside of the broken vehicle were hairy pick axes, which easily dug into the sheet metal of the roof. His briefcase and travel bag flew by him and out the shattered windshield.

I don't want to die.

He was about to follow them when all of a sudden, he was forced to the back seat by the momentum of his car flying through the air. The car landed on its side and then rolled over onto its wheels. Albert pulled himself up and looked in the direction of the monster. It was too dark to really see anything, but he could see a shape, and it was pounding the ground over by where he was parked. Albert looked back at his steering wheel. The keys were dangling.

Would you start, girl? He wondered.

This was probably his only chance, while it thought it had him on the ground. That is if his car would start. He jumped in the seat and cranked. She tried, moaning, as the motor tried to answer his call. A deathly scream came from behind him. He did not look back, only held the key cranked and closed his eyes.

Boom, a backfire sounded, followed by a startled yell from the hairy one in surprise. Albert put it in gear and floored it, shovelfuls of loose dirt pounding out behind the car toward the thing. His car began to move and picked up speed quickly as the tires found firmament to connect with. He turned his lights on just in time to see he was about to drive headlong into a tree. Albert veered off just in time, ripping off his passenger mirror and scoring the right side of the mangled car. He made second gear and let the engine scream too long before shifting again. It was running after him, huge arms and legs swinging as it came. Third found the height of the engine's ability, and Albert kept it there rather than chancing fourth and loss of momentum. He did not look back, leaning forward like a 90-year-old grandmother driving like a bat out of hell to bingo.

He soon heard a great howl growing more distant. This was the first moment relief washed over him. And the same moment he realized he'd soiled himself. He continued driving dangerously fast down the logger's road, his mind clearing enough to organize thoughts. None of this had been real before tonight. Now he would have to reconsider so much of his thinking to allow this a place in his mind. *I'm one of the nuts now....*

The nuts the world wrote off as crazy, but crazy would be denying what he had just experienced.

One hour later, Albert found blacktop and, with it, more relief as the distance between him and Hairy grew. After another hour of driving, he pulled into a truck stop and shut off the engine. It rattled and continued dieseling for a good minute afterward. He stroked the steering wheel and thanked the car as smoke began to rise from under the hood. Two truck drivers stared at him as he walked by them into the dinner. Albert sat down, and a waitress brought him a coffee. The two truck drivers came in and sat at the bar, looking back at him and talking. Finally, his waitress came over.

"Honey, you need to call a cop?"

Albert looked at her, confused.

"You in a car accident? Is there anyone else hurt out there?" she pushed.

"No…nobody else…" He thought *not human anyway*. This made him smile halfway, which made him feel odd. His mind was rattled. He had not yet consolidated enough information to register the condition of his car.

"You sure, Sugar. Your car looks like you just came from the La Plata Derby. There's nothing we need to send an ambulance down the road for?"

"You wouldn't believe me if I told you," Albert answered.

She looked past him, out the window, and he turned to look too. His car looked like something out of a carton. You could barely make out what model it was. No windows, and the entire roof about six inches lower than Saab designed it to be. Wheels were bent, fenders a mess. Looking at it, Albert could not fathom how it drove. One of the truck drivers who had been eyeballing him came up next to the waitress, looking at him as if he were some new bug newly discovered. "It was Big n foot wern-it?"

Albert did not respond. He only turned back, looking at them, stunned.

"You bumped uglies with Sasquatch, din't ya?" the truck driver asked.

"Hairy…" was the only word Albert managed.

The waitress shooed off the truck driver and then brought Albert some soup. She instructed him to eat and then made a call. Later officer Lenard showed up and took Albert's report, snickering from time to time. In the end, he left, warning him that if he found another wrecked car down the road, that Albert would wish it were Bigfoot who had hold of him.

After the sheriff left to go "Looksie," the waitress pointed to some motel rooms behind the diner. She told him to go talk to her husband, the manager, and he would give him a room and help him find his lost items in the morning light. Albert followed instructions like a tired child, and in the morning, after a free continental breakfast, hopped in the manager's pickup truck to go look. They were joined by the manager's brother-in-law, armed to the teeth.

A Bigfoot nut, Albert surmised, actually comforted by his presence.

Albert was not sure where he had come from, but the manager was sure that there was only one truck trail fitting the description into the forest within the two-hour drive Albert had estimated. They soon were on the logging road, and after about an hour into the mountains, Albert covered his mouth and pointed. The driver stopped and poked his head out his window as the other man jumped out, cocking a shotgun. A tree was broken off midway from the ground, and the ground was upturned near the pull-off where Albert had pulled over to sleep.

"We never seen 'em this close to town. Most times, they get spotted miles in the thick. Firs, time I reckon anyone spotted one this close." The manager said, shouldering his own .30/30 and snapping a holster holding a hand cannon. "You must of attracted 'em somehow."

Albert barely noticed the man talking when he got out of the truck and walked over to the place his car had once been parked. There was glass and other car parts strewn around and remnants of his bags and computer. The computer itself was shattered into many pieces sunk deep into the dirt from heavy looking blows. He dug like an archeologist for almost an hour, with the manager helping, and found his wallet and money, but could not find either his laptop drive or the external one he had downloaded the data on.

He returned to the truck, sitting in the middle while the two men looked around, smelling and tasting bark. The brother-in-law disappeared into the forest as the manager returned to the truck. He and Albert said nothing while they waited. An eight-track played bluegrass off-speed, which offered no comfort for Albert. He wanted to leave this place badly but did not offer protest for the kindness everyone had shown him.

After about twenty minutes, the brother-in-law returned with a piece of brown fuzzy hair, holding it up for them to see. It was longer than his hand, stretching from fingers to past the man's wrist, and matted, but it was the smell that caused Albert to retreat against his driver. The manager rebuked his brother, telling him to put it away. He was satisfied.

Albert was soon back at the motel. The manager told him that his car was a total and offered to buy it for scrap, for '200 Buckaroos.'

Albert took the deal, hitched a ride into the Durango, where he rented a car, and drove west. California was his destination and the home of a hacker friend who could help him. He was not giving up that easily.

Saying Goodbye

Stephen had the boat ready to sail when Peter showed up on the dock. The two acted cordial to one another while they performed their duties on the sloop. Serenity was soon keeled over in the wind about five miles west of Mission Beach. Stephen heaved-to and locked the wheel in place, causing the boat to turn and face the coast, slowly drifting.

"Thanks for coming, Pete," Stephen said as he tied off a line to the helm.

"I'm glad to be a part of this," Peter answered.

The two moved to the bow of the boat and sat on the windward side, feet hanging off. The boat floated rather calmly, though its nose would bounce up from wakes rolling in from behind every now and then. Occasionally, a bigger wake would cause the bow to point to the mountains and then dive, submerging their feet in the cool ocean water. This was Heather's favorite place to sit when they sailed, and the two enjoyed it with her silently before any words were spoken. A large wave came, and the bow dropped with a splash. Both men's legs submerged almost to the knees, and they cheered in unison from the surprise and shared memory. The ocean was their home, their sanctuary. They were members of a special club. Only those who knew it like this could understand.

The familiarity of the moment broke any ice between them, and in their revelry, Stephen placed an arm across Peter's shoulder. Peter reciprocated with a pat on his back. Any hard feelings were now dissipating into oblivion, the two men brothers again.

"She's here," Peter said.

"I know. I think she always will be. We are lucky. Even in death, our place of visit is amazing." Stephen said.

Peter nodded. "I'm glad you're back, Man. I missed you,"

Stephen looked at him with gratitude. "Me too… I guess."

"So, letting go of the past and readying for the future, yeah?" Peter asked.

Stephen nodded. He looked at the blue-green waters dancing about his feet, then over at Peter. "We need to talk about that first?"

"I'm good, Steveo. I said my piece, and I'm happy to see you walking in a better direction."

"I am Pete. And I'm sorry for all of it. To you…and Lucy."

"You don't need to apologize to me, Man. I love you and want you to be happy. Heather would want you to be happy."

"I'm also sorry about how things went down with Lucy and—"

"There's no need for that. Lucy and I were just friends." Peter cut in.

"I know you have feelings for her," Stephen said, looking right into Peter, not allowing any mistruth to exist between them.

Peter was silent.

I didn't plan for that to happen. That is all I want you to know. My heart was dying, and so was hers. We just let that bond go too far."

"Too far?" Peter asked.

"Well, I don't think Lucy and I being together would have been my choice if I were in a better frame of mind… especially because of you."

"We decided together that friends were all we were going to be," Peter said.

"Yes, and you both still acted like there could be more. I just want you to know I did not mean for it to happen like this."

"Enough said, Bro, let it lie," Peter said.

Stephen put his arm around him again and squeezed.

"So what's next? Baby, and all?" Peter asked.

"Well, we get married, I guess. I'll do right by her, but I just don't have any real desire to do all that again. It's too fresh being at a rehearsal and all that. Lucy said she didn't care and would like a wedding overseas anyway. A bunch of strangers I don't care about and bot-a-bing, it's over with." Stephen gave Peter his gangster look, which was ridiculous, and Peter laughed.

"Stick to writing buddy, acting?...Fogetaboutit."

The two looked at the beach, now coming slowly closer as the boat drifted back the way she came. Serenity was now half a mile closer to land.

"Want me to get it?" Peter asked.

Stephen nodded.

Peter jumped up and headed back to the cabin.

Stephen waited for his friend to go below and then looked into the deep.

This is it. I have to let you go. I don't want to, though. But I must try in order to be the man you want me to be. Stephen looked back for Peter, but he was still below. He looked at the water splashing at his feet.

"My soul is wrecked, like this ship run aground. It hurts too deep; my thoughts more like dreams. Yet, in my dreams, I'm free with you. Life is the dream now, and sleep is life. Only duty keeps me. My word to you. The integrity…"

Stephen leaned forward like he was telling a secret to the Pacific Ocean herself.

"Heather….I cannot lie to you. I'd still seek you in these depths here…now. My anchor in hand as I descend in search of you…"

He grew silent, looking back over his shoulder.

Only you're not in them, are you? You're someplace better.....I think... I feel your smile there sometimes, hear you calling me to…follow.

Stephen cleared his throat as Peter came out of the cabin and worked his way forward with a bottle of champagne in hand.

"I talk to Heather sometimes…" Peter said as he appeared from below.

He handed Stephen a bottle of champagne. It was Heather's plan for them to enjoy it after things settled down, and this was it. Stephen pulled the foil and thumbed the cork. It flew high. He took a sip and handed it to Peter, who took a drink and handed it back. He looked at the label and over at Peter. Stephen tilted the bottle, letting a heathy portion go to the sea. "For you, my Love, I will see you again." He said, his voice breaking slightly.

"We'll see you again," Peter added.

Stephen took another drink and handed it to Peter. He held the bottle in his lap and looked out at the water.

"She is in a better place..." he said, rolling the bottle in his hands.

"I know… she told me she found God. I know whatever she found was real for her, Pete….I need to understand that."

"I'm here," Peter said, handing the bottle back to Stephen. He took it and drank long before pouring more into the ocean. He looked over at Peter, who shook his head and then poured the rest into the water. "I love you, Heather, and will never forget you."

The bottle empty, he hugged it as he looked south. His pain deeper than the sea floor beneath them. Peter let the waves comfort him. After a few minutes, Stephen turned to Peter with a new determination.

"So, I get the angels rebelling. I have been all over the world looking into stories about star people and other mythologies. Every instance where ancient aliens are theorized to have influenced humanity is simply the fallen ones. The angels who came down and taught humanity technologies in defiance of God, manipulated humanity's natural development, and toyed with genetics."

Peter looked surprised but was smiling, so Stephen continued. "They are in every culture, though different forms. If one looks carefully, they will find similarities in how they taught humanity to worship them and helped them build great structures. They showed them how to manipulate crops, animal husbandry, and many other skills, which God wanted humanity to learn on their own."

"So they were violating the prime directive," Peter said.

Stephen laughed, "yeah! Also known as "Starfleet General Order 1."

Peter put a hand up, and Stephen high-fived him. "Even Star Trek has roots from the fallen," Peter added.

Stephen pulled out a folded piece of paper and opened it. "Samyazal, one of the 'Grigori,' meaning 'Watchers' in Greek. His name comes from the roots' shem,' meaning 'fame,' and 'azaz,' meaning 'rebellion' or 'arrogance.' Most believe he was the leader of 200 legions, which fell from heaven after the fall of Lucifer. The theory is that he led his legions to earth, taking human form and choosing women as their own."

The waves were calming, and the sailboat moved slowly closer to land. Stephen skimmed the paper for more to share.

"There is a listing of the other angels in Enoch, but the story goes that they defied God and lusted after women, resulting in all kinds of unique offspring.

"They weren't all giants. Some angels birthed horrible things with huge eyes and large skulls; others birthed very human-looking offspring with mythical gifts. The offspring of the fallen dominated the land and feasted on the flesh of humans."

Peter leaned over, looking at the paper in Stephen's hands. "I read someplace that the ideas of vampires and werewolves originated from these mythologies."

"That is an interesting avenue to research. Stephen said. "What I have discovered is that the fallen claimed different areas as their territory and were worshipped as gods. This is why there are different but similar mythological stories worldwide." Stephen read on.

"Azâzêl taught humanity the secrets of war. Let's see. um… Harut and Marut are the two Angels mentioned in the Qur'an who were known in the time of Solomon. The Qur'an says that they were a test for the people with sorcery. Dânêl taught the "signs of the sun" to humans, known today as the Zodiac. Asbeel is noted as being the manipulative voice, which first convinced Samyazal, then the rest to rebel. This one appears in many places and seems to be a real troublemaker. Also, there is Dumah, a nasty one with legends in many different cultures. We have Gadreel, who taught the art of cosmetics and the use of weapons. Penemue taught mankind writing with ink and paper. I could go on, but you understand where I am headed, right?"

Peter nodded. "I'm impressed. I had no idea all of this information even existed. So, what does this mean for you?"

Stephen folded the paper and put it away. I believe all the ancient stories result from fallen angels and demons.

"So, you follow Leroy's thinking that demons are not fallen angels? Peter asked.

"Oh, for sure. Just research the two. There are massive differences between them. I also believe aliens, lizard people, and even Sasquatch are demons or newly bred Nephilim. My hang-up is with who is right and who is wrong. Is Lucifer the bad guy? Charles challenges that Lucifer and Yahweh are both gods fighting a war. With this thinking, one might be able to accept that all these creatures are real, but still not know what side to take."

"Steveo, you may know more about the science and archeology pointing to these things than me. You sound like Leroy more than ever. It's simple, though. God has backed his claim with miracles and fulfilled prophecy; Lucifer has played sneaky games trying to undermine that plan and mimic him, but clearly not the same. Do you see any unity in all these false gods?"

"Definitely not. Only in their defiance of Yahweh."

"Did Heather describe her encounter to you?" Peter asked.

"She did…a little… She wanted to tell me more, but I wasn't interested." He looked over at Peter. "Like 'the host,' they both had similar experiences, I guess."

"The host?" Peter asked.

"Yeah. Mitch."

"Why does everyone keep calling him that?"

"The girls, Bro, they called him that. Anyway, Yeah. Him…Mitch. You talked to him….did he…Touch you or anything?" Stephen asked.

"Peter laughed. You mean in a priestly way?"

Stephen smiled, but only briefly.

"Sorry, Man. It just sounded odd the way you put it. No. No touching or anything. The guy is like talking to a stone, to be honest."

Stephen was silent for a long time before saying anything else. He sat back up, looking out at the ocean. The boat took a big wake and splashed both men, but neither made a sound as they grabbed onto the handrails.

"I touched his hand, Pete, and he showed me so much it hurt."

"You mean like a vision or something?" Peter asked.

"Yeah, like being in his head and swimming through his memories, only he guided me. I felt emotions too. I felt well…his misery. Everything flashed so fast that I felt my head was on fire. The reason I bring it up is I think he showed me his memory of meeting God too."

"Heather said it was Jesus," Peter added.

"You would know better than me. All I know is the vision I saw could have been like that. It was confusing. He told me that is because I am not used to surfing a mind."

"That sounds like something he practices." Peter offered.

Stephen lifted a leg up and turned towards him. "He has been ever since his encounter with God. He has moments where he goes away and finds himself in other people's minds."

"Wow," Peter said.

"I felt his dehydrated body as my own. He was malnourished. I think the guy had been wandering the streets for days without any food. I couldn't see them because he was protecting me, but others were in there with us. Bad things. Pushing. I could feel the heavy gun in my pocket, his hand always rubbing it, and I began to recognize the streets he was walking when he began fighting them."

"Demons…." Peter said.

"I think, but this is where it got hazy. I remember falling to the ground and seeing a cloudy image of a man appear. They talk, but it is muffled and intangible to me. The next thing I know, I feel a hand grasp my shoulder, and the greatest heat I have ever felt burning inside me. The others, the dark things, are screaming. Mitch is screaming. And there's a powerful voice speaking. It was too much. I passed out. The next moment I am being lifted up by a nurse, and Mitch is giving me a knowing look, like 'welcome to my world.'"

"Dude, I don't know what to say. It's a lot to chew on." Peter said.

Stephen felt a little relieved to unload but sensed Peter's doubt.

"Bro, all the science in the world won't show you the truth without a doubt. That would remove the need for faith, which is our only currency with God. Once you grasp the simplicity of it all, it will be easy for you."

"That Man's voice…." Stephen added.

"I believe God has touched you, and maybe…Mitch too. Listen, Steveo, I don't know about the dinosaurs or how old the earth is, but I know God is real. If he made it any clearer, it would not be special. Love is only love when it is revealed in difficult times. Light is only light when it is contrasted by darkness. I'm not sure how else to explain it. Question: If you knew without a doubt that you would see Heather, Mom, William, and Sharron again tomorrow, how much brighter would your outlook be today?"

Stephen smiled, letting this thought wash over him. "It would be awesome."

"He reveals the truth to you only as quickly as you can handle it. For some, it takes years to grow and mature; others grasp His love quickly and are like super-novae on fire, doing great things overnight. I've been a slow grower, but I also have a deep grasp of His love. God's power rests in love, and Lucifer's is based in fear. Two powers at odds with each other. Keep your eyes open for His love. That will lead you to the truth the fastest."

Stephen looked at Peter with newfound respect. Peter never ceased to surprise him. The two men sat quietly, swaying on the ocean for a while. Stephen only got up when they were in line with the channel leading into Mission Bay.

He pulled the sheets tight, righting the sails, and moved the boat onto the new tack. He did not say a word the entire time they headed in. Stephen dropped the sails while Peter steered and, when he was finished buttoning them up, sat down next to Peter while he piloted the boat into the marina.

"I saw that love in Heather…."

Peter adjusted the throttle down as they turned into the lane. "That is the benchmark of who is right, Steve."

He killed the engine as they approached the slip and stood. Stephen took the helm. Peter made his way to the bow, grabbing the line in his hand, and looked back at his friend. Stephen saw truth in Peter's opinion and wisdom beyond his years.

He turned the helm sharply, and the sailboat moved into its slip, slow enough now that Peter only had to nudge it into place and tie it off. Stephen tied off the stern, and the two were soon walking down the dock.

Well Endowed

A comfortable breeze blew as Charles and Lucy sat on the patio of a luxurious restaurant. San Diego Bay was their view. Stephen arrived and joined them.

"I'm sorry to keep you. I was tied up at the loft." He said, taking his seat and waving for service.

"The loft?" Charles asked. I thought you were moved into the house now?"

"Oh, I am. But I was working out some details with the girls next door and looking for some things I had stored in the offices." He looked at Charles. "Research."

Charles nodded, satisfied. Lucy smiled at Stephen, touching his hand. He reached and kissed her on the cheek. "You look stunning, dear." He said.

She brightened. Lucy was now three months along and wearing a very big ring. They had chosen Rome for the wedding; in truth, Charles had chosen the location, surprising them both with an estate there that made Stephen wonder how rich the man really was. It had beautiful views surrounding the property.

The endowment given to Stephen came in the form of a check for one million dollars. He had refused, and the two did not speak for two days before Lucy sat them both down and complained that they were causing harm to her unborn child. Stephen and Charles relented and shook hands. Stephen agreeing to accept, under the condition that he would choose worthy charities to give half of it to. Charles was disgusted by the insult but gave in.

Control was something Charles relinquished begrudgingly, and Stephen was not going to allow him the control he wanted. This was at the height of tensions between the two. Beginning by Stephen allowing too much control in the beginning with the wedding and even relenting on taking his wife's name for purposes of their child's future. He had accepted this ridiculousness at a moment when his integrity was weakened with drink and now regretted the power given to his father-in-law by doing so. When Charles requested their child's name be David, Stephen chose to place foot firmly on the ground, and severities rose between the two men. Lucy had promised Samuel to be the name in honor of Heather, and Stephen wasn't budging. He had won that battle and lost his Sir name in the aftermath. Now peace was beginning to flourish between the three again but was shaky as Charles was setting up schooling for Stephen's unborn child.

"David—I mean—Samuel, "Charles drawled, "Will have the finest education, giving him the greatest opportunity there."

Lucy squeezed Stephen's hand, hoping he would love her in this moment and not reach across the table and stab her father with the butter knife in front of him. He relaxed and took a deep breath. "Charles, if we.." looking over at Lucy, "decide to educate our child at this prestigious school, it will be after *we* have been there and agreed, as husband and wife, that it is in our child's best interest."

Charles leaned back in his chair, calm on his face. "Of course, Stephen, I would not presume to expect less from you. I only offer it to my grandson as a gift, if you will it."

Stephen knew he was now looking like a tyrant and backed down a little.

"Thank you, Charles. I'm sure we will love the idea as much as you, once we see it."

Lucy was now smiling and touching both men's hands. Charles, too seemed pleased. They ordered, and the rest of their brunch was cordial and uneventful, save for a brief moment that caught only Stephen's attention. A man was being escorted from the dining room by two security staff, which was not in itself very unusual, but the way that this man stared at Stephen's table the entire time stood out. Stephen excused himself from the table, and Lucy and her father continued their conversation.

He followed the path to the men's room, catching a brief look from Charles as he turned the corner. He bypassed the restrooms and walked outside to the parking garage below. There was the man talking to himself as he fidgeted his key into the lock on his car door.

"Hello," Stephen said as he walked up, startling the man.

Albert dropped his keys and leaned against his car. "Uh…ahhh…um."

"I am sorry to have startled you. My name is Stephen. Have we met before?"

"Um...no, I was just leaving." Albert managed, picking up his keys and inserting them into the lock. He had it opened and was inside quickly. Stephen knocked on the window.

"May I ask you something?" he asked.

Albert rolled the window only a crack. Putting the key in the ignition and starting the Toyota Tercel.

"We don't know each other. You're mistaken." He said, putting the car in gear.

Stephen popped the handle, opened the driver's door, and grabbed the man.

"I am no threat to you, I promise." He said in the calmest way possible. "It's him you were watching, wasn't it?"

Albert's face betrayed the truth. "I gotta go…"

"I am watching him too." Stephen said, "and believe we can help each other—"

The man backed up, forcing Stephen to let go or be dragged. As he gained distance from Stephen, he slowed and stopped the car. A hand poked out the window with a business card on it. The card dropped to the ground as the man yelled from within.

"If you want to know the truth."

The man was gone. Stephen walked over and picked up the card when a voice came from behind him. It was the voice of Charles' large driver. He was at the staircase that led from the upper level.

"Is everything okay, Mr. Rutherf—Meyers?" he asked.

Stephen hated the name every time it was used to address him, and most of their staff knew it.

"I'm great, just thought I saw an old friend." As he made his way to the staircase, the driver asked, "Did you?"

"Did I what?" Stephen asked, passing him on his way back up the stairs.

"Find an old friend?"

Stephen waved it off, looking back where he had been standing when the driver called for him. “No… I was mistaken.”

He returned to brunch with his new wife and father-in-law. After they finished, the three of them parted ways. Charles had business abroad and was flying east. Lucy and Stephen headed home. When he had a moment alone, he went into the bathroom and turned on the water. He sat on the toilet and pulled out the business card. It was a tattoo shop in pacific beach, but Stephen did not think that was where this man worked. He turned it over and scrolled on the back was a number followed by ‘Albert.’ He pulled out his phone and dialed.

“Hello?” Said a whinny voice on the other end.

“You gave me the business card,” Stephen said.

“Are you alone?”

Stephen could hear beeps and clicking of keys.

“I am. What’s this about?”

OB Peer. You know it?” the voice said.

“Yeah, I live here.”

“Be there in an hour if you want to know the truth.” The call dropped.

Stephen went downstairs and kissed Lucy. “I’m going for a ride, Dear.”

She caught his hand, looking up at him. “Be safe.”

“I will. I’ll be back in a couple hours.”

He rolled his Ducati out of the garage, and put on his helmet, looking up at the light shining down from the patio door above. Her shadow exposed her. He flipped his visor down and gunned the motorcycle down the hill. Stephen flipped out the kickstand in the lot next to the peer. He looked out at the breaking waves. It was overcast now, and mist was in the air. Not an ideal day to enjoy the beach, though some locals still made their way to surf or congregated in groups of two or three on the wall. The beach was nonetheless quieted by the weather coming in. There were a few dedicated anglers swinging rods up on the pier. He removed his helmet and made his way up the long staircase to the pier above. Stephen grasped the chin strap of his helmet, carrying it like a weapon. The end of the peer held one fisherman, and as he approached, he noticed that fishing was far from the man’s real purpose. His swing was awful, and the man didn’t even have a tackle box with him. He walked up next to him, keeping a good amount of space as he leaned against the rail.

"So, what's with all the cloak and dagger?"

The man looked over, almost dropping the pole in the water.

"You're really not good at it, by the way," Stephen added.

"This isn't my day job, Albert said. "I'm a scientist, not a spy, but the people you're close to are dangerous, and I value my life."

"The people?" Stephen asked.

"Yes, Rutherford, to be more precise," Albert answered.

"Listen, if you got a beef with my father-in-law, why don't you—"

"Aren't you at least curious why I felt safe coming to you?"

"I'm here, aren't I? Just get to the point," Stephen said.

"He and a bunch of really powerful people are planning some crazy stuff. His name comes up in all the wrong places, and the two people I trusted to help me investigate him have been killed."

"Do you have proof?" Stephen asked, moving a little closer to the chubby man.

"No, he's good. I had a hard drive but lost it. It contained files with plans that would blow your mind. Plans to de-populate the earth, viral pandemics, and instigating wars with false flag operations. Also, huge budgets designated for internment camps for US citizens who they deem a threat. There were also references to lists which had the names of all Americans who owned firearms, and flagging for the ones considered a higher priority."

"Higher priority?" Stephen asked.

"Yeah, rebels, those who speak out or could gather others in rebellion. They are going to build these huge camps under the guise of FEMA emergency shelters, but really their intent is to imprison citizens who will not give up their weapons or conform."

"Listen, I'm not interested in conspiracy theories. If you have specific information about Mr. Rutherford, then give it to me; if not, we're done here."

Stephen backed away to leave, and the man grabbed his wrist, stopping him.

"You said yourself that you are watching him…I chose to come to you because one email spoke of you as a potential problem and instructed someone to eliminate you if you began to interfere with his plans for someone by the name of Samuel…I'm not sure who this person is, but he seems to play an essential role in Rutherford's plans.

"Samuel? You're sure that was the name?"

Albert nodded. "Rutherford has his hands in everything big, and many of these plans spell bad things for our future."

"This all seems out there. How did you come across this?"

"Do you know this, Samuel?"

"No."

"I worked for a company called LSC, which does research on cutting-edge science: Robotics, software technologies, you name it. One department has designed software that will soon be able to monitor all of us. Face recognition, phone, and email scanning, you name it. This technology will all tie together within a decade giving total control of the populous. It violates more constitutional rights than you can imagine. These programs are moving forward without any public knowledge, which in itself is what I believe is most dangerous. I also believe I can prove Rutherford is involved in some very shady business worldwide."

Stephen remembered the files on Charles' desk in Jordan. Live Systems Corporation was among the names. "What exactly did the email about me say?"

"It was from a Louis Reficul to Rutherford. It said that if Mr. Meyers ceased to be of use or threatened their plans for Samuel, he should be removed. I only got bits and pieces of the original conversation because the packets I was snatching were encrypted in some new way that I barely understand myself. To be honest, it flustered me. I wrote the software to break that system down, but it must be executed from within the network for it to work. What I gleaned is that Samuel is some politician that they want to move into power."

"What do you want from me?"

"Help me get the proof I need to blow this wide open before it's too late." He handed Stephen a small envelope. "Inside is a floppy disk. And an address. The address is to the location of a server in New York. I want you to find it and insert the disk. The program will do the rest."

"What will happen?" Stephen asked.

"The truth will be exposed."

"I will think about this; that's all I can promise." Stephen began to walk away.

"Watch him, Man. He is dangerous."

Stephen hid the envelope under his motorcycle seat and left the ideas the man shared there with it for a while. He spent the next three months revising a story about a woman possessed by demons and her fight to free herself against all odds. It was during a scene where she was hiding in a church that Stephen had to stop, rocked by the realization he had just allowed information from his own past into the story. He remembered his mother's journal. He saved the document and shut down his computer. He looked around his office, now back at the loft. This was the place he liked to write, and though it annoyed Lucy, she didn't press him on this one front. Both she and her father seemed to have more control over his life than he did now, and this was one of the few things he would not budge on.

Charles traveled most of the time and occasionally would send Stephen a memo about something they found or pictures of a dig, with notes for their documentary. Charles had an office built at the Ocean Beach home that came with the newest computer system on a beautiful desk. It all sat in front of a wall of books that any writer would lust over, clearly to entice Stephen there, but his office here was his writing center, and he was good being close to Heather's friends running their business one a door away. They were like sisters now; Felix was here too, always near him when he came to write.

He got up and went over to the bookshelf. It wasn't there. He would have to go see his sister to get the answers. He picked up the phone and called her.

"I'm on my way out the door, Honey. Can we try meeting up tomorrow?"

"Of course. How bout I come for a visit?"

"That would be great. I'll be here all day. Maybe I'll bake cookies again,"

"That would be great." He said.

He hung up the phone and looked all over his office for a bible, but there wasn't one. Felix purred at his feet, and he picked the cat up, petting it. Stephan wandered, first through the busy design firm, smiles everywhere he turned, and then found himself in his loft. It was like a crypt: Dark and without the love that once permeated every corner. The smell was not bad, but stale, like opening a long sealed closet. He went to the double doors of the master bedroom and put his hand on the doorknob. It was cold, and for a moment, it reminded him of the dream. He set Felix down and turned the handle. The door cracked like a crypt as the paint, long embracing the door casing, cried out in complaint.

The room was even darker, the bed unmade. It was like stepping back in time. He closed the door behind him, standing in total darkness. There was only a faint bit of light from the edges of the windows. Heather's scent was in here. His heart began to drum like a dark symphony. Chellos began to follow its beat as he heard a death mass begin in his mind. He touched her dresser, and lightning shot across his mind. A flash of her in brilliant light smiling at him as she pulled out something to wear.

He walked to her vanity, and she was here also. This time looking up in sepia light around her. She smiled, putting on an earring. The room's darkness loomed around her, but where she sat was bathed in color. He closed his eyes and sat. When he opened them, she was gone, his lone reflection staring back in the mirror. He felt her hand touch his shoulder and looked back. She was laying on the bed, one leg revealed from beneath the covers. He got up and went to the bed. She beckoned him with a finger. Her smile almost real. He laid down with her and felt her embrace. He knew it wasn't real but decided to forget that world. Her lips felt cold but still wonderful. Her caress brought peace as she enveloped him in her arms. He was soon asleep, on a journey with his first love. The room remained dark as the man slept soundlessly on the bed.

The Grey

Stephen was sitting on the end of his bed, facing the door with a faint glow around the edges.

If God is real, so is Satan.

He felt evil around him now.

Did I reject God and allow evil to come unrestrained in the process?

He wished he could talk to Leroy or his mother. *There's Peter*, he thought.

He stared at the door, trying to remember the dreams, hoping to dislodge a clogged faucet or reopen a passage. He had been overcome with fear before, but somehow he thought that wasn't the key to finding the door again; in fact, he had an intense feeling fear was a dangerous emotion for him to hold onto now.

Fear brought them, he thought. *It attracts them.*

He remembered the light coming from behind the door and locked his mind on to that image, as well, the icy cold feel of the doorknob in his hand.

"I know I am to blame," he said to the empty room. "You tried to warn me, but I rejected your help."

The light beneath the door became brighter, and the room cooled.

"I'm sorry for that."

His face grew grievous. He was smaller. "Please show me how to find her."

His head hung low now, and a faint voice could be heard. He opened his eyes, startled by it, and saw the door. It was no more than a shimmer now, a heat phantom seen floating above a hot highway. A disturbance in reality in the shape of a door. The doorknob was different but familiar to him. It was the same doorknob his mother had sitting on a mantle when he was a boy. He remembered playing with it and her telling him that it had come from her childhood home, the only Memento from a home now long ago demolished to make way for something new.

Stephen didn't hesitate. He reached out, grabbed the glass doorknob, and felt its deep cold enter his hand. A moment later, the overwhelming feeling of smallness came again; all the air was sucked out of his lungs, followed by tininess.

Blackness became shades of grey. He felt an ancient shame, and then the odd feeling left him as grey gave way to beautiful day. The sky was clear. The breeze, sweet. Sand was under him. It reminded him of a place he had visited in San Qin Tin, Mexico. The beach was full of sand bluffs with patches of grass and small vegetation growing randomly about. The bluffs were like long lines of great stadium steps leading down to a beach with calm waves moving in and out like gentle breathing upon the shore. A small mountain protected half of the cove. A volcano churned on the other side. Small puffs of smoke rolled up from a resting giant. He stepped forward and sat on a grassy step.

The smells of the ocean entered his nose, accompanied by the sounds of sea life. He noticed he was sitting beside a grey statue of an angel looking sorrowfully down upon the waters. A little girl screamed with excitement, drawing his attention back to the beach. But before he could focus on the source, he saw a man sitting on a bluff below him about 100 feet away. He had his elbows on his knees and his head turned, following her. Stephen followed his gaze to the giggling girl about nine or ten years old. Her hair was pulled into pigtails, and her pants were rolled up to her knees. She was running from the surf as it followed her up the beach like a puppy after its master, and she screamed with glee as it rapidly caught up to her, touching her feet. It receded, and she chased it back down the beach.

Stephen thought of Heather, not much older, doing the same thing when they were kids, and for a moment, the girl looked like her. With her shimmering dark hair. It wasn't, though, Stephen realized.

"She is beautiful, is she not?" A voice spoke from beside him. Stephen's heart slammed into his chest, looking at the once stone angel now squatting down to sit. It was no statue. The angel looked at him with a face that conveyed centuries of pain, or was it shame?

Like the shame, I felt coming here...

The angel's wings were pulled tightly behind its back as he sat a few feet to Stephen's right. His skin was smooth like polished marble but grey, like the color of wet cement. The angel's eyes were a tired blue-green.

"You startled me. I thought you were a..." He didn't finish.

"I startled you?" The grey one replied. "It's not often that a man appears like you just did."

His smile was genuine but did not carry any joy. Stephen saw regret and sorrow on the angel's face. It wasn't just his color, though he knew somehow that it was a reflection of what it felt. This angel conveyed deep wisdom, maybe wisdom achieved through a great misfortune.

The angel's voice sounded like stone if stone could speak.

"All of you amaze me, you know," Stephen blurted out.

The grey one returned his gaze to the others below without a reply.

"All of your kind, I mean... Angels," Stephen reiterated.

"You see a lot of angels, traveler?" The grey one asked.

"I've seen them in dreams or whatever this is... Where we are now."

"You don't know where you are?" The angel asked.

"A dream, I think. I touched a door."

"The Father has granted you that. For what reason I cannot see; in truth, I cannot see much about you, though, enough to see you are important to Him... To them both." The angel looked at him, penetrating his soul.

"You have darkness enveloping you, though the light leaves a way of escape for you... For now."

"Why do you say for now?" Stephen asked.

"Everyone gets a chance to choose the Father. If they reject Him, He still leaves a way for them to change their mind, but only for a time. The further they walk in denial of him, the thinner that beam of light becomes; until evil consumes it forever, clouding them in lies."

The two sat quiet for the next few moments. The little girl continued running up and down the beach, chasing the ocean and barely escaping it's counter-attack. Her laughter was invigorating. The other man did not move, only followed the girl with the turn of his head.

"I've seen white angels and others who are less, but no grey ones. Some of them change from white to black at times. I think it's like a reflection of their anger or evil or something. Is that why you're grey, because of your sorrow?"

"You feel my sorrow, young one?" The angel asked him.

"Yes."

"Father has touched you, in deed. Did he show you the future, as well?"

Stephen put his head down. "A couple of times, I dreamt of things, but then I asked Gabe to leave me alone, and they stopped."

The angel shook his head. "Humanity, you never fail to amaze me. Father blesses you, and you think you accomplish great things all your-selves. He gives you gifts, and most worship his enemy with them... Or reject them."

Stephen felt foolish. "I've had a hard time getting my head around all of this."

The angel gave a short laugh. "That is the lie. We are what is real; the world humanity clings so desperately to is spurious. Angels, demons, the Father, and His adversary are very real. More real than the water in your oceans or the sand beneath your feet. Heaven is real. The rest…" He gestured with both hands around them, "all of this... It is not real; it is a construct."

Stephen looked down at the man. He recognized him when he turned to get up. It was... *the host…*The man found a new place, closer to the girl, and sat.

Stephen looked at the angel. "Why sorrow... Why are you..."

"Grey?" The angel finished. "It's my shame, and I do not try to hide it. Our sin, our rebellion, soils us. My color is evidence of the loss of my purity. I disobeyed Father, and now I am unclean—fallen."

"But the others I've seen, who seem far more evil, appear radiant, at least some of the time," Stephen asked.

The angel closed his eyes and opened them again. His eyes were now brighter, deep blue. His skin started to lose its shabby grey color, starting around the eyes and spreading throughout his face. The last of the grey vanished from his fingertips. His skin was now a flawless and pure-living-white. Thc angel now had the brilliance of energy and light within him, like the guardian in Stephen's dream. His ashen hair now held a platinum cadence.

Beautiful...

Then, as fast as he had brightened, the angel began to dim. He seemed to exhale and relax as his ashen color returned. His eyes returned to their tired blue-green hue. He was once again grey.

"The others hide their shame, some better than others, but when their focus goes to rage or battle, and they stop concentrating on their appearance, ugliness, their true color, breaks through. Some are horrible to look upon. Their evil deeds so atrocious that their eyes have become black pits. Those fallen are so treacherous and evil that they cannot come close to their former glory. At best, they can only mimic human beauty. No eyes at all, though they don't need them anymore."

"You speak as if you are not fallen, yet are. I'm confused." Stephen said.

"I did not rebel with Lucifer; I fought with the heavenly host in the first war in heaven. No… it was much later that I allowed envy and lust to enter my heart. I let a fallen brother trick me, Asbeel. He led me to a desolate place where a woman was going to end her life."

He stopped speaking, and Stephen looked over at him. Seeing his contemplation.

"I gave up my glory for the ability to be a man to her and made her mine. I allowed a moment of weakness to separate me from glory forever."

"So you *are* a fallen angel then," Stephen said.

The angel looked at him, shame on his face. "Man puzzles me, always needing a label, always combining the complex into little jars for storage, always missing the real image. I fell from grace, but I refused to rebel further. I refused to join Lucifer, so I became outcast, rejected by both sides. Father spoke to me one last time when he changed my name and has never spoken to me since. I feel his glory shine on me from time to time as if looking in on me, and when he looks, I bow in acknowledgment of my evil in submission to his righteous judgment."

"So, I don't understand," Stephen asked. "That's it? Game over? What will happen to you?"

"I will face judgment at the end of days."

"Why can't He forgive you like he has humanity?"

"Humanity had a man, perfect in all his ways, take your place. I'm not a man with a soul like you. So that pardon does not apply to me."

"So, you're an outcast and now do nothing?"

"I do what I can where I can. I am no longer empowered by God and have refused empowerment by His enemy, so I am limited in what I can do."

"Are you good or evil?" Stephen asked.

"Everything I do, I do in hope of glorifying my Father. No reward or pardon needed. It is up to him to do as he pleases with me. I find peace in my maker's judgment, greater than any offered on earth. Death in His hands is far greater than eternity out of them."

Stephen looked down at the beach and saw the man watching the girl. He was about to ask another question when the grey one spoke again.

"She is his….He, mine…Enough about this. Why are you here?"

"I don't know…I was hoping to dream again and was trying to…when… well, I came here. I know the man below, or I think I do. Mitch is his name."

The angel nodded.

"He is your…what…"

"Father has brought you here to show you something."

"I guess Mitch has something to show me?"

"I think you have something to show each other." The grey angel said. This man needs your help also."

Stephen looked over at the angel. "How can I show him anything? I barely understand how I got here."

"Find him, share what you know and have seen, and listen to his journey. I believe you will help each other in this way." The grey one said as he stood.

Stephen stood up and followed the angel, now walking along the bluff. The girl was far ahead, and the man followed her. This angel seemed to be watching over them.

Father brought another man here once, long ago in your years. He wept over the future he was shown down on that shore."

The angel pointed past the girl to a foggy part of the beach.

"Daniel?" Stephen asked.

The angel nodded, pleased with his new pupil.

"You are telling me that this is the place Daniel was shown the beast?"

"He was shown a great many things, some of which you may also see. His role was to warn the world. You, I believe, may have another job. The world has had all the warnings it can reject. I can only surmise that you are to prepare those He has chosen for the coming war."

They walked on.

"I have one more question. Is Heather's Jesus real?"

"The angel stopped, looking at Stephen with a renewed smile. "You would not be here if He were not."

Stephen lost his breath as he was pulled back from his walking companion. He could see the angel watching him fade away for a moment before Blackness took hold. He opened his eyes, taking deep breaths as he woke on the floor of his old room. He felt peace.

"I believe you… I understand….Show me."

His voice was the only sound in the room, still dark. He got up. Stephen walked to the window and pulled open the blinds letting more light into the room. He made the bed, went into the bathroom, and took a shower. His mind was swimming through all the information in his head, putting the puzzle together.

***

Stephen spent the next three months working feverishly on research, locking himself away in his office for days, writing. Lucy would see him for moments and meals, and then he would be gone again. Peeking in while he was out revealed piles of balled-up paper and stacks of open books around the office. He always treated Lucy lovingly. In fact, his way was disturbing to her somehow. He was always bright, never low. He showed no more signs of grief and even spoke openly about Heather. Entering her third trimester now, Lucy never had the chance to feel insecure about her body because his appetite for her seemed to grow alongside her pregnancy. Lucy was content with his desire for her, but a part of him she could never touch. At one point, he took her into the bathroom, where he had drawn her a bath. He made careful love to her and held her, washing her afterward. She was amazed and pleased. He dried her, brought her favorite nighty, and kissed her forehead. He looked at her with his salesmen's smile. She knew he wanted something.

"I must leave you for the night, Dear. I have something important to get done, and it cannot wait."

"Now… It is ten o'clock?" she asked.

"Yes, Dear. I must write before I lose it. This is important. I am almost finished. I want to have this done before the baby comes. After this, I will be all yours; no more work until the birth."

"Okay." She said and kissed him.

He caressed her hair and lay with her until she fell asleep. Stephen slowly got up and slipped out of the room, closing their bedroom door with a gentle click. Soon the garage door was opening, and his Ducati could be heard driving away. Lucy opened her eyes wide awake and looked out the window.

Underground

Stephen had the fourth floor all to himself. The design firm was closed for the weekend, and the house was empty. He felt peace returning to his old home and safe because no one else ever came. Felix was there, and so was Heather. He brewed a pot of coffee and unlocked the front door before entering his office. About an hour later, his phone rang.

"Yes." He said, knowing who it would be. "Fourth floor. Then the first door you see. It's unlocked."

He hung up the phone, closed a journal he had been working in, and placed it behind some other books on his shelf. Lucy snooped; he knew it, though it didn't really matter. He was simply postponing the inevitable conversation, but he needed time now. He locked his office, went through the design firm into his loft, and met Albert sitting at the bar. He smiled and topped off his cup of coffee, lifting it in question to his guest. Albert shook his head. "I'm nervous enough as it is, no caffeine for me, thank you."

Stephen smiled. He liked this guy. He was a nervous wreck most of the time but brutally honest, something He appreciated. Lately, his trust in others around him was faltering. He believed Lucy wasn't playing games with him, but he was sure there were things she withheld. His last conversation with Peter concluded with Peter telling him how Heather and he felt about her involvement with whatever was happening. This and Albert coming to him made it hard to doubt. Things were much more treacherous than they appeared. He was unsure how Charles played into it or what he wanted from him and his unborn child, but the thought made him sick inside, and he needed to figure it out. Albert and Stephen went over notes from each other's investigations. All that had been confirmed was that Charles had some form of ownership or involvement in several companies and organizations at the top of Albert's list.

"I can't confirm anything in regards to where this server is, Man. I have snooped and, a few times, nearly been caught." Stephen said.

"What about your wife? Could she be brought in on this?" Albert asked.

"No. I have thought hard on this. I don't think she has a hand in any of it, though somehow she is important to her father. He controls everything in her life and is almost nervous about her safety. My friend Peter—"

"Woa. Woa, whose Peter? I never agreed to involve anyone without talking about it first." Albert whined.

"I know, but I can trust him, and besides, all he knows is what I have suspected. I have not mentioned you…Yet." Stephen said.

"Yet? Who is he? How do I know I can trust him?"

"You can trust him more than you can me."

"That is not very reassuring…" Albert said.

"He'll be here soon, so I need you to trust that I trust him. He would give his life for mine if it mattered, okay?"

Alright, but for the record, I don't approve."

"Here is some good news. I have decided to set you up. I have money set aside for the purposes of an underground group I want you to help me create."

"I'm not hearing the good news yet, Man. I'm hearing me getting my ass in a sling, and I don't particularly like anything that is underground."

Stephen laughed. "You crack me up. The biggest scaredi-cat I have ever met, yet with his hands in the back pockets of people he thinks are trying to take over the world. So which is it: You a wuss, or Batman?"

"I prefer Robin….or maybe Alfred?"

Stephen laughed again. "You need a safe network to work in. Hidden, off the grid. We also need help. I met a couple of interesting boys up north who also have a lot to say about your conspiracy theories. They are arming up and digging in. They need leadership and ways to communicate without getting caught. You asked me to risk my neck to get that disk into that server. I'm not doing it unless there is something in place to utilize the information."

"You want me to team up with mercenaries and crazy militias or something?"

Stephen's patience was thin. And it showed. "These are good people with families and land, lots of land. We need land to build bunkers and other hidden places. You set up a network to work from, and they help watch your back."

"Where did all this come from, Man? I'm seriously baffled."

"A dream," Stephen said matter-of-factly.

"A dream....Really?" Alberts face flushed, mouth slowly opening.

"Where are you hacking into these systems from?" Stephen asked.

I'm not at liberty—"

"A garage in Irvine, probably one of your college buddy's," Stephen finished.

Albert was stunned. "You followed me? That's not cool, Man."

"If I know this, how hard will it be for someone with millions to spend to find you?"

Albert looked defeated and, for once, not the smartest man in the room. It is my grandmother's house, for your information."

Stephen smiled as he unfolded a map of the United States.

"For starters, we have land here, here, and here in California."
He placed a finger on a point between Warner Springs and Palomar Mountain.

"This one is already equipped with a well and farmhouse, but behind the home in the woods are 12 sea containers sealed and buried. They make up a complex with a natural water supply that runs underground through one of them. It drains back down and into the home's septic system. There is fresh water and some power, but still dependent on the grid. One of your jobs will be to make it self-sufficient and undetectable. Your other job will be to set up a secure connection to it."

"You're serious about all of this, aren't you?" Albert asked. Excitement sneaking into his expression. "All this from some dream?"

Stephen looked at him, hoping he was listening. "I am not going to argue my reasons with you, not now, but yes. An angel told me...well, showed me... I think it was an angel."

He looked for Albert's poke, but it never came.

"At one point, I would laugh, but not after Colorado. I saw some shit there that turned my hair white. See this?" he pointed to some greying in his temple.

Stephen ignored it and moved his hand west on the map. This area will eventually be cut off, so keep this in mind. Any recourses will need to be from the northeast of this dot." He looked over at Albert. "Are you getting all this?"

"What do you mean cut off?" Albert asked.

"Gone, everything west of here," Stephen answered. "Are you following me?"

"Yes," Albert placed a hand on the map and pointed to the red dot. "Set up power and communications here, avoid any development west. I will also set up surveillance if the money is available."

Stephen smiled. "One hundred thousand to start. I hope you can prepare this first site for half of that because I'd like to set up six more after this."

"A hundred K, Man? I was hoping for 20. Give me 50, and it will be the best of the best." His eyes grew bigger.

"The individuals I send you to are good people. Trust them, but no one else. If they don't know them, or I don't know them, then don't trust them. Albert, this is number one. This is more important than busting the elites you are targeting. Understand?"

He nodded, but then a question came over him. "This is beginning to look like doomsday preparations, Man. My goal was to stop it, not survive it" Albert sat on the stool next to him.

"We will, but first you secure the line, then battle the enemy…."

He hesitated, wondering how much to tell Albert.

Less is more. Don't overwhelm him with the end of days.

"Okay, I am in charge of setting these places up with power, security, and communications. Are they going to listen to me?"

"They are eager for your arrival. There are horticulture and organic farming experts there, and many are trained in military tactics. You are Tech, and while it is being set up, they are under your command."

"This is all real, isn't it?" Albert asked him, worry crossing his face now.

"Yes, it is, but we have time, how much I am not sure, but I would bet those places will be life to many in the future."

The doorbell rang. Albert squealed.

Stephen looked at him, concerned at how shaky this man really was. "Are you sure you are up to this?"

Albert nodded, "Sorry, I'm just wound up right now." He grabbed a candy bar from his pocket and peeled the wrapper.

Well,man-up, okay?" Stephen said, walking to the door.

It was Peter. He came in, and Stephen locked the door behind him. Albert, this is my best friend, Peter Armstrong. Peter, this is my computer expert, Albert Redding."

Peter put his hand out.

"You said you didn't tell him anything about me." He said, shaking Peter's hand.

"I only told him I had a computer expert interested in teaming up with our cause."

"It's a cause now?" Albert asked, now munching the candy bar.

Stephen gave him a look, which said he was out of patients, and Albert caught it.

"Sorry, yes, that's me, on board and ready to build." He smiled nervously at Peter.

"Peter is my contact with the land owners. Some of them are friends from his church and others through that same network. He will be introducing you to Paul, the man with the plan and backhoe near Warner Springs."

"It's great to meet you, Albert," Peter said. "We are in great need of your expertise out there." The two men got better acquainted as Stephen retreated to his room. Inside he moved Heather's dresser aside and opened a safe. Inside were seven stacks of new currency. Each with four bundles holding $25,000 in each. He grabbed one stack and placed the bundles in an envelope before closing the door.

I hope I'm doing this right...

He returned to the great room and handed the envelope to Albert. "One hundred thousand, Albert. Please make it last, and be careful."

Albert took it, feeling better about how serious Stephen was about all of this. "I promise I will do my best not to waste a dollar."

The three men spoke for another hour before Albert left. When he was gone, Stephen and Peter looked at each other, surprised that they were actually doing all of this. Peter's smile grew, anticipating tonight's black-op. "You ready, Man?"

Stephen's own smile grew, "I am."

They left the loft and drove in Peter's Volvo to Fiesta Island, a little hand-shaped island jutting out into the more shallow part of Mission Bay. The two men drove around the island to where several vehicles were parked. This part of the island had a small C-shaped inlet where children often played. Tonight it was only adults. The two got out and walked towards the crowd formed at the edge of the small pool. Peter's arm was around Stephen's shoulder as they arrived. Shelly was the first to grab him, hugging him hard enough to make his eyes bulge.

"I'm so excited, Honey. Mom would be so happy. Heather too."

Shelly kissed his cheek and stepped back while several church members shook his hand and hugged him. Pastor David called him as he waded into the water.

"We have come here tonight to celebrate a new brother, in Christ, and witness his statement of faith and obedience to the Father. Stephen followed him with a couple whoots and a whistle from Peter. Tears filled the eyes of his sister and some of his childhood friends. As he stood next to Pastor David, he felt the preacher's strong hand upon his shoulder. He looked at Stephen thoughtfully and spoke in a voice only Stephen could hear.

"From now on, you are an enemy of the prince of darkness. You understand this, right?"

Stephen nodded. Pastor David smiled.

I have watched Stephen and the rest of the Meyer family as they all, one by one, found and served our Father. I prayed for this day with both William and Betty on more than one occasion and again with Leroy more recently. I have suffered Shelly and Stephen's losses."

Many in the group had tears in their eyes now, both of joy and remembered loss. Shelly held onto Peter, who hugged her, not taking his eyes off his friend.

He looked at Stephen. "Do you acknowledge before all here tonight that you were a sinner and in need of salvation, Son?"

"I do."

"Son, did you accept Jesus as your savior and sacrifice for your sins?"

"I did."

Pastor David placed his other hand on Stephen. "Because of your open declaration of faith and acceptance of Christ. I baptize you in thc name of the Father…"

He pulled Stephen back and under the water. Stephen could hear the words "of the Son" muffled through the water. Light filled his sight, and he found himself standing on the bluff again. This time the man and child were not there. He looked to his right and could see the statue of the angel far down the beach. To his left, a man sat down. The waves were gentle still, like the ones in the bay, where he supposed his physical body remained. The man was wonderful. The perfect depiction of love and grace.

"I am very happy to have you as my own, Stephen," Jesus said.

"I am…." He didn't know how to respond. He was overwhelmed by the joy he was experiencing. Jesus' smile overwhelmed him.

"You were meant for evil, but My will is for you to do good. You will have to sacrifice for this good to be accomplished; however, your rewards will be indescribable. They are waiting, and this is where your life will begin."

Stephen felt weak, being in the presence of God. He found that place he knew Heather dwelt, and it was greater than he could imagine. Before he could speak, he fainted, and blackness washed over him. The next feeling was the cold of the water and the sound of a voice above. "..And the Holy Spirit."

He was moving up through the cold water; light became brighter, and soon air filled his lungs. He saw the face of Pastor David, and the stars above him. He was now standing, embraced by many hands. He could see Heather there in the crowd smiling at him, so beautiful.

I am so proud of you… and then she was gone.

Stephen made his way to the shore and was handed a towel to wrap himself in. They stayed there for almost an hour, saying congratulations and then goodbyes. Shelly was the last to hug him and request he visit her soon before getting in her minivan and driving off. Peter and Stephen sat on the hood of Peter's car, looking out at the bay.

"Well, now you are really my brother," Peter said.

"It feels great, Man. Thank you for sticking by me." Stephen said. He looked down at the sand, a little pinch of sadness knocking at the door of his joy. "Lucy wouldn't understand this… you know that is why I did not want her here, right?"

Peter understood all too well. His own joy drained over the concern for the girl. "I have prayed long and hard for her, Steveo, and you. But I always feel a brick wall there when I think of her. It's like she's blocking the truth."

"I know. She is so loving and sweet most of the time but has this dark side that seems to rear itself at the mention of God. She cannot even stand my writing about demons, always making negative comments about the subject. I didn't want that energy here tonight."

"I understand, Man, really… I am glad for you, though. Do you see how things appear completely different now?"

"I do. I am amazed by how much clearer the world looks." He wanted to share his vision but decided not to bring it up.

"So what now. What are you going to do about Charles and everything you've learned."

"I have a child on the way, and that complicates the situation. I must play a careful game, Man. I think we should keep moving in the direction we have planned and hope for guidance. Yes?"

Peter smiled, proud of his friend. "I could not have put it better. I think you should just leave Charles alone altogether. If Albert's right about him, he could be following dark guidance himself."

Stephen cringed at the thought of tangling with the man. "I know. I will play nice; make him think I am under control, but I need to look into things if given a chance. Charles is annoyed with me now because I have defied him regarding my child. I think I will go to Rome next week. Take the initiative and look into this school he has offered to pay for. I must tread lightly; this much is certain."

"Just be careful, Bro. I will make sure everything we have begun keeps moving forward."

Stephen stood up, pulling the towel off of his shoulder. "That reminds me. You remember the combination to the safe in my loft, right?"

Peter nodded.

"The rest of the money I pulled out of the account is therc. You know what it's for. No matter what, that must not fail. Also, my last will and testament and everything you will need if something happens to me is there. My journals, too."

"Stop talking like something bad is going to happen, Bro. I don't like it."

"Nothing bad is going to happen. We may suffer losses here and there, but they're temporary, right?" Stephen poked Peter's belly.

Peter smiled, "Yes, they are, and if something does happen, I promise to take care of things."

"I need to get back. She is ready to pop any day now."

The two men got in the Volvo and drove into the city.

100 Days of Blood

Lucy's water broke on the morning of April 6th, and labor lasted until that afternoon, which was the 7th on the other side of the world. I remember the timing of this birth well because it was in concert with first the downing of a political flight in Rwanda and later the beginning massacre of 800,000 Tutsi people in Rwanda. Many angels battled outside the dimension of man's vision over these events, and Lucifer oversaw the blood bath himself.

As the young boy was being delivered from the loins of Lucy Rutherford, one hundred Tutsi mothers had their blood spilled. As well, one hundred days of blood followed. The holy angels overcame evil and empowered those who fought to stop the bloodshed, but not before many innocent lives were slain.

Lucy named the nine-pound-six-ounce baby Samuel Nathanael Rutherford, pleasing both his father and grandfather with one pen stroke. Stephen despised taking her family name but knew more critical things were at stake. Charles was overjoyed with his prodigal son-in-law having a change of heart and grandson to adorn with all his wealth. They flew to Rome as soon as mother and child were able to travel and soon made themselves comfortable in their gifted home. Stephen finished writing the novel, making several changes to the final draft to satisfy his partner's requests.

***

When Charles came out of the den with the finished work in hand, he looked pleased with himself.

"I felt like I was there, Son. She is fascinating heroine. I would tremble to be a demon in her sights."

It's crap, Stephen thought with a smile on his face.

Stephen and Charles flew to New York and had one last meeting with the publishers, and the book went into production. His second book, the nonfiction, never made it to print. He realized this was the plan all along. This was just one of the ways Charles got what he wanted, and Stephen really didn't care anymore.

He wants your son, though...

He disagreed with almost everything Charles believed and wanted to keep working on his private work. This was his passion now; no one was permitted even a peek. He was writing 'a handbook to the end of the world'. Stephen would dream of something and map it. An earthquake in Haiti, or a tsunami in Indonesia, he wrote it all down. Waking in the middle of the night and sneaking away to work. Many times he was not sure about the order of things he witnessed or when a specific event occurred, but often there was a sign or marker, such as a local event in the news, he could tie it to.

This begins to become confusing when one looks back upon the future as if the past. Time is relative to the place where one exists. For those of us free of this constraint, it is a different creature. For Stephen, at times, his mind would fracture with the strain of differentiating the future from the present. Sleep was the only cure for these weak moments, and often when he awoke, the result would be broken fragments of events. These fragments, were laid out in journals to be given to another chosen to stand after him.

***

Lucy was beside herself, always bringing Samuel out to show him off to company, most strangers to Stephen. He felt alienated in Rome, missing the fellowship of other believers for over six months. It was after one of these dinner parties ,watching Lucy prance the baby around like a toy, that Stephen decided he needed a break and left the following morning for San Diego. He left Lucy a note stating he had business there for a week.

Lucy waited a day and then called him. After not getting an answer at their home in Ocean Beach, she called the loft. She eventually got one of the girls in the design firm on the phone, who confirmed that he was there, locked away in his office. Lucy left Samuel with the nanny and flew to the States.

The Last Prophet

It was raining hard in San Diego. The streets were shallow rivers, and thunderous clouds blanketed the city for days. At about midnight Stephen finished writing. He flipped through several pages at the end of his writing, then tore them from the journal. He sat back in his chair, looking out the window, with the pages crumpled in his hand.

He burned the pages, dropping them in the trash can one by one, and then got up and returned the furniture that had been blocking the doors to their regular positions.

Stephen slept soundly for over sixteen hours after that and did not wake when Lucy came in and tried to speak to him. Frustrated, she dug out his keys and went to his office. Thunder pounded, shaking the windows and making her uneasy. She sat down at his desk and began reading what he had written.

> *God has chosen to reveal a warning to me about the future of our nation. First, God loves each of us equally. Straight, Gay, black, white. We are, every color, shape and size, his beloved children and His grace awaits ANY who reach for it.*
>
> *I was not a believer when these dreams and visions began, but now I am. We have done this to ourselves. We have turned our backs on the creator of our universe and Father of us all. How arrogant we are to have done this. We do not deserve mercy for this betrayal, yet it is still offered to those who accept it.*

God became a man to accomplish what none of us could; pay the price for our arrogance as an innocent. I accepted that payment on my behalf and now have peace. I am no longer afraid of dying or what comes next.

America is not revealed in the scriptures that speak about the end of days because America will no longer exist as it does today when those prophecies come true.

This may be hard for some to digest, but it is true, all the same.

America has been an example to the world of God's blessings, and soon as a final example and warning of His wrath.

America was founded under one true God, and Christianity was at the root of her foundations. Because of this, America became the most powerful nation on earth. She was Israel's ally and blessed Israel in her political decisions.

God told Abraham he would bless those who blessed Israel.

If you want to see the future of America, simply read the Old Testament. It is full of nations prospering, then crumbling, and being destroyed because of their wickedness. If one looks back at history, they will see America is no different.

We are turning our backs on God and becoming a wicked nation,

The future is shocking in both the wrath we will suffer as a nation and the level of debauchery and corruption this nation will embrace.

Our nation will become controlled entirely by Lucifer, and this is already in play. Lucifer is already in control of many in true power.

Our government will be responsible for robbing and murdering tens of thousands, and God will be pushed out of our schools and ejected from our monuments. He will also become enemy to most Americans; He and his followers will be mocked and ridiculed by the nation.

Sexual immorality will rule this nation, and family values will cease to exist.

Those who try to follow God's principles will be forced to embrace sin and have their children indoctrinated with false teachings that are enmity with God.

America will become a modern-day Sodom and Gomorrah, and immoral behavior will not only become acceptable but legally forced upon all Americans to accept and embrace. This was how the cities of Sodom and Gomorrah were just before they were destroyed by God.

Marriage will have no true place in this nation, and sex will be as casual as a handshake between strangers. This, coupled with America's political decisions, which hurt Israel's cause, will be the last straw with God.

He will, once again, use America as an example to the world; this time, His final warning before unleashing His wrath upon all the earth.

God brought me to high places at different times in our future, shortly after land is rescinded from Israel and given to her enemies.

Great storms will begin to wreak havoc upon the world. A city in America will plan to celebrate an official 'Day of Sin' when God sends a brutal hurricane to destroy it. Three more storms will hit our nation, each devastating us; other acts of nature will also increase in frequency and intensity around the world.

America will experience its own Northern Lights as evil runs unchecked throughout our the country. Political divides will become violent, and rumors of civil war will be on the lips of many. Weapons will begin to be hidden away by those who see the signs, and quiet revolution will become the subject in darkrooms. Different states in our nation will become more divided than they were during the civil war as our government slowly and methodically takes more and more freedom away from its citizens.

Personal firearms will be outlawed, and this is when the battles will begin. First, rebellions will form out of those who refuse to give up their arms, then factions of our Military will mutiny, and civil war will break out.

At this time, the government will control media, power, communications, and healthcare. There will be secret prisons built under the guise of emergency FEMA camps, but they will end up being used to imprison all citizens who resist.

The North American Lights will cease to be an interesting phenomenon and will be followed by solar flares that will wipe out our power grids and do massive damage to our infrastructure. These will plunge our nation into total mayhem, with riots and looting out of control. Murder and rape will be commonplace on America's streets, and the government will be too overwhelmed to combat it or even deal with the dead.

America will be forced to make deals with foreign powers that break up her sovereignty in trade for help recovering from these disasters.

The US Dollar will fail, and its Constitution will no longer protect the people. War will break out between citizens and the government's newly formed national police force. States will attempt secession and fail, leaving America in a colonial condition.

Great earthquakes will occur, ripping 2/3rds of California and Baja California into the sea. Many will die, and the aftermath will create a new coastline for Western United States.

Superstorms, once thought scientifically impossible, will develop, some devastating the mid-east, and Eastern coast of America, while wildfires will ravage the mid-west.

The word cursed will become synonymous with America, and this will all unfold in an overwhelming rapid period of time.

However, many will repent and turn back to God. He will relent for the sake of his children, but America will never again be the glorious nation it once was.

This is not the great tribulation spoken of in the Bible; it is a precursor to those events, which will be much worse. America will be the linchpin for the prophecies to be fulfilled, and once removed as a superpower, all the pieces will fall into place in the Middle East.

I looked up and saw those lights over my own head. I witnessed, with my own eyes, California's destruction, leaving a broken string of burning islands no bigger than the Coronado's.

I saw the East Coast transformed, no longer resembling the coastline we all know so *well. Manhattan gone; Florida gone. A new east coast, miles in from the old. Many great cities gone forever. I saw these things with my own eyes. I saw the tears, the death, and the evil of those who survive. I am glad I will see my own end before this happens, but I am saddened that so many will have to live it. No one will see the 22nd century before these events transpire and God returns in glory for his own.*

October 9th, 1994

Stephen William Meyers

Lucy shut the notebook. *Is he crazy?* She left the office. Her heart was pounding.

She tried to wake him again and could not, so she left. She went to their home and called Peter. He answered on the second ring.

"Hello?"

"Peter. Is it true, or is my husband going insane? Tell me the truth, please."

Lucy…You're in town?" He asked.

"Yes, and I'm scared. Please tell me the truth. I'm willing to listen." She cried.

The sun broke through the thick cloud layer granting the city a brief reprieve from the downpour. Thunder still dominated the sky above. Shadows breathed life and faded with fast-moving patches of clouds leading in the next wave of storm clouds from the sea. As the last bit of sun gave way, shadows faded, leaving the unnatural darkness behind. These unearthly shapes crept along the floor, taking form behind Lucy on the hall.

Something new entered the home. It was no demon but a very dark fallen one. It was black as coal and had tattered back wings that folded behind it. It had a female's shape but no eyes, only dark pits, black holes within them sucking up all light. As it walked across the living room, two demons backed away, careful to keep their distance. Lucy could be heard crying upstairs. The dark one stood still and began to change. Its naked body took on light changing from coal to fair, human skin. Its long raven hair transformed into a beautiful blonde. It was her, Lucy, standing there now naked. The two demons watched from a distance. These fallen were unpredictable and often ate demons when they got too close. It was now Lucy in every way except its eyes; they remained black holes.

"Lucy, tell me what you are talking about, and I'll answer you."

"The WORLD COMING TO AN END, PETER; what else would I mean?" she cried. "I am happy, for once in my life, and now this?"

"Lucy, it's not going to happen tomorrow, but it is going to happen. We still have time, and both Stephen and I want you to join us." He said.

"Join you…? Where... on the alien spaceship?" she was crying harder now. "Do you realize how crazy you sound?"

"Honey, God is going to return for His own before much of it occurs. Heather is with Him, and Stephen and I will go too. Will you consider what I have to say to you? We want you to be with us."

Thunder rattled the entire house, shaking her where she stood. The day got even darker, and the torrent of rain resumed. It pounded the roof and blinded the view out the window. She broke down, crying. He waited for her to respond. Lucy grabbed a tissue and wiped at her eyes. "Peter, I'll go wherever you are going. I'll believe whatever you say I should believe. I don't want to be left behind. Please come over."

"I'm on my way."

He hung up and called the loft but got the answering machine. He hoped he would have the right words to say as he got in his car. He turned the key and got nothing. *Damn it!*

Lucy dried her eyes, feeling some hope at letting go of her fear and hearing them out. She loved these people and saw their peace, and wanted to be a part of whatever they held in common. After gathering herself in the bathroom, she came out and stopped frozen in the doorway. She was looking at herself standing on the other side of the room. A naked copy of her, smiling. Its eyes were now like her own.

"Do you like what you see?" It said in a changing voice.

"Who…who are you?" Lucy choked, backing into the bathroom.

"Why I am you Dear… can you not see this?" it cocked its head, looking at her. Its voice now more like hers.

She backed into the bathroom, kicking the door shut between them. She looked around for something to defend herself. Thunder pounding the walls like another monster trying to get in.

The dark one walked through the closed door as if mist and then solidified, only now its eyes were black pits again, and its beautiful body now both male and female. Its dark wings ruffled but remained set as the pure blackness of its empty eye sockets crept out, spreading across its face from cheekbones to chin, then down her neck and over its breasts. The thing was like night, its teeth sharp in its open mouth. Lucy turned, her face cringing. There was no hero to protect her. She was alone. It grabbed her by the throat and licked her face. She screamed, but it covered her scream in an awful wide kiss, almost choking her with its long tongue.

Downstairs muffled screams could be heard as demons filled the room. First three, then eight, and finally dozens. They were drawn there by the anguish being experienced by the girl upstairs.

Peter arrived by taxi an hour later. He rang the doorbell several times with no answer. This worried him, so he went around to the garage and tried the code. It opened. He called out for Lucy twice as he climbed the stairs, but there was no answer. The place was cold. The sliding glass doors were all open, letting in the rain. He shut two of them and called for her again. No answer. This time he found his way up to the third floor and made his way down the hall, calling her name. "Lucy…You up here?"

In the master bedroom, he pushed the door open and saw a mess. The bed was pulled apart, pillows were on the floor, and the sheets were gone. The comforter was piled up in the corner. He entered, now fearing another scene like the one that occurred almost two years before. But as he turned to look in the bathroom, Lucy appeared, smiling.

"Oh, Peter, I'm sorry. I was in the bathroom. Have you been here long?"

She was unsure of herself, hiding something; this was clear. There was blood on her nightgown below her waist, and she covered it by wrapping her robe around her and tying the waist belt.

"Are you okay?" He couldn't help but look down, and she noticed.

"Oh, that, yes, Peter. I started my period early and woke up with a surprise. I'm okay. All the pipes are plugged now."

He cringed at the image she created with her vulgarity. "You sure you're okay? You don't look well." He pushed.

Her voice was different also, deeper, *maybe a cold.*

Anger crossed her face for a moment and then cleared. "I'm perfect, Peter, wonderful husband, beautiful son, and all my dreams coming true. Why do you ask?"

"You were very upset when you called."

She seemed confused about this but faked it. "I'm fine now. In fact, I'm so well that I decided to leave for Rome tonight. Stephen is busy, and I miss the child."

"Well, maybe I can take you after we talk—"

"NO!" she barked, almost feral. Her face was again ugly for a flash, then back to Lucy's beauty. "No, Peter. I need to be alone. I am sorry you came all the way out here, but I must ask you to leave. I'm packing and leaving. Do understand, please, there is nothing more to discuss. You and Stephen can dream your dreams, and I will remain in reality. I will not discuss this again."

She left the room, and he followed, only to be led to the door. Peter was dumbfounded but did not push. He tried one last attempt to speak but was met with swinging door in his face. His heart troubled him as he walked in the pouring rain down the hill to catch another taxi.

Something terrible just happened...

Peter got a cab and went to the loft, where he used his key to get in. Felix was there purring when he came in, and he set his keys on the counter as he knelt to give the cat a pat. He found Stephen out cold and watched television while he waited. After about an hour of science television, he dosed off too. He woke to a chatter in the kitchen and got up to investigate. It was now very early in the morning. He turned on the kitchen light and immediately noticed that his keys were missing.

Felix

"Felix, where are my keys," he said. The cat was nowhere to be found. He bent down and looked into Felix's cat castle and didn't see them, so he pulled the roof off and found a booty. Two earrings not matching, a quarter, and his keys.

"Not too bad a haul boy," but wait, there was something else, a cassette tape. Peter reached down and dug it out. It was a microcassette. He replaced Felix's roof and sat at the bar looking at it.

This must be one of Stephen's dictations. The thought intrigued him, so he pulled a couple of drawers open, looking for a player. Stephen had half a dozen because everyone bought them for him as gifts. *What else to buy a writer: paper?* Peter himself had bought him one four years ago as a gag gift.

Nothing here.

He went into Stephen's office, nearly tripping over Felix, who was napping at the door. He found a recorder on the first shelf he chose to look on. Peter sat at the desk and inserted the microcassette.

“Hello, Darlings. You have reached the home of Heather & Steve. Leave us your goodies, and we will call you back.”

“Peter clicked stop, floored by the sound of her voice again.

“An answering machine tape, what an odd a thing for you to steal. You must have had mom and Dad trip’n over that move,” he said to the cat.

He thought about trashing it, thinking Stephen did not need any setbacks, but then decided that would be cruel. He listened to her voice again, and this time it hurt less. He closed his eyes and tried to remember her standing in the kitchen. And the cat jumped on him, causing him to drop the recorder. It went under the desk and continued playing. The next message was from a realtor talking about closing costs and other stuff. Peter stood up, placed Felix in the chair, and then bent down to fish the recorder from under the desk. He was just about ready to click stop when Leroy came to life on the tape. Peter hit his head on the underside of the desk.

> *Stephen, Heather, will one of you call me the moment you get this? I have some startling information you must hear. I fear for your wellbeing, and it is that Man, Rutherford. He is not who he says he is, or I have lost my last screw. I believe he is a servant of Satan and possibly a fallen one himself. I found information on his family line, and it is very odd, to say the least. For one, he is either an exact twin to his great-grandfather, who I am holding a picture of, or he is over 200 years old. Call me before you speak to anyone about this. Please, children. I believe you are both in great danger.*

Peter stood again, clicking rewind as he left the office. Felix chased behind, bouncing at his heels. He played it again as he entered the loft and rewound it once more as he opened Stephen’s door.

“Steveo! Man, wake up!” He slapped him on his face hard and went to the bathroom to fill a glass of water. On his return, his friend was wide awake and looking annoyed. “Why di—”

"SHOOSH," Peter said. Listen to this man. It's bad, really bad."

Stephen was waking now, concerned with Peter's erratic behavior,

"Did you just shoosh me?" he asked. His thinking froze once Heather's voice came on, and Peter cringed when he realized his mistake.

"I'm sorry, Man, I went too far." He fast-forwarded it before Stephen could protest. All of this was happening too fast for Stephen, still half in dream.

Leroy's voice grabbed what was left of Stephen's dream state and poured a bucket of water over top of it. They listened three times, Peter rewinding it and playing it again before a word was said.

"It all makes sense," Stephen said. "All the questions."

"Stephen, my attack on the road was demonic, this is sure. Leroy died violently the night he left you this message. Albert talked about someone named Samuel being important to Charles. He also had a run-in with something hairy and scary in the woods, which conveniently destroyed and ran off with the only evidence he had on Rutherford. The man is evil, dude. I feel it in my bones when I'm near him."

Peter stopped talking and looked at his friend, putting the pieces together. This does not explain Samuel; maybe he just mixed up a personal conversation with business. He is his grandfather."

"Calling him Samuel before he is born?" Peter asked.

"Maybe Lucy told him we were talking about that name," Stephen responded, still digging ideas out to consider. Heather was in this too, somehow fitting into it all, and this turned his guts into knots. He is playing games with our lives, and Samuel is at the heart of what he has planned…"

"You need to bring the kid home, Man," Peter said.

"Lucy's with him. He'll be fine."

"No, that's just it. She's not, and she's not okay either. She's here, Man, and something strange is going on with her too."

Stephen looked at Peter, confused. "How long have I been asleep?"

"Look, she called me. She said she read your journal about the world ending and wanted to know the truth."

"Truth about what?" Stephen asked.

"Is it all real! Man, catch up already. She was reaching out, Bro. She was crying to me on the phone, saying she wanted to believe what we all believe and was scared. I tried calling you, but you were on a vision bus or something, so I went over there. The crazy thing is when I got there. She was a completely different person. Cold and mean. She shot me down about talking about anything and said she was returning to Rome, that Sam needed her."

"That doesn't sound all that crazy. Pete, she has never been interested in God or talking about it and was probably being defensive with you."

Dude, will you trust me? I know Lucy too, and that was not her." She had blood on her nightgown and made some reference to plugging up her hole when I asked if she was okay. Lucy can be blunt, but she's not vulgar. She said it was her monthly, and that could be true, but still, Lucy never—"

"No….. Her period ended a week before I left. I know. I sleep with the woman. Let's go over there now." Stephen said.

Peter nodded, and both men left for the other house.

The house was unlocked and a mess. Not so much torn apart as left by someone with no care for its condition. Fridge open, sliders open bedroom a mess, and Lucy's clothing all over the bed. She was gone and in a hurry. Stephen and Peter made a plan.

I will act as if everything is okay and see what I can figure out. Also, Mitch, I need to talk to that guy."

Peter nodded, "I will go look through Leroy's estate and see if I can find out more about what he was saying about Charles.

When Peter dropped Stephen off at home, he pulled his arm hard as he was getting out of the car. "The minute you think you or Sam are in danger, get him back here, Man. Promise me."

"I promise, Pete. Just do your part, and I'll call you in two days."

"I will, Bro, but I'm worried."

Stephen nodded as he entered his building.

Followed

Charles was sitting in his office looking across the room at the balcony, which held a view of Central Park below. His face held unease. The man, who always seemed to be prepared for everything, was unsure about things, which was a first for him, or at least in a very long time. He recalled the last time things seemed problematic, and it was when over 74 million lives were eradicated in a failed attempt to eliminate his enemies and create a perfect race of his own.

This was also the last time one man would be empowered to enact the plan, which resulted in a miserable failure. This was a mistake, putting so many arrangements in the hand of Adolf Hitler; though as a boy, he appeared easily able to accomplish anything they desired of him.

Such a powerful will, that boy.

But his pride made him too uncontrollable.

Charles inadvertently put a hand up to caress the place his SS emblem had once rested. This was a time of great hope for him. The blood of his enemies flowing like the Rhine, and great leaps and bounds made in genetic breeding between his kind and the promising ones. Before this, entire lines had been born with little resemblance to humanity. Though they were used greatly in battle, what they wanted now was a race to replace humans, a more beautiful humanity. Thousands and thousands of these youth wearing the brilliant hair of the angels, and blinking pure eyes, like his own, meant the beginning of greatness, but it was all smothered, burned, and bombed to hell.

This time he would have ten Adolfs to command and their own boy to lead. His mood lightened at the thought of it all. There was a knock at the door, pulling

Charles from his reverie.

"Yes, enter."

The door opened, and two men stood ready to approach. He nodded, and his assistant opened the door wide, allowing them in.

"We will be busy for at least an hour, Stewart. Please hold all my calls," Charles said, standing to greet his associates.

Stewart nodded, closing the door.

"Scotch?" Charles asked, walking over to his bar top. They both nodded and sat in the finely crafted chairs facing his desk. He brought them their glasses and returned to his desk, picking up his own. "To the child." He said.

"To the child." They repeated and drank.

"What have you got for me?" he asked.

The first, a strong-looking man in his thirties with greying hair, leaned forward, looking at his partner, another man well-built and seeming to be either from law enforcement or at least trained in ways of the gun. He nodded for him to begin.

"We have been following the subjects day and night. And have photos of everyone they have interacted with…" He looked back at his partner again.

"Tell him." the second man said.

"Well… except for one who has alluded photographing in one way or another. What photos we did snap of his face did not develop." The first man said.

Charles was not surprised, but anger shimmered under the skin. "Continue; we will come back to this man."

"Well, Sir, Mr. Meyers…I mean, Rutherford has met with this man several times. Always someplace different. We have no idea how they communicate outside of these meetings but believe there must be a way because twice, Stephen has been sitting someplace as if waiting for someone and then gotten up suddenly and left, taking us on long trips through town. Once, he jumped the Trolley and lost us in the San Diego State trolley station. We picked him back up when he arrived back in the Downtown area."

Chares nodded, making a note on a pad of paper. "When was this?" he asked.

"This event was on the 13th of last month. I only make comment about it because I believe the two have a way of changing their meeting places on the fly, but we are not sure how yet. We will discover this soon, Sir."

The other man leaned forward. "We have more success following the other parties. This Peter Armstrong is uninteresting. He attends church events all the time and feeds the homeless three nights a week; this *was* only once a month, so the increase was noted. We have two men who are there all three nights and yet to find anyone who stands out."

"That is where he is meeting them, I am sure of it. Follow the homeless, and if any of them stand out to you, you know what to do." Charles said.

"Will do, Sir," said the first man. He opened an envelope and slid some photos across the large desk. They were photos of Peter serving food, with some good shots of the homeless as they turned away with full trays. Charles looked at them carefully as the man continued.

"We have not found Mr. Redding yet, but have his computer buddy in Irvine under surveillance. He has not shown up there yet. He shipped a package to the Downtown homeless shelter, which is why we doubled up surveillance there but have not made any concrete connections yet. His bank records have no irregularities, save for one donation of 5.00 to the shelter."

"That was a message to Peter. Was it a check?" Charles asked.

"Yes, Sir, we are working on getting a copy from our contacts at the bank; this is more difficult, though."

"I'll get the check. Focus on the man. He is the connection to Albert, and Albert needs finding and eliminating."

"We could just pick him up, Sir," the second man said.

"No, Albert is too smart for that. You will end up torturing an ignorant man for nothing. He would not give the others that information. It is a one-way relationship: Albert determining when and where they meet. He will behave erratically, and that is when you will follow him to Albert."

"Stephen has been very routine, Hours at his office in San Diego and then a stop at the Ocean Beach home at least once before returning to Rome. The only other moves he makes are the bus rides, which seem to be to nowhere. We did catch a conversation between him and Armstrong, where he mentioned that he takes the rides to help him think. It could be as simple as that if not for the other man we have seen him talk with at random places."

"This man is a thorn in my side, a mistake I will wipe off this planet. He alludes me for now, but this will change. If you see him again, I don't care who is in the way. I want him dead. You still have a connection to the Bureau, do you not, Frank?" Charles looked at the first man.

"Yes, I still consult for them, so I can use resources to a degree."

"Good, good. This man's name is Mitchel Falcone, and he is a priority. He has no business conversing with my son-in-law, and if we are sure it is him…..Well, then, my son-in-law will most likely be compromised too. I must be sure of this, though, before anything is allowed to happen to Stephen."

He looked through the rest of the photos. There were two with Stephen sitting on benches, one at a bus stop and the other at the beach. In these two photos, a man was sitting next to him. The photo was blurred so that the man could not be identified, but it seemed certain it was the same person.

"What about his friend Peter, Sir?" the second man asked.

"I cannot tell if he poses a threat. If you make a connection with the missing Scientist or this other man, eliminate him as well. Here, right here…" Charles lifted a photograph and placed a finger on a homeless man. He is in every photo, and Peter seems to be talking with him right here after he sits down. Maybe a simple check to see if the man is enjoying his meal, or maybe not. Find him and follow him. I have a feeling about this one." His finger was on the head of a chubby man in dirty clothes. "This could, with a stretch of the imagination, be our missing Albert Redding."

Charles downed his drink and went to the bar to refill it. The men sat watching him. He returned to his desk and opened a drawer removing a photo. He walked around his desk and handed it to the second man. "This is Mitchel Falcone. I need a positive ID on him. Even if you cannot get a photo or a good shot, the moment either of you sees him in proximity to my son-in-law, you notify me. I need notification before you move on him, though. Do you understand?"

They both nodded. "If we have a clear shot, do you want us to take it?"

"I'm afraid that if you have him in your sights, he will already know it. He is far more dangerous than you can imagine. I am not sure he even knows this, and I am counting on that. However, to be on the safe side. First, you call me; then we move on him."

"Sounds good to me," the second man said.

***

Stephen and Mitch sat on the bluff overlooking the beach. The little girl played far below, unaware of the men above. Stephen tried to get a better look at her face, but it seemed obscured. He could not remember if this was the case before, and as he tried to remember, he could not.

"Who is that?" he asked Mitch, pointing down at her.

"I don't know," Mitch answered, looking at her himself. I think she is my dead daughter, though I can never see her face clearly enough to be sure. I tried to run down to her the first time I found myself here, but no matter how fast I ran, she always remained the same distance away. It's a mystery I hope to one day solve. I like to watch her, though."

Stephen looked back down the beach and could see the statue a little ways off. Still standing in the same exact position it was before. He thought to ask about the grey one and decided against it.

"You're going to Portland…." Stephen said.

Mitch looked at him, questions on his face. "And my business there?"

"I'm not sure. I only know that this is where our journeys split, at least for the known future."

"I keep dreaming I am someone else there. Someone evil." Mitch said.

"Maybe you are seeing a target?"

Mitch didn't answer.

"I saw you in a taxi, and there was a young girl…."

"And roses…" Mitch finished. "always roses."

Mitch was still a stone, showing little emotion, but Stephen recognized the source of this cold heart and was able to understand him.

"Wouldn't mind a sit down with your guide, but it seems that's not in the cards." Mitch finally said.

They sat quiet for a moment longer. Both watched the little girl running down the beach. There was a little boy further down running towards her, and both men stood to get a better look. The two children met and grabbed hands while running towards the water again.

"You must find out what they want from your son, "Mitch said.

"I intend to. I know Charles is evil. Lucy, too, seems darker now. Very cold and unfeeling, only caring for Samuels's future, not really loving the boy."

"I do not see the woman anymore when I look at her; I see something else," Mitch turned to him, facing him now. "I think Lucy is gone…I fear if I get close enough to tell you more, they will see me too."

"Do you think you can focus your gift on a specific person and see through their eyes?"

"I'm sure that's what I am doing when I travel to Portland. I see through a very evil man's eyes."

"Maybe that is why you need to go there…to stop him.. maybe that girl needs you?

"I believe you may be right." Mitch said. "Ever since my encounter, I see the dark ones swarming around some people. As if my eyes have been opened to that unseen world around us. Like this world and ours mingle somehow."

So what do you think?"

"You mean Rutherford?"

Stephen nodded.

"I don't fully control this, and if I could, I think that would be dangerous. I think he would be able to look back."

"Yeah, you're probably right," Stephen said.

"If *you* were here, I might be able to, though." Mitch added.

"I see futures all around the world. You see memories…people. When we are together, it does become something stronger."

“This place is not future or past, though, and we both are able to come here,” Mitch added.

“Yes, and here we might be able to safely peek.” Stephen said.

“Rutherford then,” Mitch said.

The Keys

A diner bustled with the clanking of silverware on plates in the small town of Cedar Key, Florida. Porcia set plates of steaming food down in front of two men, smiling at them as she finished. A lady in the next booth waved at her, and she nodded.

"Anything else for you, gentlemen?" she asked.

"No, we are looking good, gorgeous." One said. The other was already filling his mouth but winked to confirm.

She made her way to the next booth and grabbed an empty plate. "What can I do for you?" she asked the woman.

The lady pointed at her plate. "I'm not feeling these potatoes. Can I change to the fries?"

"I'm sorry, Sugar. Is there a problem with them?" Porcia asked.

"No, not really. I just want fries instead."

Porcia smiled at the woman. "Not a problem. I'll add a side of fries on the house, Hun."

Porcia made her way back into the kitchen and jammed a ticket into the cook's wheel, winking at him as she went by. She sat down in the back for a minute, counting her tips, when another waitress came in. "Porcia, what are you still doing here? You were off hours ago," the thick woman said, sitting down. She looked and acted motherly, and Porcia loved working with her. She reminded her of mom.

"I know, but sandy is having car trouble again, so I said I'd cover for her until she got here."

"Girl, go home. I'll cover your tables until she gets here. Don't argue with me, neither."

Porcia smiled. "You sure? I don't mind."

"Go, Darlin'. You have that sweet little girl waiting for you. I got things here."

Porcia got up and stuffed her tips back in her apron as she swung her purse over her shoulder. "Okay then, I'm gone, Honey."

The thick lady smiled, reminding Porcia of her mother again. She climbed in her mini-van and drove away. About 3 miles down the road, she stopped near a grocery store and got out, leaving the engine running. Several homeless people were sitting at the base of the store wall near the dumpsters. Their expressions livened with seeing her. One elbowed a sleeper next to him as she turned the corner. She pulled the tips back out of her apron and stopped in the middle of the group.

"You 'all been sharin' right?" she asked.

They nodded. "Why you so good to us, Missy? You need that money. Look at your dump of a car over there." A raggedy woman replied as she took the money from the Porcia.

"I am just fine, Sugar. Besides, who's going to take care of you if I don't?"

"God bless you," another man said, taking his cut from his lady friend. "God bless you an ur'own." He repeated.

"He always does, Hun." She said as she walked back to her van. She waved to the group as she backed up and drove away.

She unlocked the door to her tiny apartment and immediately knelt to catch a waddling toddler coming at her like a little linebacker for a tackle.

"Yo chil' never cease to amaze me Dearie; already taking steps at a year and six." The sitter said from the couch. "She sum-pin special that what she is."

"Hi, Precious," Porcia said, picking up her daughter. "How was she?"

"A blessing, as usual, Miss Mitchel. "Always a blessing. That little one. Smart as any bean counter already too. She was trying out the sounds of the number be'in said on that kid show with the bird. She'll be saying them by end-O-the month."

The sweet old lady stood up and grabbed her purse. Her silvering afro was barely contained under the silk scarf she pulled over it. She looked like she stepped right out of the seventies with her handmade dress and blouse. She was in her sixties now, but her face revealed a great beauty once prominent in her younger years.

"Aunty Elouise will come by to play any time you want, Honey."

She kissed the baby on the cheek and then put a hand on Porcia's shoulder. "You need to get some rest, Dear. You look a little peaked."

"I worked a double again. I have tomorrow off, though, so I will sleep in."

The old lady made her way to the apartment door and opened it. "Well, good, then. I will see you Monday, Dear," and she was gone.

Porcia held up Seraphina and looked into her eyes. "Did you have fun with Aunty Elou—"

"How may I help you, gentlemen?" Elouise said from the front door as she reached in, locking the door before pulling it shut behind her.

The voices were now muffled but becoming louder—two, maybe three, male voices. Something clicked within Porcia, and she moved with a quickness. She darted into the bathroom with Seraphina held out in front of her. She kissed her daughter and set her in the tub, pulling the curtain closed. Porcia locked the bathroom door and ran over to her nightstand, opening a drawer, when she heard a muffled pop and saw a beam of sunlight shoot into the room, pointing at the bathroom door. Little splinters of door and dust floated to the carpet.

Oh no, Elouise

Before she could give her friend another thought, a loud crash shook her. The door held, but the jam was hanging loose now.

She pulled out a stun gun and rolled over the bed as the door flew open. Two men charged in, with another behind, dragging Elouise in and dropping her lifeless body on the floor.

The first two were on top of Porcia so fast she dropped the stun gun under the bed. One had her legs, and the other wrapped an arm around her waist, grabbing her free arm. The other arm was blindly searching the floor under the bed for her weapon. She kicked, gaining a bit of ground toward her goal, but was dragged back.

There! Her hand found the stun gun just as she was dragged to the middle of the room. She plunged it into the armpit of the man holding her other arm and clicked send. He froze as if God himself had paused the entire event. His eyes big for a moment and then closing tightly as he began to shake.

The next moment pain raced through her body and mind. The other man had kicked her between the legs with real force. She choked, and tears flooded her eyes. Before she could regain clarity, another blow came; this one to her guts, as his huge foot came down. The third man came around as she curled into a ball of pain, dropping her weapon.

His smile was ugly and dangerous. His knee dropped onto her shoulder and face as the sounds of her child began to fill her mind. Seraphina was crying. The cry was terrible, full of fear, and Porcia's only thought was an uncontrollable desire to burst up from the floor and get to her little girl.

"Where's the child!" The man kneeling on her face barked.

Seraphina's cries were getting louder, and Porcia was confused.

They can't hear you?

"Where's the kid?" he barked again. "Check the bathroom," he said to the other man.

The stunned man was climbing up on the bed, regaining himself.

She kicked with her free legs and got the guy kneeling on her in the face with a foot, but he caught the other. They wrestled as she got free from under his knee. He was choking her with one hand and punching her in her side with his other as she managed to get onto her belly, inching toward the stun gun.

The other man trying the bathroom door saw this and returned, stomping on Porcia's hand. A horrible scream came from her, startling both men. It was full of pain and rage.

The toddler's screams were louder now, and the invaders could now hear them. They looked bemused at one another as a buzz of energy formed in the air. Porcia reached down within herself for the power to get up. She managed one pushup under the weight of the men then everything went dark as a fist cracked the back of her head.

In the following moments, everything was distorted, but Seraphina's cries were now filling the room. They became siren-like, causing Porcia's ears to ring and her head to hurt. She felt the weight on top of her lift and air wash over her cheek as the room became a violent cyclone. Everything was flying around the room, including the three men. Bedding, clothing, and toys whirled around her field of vision, gaining speed.

Porcia's vision began to clear, but it became hard to breathe as the force spinning in the room sucked everything into its vortex above her. She dragged herself towards her daughter as the men's screams broke out. The sound of her daughter was now being masked by the terrible sound of the wind force screaming around the room. The men were now spinning around like pinwheels as they circled the room, violently catching the corners of walls and crying out with each blow.

Porcia reached out to the little girl crying in her head.

I love you, Sera. It's okay now. Mama's here, Darling. Another man crashed head-first into a wall with a crunch, and his blood spread out within the cloud of debris, changing the hurricane into a crimson storm. The men's screams were gone now, leaving only the sound of the hurricane spinning in the apartment and her child's softening cries. And then everything stopped, falling to the ground. The three men lay dead, and their blood sprinkled the entire apartment. She managed to get up on her knees and crawl over to the bathroom door. She stood up and forced the door open with a shoulder. The jam gave, and she entered the bathroom holding her side. The toddler's tear-filled eyes lit up as Porcia lifted her into her arms. Porcia held her against her chest and closed her eyes.

Thank you, God.

Trouble Makers

The security team assigned to Stephen was now doubled as they walked out to Peter's Volvo. He knew that it was because there was also a team assigned to Peter now. They both got in the Volvo. Peter handed Stephen a photo. It was a faded back and white photo of some SS Officers and Nazi high command. One face was circled. "who does that look like to you, Bro?" Peter asked.

Stephen's jaw dropped. It was Charles, unaged. "Where did you get this?"

"Leroy's belongings, in his Bible," Peter answered.

Peter started the Volvo and drove to the airport. He circled through the drop-off section but did not stop. They used the slow traffic and hoped for a secure conversation, cruising in a no-fly zone. Peter blared the radio as they spoke.

"You can no longer meet Albert at the shelter, Pete."

"Yeah, I know. I will make arrangements." After a second drive through the terminals, Peter stopped. The two hugged. "I love you, Man. Be safe." Peter said.

"You too, Bro, be careful—no more chances. Let things take care of themself until I return with Sam. Check the email account."

"Will do," Peter said.

Stephen grabbed his carry-on and waved as he entered the terminal. Peter folded the photo stuffing it in his shirt pocket as he drove away.

***

Albert and eight others rode ATVs deep into the woods. Two of them towing small trailers packed with equipment. It was getting dark, so they made camp for the night.

"I really didn't want to have to sleep outside, Man. How much farther is it to the entrance?" Albert asked Carlos, The only man he felt he could trust. The others, like Carlos, were hardened men, most with military backgrounds, but Carlos was patient with him and one of Peter's close friends.

"Al, it's too far to reach tonight. The extra load we are towing makes for a longer trip, so suck it up and get your tent out."

All the others were already setting up camp, one of them building a small fire. Albert pulled the string, and his tent dumped out on the ground.

Carlos looked at him. "This is going to be a long night. You sure you're the best man for the job?"

Albert shook his head, "Yes?"

Carlos grabbed his tent and helped him get it up. Within an hour, everyone was set and eating. The night grew cold quickly and very dark. There was no moon, and the thick trees created a cover for much of the starlight. Albert stayed close to the fire. The men talked about firefights and ambushes in other worlds while Albert listened. His soup tasted like dirt; everything tasted like dirt, but it was hot and made him feel better. He kept looking back at his tent, wishing it was closer to the fire. Carlos always had an eye on him, though. He noticed this.

Peter probably asked him to watch me.

He liked Peter right away. He was calm and patient with him too, so if Peter liked Carlos so much, he must be trustworthy.

All the men became silent at once. One of them doused the fire. Steam rolled up for a moment, and then Albert heard the small whine of something electronic powering up. Like a camera's flash charging. It was completely dark now, and he reached for his flashlight. A cold hand clasped his own, stopping him from turning it on. Carlos grabbed his face and whispered in his ear. "Put these on, and make your way to your tent."

Carlos handed him something heavy and cold.

Goggles.

When Albert did not move, he took them back and jammed them on his head.

"Ouch."

"Shhh!" Carlos pinched his lips.

His own night vision goggles powered up with a whine.

Like the movies!

Everything was green, but he could see men arming themselves now. They were facing in every direction. Carlos turned him toward his tent and gave him a shove. Albert obeyed, climbing in and zipping the door closed. Rustling around the camp was the only noise he could hear now, and not being able to see was worse, so he carefully unzipped his door just enough to fit his fat head out. All the men were crouching with guns ready.

Blop! Blop blop!

Sounds of something hard hitting the trees began to resound all around them. It was as if someone was beating on trees in communication. Moaning cries rang out all around now, and Albert knew this sound all too well. *Oh no!* He closed his eyes, backed away from the tent opening, and realized he was no safer inside. He climbed out and found Carlos.

"I know what this is—" Carlos covered his mouth. He backed away, freeing himself, and repeated it. "Listen to me. I've run into these things, and we gotta run for it. Now!"

"Shut up," Carlos whispered.

"Sasquatch, Man." Albert whispered, "One nearly ate me in Denver."

There were four monstrous screams from different locations all at once. Carlos looked at Albert now with doubt on his face. He put on his own night vision and looked around. Another man moved closer to them.

"They are about 200 yards out, I think. What arc they, Bears?" he asked.

"Bears don't sound like that, Man; more like Apes." Said another, still pointing his rifle out into the darkness.

"No apes around here; that's Africa," Albert said.

Carlos looked over at Albert and then back at the two men shaking his head.

One of the things would call out, then another from across the distance.

"I think they are trying to find us," Albert whispered. Maybe echolocation or something?"

"Shut up, Al," Carlos said.

Branches shattered to their backs, and everyone fumbled. One man tripped, knocking over something, and the howling stopped for a moment before beginning again.

Their closer, Albert thought.

A new scream rang out like a Primate warning; it began from one direction and was repeated all around. Their cries and howls did not cease but began to grow distant.

"They are moving away from us." The other man said to Carlos.

He pat Albert on the shoulder and stood up. All the men crept out around their camp, enlarging their perimeter.

"Over here," a voice called from the west. Albert and Carlos both walked over and saw one of the men sling his gun over his shoulder and hug someone.

Peter? What's he doing here? Albert thought.

He rushed over to him and shook his hand. All of the men came back to the center of the camp and silently listened as the herd moved farther and farther away. There were howls and thuds still, but the sounds were growing distant. Albert looked over at Peter, who never even looked around. He was sitting calmly on the ground. After about an hour of stillness, someone lit the fire again. Albert was grateful to take off the heavy goggles.

"They won't be able to find us tonight," Peter said, and this disturbed Albert even more.

And you know this how?

Carlos and Peter spoke quietly for about an hour at the edge of the camp before Albert fell asleep. In the morning, he woke late. Everyone had already packed up. He stuffed his tent in a bag and climbed on the back of one of the ATVs before noticing Peter was gone.

"Where's Peter?" he asked the man driving.

"Gone before I was up. Ask Carlos." He said.

The group rolled along most of the morning before finding their base.

An entrance was well hidden within bushes set in a hill. The opening was just big enough for a quad to push between them into a buried sea container leading them deeper still.

"Welcome to your new home, Al, Carlos said. "You got your work cut out for you here. Lots of work to do."

They dismounted the ATVs and walked deeper into the mountain, dimly lit by lanterns.

"Lighting might be a good place to start." Another man said as they walked.

"This is not my home."

"From now on, it is, Man," Carlos said. "If you want to live. I will fill you in once you are settled, but you are blown in town, and a dead man walkin' if you go back."

Albert moaned, and Carlos put an Arm around his shoulder. "It's gonna be fun, trust me."

Albert liked Carlos.

Rome Again Rome Again

Stephen was not home for more than an hour before guests began arriving for another dinner party at their home. He greeted strangers for thirty minutes before sneaking off to check on his son. He had avoided Charles altogether, fearful that he would give away the truth in his expression. But as soon as he found Samuel, there he was, his son sitting on the monster's lap.

"Stephen, there you are. You ready for the festivities?"

Stephen smiled but imagined the rocking horse sitting next to the man in his own hands, coming down hard on the bastard's head. "What's the occasion this time?" he asked.

Charles looked offended. "Why, our publishing son. You feeling alright?"

"Yes, I'm sorry. I am tired and hoping for a quiet night with my son."

Charles got up and handed the boy to him. "Spend some time with him, then come join us. I'll let everyone know."

There was no getting out of this. Stephen was not sure how he would even be able to escape with the boy. *I'm just going to have to bide my time and wait.*

The night was like so many others: plastic people telling each other lies, handing out plastic compliments of no worth. Stephen found it hard to play the game but let his son's well-being strengthen his resolve. Months passed like a blur of stupidity; only Samuel's first birthday was meaningful to Stephen. His communication with the west was sparse, but Peter's arrival last month was when he knew the time for waiting was over. He sat in Samuel's playroom, looking out a small window, thinking about Peter's words.

"You don't know how good it is to see you," he said, grabbing hold of his friend.

Stephen, I had to come. Is there a place we can talk?"

"Sure, but they know you're here. I had to tell them, otherwise, they would be suspicious. Do you think you could manage a lunch with them?" Stephen asked.

"If I must. Listen, we need to talk." Peter repeated.

They walked to Stephen's Range Rover and left the airport. The two men arrived at a small coffee shop in a touristy part of town. They sat at a small table and drank coffee. Stephen gestured as he took a drink. Peter followed his gaze and noticed two men sitting in a dark SUV.

"Is that for us?" Peter asked.

"Um-hm. Charles will most likely appear surprised to see us, next."

Peter set down his cup and looked at Stephen. "Listen, I don't care about any of that. I came here because I've spent hours reading over Leroy's notes and clippings regarding Charles."

"What is it?" Stephen asked.

"Charles planned all of this from the beginning. You and Lucy, too. In fact, both of your mothers….."

"What? Spit it out." Stephen asked.

Peter hesitated. "That isn't important. What is important is that you both were chosen for one purpose: to birth a son."

Stephen rolled this around in his head.

"*The* son, Stephen. *his* son, Peter said."

"Whose son?"

"The Destroyer."

"Are you trying to tell me my son is going to be the antichrist?"

"Yes, Brother. Without a doubt," Peter said.

A Mercedes pulled up across the street.

"He's here. Try and act calm, Pete." Stephen said, putting on a smile and waving as the man got out of the car.

"Is that you, Peter?" Charles said as he walked over. "I was on my way into town and thought I recognized Stephen, but what a wonderful surprise."

Peter stood and shook the man's hand. "Just for the day, Sir. I wanted to stop in on my way to visit family. I haven't seen my friend here in a while."

"Of course, of course, Can't you stay longer? There's so much to see. Lucy would be delighted, and Young Samuel too. You know he's just started walking."

"Yes, Sir Stephen fills me in."

"Of course he does," Charles answered, glancing at his son-in-law. "I insist you come by the home for a visit before you depart."

"We were going to go out, "Stephen began.

"Nonsense," Charles said. Samuel needs to see his Uncle as well."

"That would be fine, Sir," Peter said.

"Great, I'll let Lucy—"

"No," Stephen said. "I'm sorry, Charles, I want to spend some time with my friend, without a room full of strangers."

Charles actually took a step back in shock. It had been a while since the two had any conflict.

"It doesn't have to be like that."

"Still. I'm spending the day with Peter. We have already made a plan. If Lucy would like to bring Samuel out to meet up with—"

"That won't be possible; they have company coming to the house," Charles said.

"Mr. Rutherford. How about if I come back this way on my way back and stay for a couple of days? That way, I can see Samuel and Lucy as well?" Peter offered.

Charles smiled, unsatisfied, Defeated in his attempt to maintain total control. "Sure, that would be fine. We will make a plan, and I insist you stay at our home. When do you expect to be coming back to Rome?"

"Well, I will cut my visit with family short by one day, so let's say next Monday?" Peter and Stephen took their seats, leaving Charles to take the hint.

"Wonderful. I will let Lucy know. Will you be back for dinner, Stephen? You know we have gues—"

"No, Charles. Please convey my apologies. Tell Lucy not to wait up."

Charles looked annoyed. "It was wonderful to see you again, Peter. Enjoy your day." He reached out to shake Peter's hand again, this time with a much firmer grip. Peter and Stephen watched him get back in his car and waved as he drove away.

"See what I mean?" Stephen said. "I have no idea how I will get away with Samuel."

"God will open that door," Peter said. "Let's discuss the hurdles. When does he leave again?"

***

Samuels's laughter brought Stephen back from deep thought. The grass outside was covered in dew. The sun was just beginning to take it away. The flowers in the garden were just beginning to open. He took Samuel for a walk. His son loved the gardens separating the main house from the pool, so a bench along that path became a familiar place for him to think and often pray. He felt like every day was a painful waste, but he could see no other way.

Patience, He'll provide a way..

As the next few weeks went by, Lucy and Stephen grew further and further apart. Her once devoted love for him and his son was gone, now changed. Samuel was a prize for her, and Stephen a plaything. Most of the time, she was cold and distant with him and the child unless company was near or she was having one of her midnight cravings. Waking him for vulgar sex before vanishing back into her own room. He hated it here.

Sam's playing was uplifting. Today was special also because he found the server and installed the software for Albert. He was excited to imagine Albert's code chomping away for their cause. He only knew he had accomplished what Albert said was crucial. He was sure the one security guard who had stopped him leaving the security building would be reporting to Charles, so this meant the timeline had begun.

"We must leave, Son." He said to the toddler." Kissing him on the forehead. The child waddled to a ball and fell on it with a giggle.

time to go.

"Oh... there you are," Lucy said, looking at her husband in annoyance. Their nanny was coming up behind her. "Take him and clean him up. He's a mess. And I don't want our guests seeing him so disheveled."

You're disheveled.

"Yes, mam," said the nanny as she lifted the boy, now beginning to cry.

"When was the last time you actually touched our son?" Stephen asked.

"Don't start. I'm not in the mood for your emotional clamor. Please be ready on time tonight. It would be nice if you would make a little effort for your guests now and again."

"You mean *your* guests." He said.

She rolled her eyes and walked away. Six O clock, Stephen, don't be a disappointment. Oh, and Daddy called. He said to tell you he will be back tomorrow and needs to have a talk with you, so please don't go anywhere."

Damn it, He knows.

"Where else would I go, Dear?" Stephen said, following her back to the house.

After his shower, he dressed in the fine clothes she had laid out. He looked at himself in the mirror, a completely different man than the one in New York five years ago. That man was in love and had a bright future. Now the man he saw looking back at him had… *What do I have?*

"I have my son. I have a plan…"

It must be tonight.

Stephen got an email off to his old office, where he knew Peter would access it later. The email was to a newspaper about an article he wanted to write. The article did not exist, but the beginning word of each line told Peter everything he needed to know. This was the only way they found to communicate, and the end of this message read: "we leave tonight."

The party was a loud debauchery of drinking and bad behavior, which Stephen politely avoided. As soon as his wife was heavily intoxicated, he quietly stepped away. He packed a bag for Sam and put their things in his Range Rover. Now all he had to do was wait for the guests to leave.

The party ended late, and Stephen went to bed, hoping to hasten Lucy's own bedtime with the boredom of silence. He knew if he stayed up, she could go on until the wee hours of the night, so he lay in bed silently waiting to hear her bedroom door close. Two in the morning, and the music finally stopped. His heart was racing. He wanted to be on the road already. The door opened, and she stood a silhouette in the doorway. He tried to pretend that he was sleeping, but she did not fall for it.

"I know you are awake, Husband. I can always tell by your breathing." She walked to the foot of his bed and removed her dress. "I'll have my husband in me before I sleep." She said

She pulled the covers off of him and mounted him. Her eyes were different tonight, not Lucy's. She began kissing his neck, touching him, and then sat up on top of him. Her stare was penetrating. Her eyes cold.

"I know what you want," she said and then kissed his neck. When she looked at him again, it was no longer Lucy on top of him but Heather, and he let the rest unfold. That night he had Heather once more, and then sleep took him deep. It was early the next morning that Stephen awoke with a start.

The sun is up! Damn!

He jumped out of bed and dressed quickly before going to his son's room. The nanny already had the boy in the kitchen eating breakfast when he found him. "Antonia, please have Samuel ready in fifteen minutes. We have a day out for play. I overslept, and we are meeting friends in town."

"Out, she asked. "But Mrs.—"

"I don't care what Mrs. Rutherford said. I am his father, and we have plans in town. Have him ready."

The nanny frowned but nodded as she picked up the child and exited the kitchen. Stephen downed a cup of cold coffee and finished getting ready. Before going back for the boy, he crept to Lucy's room and cracked the door.

She never even made it to the bed.

She was sprawled out on the floor naked. *Good, she won't be up for hours.*

Stephen found the nanny preparing Samuel slowly and scolded her again. "If you cannot do what I ask, I might have to demand we hire another nanny."

The woman obeyed, and Samuel was soon dressed and in his car seat. The nanny's expression was grave, and he knew the moment he left, she would wake

Lucy, so he had to think of another way.

"Go get ready, Antonia. I will have you go with us today."

She brightened a bit, perhaps feeling better about not allowing the child out of her site.

"Five minutes, and we leave." He called as she ran off to change.

She was soon back, putting her hair into a bun as she climbed into the backseat.

I'll have to ditch her someplace where she won't be able to warn anyone. The thought of being cruel to the nanny did not sit well with Stephen, but he had no other choice, it was either that or knock her out, and that was out of the question. About four miles down the road, he turned, taking them away from town and into the mountains. He saw the concern on her face in the rearview mirror. "I thought we were going to the city?" she asked.

"We are. I just need to pick up a friend who broke down."

She did not believe this, and he knew it. The two were now playing a careful game in the mirror, watching but not. She kept looking around in the car and at the boy. It was clear they both knew the other was a problem, and one had to make a move.

Stephen wanted to get as far away from the main road as he could before stranding her but was not sure how long it would take for her to make her move. A moment later, he saw her looking in the back and realized she had made a choice. He pulled the Range Rover to the side of the road while she reached back and grabbed a tire iron.

It's on.

He barely had time to stop the car before dogging her first attack.

"Auuugh!" She screamed like a wild bear defending its cub.

The first swing denting his headrest. She swung again, this time hitting him on the shoulder and causing him shooting pain. Samuel began to cry. Stephen caught her third swing with a sting in his left hand. His other went right for her hair, grabbing a fist full and yanking her into his seat.

He got out of the car, pulling her with him. The two were standing on the mountain road. She tore herself free, giving up much of her hair in the process. She was like an animal, eyes like fire, an evil he never thought possible from the quiet girl.

She swung. He dodged and clocked her hard with a hook to her temple.

She went down hard, her face hitting the road. He was sure she would be out cold. He approached to carry her off the road. She got up fast, throwing the tire iron like a tomahawk. It whistled by his face. Samuel was still crying in the car.

She charged, and Stephen parried, grabbing hold of her dress and using her momentum to swinger her off the road. The dress ripped from top to bottom, and she was flung into a tree with a thump.

"Stop. I don't want to hurt—"

"Eeeyyuugghh!" She screamed as she got up.

Her face was ugly, bloody, and monstrous. She stood there in her underwear; her only focus was him.

She spotted the tire iron and went for it. Stephen beat her to it and kicked her as she reached. His foot planted firmly in her face. Like a football player's punt, she went up and backward, this time letting out the first human cry. Rage was gone, and only a whimpering came from the downed girl. He approached her carefully, her face soft again.

"I'm sorry."

Returning to the Range Rover, he found a blanket in the back. He grabbed it and then her dress on the road on his way back to her. Stephen laid both on top of her and backed away. "I'm sorry, but my son is more important. You'll find your way back."

He got in the car and calmed the baby before starting the engine. As he turned the vehicle around, he noticed the nanny was gone. She was now running full out through the woods and in the direction of the house.

Shit!

He flattened the gas pedal, and the Range Rover screamed down the road. He had chartered a direct flight, knowing timing was everything. Peter had advised that he get on the ground as soon as possible just in case they tried to report the child kidnapped. The plan was to get on US soil as quickly as possible, then meet Peter, who would drive them west. So far, he was late, and alarms were soon to be ringing.

We forgot to figure in the nanny.

He assumed that even if she could run that fast the entire time through the woods, it would be five hours before she made it to the house. All he could do was hope for the six to eight with her resting and walking. This would put him on the ground before authorities would be involved.

I should have knocked her out.

Back to the Beginning

Peter got Carlos on the radio. "Man, you have to button everything down. Whatever's unfinished will have to wait. I'm heading to New York to meet Steve and Sam."

"Ten-four. Is there anything we can do to help?" Carlos asked.

"Pray, Man. Pray. Over and out."

Stephen's flight landed at nine-thirty that morning. He was in a car and downtown by the time anything was coming over the radio about a kidnapped child.

Now we lay low until Pete gets here.

He decided to take Samuel to Central Park and let him play. Peter would make contact within the hour, so keeping a low profile was vital, only this wasn't how things worked out. Samuel was feeding the ducks when Stephen heard his description over a nearby police radio, and it was scary how much information they already had. They knew his flight and even had a good description of what he was wearing. He pulled out a baseball cap and left his jacket on the bench he was sitting on. He picked up Samuel and started making his way out of the park when he noticed someone pointing at him from across the park. That's when he ran.

Peter's flight landed fifteen minutes early, but traffic was horrible getting to the park. He was a block away when several police cars flew by him, and then he noticed officers outside the park.

Damn Steve, please tell me they didn't get you, Bro.

"You can let me out here," he said to the cab driver, flipping him cash. Peter made his way into the park and stopped some bystanders looking in the same direction.

"What's happening?" he asked one of them.

"The police are searching for a man who kidnapped a child. He was in the park, but now they can't find them."

Peter's heart dropped. He left the park and walked north, hoping for a sign that might lead him to his friend, and he got exactly that. Three police cars flew by, and after running a couple of blocks, he came upon the scene.

Oh no, Steve.

Several police cars were blocking the road, and a crowd was forming. His heart sank when he finally got there and noticed everyone was looking up. There, high up was a dark dot on the edge of the rooftop.

No Steve. Please.

Everything had gone wrong, and his best friend was now trapped. He thought about trying to explain to the police, but what would he say? His only chance was to get his friend down safely. He looked around for their enemies.

Peter found the officer in charge and told him he was Stephen's friend. He tried to tell a story about a father desperate to leave a controlling wife with his son, but they were not softening. He asked the man for a chance to talk him down, and surprisingly they granted his request. The next thing he knew, he was following an officer up to the 47th floor.

When they came out onto the rooftop, Peter's heart broke at the sight of his friend in this position. Stephen appeared relieved at seeing Peter. Norton and Thompson talked for a moment, and then Thompson motioned Peter over.

"Talk to him if you want, but try and get him away from the ledge. Everyone will calm down if you can get him to sit on this side of the wall."

Thompson looked over at Norton now. "I'm going back down. Richards just called me. You got this end?"

"Yeah, less is more. This guy doesn't want to hurt his kid, so I'd like police presence to be light up here."

"Agreed," said Thompson as he left.

Peter liked Norton right away. He knew this was the one person up here that may help them if things got thick. "Can I go to him?" he asked.

Norton nodded.

Peter hugged Stephen as soon as he got to the edge. Stephen never took his eyes off of the police, though. Peter held out a fast-food bag and smiled.

"Can we sit on the ground here, Steveo?" he asked.

Stephen gestured for him to sit a foot away and squatted down. The officer's shoulders dropped, a small step toward a resolution. Norton backed away and was talking on the radio.

Peter and Stephen sat looking at each other while Samuel cooed as if it were another day in the park. "He's so resilient," Peter said.

Stephen looked at his son's face and nodded. "He is. He will be a strong leader."

"There is no way we will convince them of what is going on. You know that, right?"

"Yes. I have been trying to work it out and see only two choices. Give them my son, and watch Charles turn him into something evil, or kill him and give him to God."

"You couldn't kill your son Steveo; you know that."

"I think I could. I just can't get past the fact that I've missed something."

"Yeah, you missed our rendezvous."

They both laughed though not wholeheartedly."

The officers looked at each other, a little surprised. The energy was already changing on the roof.

"I'm glad you're here, Pete. I'm scared, and you're the only one I really trust."

The Lord is with us, Man, don't forget that." Peter said.

"Hey, Chicy Nuggets," Peter said, lifting the box of chicken tenders out of the bag. He smiled at Samuel, who smiled back at his uncle.

"Chicky Nugga," Sam repeated, taking one from his uncle.

Stephen smiled. "You know Lucy would kill you if she knew you were feeding our son that crap."

Peter and Stephen both broke out in laughter again. Norton looked surprised and approached. "Can—"

"No." came in unison from both men sitting by the wall. Peter put up a finger to the officer, and he nodded and backed off. Stephen and Peter both looked at the man. "I like him. I can tell he is the real deal." Stephen said.

"Yeah, me too. Maybe God is already setting up our hand here."

This moment was surreal to both of them. Peter opened a burger wrapper, handed it to his friend, and then grabbed his own.

Stephen looked at the building noticing the carved edifice of gargoyles and angels framed by jade glass. He felt dumbfounded that he had not noticed this before. "Now, if only those were real, maybe we could fly out of here." He nodded toward the stone walls, and Peter smiled.

"We need real angels, man."

"I'm not handing Sam over," Stephen said, breaking the peace

"Steveo, if it is God's will for him to fall into the hands of Satan, nothing will change that. If it is His will that he be used for greatness, not even Satan can stop…." Peter stopped noticing Stephen's expression. "What?"

"You just said it, Bro. God's will. It all makes sense now. The story about my mother and Heather's choice. I know what to do, Pete."

Before they could say another word, the radios began to squeal. "Norton," screech, crackle. "Another"… squelch…crackle "Coming up" The radios were full of static.

"What, Sir, I did not read you?" Norton returned. Nothing but static came back. Norton looked at the other two officers, and they also tried their radios. Static.

"Gentlemen," Charles said from the doorway. "Your commander has authorized me to come up here and help resolve this issue. That is my son and grandson over there." Charles peered past the officers at Stephen with a gracious smile.

Loving Grandfather. Right, you fake! Stephen thought.

"Sir, I'm going to have to ask you to go back downstairs," Norton said, putting a hand up.

"Your commanding officer sent me up," Charles said.

Stephen put a hand on Peter's arm while looking at the sky. Peter followed his gaze and noticed flashes of light above, like little balls of lightning exploding everywhere. Even in the bright daylight, they flashed brilliantly. Peter did not know what to make of it. He looked over at Stephen, who met his eyes. "They're fighting up there…" he said, looking back up. Peter opened his mouth to speak, but nothing came out.

"Peter, buy me some time," Stephen whispered.

Peter regained focus and was up in a flash.

"That man is responsible for the death of my friend's fiancé and is a danger to both him and his child." He yelled as he approached the police.

Charles' expression delivered his deadly rebuke from behind the officer's backs. Everyone was now on edge again. Police hands fell instinctually to their side-arms.

Stephen found that place where time rests and looked through. All along the edge of the rooftop, fallen angels were landing and drawing swords. His heart began to pound, and one thought possessed him: *Hannah and her child.*

He could still hear Peter yelling, but it was as if he was in a faraway place.

He knew what to do but was not sure if he had enough time. He knelt, taking hold of Samuel.

"FATHER, I come before you undeserving. A wretched man, yet one you have redeemed. I thank you for this gift of new life…."

A massive bolt of lightning erupted above, and Stephen noticed larger Archangels battling overhead. The officers did not seem to notice, but he was sure these were the most powerful of their kind. One was swinging his sword and blocking a blow from another. This one flared in blackness with the impact, and its wings doubled in size. It was bigger than the other two now. Changing into a black dragon-like creature. Several other angles joined in his defense, the sky a light storm.

Charles' eyes grew darker, and his face shimmered with rage. "ENOUGH of This. Let me pass." He growled at the officer.

Peter recognized the danger Norton was in and pulled on the back of his shirt. At that moment, Charles looked at the two other officers, and their expressions glossed over. They both grabbed for their side arms and began firing across at each other with Norton in the crossfire. Peter and Norton fell backward, but not before the officer was hit in the leg and stomach. The other officers kept firing blindly until both were dead. Charles went after Stephen praying up to God, but Peter pulled Norton's gun and fired blindly from under the man. Charles fell backward as Norton's gun emptied in Peter's hand. The only sound was the last dancing shells bouncing on the rooftop and a powerful prayer.

"You are my God. My sweetest friend. All I have is from you, and I thank you for this beautiful boy. Samuel is my first fruits, my sacrifice to you. Please take his life and make it wondrous. He is yours, Father, my son I give to you."

"You stupid fool! I'll have your entrails spread across this roof and that bug you hold now too."

Charles' rage was unrestrained, and his features were sharp, deep, and dark." He kicked Peter knocking the gun from his hand and causing him to slide across the roof. Norton was lifeless.

Stephen held Samuel close, "You're safe, Son." He did not know what else to do.

Charles approached him, a small blossom of red growing in his chest. Stephen crawled backward with his child in his arms. The edge still held the only alternative, though he knew his son was no longer of use to Lucifer.

"I'm going to rip that child into pieces in front of you; then you can die!"

Charles was two steps away when another voice interrupted.

"Hey, dumbass. I heard you were looking for me."

Stephen looked past Charles and saw Mitch come out of nowhere. He was walking out of the wall; behind him, the giant edifice was coming to life, and the grey angel followed.

Peter gathered himself, still stunned from being kicked hard. He began to crawl around toward Stephen and Samuel. Charles turned to Mitch, and his rage only increased. His features grew larger, and bulges formed under his shirt. Hidden wings began to slowly birth underneath. He charged Mitch, who did not move. The moment Charles was on him, Mitch grabbed for his neck and face. Charles began to scream in agony and rage. A deep orange glow welled up inside him entering him through Mitch's hands. It looked like the sun was burning him from within. Like the color, a child sees holding a flashlight up to his hand.

Charles lifted both fists to crush the man but began to shake instead. He was being drained of power or devoured from within. The fallen angels on the ledge came to his aid, and the grey angel, much larger than any of them, came up behind Mitch. He created a great shell of protection over Mitch with his wings.

The fallen began swinging their swords down upon him with great flashes of light. Each blow cut deeply into the Grey, who shed this light like a man sheds blood. They were killing him, yet Mitch remained safe. As the Grey began to fall, he took Mitch down with him, cradled in his protective embrace.

Charles was free now but stunned by Mitch's touch. He was slowly regaining his strength. This was the only chance Stephen had to end him. He handed Samuel to Peter. There was no more fear in his eyes, only determination and peace.

"I know what comes next, Pete. My sacrifice wasn't Sam. It was me. Take care of him. And when he's ready, let him read."

Peter took the boy. "Steve, wait."

Stephen looked up to the sky and smiled as he got up and walked over to Charles. He grabbed him from behind. The man was still weak, only a man now himself, so he could not break free. Stephen backed up with Charles in a chokehold.

Many lesser angels were swarming the great angels in the sky, and the light danced all over the place like a distant light show. The dragon began to dive for the roof but collided with three other heavenly angels, who again locked him in battle. Several others swarmed them, making it another ball of firelight in the sky. The only angels able to reach the roof were still swinging down upon the Grey.

"Is that your master up there fighting to come save you?" Stephen mocked.

"You haven't won, boy." Charles groused, grasping for air in his mortality.

Stephen pulled his chokehold tighter and continued to back up.

"Even now, she is with child again. All you've done is postpone the end."

The fallen angels turned from slashing The Grey, now a lifeless heap. Arphax, Phanuel, Sarakiel, and Raphael came crashing down in front of them and drew swords. More holy angels landed all around. Michael, among them, had disengaged Lucifer, who was still swarmed by heavenly host. At the sight of them, the fallen took flight one by one, vanishing into the sky. Two intercepted their master and defended him. Stephen reached the edge and put one leg over, Charles locking a leg on the wall, stopping them both.

"You have not won, boy, not even by killing me."

Stephen saw Mitch now getting up from under his protector, then over at Peter and winked. "The victories' not mine to attain. God's got the rest."

He kicked out Charles' leg, and both of them went over the edge.

Peter jumped up and reached over. Stephen was falling backward with outstretched arms, his face full of peace. Charles was screaming in a bloody rage. They both ended on the street below. Samuel's soul was now safe. A story that began years ago, with another Hannah and a beloved son fulfilled.

Stephen's last vision was of the heartache on his friend's face as he fell away and then darkness. He was sure he was dead now but could still hear sirens and screams.

These sounds began to fade like pulsing waves, and the world gave way to water. The sound of water lapping gently on a bay. Then there was the sound of laughter, followed by overwhelming love. His eyes cracked open, and at first, there was only white. Someone was kneeling over him, though his vision was still a cloud. The silhouette of an angel there to greet him, Heaven's first sight. A joy filled him, replacing the blood that once flowed in his veins. And his vision became clearer as he heard her voice again.

"Hi, Love." Her big green eyes, so bright.

"Beautiful…" was all he could muster, too overwhelmed to speak.

"You're home, my Love," she said and kissed him.

Heather…

***

"I saw it all. I saw." Norton managed as he braced himself against the ledge. The massive angel, Michael, looked at Peter and smiled.

"It was you on…the road…and in the woods, wasn't it?" Peter asked.

Arphax and Phanuel picked up The Grey and took to flight. Sarakiel and Raphael followed next. Michael gave Peter a wink as his great wings filled the rooftop and flew away.

Peter looked at Norton. "You might be careful about who you try and tell this story to. But I'm grateful all the same." He looked around for Mitch, but he was nowhere to be seen.

You're a slippery one, Mitch.

There was a glimmer from the green glass edifice, which Peter caught out of the corner of his eye. Mitch was there for a second, and then he was gone.

Somehow, through all of this, Samuel came out unscathed. The little boy was smiling at his uncle. "You're a tough one, Kid. I guess that's a good thing."

A flood of policemen filled the rooftop with weapons drawn. Some of them surrounded Norton, calling for medical. Others pointed guns at Pete until Norton yelled at them.

"He's alright. Leave him alone."

Peter got up, aided by the other officers. He looked back at the place his friend had gone over. Everyone he loved was dying. A tear rolled down his face as he pulled the boy close and walked away.

Justice

Six months had passed since Peter walked off the roof without his friend. The miracle was that Samuel was out of Lucifer's reach. Or Peter thought until a tribe of Lawyers holding briefcases instead of spears came and ripped him apart in court. Lucy had not even shown her face, and still, the courts granted her custody. Even after officer Norton testified to her father's behavior, which was objected to and sustained, the court sided with the mother.

Peter sat in a coffee shop outside her hotel, sipping espresso, hoping to glimpse his nephew as they left. Carlos was there with him, and Albert too. Albert was the one who found her, and so he was allowed to tag along.

"Four hours of coffee and dry crackers. Don't these places serve anything deep-fried?" Albert complained.

"You wanted to come, so defrag, floppy disk." Carlos said.

"That's not even accurate. Floppy disks don't—"

"Shut up, that's them." Peter sat up, wanting to run to the child. His face grew grim. Lucy came out visibly pregnant again, just as Charles had said. She yanked on Samuel's little hand, causing his head to snap back. "He's barely walking," Peter said, clenching his fists.

"Wow, she's really prego, ain't she?" Albert said, chomping on a cookie.

She was followed by two men carrying shopping bags and luggage.

"She can't even stand the kid, so why fight so hard to keep him?"

"Vengeance, Man," Carlos said. "To hurt those who love him."

"So, how we getting him back?" Albert asked.

Peter and Carlos looked at each other, and smiles began to surface.

The woman got in a limousine and drove away.

"How well do you know Rome?" Peter asked.

The End

Afterword

The Eve After

5 Years Later

Two men lay camouflaged in the landscape 100 yards from their objective,

"Is the boy in sight?" one said to the other. The other man had binoculars held up to his face.

"Yes, both of them. This will go to hell fast if we can't separate him from his brother and mother." Said Peter as he lowered the optics from his view and looked at his comrade.

"We're going to have to wait this out. His mother and brother have too much security on them, and these people never take their eyes off of them." He handed the binoculars to his friend.

"There's just no way to snag Samuel tonight."

The other man was looking through the binoculars at the targets in their home.

"Damned, I thought mommy was taking the little bastard out tonight?" He looked at Peter, "This makes an already shaky situation almost impossible. Pete, do you want to abort?"

"No, we have put too much time into this, and everything is in place. We wait." The other man toggled his mic.

"It looks like a no-go tonight, boys. Get comfortable. We'll try to snag the package during morning swim." He looked at Peter, and Peter nodded. "Stand down and set up close, but stay ready for anything," Carlos said.

A voice came back, "roger that, Lead. We will hold position here one man up for watch."

Peter's partner in crime was a hard man in his mid-thirties named Carlos. He retired early from the navy seals after being injured in a firefight but was no less lethal.

Carlos was pivotal in recruiting several other seasoned warriors to their cause.

Peter and Carlos formed a resistance in preparation for the future war against the world government, which would eventually remove all civil rights from the US Constitution and throughout the planet. They stockpiled guns, food, and other essential provisions in various locations around the country and were in constant contact with other similar organizations in other parts of the world.

Each cell was independent of the others, so if one was discovered, it would not lead authorities to the others.

Many of their plans were drawn up based upon dreams the late Stephen Meyers had written down about the coming end of days.

Tonight's mission was the kidnapping of Stephen's first-born son Samuel. Peter was adamant that Samuel was crucial to this future cause, and he had promised Stephen that Samuel would be taken care of and prepared for his future role.

Peter had spent two years watching and planning for this night and would do whatever it took to free his godson from his unloving mother. While doing recon, Peter witnessed the poor treatment Samuel received from her. She acted as if he was trash to her while at the same time treating her second son like a king. Samuel always walked behind his mother and brother as if unwanted and withstood disdainful looks from his mother as she coddled his younger brother, David. They planned to act upon the lack of care and snatch Samuel from under their noses.

Carlos looked through a scope, "I could pop that little devil's head like a balloon right now. Pete, you sure that's not the right thing to do?"

"No, this is all meant to happen; It's part of God's plan. All we can do is our part. Besides, all you would be doing is murdering an innocent little boy. He won't be indwelt by Satan until later."

"Yeah, Bu—" Carlos was interrupted by their radio.

"Queen mother and the prince of darkness have decided to take a night swim. They are heading out now. Samuel is alone in the house. Should we move?" came the voice of Matt over the radio.

"No, wait, let's see what they do first," replied Peter.

Peter and Carlos dug in deep and were deathly quiet as Lucy and her second-born approached them, led by two security personnel and followed by two more. Peter could only see their feet now through the brush, and it looked as if they were headed straight for them. Peter and Carlos were nestled in the foliage near the path that led into the property's garden and swimming pool. They held their breath as the security personnel stopped inches from where they lay.

"We are at the entrance to the garden," said one, followed by a moment of silence, his hand touching the com-set in his ear.

"Confirm. We are heading to the pool."

He put out a hand, gesturing she proceed.

Lucy and David walked by the hidden men, followed by two other security personnel in black suits. The two lead bodyguards stayed where they were, watching the group walk towards the pool.

Peter looked at Carlos with a nervous look on his face. Carlos mimicked putting a knife to someone's throat and slashing it. Peter looked impatiently at him, shaking his head. Carlos smiled.

"Miss Rutherford and David are at the pool. Make sure you do a perimeter check before returning to the house." The first bodyguard said to his partner.

The other man nodded and left, circling around the garden area. The first man just stood there, waiting. Peter had a terrible urge to sneeze and covered his face with both hands. Carlos pulled out his knife, ready to deal with the problem if it came to it.

The urge passed, and Peter relaxed. Then the bodyguard turned and walked in the direction of the pool.

"Man, that was close," whispered Peter, "I thought I was going to blow."

Carlos returned his knife to its sheath.

"His partner just rounded the bend near the utility building," Carlos said, "I can see his flashlight bobbing."

He toggled his mic, whispering, "Rico, you have one headed straight for you. Stay low." "Roger that, we can already see his light," Rico responded.

Peter looked at his watch and then addressed the team over the radio.

"Okay, this may be our best chance. Rico, after you're clear, backtrack to the main house and confirm Samuels's location. If he follows after his mother and brother, his security will be light, and we may be able to grab him right when he enters the garden."

"Roger that."

"You may need to silence any issues from that end."

"Copy."

Peter looked at Carlos, who was smiling, obviously in his element. Peter was scared to death.

"You really love this stuff, don't you?" Peter said.

"Yep, it's in my blood." Carlos looked at his watch and then at Peter.

"Listen, Pete, I don't want any argument. When the time comes, you grab Sam and run. I don't care what you hear or see. From here on out, your job is getting Sam safely away from these bastards."

Peter gave him a reproachful look, but Carlos put a hand up before he could say anything. "Someone's coming."

They both looked and saw the light coming from the bodyguard's flashlight as he finished his perimeter check. The well-built man was coming back around the last corner towards them. Peter and Carlos lay low and waited as he came all the way around. The man came to the edge of the path into the garden area and stopped right next to Peter.

Rico's voice came over their headsets. "Sam is coming, Pete, and fast. He only has one bodyguard following behind him. You have 60 seconds before Sam rounds the corner."

Peter looked at Carlos with an alarmed look, then pointed up towards the bodyguard in their path. Carlos pulled his knife out and backed up into a squatting position, ready to pounce. Peter waved him to stop and shook his head.

Carlos looked at him and then signaled for him to get out of there, pointing towards their planned escape route.

Rico came back over the radio, “He’s turning the corner now. I’m pacing his bodyguard.”

Peter got ready to jump up and saw Samuel running towards them, followed by his bodyguard, yelling for him to slow down.

Peter also spotted Rico moving stealthily behind the bodyguard. He looked like a tiger stocking his prey. Peter realized if he could see Rico, then the guard on the path next to them would soon see him too.

Without thinking, Peter reached out from the brush and grabbed the man’s ankle to divert his attention. The man, startled by the unexpected touch, dropped his flashlight. The bodyguard looked into the brush and spotted Peter.

“Howdy,” Peter said.

He went for his sidearm and opened his mouth to yell but never got out more than a muffled cry.

Carlos was behind him in a flash, covered his mouth, and stabbed him in the chest.

Peter looked towards the child and saw Rico down the guard behind Samuel simultaneously. Both bodyguards were being pulled out of sight when Samuel made it to where Peter was hidden. The boy stopped, with confusion on his face, as he saw the feet of the guard disappear into the brush.

Peter stood quickly, “Sam, it’s me, Peter.”

Samuel looked even more perplexed as he looked at Peter.

“Come here, Sam, hurry.”

Samuel just stood there and looked at Peter, then right when Peter began to move, he smiled, “Uncle Pete?”

“Yes, Sam, it’s me,” Peter said in a low voice. “Come here before someone hears us.” Carlos exited the brush on the opposite side, and Samuel startled at the appearance of the fearsome-looking man. He ran straight to Peter, looking over his shoulder at Carlos. He landed in Peter's arms, afraid.

"It's okay, Sam, that's my friend Carlos; he's here to help. Trust me, okay?"

Samuel gave Peter a bewildered nod and embraced him tightly. Peter lifted him and headed through the brush. Carlos signaled Rico, who changed directions. He disappeared back into the tree line on the other side of the house.

Carlos toggled his mic, "Meet me back at the trees in front of the house."

"Roger that, headed to rendezvous," answered Rico.

"What's going on, Uncle Pete?" Samuel asked nervously.

"I will explain in just a second. Just trust me, Son."

They headed through the trees toward the Storage building.

Carlos was already ahead of them and crouching down at the end of the tree line when Peter and Samuel reached it.

Carlos looked all around, then pulled out a silenced Walter pistol and popped off a round. The light over the storage building went out with barely a noise.

He waved Peter on. "Go, and don't be long, Man. Rico and I will hold up the rear until you're clear."

"I just need a minute to talk to Sam, and then we'll move."

Carlos nodded at Samuel with a smile. "I'm glad to meet you, Sam."

Samuel looked at Peter, still confused, then back at Carlos as they ran to the building. Matt came from behind the building to meet them, giving Carlos a nod, and then opened the door for them. Peter, Samuel, and Matt entered the building and closed the door.

Carlos toggled his mic, "Rico, how we looking on your end?"

"Not good, Man; I think they are aware they're missing men. Two more bodyguards just exited the back of the house and are looking around with guns drawn. We need to step this up if we're going to make it out. Do we have the package?"

"Affirmative, Peter is confirming departure with him now. Matt has his six. I'll meet you at our starting point so we can be ready just in case we need to start the fireworks."

"Copy that, be there in two."

Peter sat Samuel down on a folding chair next to a workbench and knelt in front of him.

Matt was looking out a window with his own gun drawn.

"Sam, I know this is all confusing, but I need you to make a choice and fast, Son. I'm here to take you away from this place. I promised your father I would look after you, and I want you to come live with me. I know you're not happy here. Will you come with me?"

Samuel looked so surprised. "Pete, they won't let me go, not ever, mom says."

"We have a place they will never find you, with people who have become a big loving family. You will be cared for if you will trust me. But we have to go now."

"What about David?" Samuel asked.

"You know the answer to that question, don't you?" Peter asked.

Samuel nodded reluctantly, "He's theirs; that's why they treat him like a prince or something and treat me like a. . ."

"You're special to us, Sam, you have so many people who love and miss you. I know it has been hard on you since your mom took you away, but I've always been watching, waiting, and planning your escape. Will you come with us?"

Samuel nodded and smiled, then put his arms around Peter's neck. He had tears building in his eyes as he muttered I've been lonely, Uncle Pete."

"We have a little danger ahead of us, so do what I say when I say it, okay?"

Samuel just nodded and held on to him. "We'll get a chance to catch up on everything soon. I missed you, Bub."

Peter looked at Matt, "We're ready."

Matt nodded and cracked the door. He looked out and then clicked his headset. "Package is ready for shipping. How we looking?"

"Hold tight, Fed Ex. We have a roadblock we need to clear. You're going to have to go the long way. Wait for the fireworks, over."

Peter and Matt looked at each other, "Well, it's about to hit the fan, my friend." Peter said. Matt smiled at Samuel, "You like Fireworks, Kid?"

Samuel nodded with an excited smile.

"Just keep your eyes on me, Sam," Peter said. "And keep up, okay?" Samuel nodded. "I'm a fast runner, Uncle Pete."

"Good, because we may be doing some running."

The three of them readied by the door. Matt looked out carefully.

"Shows starting in 1," came over their headsets.

Peter came back, "Roger that, standing by."

Carlos and Rico were at opposite ends, over by the front of the house, almost 100 yards from their friends. Carlos nodded to Rico then both slowly moved in a low walk toward the sides of the house. Immediately there was gunfire on Rico's side, and Carlos pulled the trigger on a detonator that lit the sky over the back of the house. There was a huge explosion from behind the house, followed by two more. The back part of the compound was engulfed in firelight. The bodyguard, who had opened fire, turned and looked behind him when the first explosion went off, then darted behind a tree.

"We are under attack. Secure the residents." The guard screamed into his radio.

Rico snuck up around to the bodyguard's left while he was on his radio and pointed his gun in wait. The guard peeked and died as Rico pulled the trigger.

There was more gunfire on Rico's side from farther back as more security came out. Carlos pointed and shot, laying down a barrage of fire at the corner as they came forward. Two dropped, and the rest backed behind the wall.

Gunfire erupted on Carlos' right, and the tree he was pressed against exploded with impacting bullets. He barely evaded being shot by dropping and rolling around to the other side of the tree.

As soon as the explosions went off, Matt opened the shed door, knelt on one knee, gun out, covering Peter and Samuel's escape.

"Go, and don't look back. If I'm not behind you when you get to the suburban, just go. I'll catch a ride with the others."

Peter gave him a long look, then ran, holding onto Samuel's hand.

The two ran across a small meadow towards another tree line, which was near the end of the property. Samuel was faster than Peter and let go of his hand, running ahead of him for the trees. Peter looked back once and saw Matt circling around and following them.

There was gunfire going off far to their right, and as Peter crossed the meadow, he could see the muzzle flashes in the distance. Samuel stopped at the trees and looked at Peter, then towards commotion. More gunfire erupted from behind Peter.

Samuel and Peter fled into the trees and then stopped, looking back for Matt. He was nowhere to be found. Peter scanned the area and saw a body lying in the middle of the meadow. His heart stopped; he knew it was Matt. "Oh no, not Matt. Please, Lord."

Peter did not want to leave him behind but knew this would all be for nothing if they lost Samuel.

Two bodyguards came out of the trees from the garden area, one directly in line with Matt and the other about ten feet away. Peter and Samuel sat frozen, watching them approach.

Gunfire continued to roar over by the house. Rico crouched behind the tree and clipped the radio taken off the dead bodyguard to his belt. He fired off the last three shots at the side of the house, then leaned against the tree and reloaded.

"I don't have the ammo for a long exchange Carlos, so what's the plan?"

"Drop every toy you have left right where you are. When I start shooting, get to the road, and blow it on my signal."

"Roger, that Man, be careful, Bro."

Carlos dropped a guard on his side of the house and then aimed at Rico's side of the fight.

One guard stepped forward and breathed his last.

Pop! Went Carlos' gun, as the man dropped like a sack of bricks. He looked over at Rico and then unloaded a clip into the corner of the house and trees nearby.

Rico peeked out long enough to see two guards take cover from his partner's fire, then used the cover fire to escape, running all out.

Carlos ran for Rico's position and dove right as fire rang out. He leaned against the back of the tree and blindly fired his gun in the direction of the gunfire.

Rico made it to the road and slid down into the gully. He turned and crawled back up, gun in one hand and detonator in the other, waiting for his partner to follow.

The bodyguard was almost on top of Matt when Samuel yelled, "Hey! Chicken Head! Aren't you supposed to be watching me?"

Peter grabbed Samuel to run and cried, "Why di— "

Pop. Pop.

Pop.

Matt shot the man, then turned and shot the other guard several feet away. He was up again, hobbling toward them. Before Peter could do anything, Samuel ran out to meet Matt.

Peter ran after him. "Sam, Stop."

Samuel reached Matt and put his arm around his waist to help the man across the meadow.

"Kid, you shouldn't be here. Can't you see people are risking their lives to save you?"

"I am not going to watch you die. Come on, we'll help you." Peter was there too. They both helped Matt to the trees and vanished.

Carlos took fire from his old position and from behind. He returned fire in both directions and then pulled the trigger on another detonator. There was an explosion next to the tree he had first used for cover, followed by a scream of pain.

"Dunt dunt dunt, another one bites the dust," he sang.

He peeked around the corner of the tree and saw three guards creeping up. He jumped out, popped one between the eyes, and darted back behind the tree.

"Total amateurs."

Carlos unloaded another clip blindly around the back of the tree, sending the security for cover.

Without looking, he ran all out for the road. He heard shots from his left, where more security came around that corner. Carlos felt a burn in his neck and abdomen but kept running. He looked back as he made it halfway across the meadow and saw two bodyguards approaching the tree. They both fired but missed as Carlos dove to the ground.

"NOW," he yelled.

Rico didn't hesitate. He pulled the trigger on the detonator.

Click… BOOM!

Two more guards were killed as the tree where Carlos and Rico had both taken cover exploded.

Carlos got to his feet quickly and ran for the end of the meadow. He dove into the gully and lay there breathing heavily. Both men were dirty and sweaty.

"We got to go, Man," said Rico. "We got more company coming."

He put a hand out to Carlos, who grabbed it and was back up again. The two stayed low and moved quickly to their hidden vehicle. As Carlos opened the passenger's door, Rico noticed he was bleeding from his back and neck.

"You're hit, Man," Rico said.

"Grazed, let's get out of here. You're driving."

Rico got in the driver's seat started the suburban. They tore off through a rough path in the trees onto the road. Carlos tried contacting Peter and Matt on their radios but got no reply.

"They could already be out of range," Rico said. Carlos nodded and started to dress the wound on his neck.

The Security radio Rico stole off the bodyguard was squawking with chaos, and they learned that they took out three guards with the first explosions. In addition, two other bodyguards were found dead in the other meadow where Peter and Matt were headed.

"Sounds like they got out okay, eh, Bro?" Carlos muttered in pain.

"Yeah, Man, sounds like it. They don't seem concerned at all about Samuel, though, just their precious David."

"They might not even know we have him yet, but I'd bet you're right, though, from what Peter told us."

"Can you tell me again why we didn't just cap the little bastard when we had the chance, man?" Rico questioned.

"Something about fate, Bro, and him still being an innocent. Could you really kill a 5-year-old child?"

"If he was the Anti-Christ? Hell yeah." They were both silent for a couple of minutes as they sped down the road.

Peter drove down a long dark road and then turned into a long driveway surrounded by trees, as Matt applied a tourniquet to his thigh and then pulled out his cell phone.

He dialed Carlos' phone, but there was no reply. He dialed Rico's phone next and got an answer on the third ring,

"Zero's Pizza, how may I help you?" It was Carlos.

"Are you two okay?" Matt asked.

"We're a-okay; we are about 10 minutes away from the rendezvous."

Rico took the phone from Carlos, "We are going to need medical attention soon. Carlos was hit and lost a lot of blood

"I'm fine, I told you, just a couple grazes," Carlos cut in.

Rico ignored him and continued. "Carlos says they are superficial, but there is a lot of blood. Can you call ahead and make sure they are ready for trauma?"

Carlos just looked out the window with an irritated look on his face.

"We just arrived. We will change vehicles and be ready to leave the moment you arrive, I already called ahead, and they are set up and ready for us."

"Sounds good. We'll see you soon," Rico said and hung up.

"You don't look good, Man; that is a lot of blood."

Just get us back, and everything will be fine, Man."

Carlos closed his eyes and rested for the rest of the drive.

The four men and child were soon in another vehicle and on the road again, headed to a safe house and medical attention.

After being bandaged up, the group smuggled themselves and Samuel in a cargo plane. They would have to hold tight for better medical attention when they reached a safe house.

When they finally emerged from their hiding place, friends in arms, who had arranged their escape, greeted them. After a few hours of driving, the group stopped, and they emerged into the shady light of the mountains outside Olympia, Washington.

They all jumped on ATVs and traveled the rest of the way deep into the Olympic National forest. Their Camp was based near a farmer's property that bordered the National Forest.

They had a hidden underground bunker, which got its power from a small-concealed hydro generator from the creek. They parked all the ATVs down a ramp into the ground and pulled a cover over them. The group was soon underground and able to rest.

Samuel was cleaned up and had several people taking care of him. Matt and Carlos were taken to medical.

Samuel smiled at his rescuers as they left him in his caretaker's loving hands. Peter rubbed the hair on the top of his head and knelt down, looking him in the eyes.

"You're safe now, Sam, and surrounded by people who love you. Get some rest, and tomorrow I'll tell you an important story."

Samuel hugged him tightly and held on for a minute before letting go.

Peter left Samuel and followed Rico to check on Carlos and Matt. In the medical unit, Matt was being stitched up, and a medic was looking at Carlos.

"You two went above and beyond out there, and I am in debited to you."

Carlos waved him off as if it was nothing, and Matt smiled at him. The medic looking at Carlos turned to walk out and whispered to Peter as he passed. "We need to talk."

Peter looked at Matt and Carlos and smiled, "You too, relax and take it easy. I'll see to it your loved ones know where you are."

Peter exited the medical room and found the medic waiting for him down the hall.

"So what's going on, Dan? Is everything all right?"

"Well, it could be better. The bullet that hit Matt barely missed his femoral artery. We were able to stitch him up, and I will put him on antibiotics.

Carlos is another story."

"What is it, Dan?" Peter pushed.

"His neck wound was closed, but we were able to clean it up and suture the wound. However, the wound he sustained in his abdomen did some damage to his spleen. He has lost more blood than I am comfortable with, so aggressive surgery might kill him."

"He sounds good. How is that?" Peter questioned.

Dan rubbed his face. "To be honest, Pete, I don't know how he is even conscious. We are going to get him blood and then try surgery. The truth is it could go either way.'

"Does he know?"

"He knows there's a problem, but I did not lay it out. I want him calm." Peter ran his hands through his hair, taking a deep breath.

"Dan, do everything you can. What do you need from me?" "Blood is on the way. I guess just get Patty and his boy down here to see him."

"To say goodbye?" Peter asked.

"To keep him calm and happy until we can take him to surgery, so he can see them in case things turn for the worse."

"I am sending Matt out as soon they finish with his sutures. It's up to you if you want to tell anyone else. Anyone who comes to see him needs to be calm and positive."

"I got you. I will have a talk with Patty, as well, as Matt and Rico, about what is going on. For now, we'll leave it at that. We will be praying for you and Carlos the entire time Dan. Just do everything you can. Please."

Dan put a hand on his shoulder. "You know I will."

Peter went back into the room and popped open a wheelchair for Matt.

"Looks like these are going to be your wheels for a few days, brother."

Matt was already sitting up. He got off the table onto his good leg holding the injured foot off the ground. Peter wheeled the chair over to him, and he sat down.

"Dan, can you take Matt to his quarters so I can talk with Carlos?"

"What's up?" Matt questioned as Dan started to wheel him to the door.

"Nothing, I just want to debrief Carlos while it's fresh. I will be right behind you. Find Rico, so I can talk with the two of you when I'm done."

"Alright, I'll see you in a bit, tough guy," Matt called to Carlos with a hand in the air.

Carlos put a hand up and said something inaudible.

"Is he going to be okay? Matt asked. Dan wheeled him out the door. "He lost a lot of blood. He needs rest."

Peter went to Carlos' side. He grabbed his hand, and Carlos opened his eyes. "How you doing, Bro?" Peter asked him.

"I'm just tired. I need sleep," Carlos replied. "Am I in trouble here, Pete? Don't bullshit me, Man. God doesn't like liars."

Peter squeezed his hand and halfway laughed. "Things could be better; I can tell you that.

Listen, you need blood; that's first, then we need to do some damage control."

Carlos smiled at him, "Did you hear the one about the Rabbi, the Priest, and the Baptist Preacher?"

"No, why don't you tell me."

"God... He. . . came…" Carlos drifted out.

Peter put his head down and could hear his friend's breathing, and this relieved his fear.

"You rest, my friend. Patty will be here soon."

Peter put both his hands on Carlos' face and kissed him on the forehead. "I love you, Man. Thank you for saving my family."

To be continued...

Made in the USA
Middletown, DE
08 July 2023

34743113R00288